M. A. Hunter has been a huge fan of crime fiction series since a
~~~~~~~~~~~~~~ ~d al ays fancied the idea of trying to write one.
~~~~~~ signed
The Missing Children Case Files.

Born in Darlington in the north-east of England, Hunter grew
up in West London, and moved to Southampton to study law
at university. It's here that Hunter fell in love and has been
married for fifteen years. They are now raising their two
children on the border of The New Forest where they enjoy
going for walks amongst the wildlife. They regularly holiday
across England, but have a particular affinity for the south
coast, which formed the setting for the series, spanning from
Devon to Brighton, and with a particular focus on Weymouth,
one of their favourite towns.

When not writing, Hunter can be found binge-watching
favourite shows or buried in the latest story from Angela
Marsons, Simon Kernick, or Ann Cleeves.

 twitter.com/Writer_MAHunter
facebook.com/AuthorMAHunter

Also by M. A. Hunter

The Missing Children Case Files

Ransomed

Isolated

Trafficked

Discarded

Repressed

Exposed

MUMMY'S LITTLE SECRET

M. A. HUNTER

One More Chapter
a division of HarperCollins*Publishers*
1 London Bridge Street
London SE1 9GF
www.harpercollins.co.uk

HarperCollins*Publishers*
1st Floor, Watermarque Building, Ringsend Road
Dublin 4, Ireland

This paperback edition 2021

1

First published in Great Britain in ebook format
by HarperCollins*Publishers* 2021

A catalogue record of this book is available from the British Library

ISBN: 978-0-00-840906-7

Printed and Bound in the UK using 100% Renewable Electricity
at CPI Group (UK) Ltd

*Dedicated to all the parents who held
their shit together during home-schooling*

Chapter One

Before - Jess

I f the little girl hadn't been deathly pale and trembling as she'd hesitantly whispered, I probably wouldn't have thought twice about it. *She's not my mum.*

My instinct is to frown and internally question whether I've simply misheard. Her eyes are shining in the late afternoon August sunshine, and as I continue to study her face, her lower lip wobbles, like she wants to say more, but can't find either the words or the strength.

Over the girl's left shoulder I catch a glimpse of Grace squealing with delight as she swings through the air, pushing her legs out and then promptly tucking them beneath the plastic seat, as the chain overhead squeaks under the strain.

'Mummy, look at me,' Grace's voice carries on the wind.

I raise my hand to acknowledge her, but my focus remains on the other girl's face. Perhaps what she actually said was she's *lost* her mother. From my seated position it is difficult to see beyond the playground apparatus. The giant climbing frame shaped like a pirate ship blocks out the horizon to the right, and beyond Grace and the swings, the forest of green shares little of the secrets it holds.

You wouldn't believe it is the height of summer. It's been over a week since we last donned shorts, but at least there's no rain today. Talk of an imminent heatwave in the weeks to come doesn't fill me with joy.

From the way the girl is gripping the arms of my chair, her knuckles an unnatural shade of white, experience tells me that something is very wrong.

A flashback to the hushed conversations between the midwife and doctor flickers before my eyes, as I'd sucked hard on the gas and air. I'd known back then that something wasn't right, even though they'd yet to tell me just how bad things really were. Their faces had failed to keep my pulse from rising, and this terrified child is doing little to ease my anxiety. I shake the memory away. Now is not the time.

As I open my mouth to ask the girl to repeat what she said, there is an explosion of colour in the corner of my eye.

'Daisy? Daisy?' The Scottish accent echoes across the protective carpet of soft rubber that stretches beneath the playground equipment.

The girl's arms tense and her eyes seem to widen in greater panic, but her stare remains locked on mine, as if she's trying to assess whether I'll admit what she's told me; begging me to keep quiet.

A foreboding shadow falls upon us, and I am forced to glance towards the sky, now seeing the tall figure hovering over us. A pale blue cardigan pokes from beneath the large waxed overcoat, the rancid smell reminding me of childhood visits to farms.

'Daisy? Ah, there you are,' the woman says. 'Leave this poor lady alone.'

She is much older than I'd expected. A shock of auburn hair interspersed with wisps of grey, and subtle blonde undertones. The skin above her cheeks is mauve and hangs, while the lines beside her eyes are tight and strained. Maybe she's the child's gran or minder. Certainly not her mother.

'Sorry if my daughter is being a nuisance,' the woman continues. 'Daisy, how many times have I told you not to wander off?'

I look back at the girl. She doesn't look like a Daisy. If I had to guess I would say she was a Ruth or a Sandra, a name that would conform to the direct stare and determined scowl. The name Daisy belongs to a fair child with a playful smile and a mischievous look in her eyes. This girl has neither quality, yet there is a subtle femininity to her features: firm but fair.

The waxed coat sleeve reaches out and extracts the girl's hands from the arms of my wheelchair. 'Come along now. Places to go, people to see.'

'She wasn't being a nuisance,' I offer quickly, feeling drawn to engage with these strangers, but unsure why. 'Really, no bother at all.'

The woman pauses and looks down at me, almost astonished that the cripple before her in the rickety old wheelchair has a voice. 'That's kind of you to say.' She turns to move away, before hesitating, and looking back at me, extending a hand as she does. 'Morag.'

I blink in surprise, but shake her hand. 'Jess.'

'That's your wee one on the swings?' she asks, nodding towards Grace, who is still squealing in delight.

'Yes,' I say, feeling heat rise to my cheeks. 'She gets her crazy streak from her dad,' I add, nervously.

'I'd say we both must be pretty crazy to be at a deserted park on such a chilly day. The things we do for our kids, huh?'

Something about the way she says it puts a flicker of doubt in my mind that I struggle to push away.

'Worth it to witness such unbridled excitement though,' she adds.

It was only because Grace had bleated on at me for close to an hour that I'd eventually caved and agreed to bring her down here. I don't know if that makes me a good parent for bringing joy to my four-year-old's sheltered life, or a weak one for giving in. Deep down I know I only agreed because I want to make as much of the little time we have left together. Within a week she'll have started in reception class at the local primary, and I know a part of us will be lost for ever. Right now I am her whole universe – well, Charlie and I are – but once she steps through those school gates we will be relegated to the fraction of her life not dominated by learning and playing with her newfound friends.

Daisy is staring at the dark ground before her. For someone so worried about losing her mother, where is the joy at being reunited?

I recall a moment before my paralysis, when I was at the supermarket with Grace. I'd told her to stay by the shopping trolley while I went to choose a fresh loaf of bread, and when I returned she was out of sight. I'd breathlessly searched the two aisles closest to the bakery area without success, and had been about to flag down the security guard near the main entrance when Grace had come rushing back to the trolley, a children's magazine gripped in her hands. I'd dropped to my knees and hugged her tight, wanting to chastise and cradle in equal measure. She'd quickly apologised before lecturing me on the dozen reasons why I had to buy her the magazine, when clearly the attraction had been the cheap plastic sunglasses taped to the front cover.

I can't dispel the curiosity sweeping through me. 'You're not from around here,' I say, as Morag tugs on Daisy's hand, ready to move on. It's a statement more than a question, and although I can't claim to recognise every face in our small town in north-west London, Morag's certainly isn't familiar.

Morag looks back at me again, and I'm sure I see a hint of annoyance as her eyebrows dip together. 'What was it that gave me away?' she coos, her accent deliberately more pronounced.

She must notice my face reddening, as she suddenly steps closer. 'No offence intended.'

Before I can respond, Grace is at my side, breathless.

'Did you see how high I went, Mummy? I was *actually* flying.'

The cool wind tempers the burning in my cheeks, and I take in every inch of my daughter's beautiful face. She is more than I ever could have wished for. Articulate, eager to learn, and with a healthy interest in outdoor activities. When I think back to the shy, awkward child-version of myself, I don't really feel like I've changed that much, aside from the four wheels now keeping me off the ground. Grace is the polar opposite of me as a child. Whereas I spent hours with my head in books, devouring the fictional lives of the characters I so admired, Grace is already creating her own stories, filled with vibrant colours, language beyond her experiences, and a positivity that warms the heart. I now find myself wanting to be a character in one of my daughter's stories.

'Hi, I'm Grace,' my daughter says, stooping and forcing eye contact with Daisy. 'Do you want to go on the seesaw?'

I'm even envious of my daughter's unabashed self-confidence. It's as if nothing daunts her. I've never once heard her admit to being scared of anything. Even as a toddler when I would read her adventures involving sea monsters and ferocious beasts, she would snuggle close, but beam as I closed the book.

I notice the hopeful yet despondent look that Daisy fires at Morag, who seems to consider the proposal, before nodding. 'Aye, it's okay. Off you go.'

Grace grabs Daisy's hand, and the two girls tear off towards the seesaw directly in front of us, leaving Morag to watch. Daisy can't be much older than Grace as far as I can tell. They are a similar height and build, and given that Grace will be one of the oldest in her year group, I can only assume Daisy is in the year above.

I know we should be getting home soon. It is Charlie's birthday, and the cake that Grace and I baked earlier today still needs to be iced before he returns from work. I do hope he isn't late again. He promised this morning he would be home by six at the very latest, and the fact that he has yet to message fills me with renewed hope that he will live up to the promise for once.

I can see Grace is imagining that her end of the large beam of wood is a horse or a dragon, as she is gripping the safety bar with one hand, while the other flails overhead. Daisy on the other hand is staring right back at us, no sign of any enjoyment. Maybe she is wondering whether I'm going to tell Morag what she said.

'The girls look like they're having a good time,' Morag comments, but I'm not sure for whose benefit she's said it.

'Yes,' I concur. 'How old is Daisy?'

'Five next week,' Morag says after a moment. 'They grow up so quickly, don't they?'

This statement I can't disagree with. It seems like only yesterday the blob of pink and white was being passed to me in the hospital. Charlie was too busy snapping photographs on his phone to really take in the fact that we'd now been charged with the responsibility for this tiny life.

A further flash of memory of the midwife and doctor conspiring with each other fires in my mind, from the last time I'd been rushed to the maternity hospital, and I bite back the stinging tears that threaten to explode.

'I can't believe she'll be starting school in a week,' Morag says, dragging my attention back to the park.

'I know what you mean,' I say absently, looking back to Grace and Daisy. 'Grace is starting too.'

I feel Morag now staring down at me. 'Is that so? Maybe they'll be in the same class. Ah, wouldn't that be nice for them to already have friends when they start school?'

I don't mention that Grace will know at least a dozen other children in her year group from encounters at pre-school. 'Yes,' I comment instead.

'Maybe we should fix up a playdate in the next few days so they can get to know each other properly. What do you say?'

I'm not used to strangers being so direct with me, and she must sense my hesitation, as she quickly adds, 'Only if you want to.'

I think about all the pitying looks Charlie has given me since I was assigned this chair, all the encouragement he's offered when I haven't wanted it: *you will get through this.*

I know it's bitter to question whether he'd still be so positive if it was him facing a lifetime confined by no legs, but I can't help it. It didn't happen to him, it happened to me. *I'm* the one who will suffer every day as a result of my actions.

'I tell you what,' Morag offers. 'I passed a small coffee stand on the way to the playground. How about we take the girls for a juice and some cake. God knows, I could do with a refreshment.'

I think about Charlie's pitying stare again. 'Why not,' I say, knowing Grace won't want to miss out on a sweet treat.

'I'll go and tell the girls,' Morag says, and before I can offer to go with her, she is already striding across the playground to the seesaw.

I watch as Grace punches the air in excitement at the news, while Daisy fires a look in my direction, before dismounting the seesaw. In that moment, I can't ignore the nagging doubt in my mind: what if she really did say what I thought I heard?

Chapter Two

Before - Morag

The woman across the table from me looks frustrated and tired. I daren't ask what unfortunate circumstance has seen her wind up in that rickety old wheelchair, but I can't deny I'm curious.

'Aberdeen,' I say in answer to her question about where I'm from. 'On the east coast. You've not experienced cold until you've felt the gales blowing off the North Sea.'

We are seated around a wobbly plastic table, the kind they sell cheap in DIY stores. The stains and scratches in the once white surface suggest the table is far from new, and probably stored outside overnight. The hut where we have purchased our drinks is little more than a painted shed with a window cut out of it. Despite the limited space, there is a wide selection of biscuits and individually wrapped cakes on display on the counter, and behind the moustachioed man running the stand sit two large metal drums for boiling water. Two of the other four tables are occupied, but we are too far away to overhear their conversations.

'Have you always lived in London?' I ask Jess politely, putting the bottle of water to my lips.

Angus is the one who has to remind me that the leafy suburb of Northwood is captured within the boundary of Greater London, just about. There are no high-rise towers here, just a few bespoke businesses struggling to make ends meet. It's not dissimilar to other towns we've lived in over the years, but at least we chose this one. I can only hope we have the chance to put down some roots, before we have to move on again.

Jess raises the cup to her lips and blows gently on the tea to cool it. 'I was born in Southampton,' she says, and I'm surprised that she is being so open, as the suspicious look hasn't left her eyes since I introduced myself.

I don't like the way she keeps glancing over at Daisy either. When Daisy ran off at the playground, I was relieved she hadn't stumbled across some predator, but she was out of sight for two minutes, and God only knows what she might have shared in that time. I need to know what Daisy has told her. Daisy's always been so trusting; doesn't understand how cruel the world can be, nor how one slip to a perfect stranger can come back to haunt you later on. We've only been in Northwood for six weeks, and I don't think Angus's heart could take yet another move so soon.

'I've never been to Southampton,' I say, in an effort to keep the conversation neutral. I can't just demand to know what Daisy has told her, but ultimately it might be easier, even if it does make me seem odd. If she knew my motivation, she would probably understand better, but that's something I'm not prepared to share with another living soul. I did once, and I have no doubt that's what led to *him* nearly finding us that time.

'It's a beautiful part of the world,' Jess says, but there is a sadness to her tone, which she quickly pushes away. 'What brings you to Northwood?'

Ah, the dreaded question I was hoping to avoid. It's perfectly natural for people to question why someone with such a broad Scots accent would move so far south, but it doesn't make it any easier to lie to their faces.

Opening the packet of shortbread biscuits, I snap one in half, breathing in the aroma. 'These always remind me of home,' I say, ignoring the question. 'My grandmother was forever baking shortbread. Unfortunately, I didn't inherit the baking gene.'

Daisy hasn't said a word since we took our seats, and I'm relieved she's not giving the game away. She is slumped in the white plastic chair, an open carton of juice on the table before her. Thankfully, Jess's daughter Grace hasn't stopped chattering to her, but from where I'm sitting it is obvious the conversation is one-sided. I've never seen a child look so unhappy at being bought juice and Jaffa Cakes. I wish I could somehow make her smile again; make her understand why we did what we did.

'What did you say your husband does?' I ask, keen to know more about the person I'm allowing to get close to our world.

There is a look of confusion on Jess's face as she answers, as if she isn't quite sure what job her husband has. 'He's in stocks and shares.'

That's as vague an answer as I've ever heard, that's for sure. Is it because she genuinely doesn't know, or is it because she can't remember what fictitious background she invented for him? You can never be sure who is what they say they are and who plays the person they think you want them to be.

'Oh, really?' I probe innocently. 'How fascinating. Is he one of those you see in the movies, standing around staring at share prices, shouting and bidding?'

'Something like that,' Jess replies, but the uncertain expression remains.

She shuffles uncomfortably in the chair, and if I didn't know better I'd say she is close to tears. As a former nurse, you notice when people are trying to hide their discomfort, and when they're putting it on for effect. Despite my doubts about Jess, I don't think she is putting it on.

'Are you all right?' I ask. 'I've got some ibuprofen in my handbag if that would help?'

She shakes her head, but even that looks like a strain. 'I'm fine,' she says, and winces.

Her phone beeps on the table, and she snatches it up and reads the message, disappointment flickering in her eyes. Bad news, I would assume, but she doesn't appear ready to spill the beans.

'I can't get over how peaceful it is here,' I offer, taking in the vista of the park behind her. 'I always thought London was so urban, but it's so green here.'

Jess lowers the phone. 'Many assume that London is just made up of skyscrapers and the usual tourist landmarks, but even in the heart of the city there are plenty of green parks and spots of beauty to counterbalance the grey pavements and roads.'

Her cheeks flush as she realises how abrupt her response was, but I'm not so easily offended.

She turns to look at Daisy again. 'Are you looking forward to starting school, Daisy?'

The wee girl glances at me before meeting her stare and nodding.

'She's so quiet compared to my chatterbox,' Jess comments, turning back to look at me. 'You must tell me your secret.'

If only she knew the truth, she certainly wouldn't be so breezy, sitting with us here. 'She's always been a quiet child, but takes everything in. Like a sponge. Don't let her shyness fool you.'

Jess is staring so intently at Daisy that I'm certain she must see through the veil of my deceit, but then she reaches for her phone and punches in a message to God only knows who or why. I suppose it's a sign of the times that she offers no apology for this rudeness. Angus is always telling me that I need to accept it's just the way things are, but why should I? Why can't the younger generation keep their eyes off their phones for more than a few minutes at a time?

'Is everything all right?' I ask, keeping my frustration in check.

'My husband,' she says almost too quickly. 'Says he's going to be late home. *Again.*'

The sleeve of my waxed jacket crunches as I push it up and study the thin golden watch on my wrist. 'We should probably be on our way too in a moment. Angus will be expecting his dinner on the table.'

'Is Angus your husband?' Jess asks, putting me on edge.

I nod once, trying not to give too much away. 'Aye. For thirty-four years he has been at my side.' I stop suddenly, as I realise what I've said. There's no way she won't see my slip. I can almost hear the cogs turning in her head as she completes the mental arithmetic. She looks from me to Daisy, and that tells me she is trying to calculate how old I would have been to have given birth to Daisy. I'm relieved when her phone beeps again and use the distraction as an opportunity to tell Daisy to hurry up and finish her juice.

Jess reads the message and responds once again, before lowering her phone.

It's so hard to know what she will read into our little exchange. While she's taken an interest in us, she hasn't bombarded us with questions. Just the right balance of curiosity, without prying. Should that make me suspicious? *He* only hires the best private detectives that money can buy to try and find us. Is that what she is? Was our meeting in the playground by chance, or engineered? One thing's for certain, until I know more, I need to keep an eye on her. What is it they say about keeping friends close, but enemies closer?

'It's lovely how the two of them are getting on,' I say, eager to cover for my earlier slip. 'What are your plans for the rest of the week? I would be happy to have Grace over to play. Would free up some time for you, no?'

If she is as genuine as she portrays, then it can't be easy to look after such a bundle of energy, given the obvious restrictions a wheelchair would bring.

'That's very kind,' she offers, fidgeting again.

Scrawling the number of the latest phone Angus has given me onto a napkin, I slide it across the table to her. 'I'll leave you to decide.' The waxed coat scrunches as I stand and motion to Daisy to do the same. 'It was nice to have met you, Grace,' I say, and it really was. If Daisy is to settle into her new school, having a friend like Grace will certainly make it easier. 'Are you going to say goodbye, Daisy?'

She zips up her coat, and fixes Grace with a grateful look. 'Bye.'

Something changes in Jess's expression, and for the life of me I don't know what could have caused it. Leading Daisy away, I can't help but worry that this simple exchange has set us on a path from which there is no return. All I know is that I cannot wait to get Daisy home and away from prying eyes. *He* is out there somewhere searching for us, and I'll be damned if I'm going to allow him to get as close as he did before.

Chapter Three

Before - Jess

The curtains explode in a shower of light, as Charlie's car pulls onto the driveway. The shadows return a moment later, and I hear keys rattling in the front door. I am stretched out on the sofa, television remote in my hand, but I'm not really watching what's on the screen. It is late, and I am tired, but it took all my energy to shift from the wheelchair onto the sofa and I simply don't think I will manage to get back into the chair unaided. Even if I do, there's no way I will be able to get myself into bed.

The doctor who diagnosed the injury didn't tell me just how physically draining movement would be. He explained that I would ache, that they would need to monitor my psychological reaction to the change, and that my sexual appetite might diminish.

The truth is, unless you spend time confined in a wheelchair, you can never really appreciate the impact it will have on every aspect of your life. I don't mind admitting I'd never really considered just how difficult life becomes because of the chair. Wait, no, that's not fair. It isn't the chair's fault that I cannot easily get in and out of buildings, and it isn't the chair's fault that not enough businesses truly consider less-abled members of the public. Even venues that stress they are wheelchair-accessible don't all consider just how steep some of their ramps are.

My lower back is aching from sitting still for too long at the park. That was something the surgeon had warned me about when he'd broken the news I might never walk again.

'It's important to exercise,' he'd insisted. 'The lure to just stay in the wheelchair all day is one you should avoid. Swimming is a good way to keep fit.'

It's like that was the only part of the stern talk Charlie had heard. Bless him, I know he means well, focusing on the positive, but for me there is no silver lining. It's not like I'm choosing to sit in the wheelchair, but without it I'm restricted to dragging myself across the floor with just my hands and arms for leverage.

Charlie has said we'll buy a new chair when we can afford to. He thinks that a battery-powered one will make all the difference, but I'm not sure he understands that it won't solve all of our problems. Poor Charlie, I sometimes forget how hard this change has been on him too. He tries his best, I know he does, but money isn't going to solve my issue.

Not this time.

For now, my father's old chair will have to suffice. I suppose I should be grateful that it's only my legs I've lost the use of. I could be worse off.

My mind keeps wandering back to that encounter at the

park. I know without doubt that there is more to Daisy than I dared realise. Although it was only four little words, I have no doubt that Daisy's accent isn't Scottish, but how can that be when Morag's accent is so broad? But that's not the only thing that's troubling me. Daisy's cheeks were puffy, as if she stores food in them like a squirrel. They were covered in freckles, as was her nose, but her hair was so dark, in comparison to the rouge hues of Morag's. I have no doubt that Morag colours her hair, but cannot picture her ever having hair as dark as Daisy's. Her face is as round as a ball, yet Morag's is long and more oval.

I appreciate that not all children are the spitting image of their parents – Grace has the perfect balance of Charlie's and my features – but I wouldn't have expected Daisy to look so different to Morag if they are indeed mother and daughter. It's not just the lack of resemblance though. Morag was definitely evasive when I asked questions about her background, and yet she was keen to know more about me and Charlie. And then there was that suggestion that I bring Grace over for a playdate. Was it simply a kind gesture, or are her motives far more sinister? I already know what Charlie will say if I tell him what I'm thinking. He'll tell me I'm being paranoid, that I need to take control of my wandering imagination and stop painting every gesture in darkness.

Morag's evasiveness is still gnawing at my mind like a rat with a nut. Why wouldn't she tell me what had brought them to Northwood? When we first bought the house, it was convenient for Charlie to catch the Tube into the city. But things have changed. It's now become more fashionable to live on the edge of the boundary and commute. The town is no longer how I remember it, and so much busier. More people, more cars, and yet I've never felt so isolated.

Charlie looks surprised to find me still up. He leans his briefcase against the shoe rack behind the front door. 'I'm sorry,' is all he mutters, before a pained expression sweeps across that smooth forehead of his.

To look at him, you'd never know Charlie was two years older than me, nor that he is nearing thirty-five. He's always been blessed with youthful features, albeit prior to his eighteenth birthday he'd viewed it as a curse. Even when we'd started dating, he was twenty-four but would always be asked for identification when buying alcohol or trying to gain entry to a nightclub. It used to make me giggle, and I always used to tell him he'd be grateful for that gene one day.

'Your dinner's in the oven,' I tell him, 'but it's probably cold.'

I don't mean to sound so bitter, but I can't help feeling envious that he's been out of this house all day. Save for the trip to the park with Grace, I've been a prisoner, as I am most days. It isn't that I don't want to go out, but it saps my energy so quickly. The doctor said things would improve over time, but I don't feel like I've made any progress in the six months since I was discharged.

'How was your day?' he asks, but it's difficult to gauge if he really wants to know, or whether he's just being polite. I used to be able to read his thoughts so well, but things have been different since the diagnosis, and our losing Luke.

Whenever I ask Charlie about his day job, I quickly lose interest. I know that makes me sound like a cow, but he uses so much jargon that I simply don't understand. From what I've managed to deduce he does something involving investing for bigger companies and clients, but I might be completely off track. What I do know is it gets the best part of him each day. He's usually gone by the time I wake up, and when he does eventually get home, he's too tired to do anything but slouch in front of the television and fall asleep.

I know it isn't Charlie's fault, and, if anything, I am the reason he is having to work so hard. Since the surgery, I haven't been in any position to work. It's hard enough getting through the days, but try telling the bank and utility companies that our lives have been flipped off course. Bills have to be paid regardless of the tragedy and anxiety we are suffering. I would choose to have Charlie around more often rather than a battery-powered wheelchair. I sometimes worry that Grace will forget what he looks like.

I silently admonish myself for the thought, and remind myself that Charlie is a wonderful father. He makes an effort to fix her breakfast at the weekends, and reads to her every Saturday and Sunday night. I don't get up to Grace's room as much as I'd like. Since the surgery, I have been sleeping in what was our spare room downstairs. Charlie sleeps down there with me most nights, unless he returns late and I'm already in bed. On those occasions, he will sleep upstairs so as not to disturb me. I know I'm lucky to have him, and that lesser men would have abandoned me after what happened. He remains my rock.

My breath catches, as I feel the phantom kick of Luke's feet in my womb. It should be impossible to feel anything down there. I no longer know when my bowels are moving, yet every now and again I am certain I feel Luke move within me. The gynaecologist did say women who go full-term can sometimes feel phantom movement, like an echo – a reminder that he was growing inside of me. I can't help but feel that his soul – his spirit, his essence – didn't leave when they extracted him from me. I know it's crazy, but I still feel him there, and it brings joy and sorrow knowing he is with me, but not with me.

People react differently to me since the diagnosis. It's like my inability to walk has made me a spectacle. You get the strangers in the street who will divert their gaze to anywhere but where I am pushing my wheels. And then there are the people who seem to assume that because I can't walk, I'm not able to think for myself either. They mean well, sure, but I've lost count of the number of strangers who've offered to push me home, even though they don't know me, or where I live. Thankfully, there is a third, rarer breed of people who smile politely, but don't make any effort to treat me differently. Believe it or not, these are my favourite type of people. I don't want to be thought of as different. Just because I am restricted to the wheelchair, it doesn't mean I want to be defined by it.

'Do you want me to microwave your dinner?' I ask as Charlie removes his tie and rolls it up. Always so neat and tidy is my Charlie.

His brow furrows uncertainly. 'Thanks, but Doug bought pizza so we could go over the pitch again, and again.'

I bite my tongue to keep myself from showing my annoyance at this last statement. He hasn't sent a message since the one I received at the coffee stand. Okay, his dinner is just a ready meal I put in the oven, but if he'd told me he was eating pizza I wouldn't have wasted the meal.

So typical of Doug – Charlie's boss – to think buying them all takeaway pizza makes up for keeping them working unsociable hours. I've met Doug twice, and answered the phone to him more than a dozen times. Not a particularly sociable person from what I can determine, certainly never shown any kind of interest in me. Even after I was discharged from hospital, and I next answered his call, he didn't even ask how I was coping, just demanded to speak to Charlie.

'I take it Grace is in bed?' Charlie asks, yawning, and rubbing his eyes.

'I kept her up for as long as possible, but she was falling asleep on me,' I confirm.

His cheeks contract, and it is a relief to see him looking so disappointed. I'd stressed to him how much time Grace had spent thinking about what she wanted to get him for his birthday, and in the end she'd opted to buy him some new gloves for golf. She knows how much he loves going to the driving range, not that he's been able to go in months, due to work and supporting me.

I do worry that he's working too hard, and that he needs rest and relaxation as much as I do, but he can be quite obstinate. I know that if Grace gives him the gloves and insists he spend a couple of hours at the driving range, he will listen. He will do anything for her, and I wish I had that level of control over him. He does a lot for me, but rarely does he ask if I want him to do all those things.

It's selfish to complain, I know.

'I'm sorry I wasn't here,' he says. 'The pitch to the new client is first thing, but then I should be able to relax more at the weekend. Maybe we can celebrate my birthday on Saturday instead. How does that sound?'

I nod enthusiastically, but can't ignore the nagging feeling that Doug will find something else for Charlie to complete desperately at the weekend.

'How was your day?' he asks, pouring himself a whisky

from the drinks cabinet in the corner of our tiny living room, before sitting down at the dining table we've had to move in here.

While I was still undergoing tests at the hospital, unbeknownst to me Charlie was busy converting what was our dining room into a bedroom for me. New bed, chest of drawers and wet room so that I wouldn't feel obligated to go upstairs any more. A wonderful gesture, but it made me sob. It underlined just how much my life would have to change.

Accepting I needed to use a wheelchair was a big obstacle to overcome. Not only was I coping with losing my son, but I also had to make a psychological shift that was just as hard, if not harder. I was essentially kissing goodbye to my independence. And then there is the inevitable question of 'why me?', though there is part of me that always knew karma would come for me one day.

At first, it felt like purgatory; it wasn't that I wanted to die, but I didn't feel like I could carry on living either. I would wake up each morning, and for the briefest of seconds I would forget about everything that had happened, and I would be free and optimistic, and then my memory would kick in, and my world would crumble. It's almost a relief that those brief hopeful starts have subsequently diminished. Less painful emotionally to wake and know that my life as I knew it is over.

Depression is a common side effect to paraplegia, and so I am taking antidepressants on top of vitamin supplements, and painkillers. I take so many pills every day that I'm convinced I must rattle when moving down the street.

I can't describe exactly what my depression is like. I don't feel sad, or like I want to swallow all my painkillers and make it all just end. I just feel empty. I don't feel like *me* anymore. My whole life prior to the change was about discovering myself: school; university; becoming a mother for the first time. I thought I'd found what made me tick, and then it was like a bomb went off and my internal clock was reset. If it wasn't for Grace, I might have spiralled further into depression, but she gives me reason to battle on.

'Jess,' Charlie tries again. 'I asked what your day was like.'

My head snaps round and I look at him, trying to remember exactly what happened today. It takes a moment, and then I remember Daisy approaching me in the park, and the four little words she whispered: *she's not my mum.*

I rub the goose bumps from my arms, as the image of her puffy and terrified face hovers before my eyes. My pulse is once again quickening. I know I didn't imagine the words. I've tried replaying the memory to see whether it's possible she'd said something else, but I can't make anything else fit.

'Jess, is everything okay?' I hear Charlie asking, suddenly approaching and pressing his warm palm to my forehead. 'Is your blood pressure okay? You look like you've seen a ghost.'

The doctors warned that my condition can cause fluctuations in my blood pressure, but I don't think that's what's making me feel so anxious.

'I – I – I met a little girl today,' I begin, knowing that what I'm about to say will sound ridiculous. 'And I think she's in trouble.'

He is frowning at me in confusion as he steps back. 'What sort of trouble?'

'I think...' but I don't know what I think. What do those words mean? *She's not my mum.* If Morag isn't Daisy's mother, who is she?

'I don't know.' I try again. 'She said something to me, which made me think she was in trouble.'

'What did she say?'

I close my eyes, replaying the memory again. 'She told me the woman with her wasn't her mother.'

'And?'

'The woman – Morag – she came over and acted as if she *was* Daisy's mother.'

Charlie's expression shows he still isn't following what I'm trying to say.

'The little girl looked so scared, and her reaction to Morag was ... was not that of a mother and loving daughter. She looked so scared to be at the park with her, and I just thought it was very strange.'

There, I've said it. That wasn't so bad.

A smile is starting to break out on Charlie's face. 'You went to the park today? That's so good, Jess. You went out and got some fresh air. I'm so pleased.' He leans down and kisses the top of my head, and the stench of whisky assaults my nostrils.

'Didn't you hear what I said? I think this little girl was terrified to be with the woman claiming to be her mother.'

'Who was this woman? What did she say when you told her what the girl said?'

'She didn't... I mean, I didn't ask her. How could I? But I'm telling you, Charlie, something just didn't feel right.'

He drops to his knees now and takes my hands in his, and the warmth causes my arms to pimple again. 'Jess, listen to me. I know things haven't been easy since you were discharged, and I can't even begin to imagine just how much you're suffering, but making up stories about other parents is worrying.'

I pull my hands away, and wince at the effort. 'I'm not making this up.'

He takes my hands again, and I'm unable to resist his gentle touch. 'I didn't mean you'd deliberately made up a story about this woman, but with everything you've been through, with the loss of your legs, and what happened with Luke—'

I shudder at the mention of his name.

'It's understandable that your mind could be playing tricks on you, and seeing things that aren't there,' he concludes, his eyes watering. 'Maybe we should book you another appointment with Dr Savage, so you can talk these things through. Maybe she needs to adjust your meds again.'

I'm not surprised by Charlie's reaction, and I can see his doubts are nothing more than concern for me. I didn't do a great job of explaining why I am so certain that there is something strange about Morag and Daisy.

But I know I didn't imagine it.

Chapter Four

Before - Morag

I know instantly I shouldn't have come to the supermarket today. Angus did volunteer to collect what was required, but I wanted to get out of the house, and the constant reminders of everything we had to leave behind. Renting a furnished property has its benefits, but at the same time, none of the furniture is ours, and so my new home doesn't feel like mine. Hopefully that sense of being out of place, out of time, and out of sync with my surroundings will pass at some point. At least if we do have to leave in a hurry it won't be such a wrench to part with what's there.

The car park is heaving, and I'm forced to park as far from the entrance as is physically possible. A Tube train chuffs past the wire fence lining the boundary of cars, and I wish I was on it, headed anywhere but a cramped supermarket where I will have to encounter dozens of strangers, all of whom could be working for *him*. I probably should have headed out of the town to one of the larger supermarkets in nearby Pinner, Harrow, or Watford. It terrifies me that he could already be inside just waiting to find me once again.

I hurry inside, reciting the list in my head. If I move quickly, keep my head down, and don't dawdle, there's a chance I can be back in the car within fifteen minutes, safe once more. Daisy had asked if she could come with me, but I can't risk her being around all these people. I am now certain something happened between her and that Jess woman we met at the park on Thursday. They couldn't have been alone for more than a few seconds, so how much could she have really said? Jess's quizzical looks and probing questions at the table afterwards have had my nerves on edge ever since.

I only engaged with her to try and make Daisy more comfortable in her new surroundings, but I was too relaxed, and gave away too much. Jess hasn't called to accept the playdate I proposed, and in hindsight I know I shouldn't have suggested it. I haven't told Angus that I gave my new mobile number to a total stranger. He puts on a brave face, but I know he struggles with our decision as much as me, and although he tries to hide his emotions from me, I know how much he misses our wee cottage in Aberdeen and his former work colleagues.

I wish we could afford for him not to have to work, but desperate times call for desperate measures. I've offered to go and find some work once Daisy starts at school next week, but he isn't keen. Any job I could find wouldn't be as satisfying as nursing, and it breaks my heart that I cannot return to my vocation. I tried my hand at private nursing care the first time we fled, and Angus is convinced that's how he managed to find us then.

There is a man in a T-shirt leaning across me, reaching for an onion. His chest and belly are bulging through the fluorescent Lycra top, and the cycle shorts leave little to the imagination. I can see a huge sweat patch by his arm pit as it hovers near my face, and the pong makes my stomach turn. His dark, cropped hair is dripping wet, secured by a sweat band, which clearly isn't working. His groin presses against my arm as he tries to get closer to the onions.

It's as if I'm not even here. I move away and he nearly tumbles into the carefully stacked produce crates. Our eyes meet, and his cheeks redden a fraction, but he doesn't offer an apology before sauntering off.

The overhead speaker sounds as colleagues are named and ordered to the checkouts to deal with the growing queues there. A stream of uniformed students stop whatever they're doing and gather at the customer service desk like rats following the Pied Piper, before being instructed where to go. Most of them look like they are barely old enough to be out on their own, let alone serving customers and handling their money.

I silently curse as I remember I'd meant to go to the ATM before coming in here. Although Angus and I both have credit and debit cards, we have agreed not to use them in retail outlets, save for an emergency. Receipts can be tracked and traced by trained people hunters, but bank statements are more difficult to access.

Depositing my nearly full basket in a quiet corner near the fish counter, I look around for the exit, hoping my goods will still be there once I return. It won't be the end of the world if some other shopper helps themselves to what I've gathered – it's not like the items have been paid for yet – but it will save me time if everything is as I have left it. I don't have time to worry about it though, and push myself through the gathered crowd at one of the checkouts, towards the exit.

It is much warmer outside than I remember, and I'm tempted to remove my ever-present cardigan, but decide it's easier to have it on than carry it. Reaching into the zipped pocket, I remove my purse, and search for the nearest ATM. There aren't any banks in the immediate vicinity of the supermarket, and heading left I am relieved to come across a building society a short walk away. There is a tall youth in a woollen hat standing at the machine, and at first I want to forget this whole shopping idea and just return to the car, but as I pass he is already moving off.

Withdrawing my debit card, I push it into the slot, and type in my PIN. Footsteps approach from behind, but I keep my eyes facing forwards. A shadow falls across the wall ahead of me, and my heartbeat quickens.

Of course, it's not *him*.

The shadow belongs to just another stranger eager to check their balance or withdraw funds.

There is no reason for me to be picturing *him* prowling so close.

My head begins to turn to look behind me, but I force my attention to the digits now blurring slightly on the screen before me.

It's all in my head, but I am suddenly conscious of just how exposed I am here. Jabbing my finger on the button closest to the fifty, I wait as the machine whirs, counting the notes I didn't earn, and finally the card is spat out. Grabbing the cash, I squash both into my purse, and turn to leave, daring to glance back at the figure behind me. I almost laugh hysterically when I realise it wasn't a man at all. The young woman with bright, frizzy hair and a lip piercing sneers at me for taking so long, before putting her card into the slot.

The relief is washing over me in waves as I head back into the supermarket, accepting the empty shopping basket I'm handed by a shop assistant without even thinking about it. In fact, it's only when I've wandered halfway through the shop that I even recall the basket I left by the fish counter. I'm about to head straight there when I spot Jess being wheeled along the aisle towards me. As our eyes meet, there is a shared acknowledgement that neither of us wants to be here. The man pushing the chair must be her husband Charlie.

Is it merely coincidence that they happen to be here when I am? Probably. After all, Waitrose is the only supermarket in Northwood, so probably used by most of the residents at one point or another. Yet the horrified look on Jess's face when our eyes meet would suggest otherwise. Grace is with them, chattering as she pushes the small trolley under the watchful gaze of her father. Maybe I should have brought Daisy with me after all, so that this encounter wouldn't be wasted.

It's too late for me to pretend I haven't seen them, and so with a deep breath I plaster on my most welcoming of smiles. 'Why, Jess, fancy seeing you here.' Even I think my pitch is too high, the false-surprise dripping from every vowel.

Charlie stops the chair and trolley abruptly, and frowns curiously at me. He extends his hand. 'I don't believe we've met?'

I shake his hand, surprised by how cold it feels despite the warmth of the air around us; or maybe it's just me feeling the heat. 'I'm Morag. I met your wife Jess and wee Gracie at the park the other day.'

He smiles in acknowledgement, suggesting Jess has mentioned my name to him. I wonder what else she's told him.

'Charlie,' he says, pressing the icy hand to his faded blue polo shirt, his bicep tensing.

Such a handsome man, who clearly takes care of himself. It's difficult to picture them as a couple, him in his designer shirt, and her in a crumpled, tatty tracksuit. I would venture that she didn't always look so dowdy, and it's hard to imagine he hasn't noticed her lack of effort.

'Hello again, Gracie,' I say, wanting to ruffle her hair, but feeling that Jess won't like it if I do.

'Is Daisy with you?' Grace asks, searching around the other shoppers closest to us.

'Alas, not today,' I say, my pitch still too forced. 'She's at home with her dad.'

'I'm in charge of the trolley.' Grace beams excitedly.

'And what a fantastic job you're doing.' I can feel myself smiling at her, but I don't really know why; there's just something so joyful about her features that I find I can't control what my face is doing. 'Daisy really enjoyed meeting you at the park,' I add, keen to foster any potential blossoming friendship. 'In fact, she hasn't stopped talking about you, and pestering me to take her back to the park since.'

'Maybe she could come to my house and play,' Grace says, before turning to check with her parents, whose faces are at polar opposites.

Charlie is listening intently, whilst Jess looks like she wants the ground to swallow her up.

Daisy looked so disheartened when I told her she couldn't come with me to pick up the groceries, and I don't think I can handle her moping around the house all afternoon. If these two are anything to do with *him*, then I need to know one way or another. I daren't tell Angus my darkest fears on a whim. There's only one thing for it.

'I've had a fabulous idea,' I declare too enthusiastically, the basket on my arm swinging. 'What are you three up to this afternoon?'

'We were hoping to cook up a barbecue,' Charlie says as Jess squirms in the chair, 'but they've already run out of burgers. Can you believe that? I mean, I know it's supposed to be a scorcher this weekend, but you'd think they'd account for that and order in extra stock.'

'What a coincidence,' I say, and it really is. 'Angus is due to fire up the barbecue this afternoon too. We have plenty of burgers in the freezer at home if you'd like to join us? Angus has been on at me about organising a house warming of some sort; reckons it's bad luck not to toast the walls or some such thing. Daisy would love to see Grace again, and it'll give you both a chance to meet Angus. What do you say?'

Jess doesn't look keen, but her husband doesn't give her the chance to decline. 'That sounds wonderful,' he says. 'What time would you like us over?'

'Any time after one will be fine,' I tell them both, my face starting to ache from all the forced smiling. I tell them the address, already thinking that I'm taking a huge chance, and Charlie types it into his phone.

Maybe I should have checked with Angus first. I did tell him about meeting Jess at the park, and he didn't seem worried or troubled by the encounter, but how is he going to react when three perfect strangers turn up at the house?

'Would you like us to bring anything?' Charlie asks, gently rubbing Jess's tense shoulders.

'Ah no, just yourselves. We'll see you soon.'

With that Charlie wheels Jess and the trolley away, and as I watch them disappear among the throng of shoppers, I can't keep my eyes off Grace's bobbing ponytail as she cheerfully skips along.

Chapter Five

Now

Detective Inspector Mike Ferry squeezed the bridge of his nose between his thumb and forefinger, as if the pressure would somehow distract him from the pounding ache behind his eyes. It didn't help, and so, straightening, he squinted at the small screen on the desk before him. Of all the days to forget his glasses, why did it have to be today?

The blinds drawn, the only light in the small box room came from the desk lamp, casting his disjointed shadow over the filing cabinets against the opposite wall. He had no idea of the time, other than it was late enough for his stomach to be growling. Running a hand over his closely cropped coffee-brown beard, he casually sniffed his pits, before reaching for the can of antiperspirant in the desk drawer, pushing it under his shirt and spraying liberally. He should have been home and in bed by now, but nobody had accounted for the late 999 call that would have the whole team on tenterhooks.

A short, sharp knock at the door was followed by DC Polly Viceroy's head appearing through the gap. 'You look like shit.'

Her cruel efficiency was misinterpreted as intolerance by some, but Mike couldn't argue with her conclusion. Stretching barely five feet, Polly had the tough exterior of a hardened detective who has seen and heard every joke about gnomes and dwarves and has a cutting reply for each. Rumour was that she kept her hair short and clothes neutral so others wouldn't consider her femininity a weakness. Mike had never found a weakness in her approach to the job.

'I brought you some painkillers,' she offered, holding out her fist, before emptying the contents into his outstretched palm.

There was no sign of a drink, so he threw the pills into his mouth, and ground his teeth to generate enough saliva to wash them down. He managed it on the third attempt, grimacing at the chalky aftertaste.

'Is that her?' Polly asked, nodding at the screen, as the door closed behind her.

Mike nodded. 'Yeah. What do we know about her so far?'

Polly studied the image of the woman who had been found at the bloody scene. 'Only what the first responders managed to ascertain, and I think they only identified her thanks to the debit card in her purse. Hasn't said a word since she was brought in, even when they collected her clothing for forensic examination. We're waiting for the on-call to check she's medically sound for interview.'

Mike leaned closer to the monitor. The tiny screen did little to help him ascertain age; anywhere between forty and sixty, as best he could guess. Hair tangled from the shower they'd had to arrange to wash the excess blood from her skin and hair. She hadn't moved since he'd been standing here watching. Not an inch. Maybe a sign of her guilt, or just shock at what she'd witnessed.

'You look nervous, Mike,' Polly observed. 'You've been chomping at the bit to be made SIO of a murder investigation. Don't tell me you're bottling it already.'

He fired her a scathing look. He wouldn't have tolerated such insubordination from anyone else in the team, but then Polly wasn't just anybody.

'Not nervous,' he replied evenly, 'just keeping a calm head. You know how important the first twenty-four hours are for a Senior Investigating Officer. Key decisions have to be made, which will drive the success of the investigation. Hare around like a bull in a china shop and things will be missed.'

She raised her eyebrows in exaggerated surprise. 'Someone's been cramming up on their textbooks. I'm impressed, Mike. For a moment, it almost sounded like you knew what you're doing.'

He ignored her attempt to get a second rise out of him. 'Anything more you can tell me about the victim yet?'

'Identity yet to be confirmed,' Polly said, consulting her notebook. 'Fingerprints and DNA not matched in the database, and no form of ID found on the body.'

'Has the post-mortem started yet?'

'Body was being transported to the mortuary the last I heard, but I'll follow up with the forensic pathology team. Initial conclusion at the scene was that the victim probably died as a result of a severed carotid artery, inflicted by the large blade discovered next to the body.'

Mike grimaced at the memory of the photographs of the scene he'd already been privy to. Even in a still snapshot, the scene was visceral, and enough to turn even a seasoned detective's stomach.

'And the blood pattern on this lady's clothes, is she killer or witness?' he asked.

'Too soon to say, but the forensic examiners are working on the clothing as priority. I'll chase for an update and let you know as soon as I have more information. What does your gut tell you? Did she do it?'

Mike ran a hand over his beard again, trying to read the woman's mind. 'Her clothes were covered in the victim's blood, she was the only person found at the scene, and she has yet to speak to us. Is that because she is in shock at what she saw, or because of what she did? I honestly don't want to answer that question until we know more. She's been brought in as a witness, and isn't under arrest, so the holding clock has yet to start ticking. We have time for now, but it's never enough. I want more of the unanswered questions resolved before we interview her.'

Polly turned to leave, before stopping and spinning back around. 'If she hadn't been discovered in a wheelchair, would you have already made up your mind?'

He glared at the challenge. 'I'm not discriminating against her because she can't walk.'

Polly raised a finger of warning. 'We don't know for certain that she can't walk yet. It could just as easily have been the victim's wheelchair, and that woman in the holding cell is playing on our pre-existing prejudices that less abled people aren't just as fucked up as the rest of us. If she truly is paraplegic, it doesn't mean that she couldn't just as easily have wielded that blade.'

Mike swallowed hard. Polly was right, of course she was.

The bloody tyre tracks in the crime scene photograph showed that the wheelchair had been beside the body, prior to the discovery of the witness in the hallway of the large detached house in Northwood. That didn't necessarily mean that the woman he was staring at owned the wheelchair. Only an examination of her medical history would confirm that, and even if it did turn out that she had no feeling in her legs, it didn't mean she couldn't have struck the killer blow.

He knew the first rule of investigating any major crime was to assume nothing, believe nobody, and challenge everything. Able-bodied or not, he had no doubt that the statue on the screen knew a lot more than she'd told them so far, and it would only be a matter of time until he figured out what dark secret she was keeping from them.

Chapter Six

Before – Jess

I knew going to the supermarket on a Saturday morning wasn't going to end well. Something in my gut told me things wouldn't be as rosy as Charlie had suggested, but against my better judgement I allowed him to convince me to go. Unfortunately, the weekly shop is another task I'm no longer able to undertake without help, which is why it has to be done at the weekend when Waitrose is crazily busy. Back in the day I would have avoided visiting any supermarket at the weekend.

It was his idea to put Grace in charge of the trolley. Initially he'd suggested strapping one of those custom-built baskets to the front of the wheelchair, but it's already hard enough to manoeuvre the chair without making it larger. Grace's eyes had lit up at the prospect of finally being allowed to wield the trolley, rather than being strapped inside it. On one of my good days I'd have been able to move the chair myself, but today isn't a good day. I've been awake since three, the curse of insomnia, a side effect of the antidepressants I'm taking. I'd begged Charlie to just leave me at home, but he'd said I needed a break from the house as I'd spent all Friday inside.

I know he doesn't want me to feel excluded, but I'm so exhausted that I just want to switch off from the world. I'm not sure he really understands how difficult some days get for me. He says he does, but then I catch frustrated eye rolls, and sharp sighs under his breath, and my mind fills with doubt.

I can't forget how disappointed he looked when he returned home last night. Doug had actually allowed their team to finish work early, as the pitch to the new client had gone well. Of course, Doug's concept of finishing early meant dragging the team to the pub for food and booze. Charlie was slurring as he walked in through the door at six, expecting his dinner to be waiting for him. But yesterday wasn't a good day either.

My condition and the cocktail of pills mean my life has more ups and downs than a rollercoaster. For every good day when I feel I have the strength and energy to accomplish anything, there are days when I can barely function. I think I overdid things with Thursday's trip to the park. I pushed myself all the way there and back, and now I'm suffering the consequences.

He'd hugged me tight as he'd lifted me out of the chair and into the downstairs bed, and his breath had been hot against my neck. I knew what he was hoping for, but I had to disappoint him *again*. He's always so understanding about it, but sex just isn't what it once was for me. We've attempted it once since the diagnosis – about a month ago – but it was as awkward and clumsy as the first time we ever slept together, all fingers and thumbs, and Charlie constantly checking I wasn't in pain. My loss of sexual appetite is just another worry on the pile. I can't deny him forever without risking losing him.

I've already lost too much.

My hand presses against my abdomen. We've been socially AWOL since losing Luke. I don't think our friends have been deliberately avoiding us, but I don't blame them for not wanting to hang out with a grief-stricken family, adjusting to what happened to me. I don't want to force them to tread on eggshells because they don't know what to say to us.

Before I'd even realised Charlie was pushing me towards Morag, our eyes had met, and she'd offered a small wave in my direction. Too late to turn back, I'd had to sit and watch while she introduced herself to Charlie, all charm and overly excitable chatter. Charlie might have fallen for it, but I see through her. There was no sign of Daisy today, so no chance for me to call her out on what she told me.

She's not my mum.

Daisy's words echo through my mind again. I spent a long time thinking about those four words yesterday, and even asked Grace whether Daisy had said anything to her at the park, but Grace admitted she'd done most of the talking.

Now here we are, bundled in the car, driving to their house ahead of a barbecue I'm genuinely dreading. Charlie had wanted us to host a barbecue today, and invite over all of our former friends, and even though the thought of that had filled me with dread, I'd reluctantly agreed to it to save disappointing him again. I suppose I should be relieved that Morag's invitation has meant sticking a pin in that idea, but knowing Charlie, it won't be long until he suggests something similar again.

'I don't see what your problem is,' Charlie is saying as he kills the engine. 'We hadn't arranged anything for this afternoon, and I think it was very kind of your friend to invite us around for food.'

She isn't my friend, I want to scream, but I'm conscious that Grace is in the back of the car, and I don't like her to hear me and Charlie arguing.

The house is bigger than ours and stands detached from any others, an inclining driveway bordered by a patch of yellowing lawn. There is a Land Rover facing down the driveway, and there's probably enough room for our little Hyundai, but Charlie has parked against the grass verge lining the pavement outside the property.

'We're here now,' he says brightly. 'We might as well go in and say hello. Grace is excited about seeing her friend too, aren't you, sweetie?'

Grace's head is bent low, scribbling another story in her notepad. 'Yeah,' she comments without looking up, a tinge of frustration that her father's question has interrupted her trail of thought.

I look up at the house, which blots out the cloudless sky. Large wooden struts hang down from the edge of the roof, giving it a faux-Tudor look, but judging by the size of the property and the others in the road, this street wasn't in existence even fifty years ago. There's something haunting about how dark the property's windows seem from the angle I'm looking at them, like something out of a horror movie. I can almost picture flashes of lightning against a black night sky, and kids daring each other to go and knock on the large oak door.

I shudder as Charlie's fingers brush against my arm.

'Hey, what's going on here?' he asks. 'If you really don't want to go in, I suppose we can drive away and phone them from home to say something came up.'

It's exactly what I wanted to hear him say, but his tone is desolate. I turn to look at him, and all I can see is fear and concern in his eyes. He's still as handsome as the first time I clapped eyes on him, but his face now wears an abandoned look. It is at times like this when I wish he would just open up about what happened. I want him to grieve too, but it's as if he feels compelled to be strong enough for the both of us, driving me to take on new challenges and move on with life, but I'm not ready to move on yet. It's barely six months since Luke was taken from me; why should I pretend like it's just another bleak chapter in life's story?

How can I explain that I don't want to get to know Morag and her family, when I can't even explain to myself why that is? I really wish he hadn't agreed to come here, or that he'd allowed me to just stay at home. I've been awake for ten hours, and I am exhausted. The doctor said I shouldn't overdo things, but I don't think Charlie quite appreciates how much effort it takes just to put on a happy face and pretend like I am coping with what's happened.

'How about,' he begins, glancing up at Grace's reflection in the rear-view mirror, 'we go in, and if you're still not happy after an hour, we make our excuses and leave? That'll give Grace and her friend a chance to play, and will ensure we're not being rude. You never know, Jess, you might find it's not nearly as bad as you think.'

He opens his door without another word, and I feel a knot tightening in my stomach. His door slams closed, and the car shakes as he then opens the boot, removes my chair and unfolds it. We can't afford to trade in the car for one that is more accessible for a wheelchair user, so we make do with the same car I was driving the night I was rushed to hospital, only I no longer drive it. My door opens, and I feel Charlie's strong arms shift below and around my body, and then he lifts me into the crushing humidity, plonking me into the chair, and securing my feet in the straps. He wheels me onto the pavement, before helping Grace out of the car.

'You must be Jess,' a baritone voice booms, as a barrel-chested man in navy swim shorts and a short-sleeved shirt only fastened by two buttons exits the house and proceeds down the drive towards us. 'I'm Angus,' he says with a thrust of handshakes for me and Charlie, and a pat on the head for Grace. 'Morag's told me all about you,' he adds, smiling at me.

God only know what that means; she knows nothing about me other than I'm wheelchair-bound and occasionally shop in Waitrose. What else could she have said?

'You're all most welcome,' Angus adds, turning and ushering us towards the property. 'Might be easier for you to push Jess past my car, rather than through the house. There's a gate into the back garden by the garage. I'll go through and open it.'

I hear Charlie grunt with pain as he begins to push me up the driveway, steeper than it had looked from the car. I want to offer to help, but I can barely lift my hands to brush my fringe from my eyes. Charlie soldiers on, as he always does, and despite the squeeze, we make it past the Land Rover, and find Angus waiting for us by the tall wooden gate.

'Can I get you a lager, uh...?' Angus says, suddenly realising he doesn't know Charlie's name.

'I probably shouldn't, as I'm driving,' Charlie says, pushing me through the gate and onto a large patio. 'And it's Charlie, by the way.'

The garden is far longer than I had imagined. The patio is large enough for an eight-seat square table, a swing seat by the fence, a barbecue, and one of those tall outdoor heaters. In fact, their patio is only a fraction smaller than our entire back garden. The lawn must stretch at least twenty metres, is recently mowed, and contains a large enclosed trampoline, which Grace immediately sprints over to. Daisy stops bouncing, unzips the netting, and helps pull Grace inside before the two girls start bouncing in tandem, as if they have rehearsed the routine for years.

'Ah, go on, you can have one lager without breaking any laws,' Angus says encouragingly, slapping Charlie's back, and causing my chair to shake. 'Plus, Morag will be less judgemental of me having a few if you have one.'

'I suppose you're right,' Charlie says, and the two men walk off towards the side door into the garage.

They return a moment later with a chilled can each, already talking like close friends. Angus escorts Charlie to the smoking barbecue, leaving me stuck near the gate, with nobody to talk to, and no guidance on what I should do. I can't see Morag in the garden, but can't shake the sense of being watched. Daisy and Grace are still bouncing on the trampoline, and Angus is too engrossed, showing Charlie all the wondrous gadgets that he has for the large drum-shaped barbecue. I twist awkwardly in the chair to try and get a better look at the rear face of the house, but as I do, I feel a sharp twinge just above my hip, and wince.

'Our guests have arrived!' I hear Morag declare excitedly from somewhere within the house, and a moment later she is strutting out of the back door, and playfully swiping at Angus's arm. 'You never told me they'd arrived.'

She leans in and kisses Charlie on both cheeks, and officially introduces herself, before bouncing towards me, stooping to kiss my cheeks. I've never felt comfortable with excessive shows of affection, particularly between people who don't know one another, but I do my best to hide my disdain.

'Has that brute of a husband of mine not offered you a drink?' Morag says, loud enough to interrupt Angus and Charlie's talking. 'Where are your manners, Angus?'

He offers me an apologetic nod, before returning to his conversation.

'What can I get for you?' Morag says, still stooped towards me. 'Pimms? Wine? G and T?'

My eyes fall on the large wine glass in Morag's hand, condensation forming around the lipstick stain on the rim. I'm salivating at the thought of the cool nectar flowing over my tongue and catching on the back of my throat. I can almost taste it, and it takes effort to force my eyes away. 'I'm not supposed to consume alcohol with the painkillers I'm on,' I say.

In truth I haven't wanted to since… *whisper it… since what happened*. I ask for a glass of water instead.

She gives me a confused look, but then her mind catches up, and she nods at the chair, rolling her eyes in self-deprecation, and heads back towards the house.

'Here you go,' she says when she returns, placing a

dripping glass on the corner of the table 'Shall I push you over?'

'I can manage,' I say, willing my hands to the frame of the wheels, and hoping my arms have enough to push me, but my left hand slips, and I lurch forwards.

Morag immediately rushes over, and I feel her grip the handles behind me. 'Allow me.'

She has pushed me over to the table before I can protest, and as I look to Charlie for help, all I see is the back of his shirt.

Morag drops into a vacant chair near me, and I can feel her watching me as I straighten back into the chair. 'So fortunate for us to run into one another in Waitrose,' she says, but the exuberance has gone. 'I was hoping I'd get the chance to speak to you again, Jess. I feel like there will be so many things we have in common.'

The knot in my stomach tightens further, and I have no doubt in my mind now that she knows what Daisy told me at the park.

Chapter Seven

Before – Morag

Thick smoke drifts across the patio, and I can see Jess is giving the impression it's all too much, coughing and spluttering while Angus turns the meat. I'm busy preparing salad to accompany the burgers and steaks Angus insisted on cooking.

'You want us to make a good impression, don't you?' he'd said before they'd arrived.

I suppose he's right; I don't want to give her any further reason to unpick the version of our life we've carefully knitted together.

Although I'd told them not to bother bringing anything, it would have been courteous to have ignored the suggestion, wouldn't it? If they'd invited us to their house I probably would have brought flowers and maybe a bottle of wine. Maybe that's the difference between us. I know I was raised to be gracious to guests.

I silently chastise myself for this thought. I need to play nice.

My linking them to *him* is purely circumstantial at the moment. Jess being at the park and then coincidentally this morning at Waitrose could be just that – coincidental. But then I've made that mistake before; assumed everything was fine, only to be bitten later. I hate feeling so on edge all the time. What I'd give for the freedom to just accept people at face value, rather than constantly trying to see through the façade. You can tell a lot about people from their behaviour and tone of voice. I read all about it after the first time I was tricked into believing someone's backstory.

I continue to watch her, fanning away the smoke with her hand, making no effort to engage with Angus or her own husband, if that's who he really is. She keeps glancing back towards the house, like she's sizing it up. She can't see me from there because of the angle of the sun. I know because I've sat in that exact spot before. I feel a bit sneaky watching, but I daren't take my eyes off her for a moment.

Realistically, if she is somehow – as improbable as it may seem – working for *him*, then maybe that wheelchair isn't even necessary. For all I know she's perfectly able, and only using it to lull us into a false sense of security.

'You've got that look in your eyes again,' I hear Angus say.

It startles me, as I hadn't even realised he'd come inside.

'And what look is that?' I ask as casually as I can manage, my flushed cheeks betraying me.

'Mischievous,' he chuckles. 'Like you're lost in your head, making plans to conquer the world.'

'I'm just washing the tomatoes,' I say, raising my fingers out of the stream of tap water.

He looks down at my hands, filled with the juiciest red cherry tomatoes. 'Yeah, but I reckon after the first minute of you holding them there they'd be clean enough. The extra few minutes are only going to make them lose colour.'

Have I really been standing here that long? He's probably just teasing, but I suppose I did get distracted by Jess. There is something enigmatic about her, despite the tired eyes, frumpy face and mess of hair. I imagine she was probably once quite the beauty queen, attractive in a way I never was. It seems such a pity that she's let herself go.

I quickly drop the tomatoes onto the bed of lettuce and cucumber, and carry them outside, placing them on the table, and sitting myself into the chair closest to Jess.

'Sorry about all the smoke,' I offer. 'Do you want me to move you further into the garden? Or maybe inside until the meat is ready?'

She appears to wave away my concern. 'A little smoke never hurt anyone.' Her smile looks forced.

There is a pause when our eyes meet. 'Not strictly true, that.'

Her brow furrows. 'What isn't?'

'That smoke never hurt anyone,' I explain. 'It's smoke inhalation that kills most victims of house fires. People always assume that it's the flames burning the victims to death, but more often than not, smoke inhalation kills them first.'

She is blushing now, as am I. I hadn't meant the comment to be so blunt. I seem to have forgotten myself for a moment.

An awkward silence descends, and I'm relieved when Angus lifts the lid on the barbecue and announces the meat is almost ready. As a fresh cloud of smoke drifts across the patio, I temporarily lose sight of Daisy and Grace. They're no longer on the trampoline, and I'm relieved that their bouncing didn't result in any bumps or sprains. They're now at the foot of the garden, playing in the play house Angus insisted on buying for her. It's the only purchase we've made in this house that we won't be able to take with us if we leave. Hopefully, she won't grow too attached to it.

Birds are chirping somewhere nearby. The play house is in the shade of two large sycamore trees that sit just inside the tall fence panels. It really is a beautiful garden, and I wish I was more green-fingered to keep it up to this standard but, alas, it will probably turn to ruin like the rest of us.

Angus and Charlie join us at the table, and at first I'm grateful when Angus starts talking. 'Morag tells me Grace and Daisy are going to be starting school together,' he says in Jess's direction.

Her eyes are tearing slightly, but she blinks them away. 'That's right.'

'It hasn't been easy for Daisy, having to leave her friends behind and start afresh, but at least she's young enough to start over. Not so easy when you're older.'

I fire a glare in his direction, a warning not to reveal too much about what brought us here. It's too late though.

Jess's interest is piqued. 'Morag said you moved here from Aberdeen?'

He nods, avoiding my eye contact. 'Aye, but we'd actually being living in Wolverhampton for the best part of a year before we packed up.'

Jess sits up, looking engaged for the first time since she arrived. 'Oh really? What were you doing in Wolverhampton?'

Poor Angus will see her interest as friendly, but he can sometimes be as naïve as me.

'Work,' I say, ending the conversation. 'Now, Angus, you'd best get those steaks off the grill before they're hard as bricks. Does anyone else want another drink?'

Nobody responds to my question, but Jess is staring intently at Angus. 'What is it you do for a living, Angus?'

His brow has dampened, and I think he finally realises he should be more careful about what he is saying. I'm sure the couple of beers he's already had aren't helping his judgement.

'The best way to describe it is logistics,' he finally says. 'I drove articulated lorries for years, until I couldn't do it anymore, but my boss didn't want to lose my experience, so he brought me into a behind the scenes role. I'm responsible for planning routes for our drivers, and ensuring that the jobs they're given allow sufficient downtime in between. Not as exciting as what your Charlie does.'

'It really isn't that exciting,' Charlie chimes in. 'Morag, would you mind showing me where the bathroom is so I can wash my hands?'

I like Charlie. He has a warm aura, and I find myself wanting to trust him. I assume that's why he is so successful selling stocks and shares. He has one of those faces that can so easily convince you. The sort of friendly charm that you'd hear from a politician or second-hand car salesman. A man who could lie to you with a smile on his face.

I stand, and usher him in through the kitchen door. 'We don't have a downstairs bathroom, I'm afraid. It's upstairs, turn left at the top, and you should see it.'

He thanks me, and I'm relieved to hear his footfalls on the stairs moments later. I remain near the door to the hallway, straining to hear which direction his steps go, but I soon hear the bathroom door being closed and bolted. Opening the fridge, I pull out the bottle of wine I bought this morning, now nicely chilled, and pour a large glass, which I start to gulp down. Angus has warned me about afternoon drinking, but he's hardly one to pass judgement. I know I need to keep my wits about me, but my nerves are shot to shit right now, and if I don't calm down I'm going to end up saying something I might regret. I finish the glass as Charlie returns to the kitchen.

'It's a lovely house,' he says. 'Much bigger than ours.'

I've always found it odd how people constantly compare their lives to others, trying to judge who is more successful based on material possessions like houses and cars, or holidays abroad. Granted this house is larger than we're used to, but we're only renting it. We don't own it, and as far as I'm concerned it's unhomely. I would happily swap it for our wee cottage back in Aberdeen, but that's only a shell now; the fire and water damage left it structurally unsound. The last I'd heard, some developer was looking to tear it down and start again. If only real life was so easy.

'Does Jess work?'

His features tighten. 'Not at the moment. She worked for a local newspaper before... before the accident.'

My ears prick up at this word. I'd assumed that Jess had been restricted to her wheelchair since childhood, but maybe I've misjudged her.

'What happened,' I say, 'if you don't mind me asking?'

'Sure, no, it's okay,' he stammers, glancing back out the door towards Jess, who is sitting alone again. 'Jess was pregnant with our son Luke, but there were complications during his delivery, and ... he died. During the procedure, something went wrong, and she lost the feeling in her legs. The doctors have said there is a chance she will recover, but it's been really tough on her. Between you and me, she's really struggling with her mental health. I'm sure you can imagine the emotional impact of suddenly being confined to a wheelchair on top of losing our baby.'

Wow! I wasn't expecting him to be so open about their life and troubles. That certainly explains why she's let herself go, and my feelings of distrust are starting to evaporate, replaced by genuine empathy, but then I catch myself. That vulnerability is exactly the sort of trap that would be laid to catch out a former nurse.

'Can I get you another drink?' I ask, the fridge door still open.

'Thanks, but I'd better not,' he says, regaining his natural charm and warmth. 'Do you need any help with carrying anything out?'

I nod at the basket of rolls on the counter near the back door. 'You could carry the buns out, thank you.'

I top up my glass as Charlie heads back outside and starts talking to Jess. Angus is removing the meat from the barbecue as I join them. It is such a warm afternoon, and I can feel the wine starting to make my brain swim. There's clearly a lot more to this family than I'd realised, and even if they aren't connected to the man who haunts my dreams, I suddenly want to know exactly what secrets Jess is hiding, and why she seems so interested in us. Unfortunately for her, I too have ways of extracting the truth from people.

Chapter Eight

Now

Heading to the canteen on the first floor, Mike Ferry was pleased to catch up with the first responders, hunched over the pool table, one holding a steaming beaker of tea and the other chomping on a Mars bar.

'Can I get you anything?' Mike asked, approaching the vending machine and studying the contents. There was a bowl of leftover beef bourguignon in the fridge at home that he'd planned to devour with a large glass of merlot, but murder had a way of fucking up the best-laid plans. His stomach grumbles were becoming cramps, and against his better judgement he'd decided crisps and chocolate would have to sustain him until he could get to a late-night petrol station for a sandwich. When he'd first joined the service, canteens remained open until 10pm, but budget cuts now meant you were lucky to find a hot meal even at five in the evening.

'I'm fine, Guv,' PC Wozniak replied, sipping his tea.

Mike nodded at the larger-framed PCSO with him, who nodded as he squashed the last piece of chocolate into his mouth. 'Same again. Ta.'

Mike reached into his pocket and pulled out a handful of change, dropping it into the slot and punching in the digits for some salt and vinegar crisps and the Mars bar, and carried both over to the pool table.

'You two were the first responders at the address in Northwood, right?' Mike asked rhetorically.

'Yes, sir,' Wozniak replied, resting his cup on the edge of the pool table.

'What can you tell me about it?'

Wozniak considered the question while the PCSO opened the fresh chocolate bar and chomped down.

'Like something out of a movie,' the PCSO said between chews. 'Front door looked like it had been kicked in; hanging off the hinges, you know? Smelled musty too, like somebody had died in there. I mean, I know someone had, but I mean like someone had died there years ago.' He swallowed, and took another bite. 'And the blood – Jeez – definite horror movie shit.'

Mike had seen the early SOCO photographs, so that wasn't the information he was now seeking. 'What can you tell me about the woman you found?'

'The cripple?' The PCSO checked. 'She looked like a rabbit caught in the headlights when we spoke to her. All she kept saying was, "It was an accident," but I'm not sure how you let someone bleed out like that in an accident.'

Mike frowned. 'There was no mention of that in your report. What else did she say?'

57

Wozniak turned to face the PCSO too. 'You never told me she spoke to you.'

The PCSO loudly swallowed his mouthful, the blood draining from his face at the error. 'I... um... I mean, she said it in the spur of the moment. I – I – I didn't think it was important.'

Wozniak placed his hand on Mike's shoulder and ushered him back towards the vending machine. 'I was checking the victim while he was checking the witness for injuries. I swear he never mentioned that she'd spoken to him.'

Mike nodded his understanding, remembering the shock of the first ever murder scene he'd attended, and how the nightmares had clawed at him for over a week afterwards. 'Your honest opinion: did it look like an accident?'

Wozniak took a moment to compose himself. 'Too difficult to say. The blade appeared to be from a block on the kitchen counter, which would suggest the crime wasn't premeditated. On the other hand, there weren't any obvious bruises on the witness, which would suggest she was defending herself. And then I keep coming back to the fact that no attempt was made to call for an ambulance.'

'None at all?'

Wozniak shook his head. 'I keep thinking if that was me in that situation and I'd accidentally stabbed my partner in the neck, the first thing I'd do is phone for help.'

'Were there any other signs that a struggle may have ensued prior to the stabbing? With the door kicked in, I'm just wondering whether we're dealing with a home invasion of some sort, or an aggravated burglary.'

Wozniak kept a straight face. 'The one thing I did notice was a tea towel stained with blood, along with an amber-coloured cardigan, presumably belonging to your witness. At best guess I'd say both were used to try and stem the flow of blood in some way. If the victim was the aggressor, why did your witness try to sustain life after the stabbing?'

Mike thanked the two officers for their time, and peeled out of the canteen, bag of crisps in hand. There are two sides to every story, and as he wouldn't be able to talk to their witness until the on-call medical team had given the all-clear, his only choice was to start at the opposite end of the crime: the victim.

Chapter Nine

Before - Jess

I'm feeling a bit light-headed when Charlie returns to the table and squeezes my hand.

'The house is huge,' he whispers, leaning closer to me. 'I went to the toilet, and couldn't get over the enormity of the rooms. They must have a fair wad of money too, looking at the size of the television on the wall in the living room.'

I can't believe he's been snooping about inside. I hate the idea that guests of mine might wander about our house, looking at our possessions and passing judgement. Before I have chance to reprimand him, Morag appears through the smoke, and places a jug of homemade salad dressing next to the wooden salad bowl in the centre of the table.

'I forgot to ask,' she says, looking directly at me. 'You're not allergic to nuts, are you?'

I shake my head. 'Not that I'm aware of.'

'Ah, good. I've made some salted caramel ice cream for pudding, but it contains pecans.'

This woman is putting me to shame. My cooking – and I use the term very loosely – extends to nothing more than piercing film lids and heating in a microwave. It's been months since I prepared a proper home-cooked meal for my family. I know that isn't really my fault, but it doesn't stop the guilt that is suddenly overwhelming me.

'Sounds delicious,' Charlie says in answer to Morag's comment about the ice cream.

She disappears off, returning a moment later with plates and cutlery, and sets the table, as Angus continues to work at the barbecue.

'Charlie tells me you work for a newspaper,' Morag says when everyone is seated and Angus is passing around the plate of meat.

'I did,' I say, tearing apart the bread roll, and nibbling on the crumbs that cascade onto my plate.

'I always wanted to be a journalist,' Morag continues, staring wistfully into the distance. 'I'm sure it's nowhere near as glamorous as they make out in films and television, but I liked the idea of chasing after a story no matter the cost.'

Charlie holds the plate of meat before my eyes, indicating for me to show him what I'd like. The burgers are dripping in grease, and my stomach flips as I see the puddle swishing about.

'I make them myself,' Morag says watching me carefully. 'Using the finest Aberdeen-raised beef, I mince it myself, adding seasoning, onions, bacon, and garlic. Oh, and there's a little surprise in the middle when you bite into it.'

I don't want to think about what the surprise might be, and

nod at the burger nearest to me. I'll make a show of eating it, but will focus on the bread roll and salad. Charlie stabs the burger with his fork and the grease spills over the edge of the burger, dripping onto the base of the bread roll.

'So, is journalism as exciting as my younger self imagined, or drearier?' Morag continues, still watching me.

I hate being the centre of attention, but I can feel them all staring at me now, and I just want the ground to swallow me up. I'm also annoyed that Charlie has been speaking to her about me behind my back. Presumably that's what took him so long to return from the toilet.

'It was only the local paper, so mostly stories about fete openings, and missing pets,' I finally say, meeting Morag's gaze. 'I also had to ring up local businesses to try and sell advertising slots. Definitely as dull as it sounds.'

She blinks at me several times, as if her mind isn't able to compute what I have just said. 'Oh, I see, my misunderstanding then. When Charlie said... oh, it doesn't matter. Have some salad, please. It's just a bit of lettuce and some of the vegetables from our garden. The dressing is honey and mustard.'

I'm conscious that she hasn't asked me what I now do. Does that mean Charlie has told her I gave up my job, and the reason why? I hate feeling like he's been gossiping about me. Has he also told her about the rush to the hospital when I was in labour? Or what happened when the anaesthetist recommended the epidural?

Charlie holds the salad bowl near me and I nod for him to spoon some tomatoes and lettuce onto my plate, but I shake my head at the offer of the dressing. Sealing the burger in the bun, my hands are trembling as I raise it to my mouth and take a bite. I can taste the fat oozing between my teeth, but I can see Morag staring at me, and I try to smile through the revulsion I'm feeling.

'You girls look exhausted,' Morag says turning her attention to them. 'I hope you're having a good time, Grace.'

I look over at mention of my daughter's name, wiping bap flour from the corners of my lips as I force myself to swallow. Her little cheeks are rosy, and her hairline is soaked through with sweat, but she is nodding vigorously as she pushes some of the sausage into her mouth with a generous coating of ketchup.

'The trampoline is *amazing*,' she says, swallowing the sausage. 'I wish we had a trampoline at our house.'

'That trampoline would probably take up most of our garden,' Charlie chuckles, placing a delicate arm around her shoulders. 'Ooh, you're very hot, sweetheart,' he says, suddenly recoiling, and turning back to me. 'Did you put any sun lotion on Grace this morning?'

My hand shoots up to my mouth in shock at my own omission. I hadn't even thought about it. We were only supposed to be going to the supermarket and then home, but of course we never made it home, and it never crossed my mind that she would be playing out in the hot sun and need protecting.

Morag must sense how poor a mother I am, as she quickly stands, and races to the kitchen, clutching a yellow bottle when she returns. 'It's okay, we have plenty,' she says, handing the bottle to Charlie. 'It's factor 50, and not the cheap stuff either. Please, feel free to use it, and for yourselves too, if you want. I was going to say, your face is looking a bit flushed too, Jess.'

Pressing cold fingers to my cheeks, I can now feel how hot

they are. I've definitely caught the sun, but there's deep shame there too.

Charlie is smothering Grace in white lotion, and I am so disappointed in myself for not thinking about sun cream sooner. What kind of mother allows her daughter to play in the sun without adequate protection? I can't blame this on my condition; I've been too caught up in my own issues to consider my child, and that stings more than the dry skin of my cheeks.

Charlie squeezes more lotion into the palm of his hand, and sets to work on my face and neck. I'm still wearing the thin cardigan, but I feel like I'm overheating, and try my best to pull it off, but each jerk sends a shooting pain to my lower back, and I have to wait for Charlie to wipe his hands, before he pulls the cardigan off me.

The table, and those around it, are spinning, and I can taste bile building at the back of my throat. I reach unsteadily for my glass of water, and Grace shrieks as I knock the glass over and water spreads across the table cloth. I know what's coming, and I wish I was anywhere else but here. I need to move, but my arms fail me, and as my head lolls to the side, the heat rushes up my throat, and I know it's already too late.

———————————

My throat burns as Charlie continues to cradle me, his hand pressed into my chest to keep me from tumbling all the way into the upstairs bathroom sink. The same burn reverberates up to my nose, and I can only hope that the retching is now finished; surely there can't be anything left in my stomach.

'There, there,' Charlie purrs just behind me. 'How are you feeling now?'

Embarrassed, disgusted, and ashamed probably best sum up my current mood. It's horrid enough throwing up, but to do it at somebody else's house, and all over their patio. I've had to clear up Grace's vomit from the carpet before, and those stains just never go. They can be covered with the floral scent of various cleaning products, and even hidden by strategically placed furniture, but they're always there as a constant reminder of what happened.

I feel like I should offer to have their patio professionally cleaned, or maybe even re-laid. Even if some industrial-strength cleaning fluid manages to bleach out the stain, every time they step outside they'll remember how I lolled and lurched, before I couldn't control my up-chuck reflex.

Thankfully, I managed to avoid getting any of it on my clothes. There is nothing worse than that stench following wherever you move, serving as a reminder of what you've done.

'Jess, can you hear me?' Charlie tries again, and I realise I never actually answered his question.

I'm about to tell him I think it's stopped when I feel the rumbling in my stomach and my throat contracts, forcing my lips apart, and I clamp my eyes shut so I don't have to watch as more accelerant is applied to the burn in my throat and mouth. It's as if some invisible hand has reached into my gut and is wringing out my stomach like a sponge.

Charlie keeps tight grip of me as my body convulses with each strain, and I really don't know what I would have done if he hadn't been here with me. If I'd been alone at Morag and Angus's house, I'd probably still be outside redecorating the patio. But Charlie was quick to react, offering apologies as he scooped me into his arms, rushed in through the house, up the stairs, and into the bathroom, where we have now been for the best part of twenty minutes. The whole time he's been offering nothing but positive platitudes in a calm tone that I would struggle to maintain.

I feel his hand gently rubbing my back in a circular motion, and as I swallow and redraw breath, I wish I could tell him how much I love him right now. Lesser men wouldn't have held onto me without any mention of the ache he must now be feeling in his legs, having me sat on him as he straddles the closed toilet seat. What a picture we must make!

'Okay, I think I'm done,' I say, wiping my mouth with the back of my hand. A pink and orange gloop forms a bond between my chin and thumb, and I'm grateful when Charlie quickly passes me a piece of tissue he has torn from the roll. 'Thanks.'

'We should probably wait a moment longer,' he says without judgement. 'I thought you were done a couple of minutes ago, and then... How are you feeling?'

I don't want to tell him of my shame. 'Exhausted,' I settle for.

All I want now is to be taken home, cleaned up, and laid in bed. I need sleep, and the sooner this horrible day is over the better.

Poor Grace, what must she be thinking of her heaving mother? And it happened in front of her new friend. Grace doesn't need rumours starting up in the playground about her mother vomiting. And poor Daisy too for that matter. I feel humiliated by what has happened, but I know that seeing someone being sick can be equally mortifying. How many times have I watched on in agony, holding back Grace's hair, knowing there's nothing I can do to stop her pain? I've probably psychologically scarred both children for life!

'What do you think brought it on?' Charlie asks, still drawing circles on my back with his palm.

I instantly picture the pool of grease on the burgers, and my chest strains, but I'm able to control it with my breathing. 'I don't know, but it was the fatty residue on the burgers that triggered it I think.'

The circles on my back stop abruptly. 'I don't think it could have been the food,' Charlie states bluntly. 'Grace and I ate it fine without being ill, and you'd barely had a mouthful of yours. What else have you eaten today?'

My eyelids feel so heavy, and if I was given the chance I could easily curl up in Charlie's lap and go to sleep. My brain feels so weary that I can barely remember this morning.

'I had a slice of toast and a banana,' I say, unable to stifle my yawn. 'I'm sure it was seeing those burgers.'

'Jess, you can't blame the food. I watched Angus cooking the burgers and steaks and they are definitely cooked through. You were saying how hot you were, it's probably just a bit of heatstroke. Your back and chest are still pretty warm, and the back of your neck resembles a Belisha beacon. I bet that's what it is. Too much sun, and your body overheated.'

Morag's words suddenly echo in my mind: *there's a little surprise in the middle when you bite into it.*

I don't know why her words have suddenly returned to my short-term memory, and I frown involuntarily. Could she have put something in my burger to bring on the sickness? I dismiss the thought almost immediately. How would she know which burger I would choose, and what could she put in there to initiate nausea? Considering how hot the barbecue got, with the flames caressing every burger, it seems unlikely that any kind of poison could have survived such temperatures. More importantly, why would she want to make me ill?

She's not my mum.

A chill jolts down the length of my spine. Is that why she invited us to the barbecue, in order to show me she's in control? Does she want me to know that she knows what Daisy said?

I almost burst out in laughter at the ridiculousness of the paranoid thought. Of course that's not what happened; there are too many variables for that sort of plan to succeed.

'That's two minutes since your last retch. How are you feeling now?' Charlie asks.

I'm grateful for the distraction from my troubled imagination. 'I think it's stopped,' I say, belching, and re-tasting the burger, but nothing follows.

'I think we should go back downstairs and I'll fetch you a glass of cold water,' he says as he wraps my left arm around his neck, and puts his hand behind my kneecaps, lifting me into a cradled position.

I can hear Angus and Morag's voices in the kitchen, but the door is ajar, so I can't make out exactly what they are saying. Charlie carries me down the stairs very slowly, and into what must be their living room. An enormous television set is hanging from the wall, across from a faux fireplace. The room must be at least the length of our entire downstairs, if not the width. Two enormous leather sofas stand in an L-shape, and the leather feels cool and refreshing as Charlie gently lowers me onto the cushion closest to the door. A ceiling fan blows a refreshing breeze over my head, and I can feel the warmth of my neck already starting to cool.

There is a small wooden unit built into the wall beneath the television set, containing a SKY box and Blu-ray player, but there is no sign of any DVDs or Blu-ray cases in the immediate vicinity. Two large glass-fronted cabinets stand either side of the television. One contains a variety of glasses, each shining in the afternoon's sunlight streaming through the patio door at the opposite side of the room to me. The other cabinet must be for decorative reasons, as it is filled with an assortment of teapots of different shapes, sizes, and designs. Morag must be a collector.

Charlie returns to the room a moment later, tightly gripping a glass of water, ice cubes clinking together with each step. He drops to one knee, and presses the rim to my lips, tilting the glass so the water splashes over my teeth and dampens the burn in the back of my throat.

'You should take small sips often,' I hear Morag advising from the doorway.

It startles me as I hadn't heard her approaching. Angus appears at her side. Neither is masking their concern at my condition. Of all the ways I'd imagined today would go, this had never even entered my mind.

'I'm so sorry,' I offer, as Charlie places the drink on a coaster on the small table beside the sofa, and perches next to me.

'How are you feeling?' Morag offers, and I'm troubled to question whether the tremor in her tone is brought on by genuine concern or guilt at what she might have done to me.

'A bit better,' I say, sensing how worried I would be that the sick woman might throw up again over all the delicate furniture.

The fan is working wonders at cooling and relaxing me, and I feel confident that I won't be sick again any time soon.

'Can I have some more water, please?' I ask Charlie, who reaches for the glass and holds it for me again.

'Try not to drink too much too quickly,' Morag warns again. 'You don't want to bring on another bout of… well, you know.'

'You can take the lass out of nursing, but not the nurse out of the lass,' Angus says, placing a hand on Morag's shoulder, smiling proudly.

She pats his hand in acknowledgment. 'That was a long time ago. Even so, some things you never forget.'

For some reason it doesn't surprise me that Morag used to be a nurse. I can instantly picture her in a blue uniform, taking patient's temperatures and handing out medication. Although she must be in her early fifties – if not older – I doubt she is old enough to have retired from the profession, and I'm curious to know why she would have stepped away from such a tough but rewarding vocation.

'I'm so sorry about your patio,' I say. 'I don't mind paying to have it professionally cleaned.'

Angus quickly brushes away my concern with a shake of his hand. 'Don't be silly, it's already cleaned up. High-pressure hose and a broom did for that. Good as new.'

'Is Daisy okay? And Grace?'

'They're back on the trampoline,' Morag says, her frostiness thawing a fraction. 'I've promised them an ice lolly in a bit if that's okay with you?'

I nod, making a mental note to apologise to Grace when we're back home.

'I should go and sort those lollies,' Morag says, taking Angus's hand. 'Would you two like some of that salted caramel ice cream? Might help the burn in your throat,' she encourages.

I nod, hoping a burst of sugar will help boost my energy long enough to get home.

'I'd better come and check on Grace,' Charlie says, standing. 'Will you be okay on your own for a few minutes?' he asks, staring down at me.

There's a shooting pain in my back as I look up to meet his gaze. 'I'll be fine.'

He follows Morag and Angus out of the room, and the rumble of their voices mutes into the distance. My arms are pocked with bumps as the fan continues to blow a gale down on me. I want another sip of drink, but I daren't reach for the glass out of fear of dropping it and spilling water across the carpet. I shuffle into the cushion behind my back, and allow my eyes to wander around the room again. The orange brickwork gives the room an old-fashioned cottage-like ambience. There are photo frames of different shapes and sizes dotted about on the wall. Most are pictures of Morag and Angus in a variety of tourist locations across the globe. They seem well travelled, as I spot the Eiffel Tower, Taj Mahal, and Egyptian pyramids. And then I see an image of them with a sleeping Daisy in a pushchair. The three of them are on a beach, the sea crashing in the background, but the sky is covered in cloud, and all three are bundled up in thick coats. Angus looks a fraction thinner, but Morag hasn't aged since it was taken. It can't be more than a year old.

My head scans the room again, and I can't ignore the voice in the back of my mind. There must be a dozen pictures on the wall, but only this one includes Daisy. Where are all the baby photos? Our living room and bedroom have so many pictures of Grace in various states of age and craziness as we endeavoured to capture each of her 'firsts', as all new parents do. Where are the pictures of Morag cradling her firstborn in hospital? Or the pictures of Daisy and her first baby teeth?

I don't recall seeing any photographs on the wall of the staircase, and as much as I try to convince myself that those photographs are probably just waiting to be tacked up, I can't avoid questioning whether there's another reason that the first picture of the three of them is less than a year old.

She's not my mum.

Chapter Ten

Before - Morag

Wiping the last of the plates with the dishcloth, I keep replaying the moment Jess and Charlie left with Grace earlier on. Her demeanour was so different – so cold and detached – almost as if she thought I'd somehow caused her to throw up. I mean, why would she think such a thing? Despite my reservations about her true nature and motivations, I was nothing but pleasant and welcoming, so what gives her the right to judge me?

At least Daisy seemed to have fun; that ought to make her more malleable this evening. It's been so long since I've seen her laugh and play so openly that it almost brought tears to my eyes. Even Angus seemed to enjoy himself, chatting to Charlie. I could see the two of them becoming good friends, despite the gap in their ages, and that's what troubles me most.

I can't put my finger on it, but there is something about Jess that I simply do not trust. Inviting wee Grace and her dad into our lives is all well and good, but not if it means allowing Jess in too. I can't escape the overwhelming feeling that she will be the end of all of us.

'I want some milk,' I hear Daisy say sullenly over my shoulder.

'I want some milk, what?' I challenge.

'I want some milk *now*.'

I turn so I can face her, and show that my corrections are meant as a learning tool, and not because I'm trying to be abrasive. 'I think you meant to say: *please* may I have some milk?'

She stares blankly back at me, and in that instant she is almost the spitting image of her mother, with an equal amount of spite. Turning on her heel she storms from the room without repeating her request.

I sigh loudly, closing my eyes and counting to ten as I was once taught to do. Does she think this is any easier for me? For us? It wasn't my decision to move us down here, away from her friends. Doesn't she realise I feel lonely and isolated too?

Of course she doesn't, I remind myself. She's about to turn six… five, I correct myself. She's about to turn five. That's what her doctored birth certificate says, that's what we've told the school, and that's what we've told Daisy. I need to remember that if anyone asks, she is going to be five, and is just a bit more advanced for her age.

I'm pretty sure Grace didn't notice the disparity in their heights and mannerisms. And who picks up on things like that in this day and age anyway? All children are different, and I'm sure if you compared a six-year-old boy with a five-year-old girl, there'd be little difference, as girls mature quicker at that age (at all ages, my mother would have said!).

Reaching a plastic cup down from the cupboard, I half fill it with milk from the fridge, and carry it through to the living room where Daisy is sulking on the sofa. Angus is in the armchair, eyes closed and snoring, oblivious to the rest of the world.

'Here you go, Daisy,' I say with all the restraint I can muster.

She hesitantly reaches for the cup. 'Th – thank you,' she stammers, but it's enough to break through my concern.

'You're welcome, sweetheart. It's important to remember to be polite and courteous at all times. In this house we use "please" and "thank you" whenever we can. I don't mean to be off with you at times, and I know none of this is your fault.'

I watch her drink the milk silently.

'Did you have fun with wee Gracie today, sweetheart?'

Her face brightens momentarily. 'Yeah, she's funny.'

'That's good, sweetheart. You never know, she might even be in your class when you start school next week. That'd be grand, wouldn't it?'

The sulk returns. 'I miss my friends.'

I had hoped that today's jaunt with Grace would stop her thinking back to the last place we'd been, and the handful of friends she'd made while attending the last school.

'Why can't I go back to my old house?'

She asks me this question every day, and it never gets easier to answer. I wish I could tell her the truth, but she wouldn't understand; nobody would. I did what I did because…

I shake the thought away. I'm not going back to that place. Not now. Not ever again. It's too upsetting, and I want to keep things light and positive in here today.

'Hey, I was thinking, you and I need to go to the shops and

buy you some bits and pieces for school this week. What do you say? Maybe Monday or Tuesday we could go into Harrow and pick up what you need. Your new teacher sent a list of things you'll need, including wellington boots, and a gym bag. We could make a day of it. Just us girls, leave old misery boots here on his own.'

Angus grunts loudly as if he's picked up on the fact that I'm referring to him, but his eyes remain closed and the loud rhythm of his snoring soon returns.

Daisy finishes the milk and hands it back to me. 'Maybe.'

I had hoped a shopping trip would inspire a little more excitement, but I suppose I was being naïve.

'I miss my mum,' she sighs, and as she looks up at me, I can see her eyes welling up.

Ah, this again. I've tried so hard to get her to think of me as her real mum, but every time it feels like we're making progress, something happens and she ends up mentioning her.

'As do we all,' I say, standing, not prepared to get drawn into that conversation again. Carrying the plastic cup out to the kitchen, I rinse it in what is left of the soapy water in the sink, and place it on the draining board. Then heading to the fridge, I once again reach for the bottle of wine, knowing it will only numb the memories for so long, but hoping it will keep them at bay until the morning.

Chapter Eleven

Now

The ache behind Mike Ferry's eyes was even more exaggerated beneath the harsh white light of the overhead halogen bulbs, bathing everything in its clean glow. Each of the three unused stainless steel slabs reflected the light back at odd angles, making the glare seem so much worse.

'You okay?' Dr Karen Murphy asked, her County Down accent grating.

'I'll be fine,' Mike replied, wishing he'd brought his prescription sunglasses into the lab, instead of leaving them in the car.

It wasn't the first time he'd had to come to a morgue to hear a forensic pathologist's preliminary report on a murder victim, but it was the first time he'd been the sole attendee. He could have dragged along Polly or any of the team assigned to him, but there were plenty of other urgent tasks that needed completing. Usually he only accompanied the Senior

Investigating Officer to such meetings, listening attentively as the SIO asked pertinent questions. And as he tried to replay any of his previous visits, his mind remained bare of questions.

'You sure you're okay?' Dr Murphy checked again, staring out through her protective goggles. 'You wouldn't be the first wet-behind-the-ears copper to hurl at the sight of a dead body.'

He ignored the dig, and nodded for her to start her briefing. It wasn't the purple tinge of the corpse's skin, nor the overpowering smell of bleach, that was making his stomach turn.

'Victim is male, obviously,' the pathologist began, the blue polythene over-suit crackling as she leaned across the statuesque body, pointing at the gaping wound beneath the chin. 'Death was caused by a single puncture wound to the neck, severing the left carotid artery. There is some evidence of a struggle prior to the stabbing. The bruising to the torso here is quite pronounced, but I would say was caused at least two days ago, so may be unrelated to whatever led to today's incident.'

'Or today could have been a continuation of what occurred previously,' Mike corrected, refusing to rule anything out at this stage. With domestic abuse cases on the rise, there was every chance the victim wasn't as guilt-free as she was presuming.

'Quite. The blade made a real mess of the artery and surrounding veins, so he would have bled out rapidly. I imagine the scene was a river of blood, no?'

Mike's own cheeks drained as he thought back to the visceral crime scene photographs, and the canteen conversation with the first responders; a cold sweat dampened his shirt collar.

'I would also expect the killer's clothes would have been saturated in the victim's blood,' Dr Murphy added. 'There was a witness found at the scene, or so I heard?'

Mike nodded. 'Woman in a wheelchair was at the house when the first responders arrived. Bloody tyre tracks led from the body in the kitchen to where she was discovered in the hallway. Head to toe in blood apparently. Shouldn't be too difficult to confirm if it was the victim's.'

'That's interesting,' Dr Murphy said, forming a fist above the victim's face. 'I was going to add that the trajectory of the blade looks like it was angled upwards when it struck the flesh.' She mimed the action. 'The killer was probably shorter than the victim, or on the floor when the blow was struck. But I suppose he could have been on his knees when it occurred.'

'How tall is he?'

'Five feet, eleven inches, so pretty average.'

Mike pictured the victim crawling across the floor towards the woman in the wheelchair, reaching out to her for mercy when the blade flew through the air and hit its target.

'How long would it have taken him to die?'

She considered the question. 'The brain goes into shock when the blood supply is cut, starts shutting down, like a fire sale. He would have passed out pretty quickly, knowing that something awful had happened, but probably unable to comprehend exactly what. The speed would depend on how upright he was when he was struck. Gravity is the biggest catalyst with blood loss, so if he was standing, he would have been unconscious within a few seconds. If he was flat on the floor, it would have taken a little longer, but he probably didn't suffer too much because the brain goes bat shit crazy when it's under such threat.'

Mike took a breath to steady the bile building at the back of his throat. 'Any foreign DNA discovered on the body?'

'You'll have to check with the team running the forensics. They came in and took nail clippings, and examined the body for trace examples – hair, et cetera – but they neglected to confirm whether they'd found anything out of the ordinary.'

Mike scribbled a note in his book to have Polly chase up the nail clippings. The witness in the wheelchair didn't have any scratch marks that had been noted when they'd taken her clothes for processing, but that didn't mean the victim hadn't managed to grab a handful of her hair as he'd lain on the floor, the life draining from him.

'Anything else you can tell me about the victim?' Mike asked, narrowing his eyes against the harsh white light.

'A deep scratch on his neck, so check your suspect's nails for skin tissue. Also, I found a birthmark behind his right knee.' She lifted the white sheet covering his legs, and angled the knee so Mike could see behind it. 'Might help identify him if there's no DNA or prints match in the database.' Returning the sheet, she moved away from the slab, and over to the large counter against the wall.

Mike followed her across, in awe of the array of medical machinery that beeped and whirred, none of which he understood. 'Stomach contents?'

She looked impressed by the question. 'Still being processed, but I'll send the findings across when I know more.'

Mike thanked her, keeping his head dipped as he headed for the door, willing himself not to bring up the salt and vinegar crisps before he made it out into the safety of darkness.

Chapter Twelve

Before - Jess

I'm running around after Grace in the park, when a gentle shaking of my arms wakes me. For a moment, it feels like I've fallen, and I start, until I open my eyes, and see Charlie's exhausted face in the dimly lit room.

'What time is it?' I try to ask, my mouth and throat so dry that I croak it rather than enunciate the question properly.

'Just after seven,' he says, smiling empathetically.

I glance over at the bedside clock for confirmation. How is it so late? After we got home from Morag and Angus's house I felt so tired that I told Charlie I would have a little rest. The last thing I recall is reading. The book in question is balanced on top of the bedside clock.

'I thought I should wake you, or you won't be able to sleep tonight,' Charlie continues. 'How are you feeling? Any more sickness?'

Thankfully, I haven't thrown up since Morag's bathroom, and my cheeks burn at the memory. As I replay the afternoon in my mind, it's like I'm watching someone else picking at the food, before expelling the contents of her stomach all over the patio.

'Better now,' I croak, though my stomach is empty, and my throat feels like liquid hasn't passed along it in months.

Charlie rubs my arm, and this is the first I realise how cold it feels, and shudder involuntarily. 'I can't take you anywhere, can I?' He chuckles. 'I think we should put some after-sun gel on your face, neck and shoulders just to be safe.

As he mentions each body part, I realise it isn't my embarrassment that is causing the warmth. I gently press icy fingertips against my collarbone, and flinch.

'Even with the lights low, I can tell we could fry an egg on that neckline,' he gently teases. 'Come on, I'll help you get out of bed. It's time for your medication anyway.'

He pulls back the thin sheet, and I'm relieved to see I haven't had an accident in bed. I must have been asleep for three hours or more, and I haven't emptied my bladder since we were at their house. As Charlie scoops an arm under my knees, I spot the tell-tale sign of the incontinence pants I don most evenings. During the day I'm more than capable of identifying when I need to go to the toilet. What little feeling I have left allows me to avoid the need for a catheter, which is a blessing, but the signals to my brain are not as strong when I am lying flat in bed, which we discovered very early on.

I don't remember slipping on the pants before going for a doze, and Charlie must notice my confusion, as he adds, 'I put them on you. I came in to check if you'd like a tea, and found you zonked out, your book on my pillow. I thought it would be safer if I… I hope that's okay?'

It's moments like this that remind me how lucky I am to have a considerate husband. He may be late home from work most days, but he has the patience of a saint. I lean forward and kiss his cheek, as he lifts me out of bed and carries me to my chair. Despite the lack of food in my system, the nap has had a wondrous effect on my energy levels. Charlie offers to push me out of the room, but I politely decline, gripping the side of the wheels and manoeuvring myself through the doorway, into the corridor, and to the right.

'You hungry?' he calls out, heading the opposite way to the kitchen.

'Starved,' I reply, rolling into the living room, surprised to see the television switched off, and no sign of Grace.

'How about I whip up my world-famous tortilla Española?' he asks, appearing in the doorway. 'Full of everything an unwell patient needs, and kind on the stomach.'

Essentially it's an omelette with cheese, potatoes, and onions, not exactly cordon bleu, but something he knows how to cook without weighing all the ingredients. Right now I'd eat anything he offered.

'Sounds delicious,' I reply, smiling gratefully, as my stomach rumbles.

'Great!' he says, probably relieved I didn't ask for something complicated.

'Charlie,' I say, as he's turning back towards the kitchen. 'Where's Grace?'

'Oh, I put her to bed already,' he replies. 'She was so tired from all that bouncing on the trampoline and tearing around that enormous garden with Daisy. Plus, I figured you weren't really in any state to sort her and read.'

'Okay,' I say, as he disappears towards the kitchen, but there is sorrow in my heart. I know that he's done a kind thing with the best of intentions, but it saddens me that I won't get to say goodnight to my daughter, nor apologise for any embarrassment my sickness might have caused.

The living room is so quiet without Grace haring about, and as I roll across to the television remote, I catch a glimpse of the photo frame standing on the coffee table. It's one of those frames pregnant women receive, allowing them to display the first two ultrasound scans, and finally a picture of the swaddled baby: the first ever photographs of Grace.

We did buy an identical frame for Luke too, but it's just too painful a reminder to have on display. It's safely wrapped in the old brown suitcase with all the other mementos that remind me of the short time we spent together. One day I pray I will have the courage to display all of his things, but I'm not there yet.

I lift the frame into my lap, studying the evolution from two lumps and a skinny arm, to two much larger lumps and four spindly limbs, and then the bundle of pink, tightly wrapped in white blankets. The swaddled Grace looks nothing like she does now; her hair was so dark when she was born that we were convinced she would look more like Charlie than me. Over time, the hair colour softened until it resembled my own caramel tones. Her essence is there in the picture though.

I return the frame to the table, remembering the only image of Daisy I saw on the living-room wall in the other house. Surely, Morag would have a similar frame for displaying ultrasound pictures – I don't think I've ever met a mother who doesn't own one – and would proudly display it? Even if she was a mature first mother, that's only more reason to celebrate the miracle of Daisy's life.

Certain I can't be the only one to find it odd, I roll into the kitchen, where I find Charlie peeling potatoes while a pan of water simmers on the hob beside him.

'It shouldn't be too long,' he says, hearing my tyres squeaking on the linoleum. 'Half an hour or so. Your pills are on the side there with some water. I was going to bring them through once the potatoes were on the boil.'

Ignoring the pills, I drain the glass, but it does little to sate my thirst.

'Did you notice the photographs in Morag's lounge?' I ask, wiping my mouth with the back of my hand.

He looks around, confused lines furrowing his brow. 'Not particularly.'

He's never been blessed with the greatest observational skills. He's an intelligent man, of that I have no doubt, but he often misses the minutiae.

'There were loads of images of Morag and Angus in different tourist hotspots, but just the one image of them with Daisy, and it could only have been a year old at most.'

'And?'

'Well, don't you think that's a bit strange? Think about the number of pictures of Grace we have on the walls. Pictures of her alone, pictures with you, pictures with me, and then pictures of the three of us. It's rare we have any photographs without her in.'

He slices and drops potatoes into the pan. 'What's your point?'

'I just think it's strange that they wouldn't have any images of Daisy as a baby. Did Morag mention anything to you when the two of you were talking?'

He gives me another puzzled look. 'We didn't really talk; I was with Angus most of the time. We largely discussed work and football. He's an Aberdeen fan, but said he's thinking of trying to get tickets to watch Watford's next match. Asked if I wanted to tag along, and I said why not. You wouldn't mind, would you? It would probably be a Saturday match, but I'd give you notice so we can make sure that you and Grace are all right on your own.'

He's failing to see what seems so obvious to me now.

She's not my mum.

It's time to spell it out for him, once and for all. Taking a deep breath, I blurt it out: 'I don't think Morag and Angus are Daisy's real parents.'

He starts chopping the onion without looking up.

'Did you hear what I said?' I ask, conscious that the extractor fan is whirring in the background.

He lowers the knife, and turns so he is facing me, his back to the counter and onion. His eyes are watering slightly, but I think that is the effect of the onion. 'Is this about *your* mum and dad?'

The question throws me, and my mouth opens to speak, but I don't know what to say.

He crouches down before me. 'I know that you said things were never the same between you and your parents once they told you that you were adopted, but I think you're taking a massive leap to assume that Morag and Angus adopted Daisy.'

He has totally missed the point, and I hadn't even considered the prospect that they might have adopted her.

'I get that they're older for first-time parents,' Charlie

continues, and I recognise that pitying look again. 'Being new to the area, they're maybe not as relaxed about things as other London-bred parents we know, but they've offered me no reason to assume that they aren't Daisy's actual parents.'

I wheel myself backwards, annoyed at where his thought processes have gone. 'This is nothing to do with my situation,' I snap.

He pushes closer. 'Are you sure? You have to admit, when your dad died last year it was a shock to all of us, and you wouldn't be the first to have unresolved issues about your birth parents. Maybe all this – the park, the photographs – maybe it's just your mind's way of dealing with your own issues.'

'This has *nothing* to do with my adoption,' I growl, louder than I'd anticipated, wheeling myself away so he doesn't see my own eyes moistening.

———

I wish now that Charlie had just left me sleeping earlier. As the gentle rumble of his snoring beats a rhythm in time to the rise and fall of the duvet, I feel nothing but envy. What I would give to be sleeping now.

The blue digits of the bedside clock burn a hole in the darkness surrounding us, and I know it isn't Charlie's snoring, nor the fact that dawn is around the corner, that has me lying here wide awake yet physically exhausted. I tend to spend at least a couple of hours awake in the darkness when I should be lost to dreams and rest. Had Charlie left me sleeping earlier, I might have crammed in a few extra hours before the insomnia came calling for me. How I wish I could just stop taking *all* the prescribed pills for a few weeks, just until I can get things clear in my mind, but without them I will be bedridden, and subsequently impacted by bedsores.

You've got to make the best of a bad situation, is what my dad would tell me if he was here now. I do miss his cheerful optimism. No matter how great the adversity, he always managed to find time to smile and offer me words of encouragement. I'm grateful that he never got to see my suffering, but how I wish I could hug him one more time and thank him for everything he did for me.

My fifteenth birthday was the day my parents chose to tell me I was adopted. That sounds cruel, I know, but there was nothing unloving about their intentions. As an only child, I was used to them treating me with the respect they expected me to extend to them. And so, when I was through opening my presents and we'd celebrated a delicious hot breakfast, they turned to me, and holding hands, delivered the news that would permanently alter my understanding of the world.

What I'd never admitted to them – what I've never told anybody – is that I'd always suspected something wasn't quite right. I didn't really resemble either of them, plus there were clues they'd subconsciously dropped throughout my childhood, referring to me as their 'gift from the angels'.

My birth mother, they told me, was fifteen herself when she fell pregnant, still a child herself. My biological father was not named on the birth certificate, and whether my birth mother knew who he was, she never divulged. She was a clever girl by all accounts, destined for university and an important career, and raising a child at such a young age was never on the cards.

Her parents, my maternal grandparents, were supportive of

her decision to give me up for adoption, but on the understanding that they would cut all ties. Having lost Luke, I can understand how painful it would be to see constant reminders of what could have been. Even now as I lie beneath the bedding, I can still feel the echo of him moving around inside me, and it brings back all those painful memories of what I did.

Charlie snorts loudly, and rolls away from me, as I dab my eyes on the sheet. It had been heartbreaking telling Grace that she wouldn't get to meet her baby brother. Throughout the pregnancy she'd been so excited, and I wonder now whether he heard her voice when she would talk to him through my belly. She'd tell him the stories she'd made up, and how she would share her toys and books with him. It feels now like he was the missing piece of our jigsaw, a piece we will never be able to slot into place, and so the puzzle will remain incomplete.

Is that how my birth mother felt when all the papers were signed and she returned home alone? Was there ever a moment when she woke in the middle of the night and dared to dream what her life would have been like had she made different decisions? I wonder too whether she ever looked me up or tried to make contact. I once asked to see a picture of my birth mother, but my parents said they only met her the one time when the paperwork was signed.

Charlie stirs next to me again, and I remember his suggestion that Morag and Angus might have adopted Daisy. Is that what she'd meant when she'd approached me in the park?

I close my eyes and replay the scene in my head. The way she gripped the arms of the wheelchair, her knuckles white with the strain, her eyes shining with tears, her trembling lips as she whispered those four little words.

I shake my head in disbelief. Why was she so scared? I remember feeling lost and confused in the days that followed my fifteenth birthday, but there was never any fear; my parents had shown me too much love for me to question their feelings towards me.

Daisy's panic had only worsened when Morag had come over and introduced herself, and then she'd been so quiet throughout our time at the coffee stand, and even at the barbecue earlier she hadn't spoken a word to me.

I sit up in frustration. Why am I letting this bother me so much? I know nothing about Daisy or Morag and Angus, so why am I so hung up on four little words that could have been uttered as a cruel trick as much as a cry for help? Why is my subconscious mind so determined not to let me forget about them and focus on my own life?

I close my eyes and take a deep breath, holding it in my chest until it burns, and then slowly exhaling through my mouth. Then another deep breath, holding it a second longer, before releasing. I feel my shoulders relax a fraction.

She's not my mum.

My eyes shoot open, and the tension immediately returns to my neck and shoulders. It's no good, I have to know the truth. I have to know why Daisy approached me, and why she looked so terrified. I need to know why Morag doesn't have any pictures of Daisy as a baby, and why they really moved to London. I don't know where to begin, but I'm so much more familiar with the internet than I was twenty years ago.

Reaching down to the side of the bed, my fingers scramble around until they grip the laptop. Hoisting it onto my legs, I lift the lid and search for their names, adding keywords of adoption, Aberdeen, Wolverhampton, and nursing. It's everything I know about their family, and I have hours until Charlie will be awake. I hit the search button and begin to read.

Chapter Thirteen

Before - Morag

Waking early, I creep out of the bedroom, leaving Angus still fast asleep. Despite the early hour, sunlight is already peeking through the gap in the curtains, but not enough to disturb him. After forty-plus years of marriage I've learned Angus' sleeping pattern well enough. He's been known to sleep through overhead storms before.

I collect the small bundle of clothes I secreted in the bathroom last night before we headed into bed. The last thing I want is for my sneaking about, from drawers to wardrobe, to disturb Angus or Daisy. Passing her bedroom, I open the door a crack and peer in, but she's still sound asleep too, hugging the little furry giraffe she'd held the first time I saw her. She's never slept without it; despite all the moves we've had to make.

I carry the bundle of clothes down to the lounge and dress quickly, only giving my reflection half a glance in the window of one of the cabinets. If all goes to plan, I won't see another living soul while I'm out and about, so nobody will be appalled by my lack of make-up.

The front door creaks as I heave it open, and it sounds so loud, when I'm sure it probably isn't nearly as piercing as I imagine. I remain framed in the doorway, straining to hear any movement from upstairs. If the door has woken either Daisy or Angus, one of them is bound to stir in bed, and I would be able to hear that. Only silence greets me, and I'm relieved that I can continue with my plan. Closing and locking the door, I skip down the driveway, pulling the hood of my top over my head.

Checking the time, I see it is only just after six, and on this early Sunday morning, there is no sign of movement from any of the neighbouring properties. To my relief. Turning right at the foot of the drive, I hurry along the pavement, keen to reach my destination as quickly as possible, without drawing unnecessary attention to myself. It's kind of a half-jog, half-skip. Dressed in a hooded tracksuit, if I am spotted by any half-asleep neighbour opening their curtains, I'll probably just appear to be one of those crazy people who choose to run every day for pleasure. I know they'd argue it's a healthy activity, but I was brought up to run only when necessary, as in when someone is chasing you. In my book, running for pleasure is as foreign as choosing to throw yourself off a bridge with a bungee rope. Safe to say you wouldn't catch me ever doing either.

But there is a lightness to my steps today. I'm excited by what awaits, even though I know it's a huge risk. I don't see that there is another choice. I will take the necessary precautions, as I do each year, and if I stick with the routine, there is no reason to fear.

Spotting the tall red box at the end of the third road I reach, my pace quickens. I no longer care who sees me darting for the phone box, the excitement is too overwhelming to move any slower. Bursting in through the door, it takes a few moments to settle my laboured breathing and panting. One of the reasons we ended up choosing the current property was its proximity to a public phone box. In the digital age such outlets are few and far between these days, so this one was quite a find.

Removing the two pound coins from the zipped pocket of the tracksuit, I pull out my mobile phone, and open the stopwatch app, ready to press the start button the moment the line connects. In some ways it would be safer to make the call from home, where there is no danger of my face being seen, nor the conversation being overheard, but I'm not savvy enough to know how to hide the GPS coordinates of my mobile phone. The last thing I want is to put my family in unnecessary danger, but I have to make this call. I made a promise a long time ago, and I intend to keep to it.

Lifting the receiver, I dial 141 to disguise my location, before entering the rest of the number I memorised. As I hold the coins close to the slot, the phone rings twice before I hear her voice. Dropping the coins into the slot, I start the timer.

'Gwen, it's me,' I say, covering the receiver slightly with the cuff of my top.

'Mor—' she starts to say before I quickly cut her off.

'Don't say my name, Gwen. You know who this is, but don't say just in case anyone else is listening.'

'Oh, you and your paranoia,' she burrs. 'You don't really think anyone's put a tap on my line, do you? What nonsense!'

It's so great to hear my sister's voice after all this time, and

I make no effort to wipe away the tears pooling by my eyelids. 'I just wanted to wish you a happy birthday.'

'I did wonder whether I might hear from you today,' she says, and I'm pretty sure I can hear the sob building in her throat.

'I didn't wake you, I hope?'

'No, you know what I'm like: awake at first light no matter the day or time of year. How are you, big sister?'

My face scrunches at the reference to our relationship. She might as well have used my name. I've tried explaining why we have to take these precautions, but she thinks I'm just being dramatic. That's because I've done my best to shield her from the consequences of my actions.

'I'm fine,' I say quickly to cover her slip. 'We're all fine. How are you doing? How is Rufus?'

'I left him in bed snoring as per the usual. You know what he's like. Not dissimilar to your—' She seems to catch herself before saying Angus's name out loud. 'Well, you know.'

'Have you got anything nice planned for today?' I ask, just eager to keep her talking for as long as possible. I can't believe we've already been talking for thirty seconds. Only ninety seconds left until I'll have to force myself to hang up for another year.

'Rufus has promised to take me to The Black Ox for a fish and chip supper later, but otherwise I plan to be out on the loch like most days. It really is so pretty this time of the year. I wish you could come up and see it. I bet it hasn't changed since we were babies.'

How I wish I could, I want to say, but then we'd have to get into the usual conversation about all the reasons I can't come home yet.

'I'm surprised The Black Ox is still going,' I admit, 'but that sounds like a lovely day.'

There's a pause on the line that I feel compelled to fill as the seconds tick past, and I'm about to speak when I hear Gwen clear her throat. 'There's something I should tell you... not that there's anything you can do about it.' Another pause, and a feeling of dread begins to pass over my shoulders. 'I had some tests at the hospital, and... it's not good news. The oncologist reckons the cancer is back, and this time it's more aggressive than before.'

The tears escape my face, but no longer in joy. 'Oh God, Gwen, no.'

'Now, now, I don't want you upsetting yourself. After the chemotherapy last time, we always knew there was a risk it could return some day. I've had five wonderful years of love and friendship here in Skene, and I realise how fortunate I am.'

I don't want to ask the next question, but I only have seconds left before I'm going to have to hang up. 'How long have they said?'

'Maybe six months to a year with treatment, but I'm not sure I'll take them up on that offer. You remember how sick it made me last time.'

Oh my God, it's possible this will be the last time I get to talk to my baby sister, and I want to scream and thrash, and tell her to hell with the risk, I'm coming home to spend the next six to twelve months with her, but I can't.

'Oh, Gwen, I'm so sorry,' is the best I can manage. 'I love you, and I will try and call again as soon as I can.'

I don't hear her response as I depress the lever and the call ends. I stop the timer on two minutes and five seconds, and I am tempted to dial again, but I know the danger I'll be putting myself in if I do. Pocketing the mobile, I emerge from the phone box feeling half as tall as when I entered. I'd been looking forward to this call for weeks, and now I wish I hadn't made it. I know that's selfish to think, but I'd rather not have known my wee sister is battling death again. The worst part is, I know deep down things are probably a lot worse than she's made out, as she always did try to make things easier for me to hear. The last time she was diagnosed with cancer, she didn't tell me until the treatment was nearly complete. Even though she was visiting the hospital where I was working, I had no clue she was there, nor why. It was only when I happened to bump into her one day when I was running late for work that she came clean. If she's saying the doctors has given her six to twelve months, the truth is probably three to six months.

It kills me that I'm so far away and unable to help her. The walk back to the house is tearful, but silent. When I am back inside, as much as I long for a hug from Angus, I'm relieved he is still in bed. The thing is, he doesn't know about these annual jaunts to the nearest phone box, and if I tell him I've been in touch with Gwen, he'll be angry that I've put everything – our whole life – at risk. So I will have to keep this news to myself, even though it is eating me up inside. Why does life have to be so cruel at times?

Chapter Fourteen

Now

The Scientific Services department occupied the top two floors of the building, and had an unwelcoming, sterile feel. DI Mike Ferry took the lift up to the reception area, nodded at the inexplicably handsome administration assistant behind the desk, and signed in.

'Ah, you're here about the big murder case,' the younger man said, grinning inanely.

Mike considered him for a moment. A millennial, part of the new generation of police fast-tracked into roles with too much responsibility and not enough experience. Could he really be held responsible for his naivety?

'Haven't ruled out self-defence yet,' Mike corrected, but resisted the urge to tell the kid to act with more professionalism. 'I had a call about the suspect's clothes.'

The kid began hammering the keys on his computer, talking as he read the detail from the screen. 'Dr Towser is overseeing that. I'll message and let her know you've arrived. Grab a seat. I'm sure she won't be too long.'

Mike took a seat against the wall across from the unnecessarily large desk, and pulled out his phone, opening the email app to see if any of the rest of the team had sent an update. He'd left DS Nazia Hussain in charge of canvassing the area around the house for any kind of surveillance footage that could help provide a timeline of the evening's events. The house was halfway along a residential street, but in an affluent area like Northwood, he was hopeful private security cameras and vehicle dash cams might be able to confirm the movements of the victim and suspect.

She had yet to confirm her level of success, but it was still early. Given the timing of the incident, it was also possible that some of the neighbours might have seen or heard what happened. The initial responders had been called by a next-door neighbour who had heard banging and crashing inside the house, but hadn't overheard an argument.

The secured doors to the suite of laboratories swished open and Dr Emily Towser emerged, removing the thin mask covering her mouth and nose, and extended her hand towards him. 'DI Ferry?'

'Mike, please,' he replied, shaking the hand.

She was far prettier than he'd anticipated, her mouse-brown hair tied in a small pony-tail, but he also caught sight of an engagement ring on her finger.

'Do you want to follow me through?' she said, turning on her heel, and heading back towards the doors, swiping the pass around her neck against the paddle on the wall.

The doors swished again, and as they stepped through, Mike couldn't ignore how clean the air smelled. Frosted glass cubicles lined both sides of the corridor, beyond which ghostly figures in white concentrated on their business, oblivious to the man in the tie and jacket being led past them.

At the end of the corridor, Dr Towser stopped abruptly at a more traditional wooden door, opened it, and stepped inside, holding it open for Mike to follow. A large, shiny, black rectangular table dominated the room, with half a dozen chairs around it. For anyone wondering what happened to the money saved by budget cuts and lower police officer numbers, one look at this place would answer that question.

Dr Towser handed him a thin pink paper file. 'Here's my report on the blood samples taken from your suspect's clothing. You can take that away with you to read in full, and we'll add a digital copy of it to the HOLMES case file.'

He turned it over in his hands, another example of modern policing; no more boring pastel-coloured files. 'Can you give me the highlights, doc?'

'Sure. We examined blood samples taken from the suspect's T-shirt, jeans, bra, socks, and underpants, along with samples taken from key areas of the suspect's body, notably wrists, fingers, neck, and hair. *All* samples came back as belonging to the victim. Judging by the volume of blood discovered on the suspect's clothing, she was in very close proximity to the victim when he bled out. I would almost go so far as to say she was beneath him when the fatal blow was struck, judging by the spatter pattern identified through the photographs of her taken when she arrived at the station.'

'So, you're saying she did it?'

'We never confirm one hundred per cent, you know that.'

'Has the weapon been examined yet?'

Dr Towser nodded. 'Back page. The six-inch blade is

consistent with the images of the wound the forensic pathologist sent over. Three sets of fingerprints have been identified on the handle of the knife: the victim's, the suspect's, and an unidentified third party.'

Mike flicked to the final page of the report and skim-read what she'd just told him. 'Prints not on the national database then?'

Dr Towser shook her head. 'What's interesting is that we recovered both bloodied and non-bloodied prints from the handle for the suspect, which suggests she handled the weapon both before and after it had penetrated the victim's neck. His prints were made pre-puncture.'

Mike reflected on the crime scene photographs that would remain permanently etched on his memory. 'The knife was found beside the victim by the first responders, suggesting it was removed after the fatal blow.'

Dr Towser was nodding again. 'Given the nature of the prints, it's pretty safe to conclude that the suspect was probably the one to pull the blade out and leave it beside the body. Have you spoken to her about what happened yet?'

Studying the image of the blade in the report, he noted the call-outs where the prints had been located. 'Not yet. Still trying to piece it together in my head. We're holding her as a witness until we're ready to interview her under caution.'

'You know, what amazes me is that she made no effort to clean herself up. Didn't even wash the blood from her hands. Even if she wasn't looking to cover her tracks, it's human nature to clean death's stain from ourselves.'

Mike snapped his fingers together. 'That reminds me, the pathologist said there was a scratch on the victim's neck. Any skin cells found under the suspect's nails?'

'I'll double-check and let you know.'

Mike stood, tapping his fingers against the file. 'Thanks. There was one other question I had; in your experience, did she do it on purpose, or could there be more going on that we realise?'

'I can only tell you what the evidence tells me; she was there when he was struck and she watched him die. Why that happened is your field of expertise. Good luck!'

Chapter Fifteen

Before – Jess

The sun is streaming through the dining-room window as I pick at the croissant on the plate before me. It's going to be another hot day today, but given my experience yesterday, I think I'll keep myself wrapped up and in the shade. The after-sun did wonders to cool my skin, but now my neck and shoulders feel sticky, and I'm desperately craving a shower and clean clothes.

Charlie's mobile vibrates on the table again, and he quickly turns it over and chuckles at whatever he's read.

My early-morning internet search revealed absolutely no clues about Morag, Angus, or Daisy. Without knowing their surname, there was just too large a pool of social media accounts to trawl through. The ones that did have profile pictures didn't match Morag or Angus's faces, and there were no news stories about them in Wolverhampton or Aberdeen, but that's hardly surprising unless they'd done something newsworthy. Out of curiosity, I searched my own name, and found my Facebook and Twitter profiles – neither of which I have accessed in the last six months. The only other hits for me were on the newspaper site where I worked, my name credited on the staff list. Hardly fame.

'You not hungry today?' Charlie asks, and I suddenly realise he's been watching me. 'I'd have thought after yesterday you'd be ravenous.'

'Still a little queasy,' I say, tearing at the pastry and delicately placing it on my tongue. The truth is I just don't have an appetite right now. Because of the lack of sleep, I feel like I'm running on empty, and as tempting as it is to return to bed, I know I won't be able to drop off again.

Charlie's phone buzzes again. He reads and chuckles again before placing it back on the table face down.

'What's so funny?' I ask, envious that he can find amusement in such a cruel world.

'It's from Doug.' He grins. 'He set up this WhatsApp group for those of us from the office and he keeps uploading pictures from Friday night. Hilarious! I can't remember half of them being taken.'

I don't ask to see them, as I doubt they're as humorous to someone who wasn't there.

His expression tightens. 'Are you sure you're okay, Jess? I know yesterday was unpleasant for you, but you shouldn't let it ruin the weekend. What do you fancy doing today?'

My eyes fill like some switch has been flicked in my head. I don't want to do *anything*. I don't want to stay cooped up inside, yet the thought of going out and facing all the curious questions and awkward stares fills me with dread. Before I was confined to the chair, we rarely stayed in at the weekend, even when it was bucketing with rain. We would go for a drive, stopping off at a pub for lunch, or we'd just step out of the front door and walk for miles, Grace in her pushchair. It pains me to remember how much freer we were before all of this.

'I'll be fine,' I say, pushing the plate from me, listening to the birdsong just beyond the patio doors.

'I was thinking,' he says, reaching over, picking up the remains of my croissant, and shovelling it into his mouth in one, 'we should probably invite Morag and Angus over for food at some point. Not today, obviously, but maybe next weekend? Return the favour.'

I study his face for any trace of mirth, but he is serious.

'We barely know them.'

'Exactly, but that's how friendship works, isn't it? You take an interest and get to know someone. It would be good for you, I think, to know another mum in the playground.'

I know he's trying to be supportive, but sometimes I just wish he'd lay off it. It's the same reason he keeps urging me to return to counselling. He thinks that my pain and frustration can be healed with some kind of band-aid, when all I want is time to understand my new destiny.

'I don't want to invite strangers into our house,' I say bluntly.

'They're hardly strangers, and they weren't afraid to welcome us into their home. What are you worried about? They don't strike me as serial killers.' He laughs mockingly.

'We know nothing about them! I don't even know what their surname is.'

'Kilbride.' He says it so matter-of-factly, like I'm being dim for not knowing it myself.

'How do you know that's their surname?'

Charlie wipes crumbs from his chin, and then brushes the mess from his T-shirt. 'I saw an envelope on the side in the kitchen. Redirected mail from their home in Wolverhampton. It was addressed to Mr and Mrs A Kilbride.'

A thought fires in the back of my mind. I'll have a better chance of tracing them online with a surname and former postcode.

'What was the address?'

He shrugs, and his face contorts into a ball of confusion. 'I have no idea; I didn't look at it properly. I'm not in the habit of rifling through our friends' post. What does it matter?'

I know he'll laugh at me if I tell him I still have major doubts about the backstory Morag and Angus presented.

She's not my mum.

Charlie's mobile vibrates, and again he quickly looks at the screen.

'I was thinking of going to visit my mum,' I say suddenly, though the thought has only just entered my head. 'With Grace starting school on Wednesday, I thought Mum would like to see her before. It's been a few weeks since we were last up there. Do you think you could get the day off tomorrow or Tuesday to drive us?'

His eyes rise from the screen in astonishment. 'What?'

'Mum's,' I repeat. 'Would you be able to get a day off this week to drive us up there?'

He pockets the phone, and stands, reaching for my plate. 'Are you joking?' His cheeks are flushed, and he's glaring at me as if I've asked him to sever a limb. 'You know how busy I am this week. And what kind of notice is this? Why do you suddenly want to drop everything and go to your mother's?'

'I think it would be good for her to see Grace before school starts, that's all.'

My plate rattles as he drops it onto his own, quietly seething. 'Well, no, I'm sorry, Jess, but unlike you I can't just drop everything on a whim. You know how hard I've been working to secure this new client.'

'Exactly,' I fire back in anger. 'With all the extra hours you've been putting in, the least they can do is give you some time back.'

'What's Doug going to think if I suddenly ask for a day out of the office in what could be the most important week in the company's history? I'm meeting with their Chief Risk Officer tomorrow, and then I'm away at the client's offices in Oxford on Tuesday. No. It's out of the question.'

I was not prepared for him to react like that. I know he hasn't always seen eye-to-eye with my mum, but I thought they'd put all that behind them. And it isn't like the drive to Southampton is particularly long. Ninety minutes at most, depending on traffic.

He carries the plates out to the kitchen, and I hear them crash into the sink. Have I done something wrong? My request for a lift wasn't unreasonable, and it really has been a few weeks since Grace saw her grandmother. I make an effort to call my mum at least once a week, but it's not the same as spending time there.

Charlie returns, collecting the butter and jam and leaving without even looking at me. When he returns again, I wheel around to block his exit.

'What is wrong with you? If you don't want to take me, all you had to do is say no. Why are you so angry?'

There's venom in his eyes as he glares at me. 'Because this

is so typical of you at the moment, expecting me to drop everything and wait on you hand and foot.'

My hand shoots to my mouth. I had no idea that is how he feels. I don't think I've made that many demands of him, and sometimes I do need his help because there are things I can't do alone.

He must notice my hurt, as his expression softens with regret. 'I'm sorry, that didn't come out how I meant it. I'm under a lot of pressure at work, but all the extra hours are an investment in our future. I know it's tough and I miss being around you and Grace, but it will be worth it one day. You'll see.'

I wheel myself away so he won't see the tears refilling my eyes. I hate being so reliant on Charlie for everything. I wish I could see a clear path forward that would allow me more independence and to contribute to our finances again, but it feels so far away at the moment.

A taxi to Southampton will cost too much, and the only alternative is a train, but I'd need to take the Tube to get to Waterloo. I don't feel confident managing my chair on public transport, let alone with Grace in tow.

The real reason I am so keen to return to the family home is to pick my mum's brains about the adoption process. It's one thing to read about it online, but better to speak to someone with first-hand experience. I wheel towards the kitchen to ask Charlie if we can afford for me to catch the train, but his head is bent over his phone as he taps out a message. He hears my wheels clatter over the carpet trim and looks up in panic, quickly pocketing the phone again.

I'm about to ask him what's wrong when Grace comes

bounding down the stairs, swimming goggles swinging in her hand. 'Come on, Daddy, we'll be late for swimming.'

He glances at his watch before rushing past me, grabbing his car keys, and slamming the door behind them.

I've been lying on top of the bed sheets for at least twenty minutes since Charlie and Grace departed, but am no closer to dozing off. Every time I close my eyes and try to empty my brain of thoughts, something else rears its head, such as that bloody cobweb, dangling out of reach, yet somehow watching my every move. I feel so physically drained, but I'm too alert to sleep.

I hope Grace is enjoying her swimming lesson. Charlie's been taking her to the pool regularly since her third birthday. I remember how timid she was stepping into the water unaided that first time, her little legs rippling the water with nervous energy. She hadn't wanted to let go of Charlie's hand that day. I'd been watching from the edge, subtly taking pictures of the two of them when the lifeguards' heads were turned.

To see her now, fearlessly jumping into the deep end and swimming back to the side, or diving under the water in the shallow end and swimming along the bottom of the pool, you'd never know she was that timid girl who wouldn't let go of Charlie's hand on that first visit. I'm amazed at how far she's come under his watch. I stopped going with them when Charlie asked for it to become a daddy-daughter activity – an opportunity for the two of them to bond. I remember how encouraging I'd been of that choice, and now I hate myself for how envious I am of that special time they get to spend alone. I can't remember the last time Charlie and I were alone as just husband and wife, enjoying each other's company. But I suppose that's the deal you strike when you become parents.

I close my eyes again, pushing thoughts of the pool and my little family from my mind. I try to picture just a blank void, focusing on the darkness of my eyelids, and blocking all and any thoughts as best as I can.

She's not my mum.

Oh God, there it is again. Her trembling arms, quivering lip, shining eyes, and white knuckles.

What is wrong with me? Why can't I let it go? What is it I think she could have meant? If Morag isn't Daisy's mum, who is she? Some weird jailer, keeping her prisoner? From whom and why? Or some woman who couldn't have children of her own and abducted an innocent four-year-old?

I frown at this last thought. Is that what's been irking me since the park on Thursday? It could explain Daisy's terror, and why there are no baby pictures in Morag's home, but it isn't a logical conclusion to draw. For starters, where would Morag have taken Daisy from? And apart from Daisy's terrified message, what other evidence is there of such a heinous crime? It's not like Daisy wasn't enjoying herself on the trampoline on Saturday. If she hadn't approached me in the park, I'd have no reason to doubt that she is a perfectly adjusted child in a loving family. Besides, child abductions are a trope you only read about or see in films.

Great! So much for keeping my mind clear of thoughts. This is no good. Leaning over the side of the bed, I reach for the laptop and pull it up onto my legs. There's no point in fighting the insomnia.

I try to recall the surname Charlie mentioned at breakfast:

redirected mail from their home in Wolverhampton... addressed to Mr and Mrs A Kilbride.

Opening a fresh internet search window, I type in 'Morag Kilbride' and look at the results. Facebook, Twitter, and LinkedIn are the first hits, but I steer clear of those for now, following this morning's unsuccessful review of social media. The next hits are for TripAdvisor and Expedia, but with no address or profile images next to the comments, there's no way of knowing whether they were posted by the same woman I met at the park. There's a hit on Ancestry.com, but I can't access it without signing up to the site. The remaining pages of hits either refer to East Kilbride, or individuals called Morag. There are no further hits for people called Morag Kilbride.

Returning to the Facebook hits, I scroll through the two dozen Morag Kilbrides listed. It is a narrower search than I'd performed this morning, but as I click on each name, I'm disappointed to see profile pictures that are not of the woman I'm searching for. Clicking back to LinkedIn, I don't find any Morag Kilbrides who list nursing as their profession.

Opening a fresh window, I search for 'Angus Kilbride', but the first hits here refer to Angus Avenue, a road in East Kilbride. There are mentions from Zoopla, Rightmove, and Google Maps. In fact, it isn't until the seventh page of search results that Facebook, Twitter, and LinkedIn hits appear. Facebook has only six Angus Kilbrides with profiles, and two of them live in Canada. I focus on the four in the UK, but only one has a profile picture, and this man has a long and thick beard, is dressed head to toe in tartan, and is clutching enormous bagpipes. He's too tall to be Angus. I click on the remaining three profiles, but am unable to see anything they've posted, only the dates they joined the site. LinkedIn is just as unsuccessful, as none of the three Angus Kilbrides listed mention logistics. One is an IT specialist, another a vet, and the third a sociology student.

I slam the lid of the laptop as it shuts down. How can there be no record of them? None whatsoever. It's as if they don't even exist.

I freeze.

What if their names aren't Angus and Morag Kilbride? What if their names aren't really Angus and Morag?

The thought chills me to my bones, but I'm also conscious that it's a huge leap in judgement. Here I am conjuring all sorts of theories and malicious thoughts about two people I don't know and a girl who may or may not be their daughter. There has to be a reasonable explanation for why Daisy looked so terrified, and why I cannot find any trace of Morag and Angus online.

Unlocking my mobile, I scroll through the list of contacts until Gail Rowson's name appears in the display. It has been months since I last spoke to her, though she was kind enough to send flowers and a sympathy card when I left the hospital. She represents a chapter of my life that I now deem closed, where I had a normal job and future to look forward to.

She answers on the third ring, and even though I know to expect her usual bright and cheery persona, hearing it has me stuttering my opening.

'Hi… Gail, I… uh… how are you?'

'Jess? OMG, it's so good to hear from you. I was just telling Jack how much I miss the old days when we'd have payday lunch at the pub and come back half-cut. Do you remember? Everyone here's so boring now, and it's all about delivering articles to impossible deadlines.'

The fact that she is in the office at the weekend is not a surprise.

'Anyway,' she continues, 'to what do I owe this pleasure? Are you coming back to join us soon?'

I was expecting her to ask this, and already have my answer rehearsed. 'It just isn't practical, unfortunately, not unless they make the place more accessible.'

The shabby office is on the first floor of a three-storey building, the other two floors vacant. But there are steps up to the main entrance, and then steps to each of the floors, but no elevator, or room to install one. Making the building wheelchair-friendly would take major investment, and although there may be some legal requirement for them to do that to support me, I know the costs would cripple the paper, and I don't want to be the cause of that.

'Of course, of course,' she says, without missing a beat. 'I don't see why you couldn't still do your job from home anyway. All they'd need to do is give you a laptop and phone. Probably cheaper than having another desk to provide in the office. And you were so good at selling the advertising space as well. Income has plummeted since you left.'

She hasn't mentioned my loss, or the injury I sustained during labour, and I'm grateful that she seems so willing to gloss over the last six months like they never happened.

I want to ask her to do me a favour. As a current affairs reporter, I know that she has contacts at the local council, and could find out whether Morag and Angus have registered to vote yet. She could also probably confirm what names were used to register for council tax. But how can I ask for her help when I haven't been in touch for so long, and how do I explain why I want the information? Telling her about

Daisy's message in the park will have her thinking I've lost my mind.

'We really need to catch up soon,' Gail says, disturbing my trail of thought. 'What are you doing this Friday? Maybe you could come into town and meet me and we could relive our payday lunch routine again. It would be so good to see you and catch up on all that's been happening. Go on, what do you say?'

I can't decline and then ask for her help. This was such a bad idea.

'I'll even treat you to *actual* food,' Gail adds, as if we're negotiating some hugely important contract.

Now I feel compelled to agree, otherwise she'll wonder why I phoned in the first place.

'Lunch would be lovely,' I say, cringing as the words leave my mouth, 'but I'll pay my way.'

'Perfect!' she coos. 'I'll send you an email to confirm.'

We say our goodbyes and the line disconnects. I feel strangely content that I've made some progress in my investigation. Gail's contacts at the council could be the means of finding out who Daisy, Morag, and Angus really are.

Chapter Sixteen

Before - Morag

Angus finally surfaces a little after 9am, and although I've spent the best part of twenty minutes trying to cover my tears, he seems to sense that I've been crying.

'What's wrong?' he asks, filling the kettle. 'Has something happened?'

How I wish I could tell him about my call with Gwen.

Reaching for a tissue, I dab my eyes. 'It's my sister's birthday today, that's all. It made me upset knowing I can't call to wish her all the best.'

He comes over and wraps his large arms around me, and we remain holding each other for several minutes, with neither of us speaking. There's a shared acknowledgement that what I long for is impossible. Neither of us wishes to have *that* argument again. It's always too painful, and neither of us wins.

I haven't been able to stop thinking about Gwen's news. I long for some way I could get back to see her one more time, but it isn't safe, and I don't want to put her life in danger either. Worse still, I've no way of knowing when that terrible day will strike either. The village where Gwen lives – Kirkton of Skene – doesn't have a local newspaper recording deaths of residents. The only newswire in the tiny village is word of mouth, and usually within two hours everybody knows whatever the latest news or events are. So, as and when Gwen passes, I won't know unless I'm there.

Learning that someone close is facing death certainly helps put things in perspective. I am lucky to still have my health, and Angus at my side. And then of course there's Daisy. There have been days when I've wondered whether we did the right thing, but then there are other days where I'll catch her laughing at something, and it fills my heart with warmth.

It is too easy to live with regret.

That is why, despite my reservations about her, I am going to make more of an effort with Jess. I know little about her or the pain she has suffered. Charlie told me her disability was as a result of a needle slipping during labour, and that they also lost their son. How would I be feeling if I'd had to face such adversity? It goes some way to explain why Jess comes across as closed off. Maybe she struggles to form new friendships as a result of what she has lost. I can understand that.

'What are you making?' Angus asks, looking over my shoulder at the pot bubbling on the hob. 'Smells delicious.'

'Just a bit of leek and tatty soup.'

He frowns. 'Soup? In this weather? I love your leek and tatty soup – you know I do – but it's a bit hot outside for soup, wouldn't you say?'

'It's not for us,' I say evenly, turning back to the pot and stirring the softening vegetables. 'I'm making it for Jess.'

His frown deepens. 'You've lost me.'

'Her being ill yesterday,' I explain. 'I thought maybe she's ill with a virus or some such. If she's struggling to stomach anything normal, I thought maybe a bowl of homemade soup might be more appealing.' He doesn't look convinced, and it fills me with self-doubt. 'Do you think I'm being daft?'

His expression softens. 'No, no, I think it's a wonderful gesture. How did I get so lucky to find such a caring and beautiful wife?'

The doubt dissipates. 'I found their address in the phonebook last night, so I'll drive over there when it's ready and see if she's feeling any better.'

Angus moves away from me as the kettle reaches its crescendo. 'Is Daisy up yet?'

'Not yet.'

'Good, there's something I've been meaning to discuss with you.' His tone is serious, and my immediate thought is that he heard me sneaking out this morning and now wants to grill me about it.

'Oh, aye,' I say calmly, not prepared to give him enough rope to hang me with.

'Can you leave that for a minute and come and sit down at the table with me?'

It's all a bit formal, but I don't disagree, switching off the hob and setting the steaming pan to one side. He carries the mugs of tea through to the dining room, placing one in front of each of us as we sit.

'Is everything okay?' I ask, blowing on the tea.

'Aye, fine, fine. It's just… I've been doing some thinking. It feels like we've been running away from our problems for years, and maybe we need to try a different approach. After all, neither of us is getting any younger.' He coughs as he says this, and I can't tell if it's deliberate or involuntary.

'Speak for yourself,' I say with a smile, though this serious tone is setting off alarm bells in my head.

'I think it's about time we stopped making decisions based on gut feelings. The last couple of times we moved it was because we *thought* he was getting close, but we don't know for certain that he'd tracked us down.'

I think back to our last home in Wolverhampton. It was my fear that we were being watched that led to our sudden early-hours escape.

'Are you saying you don't believe me, Angus?'

He takes my hand and rubs his thumb in gentle circles against the skin above my thumb. 'No, that's not what I'm saying. I just think we're both on edge all the time, never knowing who we can trust or how long we'll be safe for. It's time to stop being reactive, and become more proactive.'

I'm confused by what he is saying, and he doesn't look like he's too sure either. 'What are you trying to say, Angus?'

He picks up my other hand. 'I've hired a specialist to help us out. His name's Lawrence, and he used to work for the Metropolitan Police, but has since gone private.'

'You've hired a private detective? What for?'

'To keep an eye on us, and those who might be looking for us. I've invited Lawrence over to explain what he does, and then we can decide together whether it's what we want.'

This is all news to me. Angus has never mentioned such an idea before, and it troubles me that he's clearly been thinking about this for some time without letting on. Maybe my husband is a better liar than I ever gave him credit for; a thought that chills me through.

Chapter Seventeen

Now

Returning to the office, Mike savoured the hum of hard work and anticipation: keyboards click-clacking, and hurried phone conversations taking place. There's nothing like a major incident to get pulses racing and the whole team pulling in the same direction.

Within the windowless Major Incident Room at the far side of the office, pictures of the victim and suspect had been hastily stuck up on the floor-to-ceiling dry-wipe board, which hung on the far wall, away from the prying eyes of anyone passing the entrance to the room and casually glancing in. The information in this room would remain need-to-know until further notice.

A knock on the MIR door was followed by DC Polly Viceroy's entrance, open notebook in one hand, her eyes skimming the page as she spoke. 'The house belongs to one

Ibrahim Farooqi, a Pakistani businessman, whose permanent residence is in Islington.'

Mike wasn't familiar with the name and nodded for her to continue.

'All utility bills and council tax are in his name, but this is one of three properties he owns and operates through a rental agency, Bennett's. Haven't managed to get hold of anyone from the agency yet but will keep trying. The other two properties are located in Harrow and Pinner, but both are currently vacant, according to the Bennett's website.'

'Victim doesn't look like he's from Pakistan,' Mike muttered.

'Well, I don't know about that, but I *can* tell you Mr Farooqi isn't the victim, as I've just spoken to him on the phone. He wasn't happy to be disturbed so late, but he's agreed to come in first thing, and answer any further questions.'

'Was the house in Northwood vacant?'

Polly looked up from her notes to shake her head. 'Not according to Farooqi. Says it was let a couple of months ago. At first, he couldn't recall the name of the couple, but when I pushed he went away and found the email he'd received from the agency. House rented by a Mr and Mrs Kilbride, but the email didn't confirm first names. I've asked him to forward it to me, but we may have to wait until the agency opens in the morning to confirm anything further about them.'

Mike studied the photograph of the victim, which had been snapped at the mortuary and emailed over. Eyes closed, and skin an unhealthy pallor. 'So we could be looking at Mr Kilbride here?'

'Possibly. There's no print or DNA match on the database yet.'

'Thank you, Polly. Give the owners of the agency another go, but I reckon you won't get hold of anyone until the morning; don't think I've ever come across an estate agent who answers the phone outside of business hours.'

'Have we got the green light to interview our witness yet, Mike?'

He shook his head. 'Medical assessment is underway at the moment, but not looking promising. Apparently, she's becoming more and more agitated, shouting obscenities from the holding room. It's possible she's on something, or off something, but we won't know for sure until her full medical records are recovered. Vikram downstairs is keeping me updated, but he doesn't think we'll be allowed to interview until morning.'

'Have we still not got hold of her next of kin?'

'No answer on the number we found in her phone, but we'll keep trying. In the meantime, if you're unsuccessful with the estate agency, go and get your head down for a few hours. I have a feeling tomorrow is going to be a long day.'

'What about you, Mike? You look like you could do with a kip too. I don't mind you crashing at mine, if—'

'Thanks,' he interrupted, 'but probably best we keep things strictly professional.'

Her cheeks flushed with embarrassment. 'I wasn't suggesting you do anything but sleep, but whatever.' She didn't wait for him to say anything further, heading out of the room and closing the door, leaving him alone with his thoughts and the two pairs of eyes staring back at him from the board.

Given their history, he'd automatically jumped to the conclusion that Polly's suggestion had been much more than it was. He would apologise in the morning, as chasing after her now would set tongues wagging, and he didn't need any additional pressure.

Reaching for a marker pen, he wrote the name Kilbride and a question mark beneath the victim's name. If only the dead could speak, Mike mused. Investigating murder would be so much easier, though not nearly as much fun.

Checking his phone's display, he answered when he saw DS Nazia Hussain's name. 'Talk to me.'

'I've just spoken with a neighbour who lives three or four houses down, and they've confirmed it was occupied by an older Scottish couple and a little girl, who she estimated was four to five years old. The neighbour said she would see the woman and child going to the park, and knew them well enough to say hello, but couldn't confirm the woman's name.'

Mike's eyes narrowed. 'We have a male victim and female suspect, but nobody's mentioned a child until now. Where is she?'

'Your guess is as good as mine. Maybe some of the surveillance footage will help. We've completed house-to-house enquiries with everyone in the street who was home and have about a dozen feeds from security cameras and dash cams to trawl through. I'll get it back ASAP but could do with some help viewing it.'

'Good, okay, get it back here, and I'll see who we can spare to support.'

'Will do, Mike. See you in a bit.'

Leaving the Incident Room, Mike caught sight of Polly just as she turned out of the office, and was tempted to catch up with her and apologise for his assumption, but it would have to wait until morning. He had more important things on his mind; namely, where was the missing child?

Chapter Eighteen

Before – Jess

My eyes fly open as the front door slams closed, and I realise now I must have dropped off, but it can only have been for minutes, rather than hours.

Charlie calls out my name, and I holler back that I'm in the bedroom.

'Oh sorry, did I wake you?' he asks, pushing the door open.

'No, I was on the internet,' I say, nodding to the laptop still straddled across my legs. 'How was swimming?'

He remains where he is, leaning into the door frame. 'Grace did well. I had her swimming to the bottom of the pool to pick up toys and bring them back. Also showed her how to do an underwater somersault. She'll have to keep practising, but she's come on leaps and bounds. You should come with us next time.'

I fire him a look of disdain.

'I know, I know,' he says, raising both hands in mock

surrender, 'but I'm sure the staff would help us get you into the pool. I could carry you from the changing room to the pool edge if necessary.'

I can think of nothing worse than other swimmers – adults and children alike – staring at the grown woman being manhandled into the pool.

'I'll think about it,' I say to avoid confrontation.

Charlie crouches down, resting his chin on my knee. 'I'm sorry I shouted earlier. I hate it when we argue, and I'm sorry that I can't get any time off this week. Things should settle towards the end of the week, and I can ask Doug whether he'll let me have some time off the week after, if you'd like? We could get away for a couple of days, just the three of us. If you want to visit your mum we can do that, or we could go to the coast and call in at your mum's on the way back?'

I know he's trying to make amends, but I don't think he's seen the obvious flaw in his plan. 'Grace starts at school on Wednesday. We can't take her away for a couple of days the week after.'

'Why not? It's only reception class, it's not like a couple of days out of class is going to seriously impact on her future education and career choices.'

'It doesn't matter; there are rules about taking children out of school in term time now. They fine parents and threaten court action in some places.'

His mouth twists into a doubtful smirk. 'You're kidding!'

'I'm not. Once she starts school on Wednesday, our holidays will be strictly limited to half terms and summer holidays.'

'Oh,' he says, the disappointment evident in his tone. 'I hadn't realised. Well, there's always next weekend. If Doug would let me finish a couple of hours early on Friday, we could be in Southampton by supper, and spend a couple of nights in a cheap B&B, before coming home on the Sunday. Would that be okay?'

He's trying so hard, and I'm grateful that he's clearly been thinking about this morning's conversation. I press my hand to his cheek. 'That sounds lovely. Thank you.'

He checks his watch. 'Hey, I tell you what, why don't we go out? For lunch I mean.'

I suddenly realise I haven't heard Grace since he returned, and I strain to hear whether she headed straight up to her room, though usually she's bursting to tell me what new moves she's learned in the pool.

'Where's Grace?' I ask when I still can't hear movement.

'Oh, she's at Ava's. We ran into her and her mum at the pool and they begged me to let Grace go play.'

Ava is Grace's closest friend from pre-school, and is also due to start in reception on Wednesday. Her mother – Nadine – is all enhanced breasts, bleached hair, acrylic nails, and fake eyelashes. The sort of woman who thinks she could have been a supermodel if she wasn't so busy with the school run, and who is ogled by all the dads.

'Oh yes,' I say, imagining every man at the pool lusting over her bikini body, 'and how is Nadine?'

'Very well. She said she'd give Grace her dinner and I could pick her up around five. So, as we are child-free I thought we could go out. Nowhere too fancy, but perhaps a nice pub lunch. What do you think?'

A flash of the last time we went out for lunch fills my vision. A pub full of people gawping at the poor woman struck down in her prime. I'm not sure I can bear it, particularly if we bump into someone we know. At the same time, I've been crying out for Charlie and me to spend some time together as husband and wife, and with Grace at Ava's it would be such a waste to mope around the house.

'That sounds lovely,' I begin, tempering my enthusiasm, 'but can we go somewhere we've never been before? I don't want to end up at The Gate or The Black Horse. Can we go somewhere a bit further away?'

He smiles broadly. 'I was thinking the same thing. Thought we could have a bit of a drive first, and then stop off when we see somewhere that takes our fancy. Like we used to do. What do you think?'

I'm grateful that he hasn't argued, and nod encouragingly. 'I should probably change,' I say, brushing pastry crumbs from my tracksuit bottoms.

He isn't brave enough to admit I look a state, and I don't wait for him to reply before transferring myself back into the chair, and opening the chest of drawers. I used to wear skirts and dresses before my confinement, but I much prefer to keep my useless legs covered these days. I locate some navy suit trousers and a salmon pink blouse, and proceed to shuffle myself out of the T-shirt and tracksuit bottoms. I can hear Charlie moving about upstairs, and as I am fastening the buttons on the blouse, he emerges in smart jeans and a short-sleeved shirt. A cloud of cologne follows him into the room, but it's good to see he's made an effort.

I allow him to wheel me to the front door and down the makeshift wooden ramp he eagerly installed six months ago. The sun beats down, and my forehead is moistening by the time I'm fastened into the front seat. Butterflies flutter in my stomach, and I feel as giddy as I did before our first date. Today will be a good day, I tell myself.

Living in London, it can be easy to forget just how beautiful a country England is. Ten minutes after setting off from home, and I can barely remember the grubby grey buildings and smog, as all I can see now is bright blue sky – like living inside a real-life watercolour – and rolling green and yellow fields. We've been transported into rich countryside, the stench of small farms carrying on the breeze, which fills the car with country air.

The radio is playing quietly as the car picks up speed, the snake-like lane twisting ahead. Part of me wishes Grace was here to share in the stunning landscape, but I know her head would be buried in a book, missing the breathtaking vista. It feels like the weight of the world has been lifted from my shoulders, and I do all I can to commit this feeling of tranquillity to memory. It will all be over too soon, but for now I'm here, and all is calm.

I start suddenly at a squeal of brakes and a rapidly slowing car. Was I asleep? I don't remember drifting off, but outside my window the golden fields and high bushes are gone, replaced with ancient-looking stone walls, dotted with the occasional lamppost.

'Where are we?' I ask, spotting the burning red of the traffic light through the windscreen.

'You dropped off,' Charlie says, turning and smiling affectionately.

I glance at the dashboard clock. It can only have been fifteen minutes since I'd last checked it, and I have no memory of being asleep. It's disappointing that I allowed myself to miss the rest of the view, and I wish I knew why that keeps happening.

'We're nearly there,' Charlie says as the car lurches forwards. I see a war memorial to my left: bronze soldiers charging with rifles extended, and a tall stone tablet detailing their part in history.

Beyond the memorial, a sea of gravestones stretches to the horizon, a few stray wisps of cloud lying just above. The air is chillier here, and I stab at the button to raise my window, the skin of my arms prickling. The graveyard and memorial disappear into the reflection of the wing mirror, and I now see we've arrived at some kind of village, an empty market square bordered by bespoke shops. There's a bakery, pharmacy, newsagent, and café, all of them closed. Further up there's a pub, with two men sitting outside smoking pipes and glaring at the passing traffic, but it's impossible to tell if they're actually looking at us or gazing into the void. It doesn't look like the kind of pub where guests are made particularly welcome.

Something stirs in the back of my mind. 'We're nearly there?' I repeat back to Charlie. 'Nearly where? I thought we were going to stop when we saw somewhere nice.'

He doesn't answer at first, slowing a fraction to read a road sign, before accelerating again.

'I know,' he says, 'but then I remembered that pub we passed – must be last year – which we both thought looked like somewhere we'd like. Do you remember?'

I have no idea where we are, nor do I recall a pub we once saw, but my grumbling stomach won't allow me to argue. There is something vaguely familiar about the geography, and I'm now hopeful our journey will end soon, as a small wave of nausea ripples through my body. Charlie was right; I really should have made more of an effort to eat breakfast. I'd give anything to have that croissant back to gobble up.

Then, as we round the next bend, I spot the large converted barn, with a beautifully landscaped garden at its rear, and a large chalkboard advertising traditional Sunday lunch. I do now remember seeing this place before, and we did indeed comment that it looked like a fine establishment.

It's just after midday and the car park is already pretty full. Charlie locates a marked bay near the front door and pulls in, placing the blue badge on the dashboard, before exiting the car to collect my chair from the boot.

'I hope they have a table,' I say, as Charlie opens my door and helps me shuffle onto the cushion.

'I phoned ahead and made a reservation,' he says, without a beat, and I can't ignore the nagging sensation playing at the back of my mind.

Thought we could have a bit of a drive first, and then stop off when we see somewhere that takes our fancy.

Those were his words before we left home, and I know he didn't phone ahead from the car. Even though I'd drifted off, I would have heard him had he made a phone call, which means he'd already had this place in mind when he suggested we go out for lunch. Is there something sinister in that, or is it just his attempt to be romantic? I will just have to give him the benefit of the doubt, as there isn't time to go somewhere else now.

He wheels me away from the car, locking it, and then pulling me backwards through the pub's open doors. The smell of sage and onion stuffing wafts through the air, and then the sweet smell of vegetables and the saltiness of the beef waiting to be carved on the stand. I'm salivating as we stop at the table and he tells the maître d' our name. He smiles at Charlie and me before ticking us off his list, and asks us to follow him.

The wheelchair bounces as Charlie forces it over the uneven wooden floor. The ceiling hangs low, thick black beams jutting out in all directions, as if the barn was built by a child and might collapse at any moment. The windows are so small that little light penetrates, and the spotlights on the struts securing the ceiling are on full beam. Even so, it's still pretty dark in the corners we pass.

It's lucky that Charlie did think to book ahead, as there isn't a vacant table anywhere I can see, though as we head past the bar, I realise there is additional seating upstairs. I hope they haven't reserved us a table up there. I don't want the indignity of Charlie having to carry me up the spiral staircase.

I'm suddenly uneasy as we near the steps. I'd thought going somewhere where nobody knew us would keep inquisitive stares at bay, but every time I look up, I see a pair of eyes on me, swiftly followed by an empathetic and encouraging smile.

We detour past the spiral staircase, and I breathe a huge sigh of relief. I can't get over how much floor space this place has. We're now heading towards the back of the pub, and there are still tables everywhere I look. At least the pub's popularity bodes well for the quality of the carvery.

And that's when I see it. Two closed doors directly in front of us, each with fifteen or so small windows, but covered by a net curtain of some kind, impossible to see through. Why would we have a table booked in a private room at the back of the pub?

I don't have to wait long for an answer, and as the maître d' pushes the doors open, my gaze falls on the large round table, and the dozen pairs of eyes staring back at me. I want the ground to swallow me up.

'Surprise!' Charlie exclaims.

Bile builds at the back of my throat. So this is why he suggested we go for a drive today; this is why he said we could stop somewhere random for lunch; this is why he'd booked ahead; his intention was always to drag me into a room full of former friends – people I haven't seen since I was discharged from hospital. People I haven't wanted to see because of the painful memories each will drag up.

Chapter Nineteen

Before – Morag

When Angus told me he'd hired a private investigator, the first thing that sprang to mind was the old-school gumshoe in the mould of Raymond Chandler: fedora, five-o'clock shadow, and cigarette in mouth. The man who arrived on our doorstep five minutes ago couldn't be much further from that description.

For starters, he barely looks old enough to be out of school. He has one of those closely cropped ginger beards that hipsters preen on a daily basis, like an exotic facial bonsai. And far from stinking of tar and tobacco, he actually arrived on a bicycle, and carrying a transparent plastic bottle of something green.

'Kale smoothie,' he tells me, slightly out of breath. 'My partner has me on a detox.'

He's wearing a skin-tight shirt and shorts in a palette of yellows, greens, and blues. I wouldn't be seen dead outside in such an array of colours, let alone in an outfit that really leaves little to the imagination.

'Do you mind if I bring my bicycle inside?' he asks Angus. 'It's a racer and I don't want it to get stolen.'

Angus glances at me before nodding, and watches as the younger man lifts the lightweight frame onto his shoulders and carries it into the corridor, where he balances it against the radiator.

'Hi,' he says, once the bike is secured, and thrusting out a hand. 'I'm Lawrence.'

More of a surname than first name if you ask me, but I don't say this, biting my tongue instead.

'Would you like a cup of tea?' I ask.

He holds up the bottle of green. 'Thanks, but I'm off tea, coffee, alcohol, and dairy. Just water, fruit, and vegetables for me this week. All organic, of course.'

The pained expression on his face suggests that he believes his odd choice of diet makes him heroic in some way, like his abstinence is somehow saving the world.

I boil the kettle regardless, as I know it is the time of the morning that Angus likes a coffee, and quite frankly it gives me an excuse to avoid having to make small talk with this strange young man.

Angus shows him through to the living room, and when I join them with the coffee minutes later, Lawrence is leaning forward, hands pressed against the windowsill of the bay window, one leg thrust out behind him, and the other tucked up into his body. Angus simply shrugs when I look at him. Lawrence swaps legs and repeats the process, before turning back to face us.

'Sorry,' he offers, 'that must seem a little strange, but if I don't warm down properly after a bike ride, I'll struggle to make it back later on.'

I perch on the edge of the sofa next to Angus, whilst Lawrence sits at the opposite side of the L-shape, and turns to face us. It's only now I realise he is wearing a small satchel, the same colour as his outfit, and he slips this over his head and unzips it. Withdrawing an electronic tablet, he punches in a PIN, and swipes through the screen, until he locates what he is looking for.

'Before we begin, I need to discuss with you my standard contract terms. I find it is much easier to discuss matters like money and hours upfront, so we both know what it is I'm going to do and how. I appreciate discussing money can be somewhat taboo, but ultimately it's just a business transaction between consenting adults, right?'

If I didn't know why he was here, I could almost be shocked at the subtext of his patter.

He passes the tablet to Angus, who lifts it onto his lap for us both to read.

'So,' Lawrence explains, 'I charge sixty pounds per hour for surveillance, prorated to the actual time spent watching. Individual background checks are a thousand pounds each, but I will seek confirmation from you before commencing additional checks on associated parties of the person you're seeking.' He fixes us with an empathetic look. 'There is no such thing as a *typical* investigation, which means that sadly there is no "flat rate" for the type of services I offer. Every private investigator is unique, and whilst many of the techniques and processes we carry out are similar, every case is ultimately different. If you decide you cannot afford my services, I won't be offended, but I would prefer to know upfront, so we don't end up wasting each other's time.'

My head is spinning as I continue to read the screen and the range of different services and costs. 'What's this about packages?'

He glances at the screen, before nodding. 'I offer complete packages for clients who hire me to catch their spouse cheating. The silver package includes sixty hours of surveillance, photographs, and a record of the target's movements over a month. The gold package includes an additional thirty hours of surveillance, and a digital copy of the images of illicit activity. And the platinum package includes unlimited surveillance for two months, video as well as photographs, and statements from corroborative witnesses. Basically, the platinum package is all but guaranteed to achieve a client-friendly divorce settlement. Unfortunately, I don't offer packages for what you require. As I said, every situation is different.'

There is something quite sick about a human profiteering from the misery of others.

He must sense my reticence, as he adds, 'I am very good at what I do. Nobody expects me to be a private investigator, and that allows me to get closer to targets.'

'What does your wife think about all this cloak and dagger stuff?' I ask out of curiosity.

His stare hardens. 'My *husband* is fully supportive. If you have had second thoughts, or don't want to accept my terms, that's fine, I can just—'

'Don't go,' Angus pipes up. 'We need your help. Please?'

Lawrence looks to me for confirmation, and I nod, even

though I've no idea how we can afford the figures quoted on the tablet.

'Very well then,' he says, taking the tablet back. 'I've done some preliminary work on your case based on what Angus and I discussed over the phone. I have managed to locate home and business addresses for the man you mentioned, as well as a full criminal history check. If you decide not to continue with my services, there will be a two-hundred-pound charge for this information. However, if you wish me to undertake further surveillance and report back to you, I will waive the preliminary fee.' He pauses so we can consider the proposal. 'Tell me what you need, and then maybe we can agree a finance plan to help you achieve your end goal.'

Angus is about to speak, when Lawrence cuts him off with a hand. 'I should just add that if any of the information I provide to you results in police intervention, I am obliged to hand over details of any discoveries to the authorities, and that includes details of any conversations we've had.'

'I don't understand,' I say.

Lawrence looks like he is trying to choose his words carefully. 'Let me phrase it like this – and please do not be offended, as I am not suggesting that this would actually happen, but – in the event that the man you've asked me to trace winds up dead, for example, and you are in the frame for his death, I will have no choice but to notify the police that you hired me to find him, and the information you have provided. It's not a threat, but you need to appreciate that I am a professionally qualified investigator, and as such there are rules I am obliged to follow in order to retain my licence to practise.'

'We don't want him dead,' Angus chirps, though I'm not sure I can agree with that sentiment.

'You'd be surprised what drastic measures some people will take under intense stress,' Lawrence says, and it's as if he's reading my inner thoughts. Our eyes meet, and I'm forced to look away, feeling self-conscious.

'Do we look like killers?' Angus challenges.

Lawrence considers us both, and I'm not sure if he's genuinely trying to assess our threat level. He finally sighs and rests both hands on his knees. 'To be honest, you never really know anyone in this day and age, nor what they might be capable of. So many create a "best version" of themselves, whether online or in person, and in some cases the individual can even begin to believe it themselves. I'm not suggesting either of you want this person dead, I'm just hedging my bets.'

'We just want to know where he is, whether he's still looking for us, and more importantly… whether he already knows where we are.'

This last statement from Angus sends a shiver the length of my spine. I still recall the fire at the cottage, how we lost everything because of *him*: photographs, heirlooms, memories. All gone with the strike of a match, and all an act of bitter revenge. Nobody realises how hard it is to start from scratch with only the clothes on your back, wafting ghost-like through life, unable to let go of the past, but unable to return.

It's tempting to ask Lawrence to run one of his standard background checks on Jess.

Angus fills Lawrence in on our background and our previous addresses so that Lawrence can undertake the necessary enquiries on our behalf. He promises he will get to work on our case immediately, and I can't tell if that's because he doesn't currently have much work on, or whether he senses our desperation. Peace of mind will come at a cost, but if it allows us time to get Daisy settled once again, then it will be worth it. I just hope Lawrence is as good as he says he is, and that Angus's desire to be pro-active won't result in trouble finding us sooner.

Chapter Twenty

Now

Mike didn't appreciate being summoned, least of all by the Chief Super demanding an update he simply couldn't provide. Straightening his tie in the mirrored wall of the elevator, he checked no stray food was trapped between his teeth before exiting and making his way along the corridor, stopping when he arrived at the closed office door. A glow of light beneath the door confirmed the boss was still there.

Mike knocked twice, and waited to be invited in, closing the door behind him when called to do so. The Chief Super was standing by the window, framed by the dark sky and the array of lights coming from the town's skyline.

'Well?' she demanded without turning around.

Mike took in the rest of the office, the desk larger than necessary and with barely enough room for a normal-sized person to squeeze around; the laptop open and at a forty-five-degree angle, with a separate keyboard connected via USB; no sign of a mouse, but two plastic trays – one marked 'In' and the other 'Out'; nothing was out of place, and it was all in stark contrast to Mike's own desk, where it was never obvious if he was coming or going. He envied her organisation, but not her frosty demeanour. A framed photograph of her daughter stood adjacent to the laptop's screen.

'I've got a victim, the weapon that killed him, and possibly one of two suspects responsible for his death.'

He could see the reflection of her eyes boring into him, and suddenly wished he'd ignored the ringing phone as he'd been packing up to leave for the night. Not that it would have made much difference. Given what had unfolded, he probably wouldn't have made it out of the car park before being called back in.

'Still no victim's name?'

'We're checking DNA profiles, but nothing has been located yet. The situation isn't being helped by the system outages we've been experiencing across the borough. The team are doing their best.'

She made a show of pushing up her sleeve to check her watch. 'Clock is ticking, Mike.'

'Yes, ma'am,' he said, biting his tongue to ensure he didn't stray from the party line.

She suddenly turned, and he saw now just how tired she looked. Any make-up she'd put on first thing had worn thin, and he hadn't realised just how dry and wrinkled the skin around her eyes was.

'We need a result,' she said plainly. 'Whatever it takes, we need this case completed with full sign-off from the CPS to charge. Am I making myself clear? I've taken a major risk putting you in charge, and I don't want it to blow up in my face. You were lucky to escape without getting your fingers burned. Other members of your unit weren't so fortunate.'

They shouldn't have had their hands in the fire then, he wanted to retort, but kept his lips buttoned.

'I have Professional Standards breathing down my neck,' she continued, gripping the back of her desk chair tightly, 'and they'd just love it if we screwed up again, and had me out of a job. Running this station *my way* has not made me popular amongst my peers.' She paused. 'What can you tell me about the woman you brought in?'

Mike noticed how white her knuckles were as she continued to squeeze the back of the chair. 'Jess Donoghue: married mother of one, and we've now had it confirmed that she is wheelchair-bound. She was discovered at the scene along with the victim, and his blood was found all over her clothes.'

'I read the forensics report. Two sets of her prints were found on the murder weapon too. What's stopping you from charging?'

Evidence, for one thing, Mike thought.

'It's complicated by her mental health. She hasn't been passed fit enough to make a statement yet. Seems she may have been off her prescribed medication for several days, which is making her frenzied and incoherent. We're currently waiting for her counsellor – one Dr Wanda Savage – to arrive and confirm the assessment. We may have to wait until morning to speak to her.'

'And in the meantime?' she asked, not missing a beat.

'We are collating security camera footage from around the area, interviewing neighbours, and trying to figure out who the victim is. Ma'am, with all due respect, I don't think this is as straightforward as you are suggesting.'

She glared at him, and he physically shrank beneath the weight of her expectation. 'Her prints are on the weapon, her clothes smeared in his blood, and we can place her at the scene; don't make this more complicated than it needs to be. There's no budget for overtime, Mike, and at best I might be able to give you a couple of experienced uniforms to support your team, but that's it. You need to work efficiently and get this over the line. The longer it takes, the more likely that Professional Standards will come sniffing our way.'

She nodded at her door, their meeting now concluded.

He turned and headed for it.

'Oh, and Mike? Don't fuck it up,' she added as he showed himself out.

Chapter Twenty-One

Before - Jess

C harlie wheels me to the head of the table, a space between the guests large enough for three normal seats. Geordie Maggie is to my left, and immediately starts talking at me, telling me how wonderful I look, how it's been far too long since we've spoken, and how pleased she was to receive Charlie's call last week.

Her husband Trevor is busy buttering a bread roll, nodding occasionally when his wife mentions his name in some context. Beside them are Katie and Anthony. A large bulge beneath a blanket over Katie's chest suggests she is breastfeeding their new arrival. This is precisely why I haven't made any effort to see or even speak to them. I don't resent their good fortune at having a new child to care for, and I genuinely wish them the best of luck in all the challenges that will follow, but I don't feel able to fully share in their unbridled joy. It should be me discreetly breastfeeding my child at the table.

Further round, I spot Tracy and a vacant chair; presumably her husband Jack is at the bar. She wiggles her fingers at me in a childish wave, and I force myself to nod back. Geordie Maggie is still babbling beside me, though I'm not entirely sure what she's saying now. Hailing from Newcastle, her accent is still as broad as the first time we met, and I fail to interpret every fourth word she utters.

A tall man I don't recognise leans down and kisses Tracy on the cheek, before sitting in the vacant chair next to her. I watch them in confusion; where is Jack? He wraps his arm around Tracy's shoulder, and she snuggles into his embrace, pressing her lips against his, and it is all I can do to contain my shock. I look away as Tracy's eyes turn on mine, and my cheeks are flushing with something between anger and embarrassment.

'You're not angry, are you?' Charlie whispers into my ear, as he leans towards me, his cologne overpowering.

I want to tell him how disappointed I am that I don't get to spend the next couple of hours alone in his company, like he'd led me to believe. I want to ask him if there's a reason he doesn't want to be alone with me. I don't blame him for losing interest. Being confined to the chair has not aided my figure at all, and although I am generally healthy with what I choose to eat, there are some days when I just eat crap because the frustration is too great to get through the day without an endorphin boost.

'Oh, look who's here,' Charlie declares, before I can respond to his question.

Rosie and her husband James have just appeared at the two doors, and it seems the party is complete as they take the two remaining vacant chairs at the table. Rosie is Charlie's sister, a police officer no less. Tall, with blonde hair, she spends all her free time at the gym working on her core, or at least that's the way it seems. Before my confinement she would try and convince me to join her gym at every opportunity. At least that subject has been closed since.

I feel one of Rosie's muscular arms fall across my collarbone, and she squeezes gently, nearly choking the life out of me. 'It's so good to see you,' she says. 'We'll have a proper catch-up later, yeah? Promise?'

I nod, just to alleviate some of the pressure on my windpipe. James is next over, offering me a hand to shake. Despite being in-laws for more than six years, he is still so very formal with me. Rosie is definitely less inhibited.

'Hi,' is all he offers, before staring down at his feet. He isn't one for small talk, and I'm relieved when he takes his leave and sits down between his wife and the strange man with Tracy.

Menus are promptly handed around, and the chatter between guests intensifies.

'Have whatever you want,' Charlie whispers in my direction. 'I hear the carvery is the best option, but if you'd rather some pasta, that's fine too.'

Geordie Maggie is still nattering away, sometimes in my direction, and other times at her husband or Katie next to him. The napkin has been moved away and the baby is nuzzling on a toy in its travel basket just behind the tired-looking parents.

After the waitress has taken our orders, she returns with a ticket for those who've opted for the carvery. Charlie offers to get my food for me, which is just as well as I don't think I'd be able to reach the hot counter anyway.

'I'll get you a selection of the things you like,' he promises, and as he stands to leave, Rosie jumps into his chair.

'How are you doing today?' she asks. Rosie is one of the few people I have seen since returning from the hospital; having no children of her own, she dotes on her niece. She's also aware that I am taking antidepressants to try and manage the psychological trauma I experienced.

'I'm doing my best,' I say, and that may be the most honest statement I've ever uttered. Isn't that what most of us do, grin and bear it on the bad days, and cling to the good ones?

'You know,' she says, taking a sip of water, 'I was talking to one of the civvies we have working at the station – he's in a wheelchair too – and he was telling me that the civilian support team are crying out for more wheelchair-bound staff. He reckons the role is flexible enough to allow him to attend physiotherapy and medical appointments as required, and he isn't treated any differently to other more abled staff.' She raises her eyebrows in my direction like she's expecting me to be impressed or grateful for her enquiries. 'It could be an avenue back into work for you. Your closest station is probably Harrow, but Uxbridge has a larger civilian support network if you could get there? I could ask him for some more information if you'd like? Or maybe I could ask him to give you a call and answer any questions you might have.'

This is typical of Rosie. I haven't expressed any interest in returning to a working life yet, let alone as a civilian support to the police, but suddenly it's as if I have been begging her for help. I know it isn't fair to expect Charlie to be the sole breadwinner for ever, and at some point I will need to look at work opportunities, but I'm just not ready yet. It's been such a steep learning curve in the last six months that taking on more responsibility will only lead to self-destruction.

'How's work?' I ask, eager to change the subject.

'Busy, busy, busy, as always,' she replies. 'I've been seconded to a new unit – plainclothes – for the next year. It's no extra money, but good experience to add to my CV, and something different to the usual array of domestic violence cases we investigate.'

'Congratulations,' I say, reaching for my own water. 'What will you be doing?'

'I can't say too much,' she begins, which is what she always warns when she's about to tell me more than she probably should, 'but the Chief Super has put the team together to focus on reinvestigating the back book of Missing Persons cases. It's a borough-wide team, working out of Uxbridge and reviewing all outstanding Misper cases, re-interviewing witnesses, and looking for fresh clues about what may have happened. Some of these go back ten years or so. The idea is to see whether we can trace the missing person, or uncover evidence that something more sinister may have occurred. I've only been assigned a week, and I'm loving it already.'

A flash of Daisy's face fizzes through my mind like a firework. 'Do you have any missing children cases to look at, or is just adults?'

'A mixture. We have been tasked with reviewing a hundred cases between us by the end of the assignment. Of those probably a third involve children, half adults, and the remainder vulnerable adults – mental patients, you know?'

'I don't suppose there are any missing five year-old girls in amongst your caseload?' I say before I can stop the words tumbling from my mouth.

Rosie frowns at me, and then begins to chuckle like she suddenly sees the funny side of my question. (There was no funny side.). 'I wondered where my niece was today. Where have you left her?'

I see now why she is laughing, and I don't correct the misunderstanding. 'She's at a friend's house,' I say.

'That's such a shame. James and I will have to come by soon and take her out for the day. She's starting school soon, isn't she?'

'Wednesday,' I say, nodding, and it's like a pin has been pushed into my heart.

I can see Charlie returning with two plates of food in his hands, each stacked as high as a sandcastle. I grab Rosie's hand. 'Would you do me a favour? Don't ask why, but can you check your case pile for a girl called Daisy? She's nearly five now, I believe, petite, dark hair, goth-like.'

Rosie's frown deepens, but Charlie arrives before she can ask any more questions, and she has to shuffle back to her chair. Charlie pushes the plate before me, and gravy drips over the edge and onto the table cloth. There's an enormous Yorkshire pudding, with two tepid-looking sausages inside, a mountain of mashed potato beside it, peas, carrots, sprouts, broccoli, a scoop of swede, three parsnip slices, cauliflower cheese, and sage and onion stuffing balls, along with slices of pale-brown turkey breast.

'I got you a bit of everything,' he says, placing his even taller plate next to mine.

He knows I'm not a fan of cauliflower cheese, and my stomach turns as I see the cheese sauce congealing with the thick brown gravy. I push it to the edge of the plate, and dig my fork into the potato.

'Don't worry if you can't eat it all,' he says leaning in. 'Think my eyes were a bit bigger than my belly. I—' But before he can finish whatever he was about to say, his phone is ringing. He fishes it from his pocket, and checks the display. 'Sorry, I have to take this,' he says, wiping his mouth with his napkin and quickly hurrying from the table, the phone pressed to his ear.

Rosie shuffles back over, the skin around her eyes taut with concern. 'Is everything okay, Jess? Your request is a bit... unexpected. Who is this Daisy girl?'

I wish I hadn't said anything now. 'It's nothing,' I say, backtracking. 'Forget I said anything.'

Unfortunately, I know she won't and will probably spend the rest of the day ruminating on what my interest is in Daisy.

'Let's talk after lunch,' Rosie says, still watching me as my cheeks redden.

The last thing I want is for Rosie to mention what I said to Charlie. He already thinks my mind is playing tricks on me, and if he learns I've tried to rope his sister into my supposed delusion, his anxiety is only going to grow. I catch a glimpse of him outside the window of the converted barn. He is laughing uproariously at whatever Doug has just said, but as he turns and our eyes meet, he suddenly hurries away like I have caught him in a terrible lie. Maybe he just doesn't want me to see him enjoying life in case I'm jealous.

It barely looks like I've eaten a thing, but my stomach is full. More than half the plate of food remains, and as much as I hate to see good food wasted, I cannot manage another morsel. As I push the lonely sprout towards the mountain of mash, my gaze falls on Katie and her baby. Though she is barely a month old, I can already see she has her mother's brown eyes and mess of dark, curly hair. She is awake again, and Katie has propped her up, a hand securely clamped around the back of her neck for support, but the youngster seems to be enthralled by the smiling faces of the other guests, who've all come over to gush at how beautiful she is.

Not one of them has asked how I'm feeling about losing my son. Not one has come over and asked how I am coping, knowing I carried him to full term, only to never feel his beating heart against my own. I still remember how ice-cold his tiny hands felt as they placed his carefully swaddled body on mine.

'It's important that you say goodbye properly,' one of the midwives had said.

I hadn't wanted to say goodbye. Even now, I want this to all be just some horrible nightmare that I'll wake from, to still find him moving about inside my womb, waiting to burst into the world.

'None of this is your fault,' one of the other midwives had said, yet nobody could tell me exactly whose fault it was that my son came into this world without a single breath in his lungs. 'Just one of those things.'

What a copout! Somebody is always to blame. Was it because I didn't sleep at the most beneficial angle for him? Or perhaps that his father and I tried to have sex to induce labour? Or maybe it was because I simply didn't deserve to bring a beautiful, bouncing boy into this world. This was my punishment for daring to believe I could have all the cherished things other mothers enjoy.

I remember kissing his tiny fingers, and willing any God to take the life from me and pass it into him, just so that I would be able to tell him how much I loved him, how I'd felt such a strong bond with him throughout my pregnancy. I would have given anything for him just to hear me tell him how precious he was.

Katie's baby belches and a stream of regurgitated milk spurts from her mouth and all over Katie's hand. The smell of baby sick wafts across the table, and I have to put my napkin to my nose as a filter.

A knocked-over glass jolts me back to the present, and I see that Tracy has now plonked herself down in Charlie's seat. There is no sign of her new mystery man, and as our eyes meet, she is already fiddling with her wedding ring.

'You're looking well,' she says, before I've had chance to think of what to say. We both know she's lying; even in the salmon-coloured blouse I decided to put on for my trip out with Charlie, my hair hasn't been cut in months, my skin is dry and unmade, and my weight has ballooned in the chair.

'Where's Jack?' I ask, as casually as curiosity will allow.

She stands up the glass she knocked over, avoiding my gaze. 'I thought you'd have heard: we broke up.'

The news isn't unexpected, given the intimacy of the kisses she's been sharing with the new man, but I'm still surprised to hear the words coming from her lips. In our circle of friends, Tracy and Jack were the powerhouse couple; together since college, married for ten years, and living in an enormous detached house in Gerrards Cross, they'd been the couple we all aspired to be. No children, as both wanted to focus on their careers, Jack a chartered accountant and Tracy working in publishing. We'd all been expecting them to announce an extension to their family any day.

I have dozens of questions filling my mind, but give her the space to speak more.

'Caught him shagging some client he was working for up in Barnstaple. Apparently they'd been at it for months behind my back.' As she's speaking the words, I find it almost impossible to believe that the Jack I know could be so callous, yet there is no hurt or regret in her voice. It's as if she is reciting a recipe, every detail delivered with an even pace and in a matter-of-fact manner.

'He said he'd fallen out of love with me, and agreed to the divorce settlement my solicitor demanded on my behalf. Ironically, I'd say planning our wedding took longer than dismantling it. He's moved up there with her from all accounts, and that's all there is to it.'

Given I haven't seen Tracy since the week before I was rushed into the hospital, I don't quite understand why she thinks I would have heard about such shocking news and had not offered my support.

I look over to Charlie, who smiles and waves in my direction before returning to his conversation with Dave. If he arranged this gathering today, he must have known that Tracy was bringing her mystery man, and that Jack wouldn't be here. Does that mean he knew about the breakup and didn't tell me? What else is he keeping from me?

'I'll introduce you to Gareth when he's back,' Tracy continues. 'He's a fireman, and also plays rugby for a local team. So much bigger and stronger than Jack, and so hands-on with stuff that Jack would have just hired someone to come and fix. Like, I was having a problem with the car not starting last week, and Gareth was over in an instant, tinkering away with the engine, and had it up and running again inside twenty minutes.'

A waitress appears at my shoulder and asks if I've finished, and I nod guiltily. She probably assumes that my eyes were too big for my belly, and I want to tell her I never would have piled my plate so high, but what is the point? I just hope they have some kind of process in place for redistributing unwanted food to those in greater need.

'She's a cutie pie, isn't she?' Tracy says, smiling and nodding towards Katie's baby, who is once again drawing everyone's attention. 'Where's Grace today?'

'She's at a friend's,' I say, quickly looking away from the baby, and pressing my hand to where I last felt Luke kick.

'Well, it makes me glad Jack and I never had kids.' Tracy sighs loudly. 'Nothing worse than having to explain why Daddy is now living with some trollop up north.' She breaks off, as Gareth heads over, and she quickly introduces us.

'I've heard so much about you,' Gareth says, his voice not quite as deep as I'd imagined it would be.

'Not all bad, I hope,' I fire back quickly with a smile.

He smiles too, and I can see why Tracy has moved on from her ex-husband so quickly. Gareth is handsome, too muscly for me, and certainly not my type, but attractive nonetheless. They seem quite an odd pairing, Tracy so petite and barely five feet tall, but he is as into her as she him. I find myself watching them as they return to their places across the table from me, and I'm barely able to remember what Jack looked or sounded like.

I'm relieved when Charlie finally returns, and it is quickly agreed that the bill will be split rather than fathoming who ordered what and paying for individual items. Then we are away, Charlie wheeling me back through the restaurant towards the front door. The place somehow feels even busier than when we arrived, but I keep my head bent to avoid making eye contact with any curious bystanders.

Back in the car, I'm amazed at how tired I suddenly feel. Maybe it's my full stomach, or maybe it was the energy it took to keep smiling and pretending like my life hasn't been totally flipped upside down by everything that's happened these past six months. My eyelids feel so heavy, but then the car's Bluetooth system announces that Doug is calling Charlie. What is wrong with that man? Why can't he leave his staff alone at the weekend? It isn't like Charlie gets paid any extra for being at his boss's beck and call.

I'm waiting for Charlie to answer, but he cancels the call. 'Sorry,' he offers.

'No, it's fine,' I sigh. 'If you need to take it, I'll pretend I'm not here.'

Charlie doesn't bat an eyelid. 'I'll call him back when we're home.'

Is my husband turning over a new leaf? I've never known him decline a call from Doug. Back when we were trying to conceive, he once stopped foreplay to take a call. I don't know whether to be alarmed or impressed.

He checks his watch. 'We've got to collect Grace from Ava's house shortly.'

His mood has gone decidedly frosty, and I can't help wondering whether his last call with Doug ended in some kind of argument. I close my eyes and try to shut out all thoughts, figuring twenty minutes' sleep on the way home is better than none. The phone rings again, and Charlie quickly declines the call, before switching off the stereo, and thus the Bluetooth system.

I think back to my conversation with Tracy, and can only hope that my husband isn't keeping dark secrets from me. I know he doesn't want to add to my already high stress levels, but what if all the extra hours at the office and the constant calls from Doug are a sign that everything at work isn't as rosy as he's been making out? I want to ask him, but I'm not sure I could take the strain of the truth right now.

Chapter Twenty-Two

Before - Morag

L awrence's words are playing on my mind as I drive up the road, searching left and right for the address I found in the phonebook: *you never really know anyone in this day and age, nor what they might be capable of.*

I suppose there is some sense in what he was saying, though I have always considered myself a good judge of character. Not so much in recent years, it has become apparent. Take Jess as a prime example; my instinct was that she was just like any normal mother, and that the two of us might be able to strike up a friendship for our wee ones. But after our run-in at Waitrose, and the coldness she presented at the barbecue, now I'm not certain what her intentions towards us are.

Spotting number thirty-seven, I indicate and pull onto the driveway. There's no sign of Charlie's little Hyundai, and now I'm wishing I'd phoned ahead to let them know I would be dropping off the leek and tatty soup. If I'd known they were out, I would have brought it around later. I'm surprised they're not home, to be honest, as Jess had given the impression she spends most of her time cooped up. I'll just have to leave it inside their porch with a note saying who it's from.

When I get out of the car, the air is much cooler than first thing this morning when I dashed to the phone box, and there is little blue sky visible beneath the white quilt of cloud. I'm certain showers weren't forecast, but the weather down south can be temperamental. At least back home in Aberdeen you're almost guaranteed it will rain at least five days a week.

I'm just leaning in and reaching over to the lidded porcelain pot on the passenger seat when I hear an engine revving just out of sight. Straightening, I'm pleased to see they've returned, so I won't need to hunt for pen and paper. I carry the pot over to Jess's side of the car. I'm sure she's scowling as she lowers the window.

'Hello there, Jess. How are you feeling today?' The question is meant to be a sincere enquiry into her well-being after yesterday's ill health, but the way her cheeks quickly redden, you'd have thought I was accusing her of some heinous crime.

'Much better,' she snaps. 'What's in the pot?'

Her frostiness is enough to make my blood boil, but I lower it to a simmer. 'I thought you might not be up for cooking, so I made you some leek and tatty soup. It was my great-aunt's recipe, passed down from generation to generation. Best thing when you're feeling under the weather. Cures all known ills. I thought you might enjoy it. Only needs a few minutes on the stove to warm it through.'

'Sounds wonderful,' Charlie says, leaning across his wife and offering a warm smile. 'That's very generous of you, Morag. Hold on, I'll let you in and you can carry it through.'

Jess opens her mouth to say something to him, but quickly changes her mind, and raises the window again. What the hell is wrong with her? Whatever happened to good manners?

I move back to my car, keen to put down the pot, which is much heavier than it looks, but the two of them remain in the car. A murmur of their voices carries on the wind, and I don't turn because I don't want to witness their argument. Poor Grace must be hearing all of it, and I wonder if she's become immune to their bad-tempered spats. I don't think Angus and I have ever argued in front of wee Daisy, but I know she too has borne witness to bickering parental figures.

Charlie's door slams shut as he gets out. He is all sweetness and light to me. 'It really is very kind of you to make us soup,' he says. 'Leek and potato has always been one of my favourites. My gran used to make it, but my mum was never much of a cook. Guess I inherited her lack of culinary skill.' He unlocks the front door, and I'm expecting him to take the pot from me, but he pushes the door wider and encourages me up the ramp and inside. 'Kitchen is at the far end of the hallway.'

Before I can say anything more, he is already on his way back to the car, presumably to help Jess and Grace out. With no other choice, I head in, instantly struck by how homely the place feels. The wall leading up the staircase is covered in framed photographs of the three of them looking contented in sunnier climes. It's hard not to look at each image, a moment captured for ever, hinting at happier times. There are no pictures of Jess in her wheelchair, and it stirs a thought in the back of my mind; does she really need that chair or is it part of their cover story?

'Stop being so paranoid,' Angus would tell me if he was here.

I know he's right, but I can't ignore the nagging doubt in my head about this picture-perfect family. As I move towards the kitchen, the pile of plates, bowls, mugs, and glasses by the sink catches my eye. Despite all the crockery, there is no sign of any pans, and the dustbin is overfilling with plastic containers. Is this really how they live? Considering the height of the countertops, I suppose I shouldn't be so surprised that Jess isn't able to do more in here, assuming she really does need that chair. They've clearly fitted the ramp to enable her to get in and out of the house, so it strikes me as odd that they haven't made modifications to the kitchen too.

Placing the pot on the hob, I'm about to leave – I don't want them to think I'm snooping – when I notice a small collection of pill bottles near the kettle. Lifting each, I recognise the names on the labels: Oxybutynin for bladder spasms; Gabapentin for pain relief; Clopidogrel to prevent blood clots; and finally Citalopram, a mood stabiliser. I'm not shocked that Jess is taking antidepressants if everything they've told me is true. It's not safe leaving them here though, within easy reach of wee Grace. Some of these pills could easily be confused for sweeties. Do they not realise what a danger it is to leave such toxins in easy reach of a curious child?

I suppose Angus is right, *you can take the lass out of nursing, but not the nurse out of the lass.*

I can't just leave without saying something. Pushing the small container of pills behind the kettle, and therefore out of Grace's reach, I move towards the kitchen door. I can hear their hushed voices further along the hallway.

'How does she know where we live?' Jess says in a loud whisper.

'I don't know, maybe she looked us up online. What does it matter? She's done a kind thing here.'

'Has she? You think turning up at a virtual stranger's house with homemade soup isn't just a bit weird? For all we know she's probably poisoned that like she did the meat yesterday.'

There is an edginess to Charlie's voice when he speaks again, a kind of low growl. 'It was only you who got sick, Jess. The rest of us were fine. You seriously need to get a grip. Are you still taking your pills? Because you're really starting to worry me. We don't want another episode, do we?'

'How dare you! For all we know it was those bloody pills that caused what happened. And in answer to your question, yes, I'm still taking the bloody pills. You can check the bottles if you don't believe me.'

I don't want to be listening in to any of this argument, but if I suddenly appear, they'll know I've overheard what's been said. I need to remain where I am until it blows over, and then plead ignorance if they ask.

'Meeting her at the park,' Jess continues, 'then running into her in Waitrose, then the barbecue, now the soup… It's like she's trying to crowbar herself into our lives.'

'Jess, can you hear yourself? Do you think Morag is some kind of stalker? Don't be ridiculous. I for one think it's very sweet of her to be so concerned about someone she barely knows. Don't look a gift horse in the mouth.'

His voice is growing nearer, and I sense he is now just the other side of the door, but he hesitates.

Jess is closer too when she next speaks. 'Nobody in this day and age is that kind without reason, Charlie. I'm not being paranoid. There is something… odd about her.'

'Listen, she's probably just lonely,' Charlie says, barely

audible, and much softer now. 'You said yourself they're new to the area – maybe she's just trying to make friends so she'll have someone to natter to in the playground before school. It's obvious she'll probably be one of the oldest mums at the school, and maybe she's feeling nervous about that. Who knows?'

This is my moment. Pulling open the door, I pretend to be startled to see them both so close. If they think I'm a lonely old woman, maybe they'll also buy that I'm hard of hearing, even though it's as sharp as a tack.

'I've left the pot on the stove,' I explain, removing my oven gloves, and tucking them beneath my arm. 'There should be enough for four to five servings. No rush to get the pot back to me. And if it's easier you can give me a call, and I'll come and collect it when you're done.'

I'm desperate to get out of their house, before they start questioning what I might have overheard. Pushing my way past, I head for the front door, before realising that Charlie's car is now blocking mine in. He hurries after me, and confirms he will move to let me out, and it is only then that I see Grace is still strapped into her seat, and I wonder how long they would have left her there had I not insisted on leaving. She looks dejected as she stares out at me from the back seat, and I can't help but wonder whether they realise how unhappy their daughter is, and whether there's anything more I should be doing to help her. It wouldn't be the first time I've come to the rescue of a child in need.

Chapter Twenty-Three

Now

Mike Ferry grimaced as he tasted the lukewarm dregs of the Americano, and almost spat it back into the cardboard cup. Only DS Nazia Hussain remained in the office, still poring over the security camera footage she'd brought back to the station with her.

'You should head home when that one's finished,' Mike said, stifling a yawn. 'No point in watching it with tired eyes; more likely to miss something vital.'

Her eyes remained on the screen. 'I think I might have found our suspect arriving at the house.'

Practically leaping from his chair, Mike hurried to her desk.

'This is from a private security camera across the road from our crime scene,' she said, pointing at the screen. 'You can just make out the taillights of a vehicle pulling away from roughly where the house would be. Not enough to confirm registration number, but if you keep watching the screen…' She paused the grainy image and tapped the monitor with the tip of her pen. 'There, woman in a wheelchair. Can't say for certain that she was in the car, or whether it was just blocking the view.'

Mike stared closer at the screen. 'Is there any way we can sharpen the image? The long hair suggests a woman, but a fancy defence barrister could argue that that's someone else in a wig.'

'I'll have to speak to the technicians upstairs, but the important thing is, it gives us a timestamp. If this *is* our suspect, then she arrived at the house a little after five this evening. First responders weren't on the scene for another ninety minutes. So did she go to the property with the intention of killing the victim?'

'Have you seen our John Doe arrive yet?'

'Not so far, Mike, but I've barely broken the surface of the feeds I confiscated. You want a fresh coffee? I'm making myself one.'

'I told you, you ought to get yourself home for a few hours' kip.'

She cocked her eyebrow at him sceptically. 'I'll go when you do, Mike. Milk and sugar?'

'Neither. Thanks.'

Locking her workstation, she pushed her chair back from the desk, picked up her mug and headed out of the room, turning right in the direction of the small kitchen at the end of the corridor.

Dropping into Nazia's chair, Mike leaned back, closing his eyes, and focusing on their suspect's face, trying to determine whether she could be cold-blooded enough for the stabbing to be premeditated. And why that house?

The phone ringing at his own desk startled him out of near-sleep, and lurching for the handset on Nazia's desk, he sent her pot of pens flying.

'Hello? Hello?' he stammered into the phone.

'Mike? It's Vikram in the custody suite. A Dr Wanda Savage is down here, demanding to speak to whoever's in charge. Reckons your suspect is one of her patients. Are you free to come down and speak to her?'

Mike thanked him, hung up the phone, and finished what remained of the lukewarm coffee. Fresh caffeine would have to wait for now. Leaving Nazia a note, he headed out of the office, along the corridor, and down the two flights of stairs, swiping his pass to allow him access to the custody suite. The woman in the dark jeans and red hooded top didn't resemble any kind of psychiatrist he knew of, but given the late hour of the day, he shouldn't have been surprised that she wasn't more formally attired.

He offered his hand, but she ignored it, crossing her arms, clearly not afraid to challenge him in front of his colleagues.

'You've no legal grounds to be holding my patient Mrs Jess Donoghue. She is in a vulnerable state and needs to be treated with care. I have it on good authority that she hasn't been taking her prescribed medication, and until I can confirm that she is mentally sound, she is not fit to be interviewed by you.'

Mike took a step back and allowed himself a moment before responding. 'Good. We've been waiting for you. Perhaps we should go somewhere more private where we can discuss your patient's mental state?'

Dr Savage puffed out her cheeks. 'Not until I see her to check she is okay.'

'I'm happy to arrange for one of my colleagues to take you

to her. Mrs Donoghue isn't under arrest, but from what I've been told by our on-call medical team, she is in an agitated state, and so, for her own safety, we wanted to keep hold of her until an exact diagnosis could be made. It was our team that reached out to you, correct?'

The counsellor nodded. 'I'm Dr Wanda Savage.'

Mike smiled again. 'And I'm Detective Inspector Mike Ferry. To be honest with you, I'm glad you've come in. You mentioned Mrs Donoghue is off her medication; are you able to confirm what you're treating her for?'

'You know that's confidential.'

'I wouldn't want you to break your patient-doctor privilege, but I believe Mrs Donoghue witnessed a horrifying crime this evening, and I need to determine whether she could have been the aggressor in the situation. Now, if she's a potential threat to my officers because she hasn't been actively treating her condition, then I think I have a right to know.'

Dr Savage narrowed her eyes. 'I can't comment on the safety of your officers until I've spoken to her. I would like to undertake an assessment of my own, and it might be that I need to temporarily have her moved to a secure facility until her condition, as you describe it, is under control.'

Dr Savage's unwillingness to say that Jess wasn't capable of violence told Mike all he needed to know. 'Very well, please carry out your assessment, but I'd like to observe too.'

She considered his request. 'I'll ask her if she minds, but I can't guarantee it. If she's not under arrest then she's within her rights to leave here of her own volition, and there's nothing you can do to stop her.'

Mike knew she was right, but he was reluctant to allow his

key witness, and a possible killer, to leave the station without a fight, even if it meant playing his hand and having her arrested.

Chapter Twenty-Four

Before – Jess

I start as the alarm sounds loud on the bedside table, and quickly reach over to snooze it, conscious of disturbing Grace upstairs. The curtains are doing little to shut out the bright sunshine, and as I feverishly rub the sleep from my eyes, I notice the space in the bed beside me. As always, Charlie has folded his pyjama shorts and T-shirt set, and left them on top of his pillow. There's also a travel mug of tea on the bedside table in front of the clock. The gesture always makes me smile, a reminder that he does love me despite all the difficulty my condition has caused to our lives.

I adjust the pillows behind me, so I can sit up in bed and drink the tea without slopping it all over the summer duvet. Incredibly, there was no middle-of-the-night insomnia to contend with, and I genuinely feel well rested. I have two days of Grace to myself before school starts on Wednesday, and am determined to make the most of every second. I haven't felt this level of energy coursing through my veins in several days, and the positivity is washing through me like waves.

Reaching for the travel mug, my eyes widen when I catch a glimpse of the clock display.

That can't be right! It can't possibly be half past eight.

Arriving in the hallway, I'm surprised to hear voices behind the living-room door. Pushing it open with the chair, I gasp as Grace's cheery face greets me. She's stretched out on the sofa, and some cartoon is playing on the television.

'Morning, Grace,' I say, keeping my surprise in check. 'What are you doing up?'

Her eyes remain glued to the screen as she responds, 'I woke up and came downstairs. You were asleep, so I let you rest. Can I have some breakfast now?'

A happy tear threatens to escape, but I maintain my composure. How many children would have woken their sleeping parent to demand breakfast? Not mine. So considerate of her to leave me sleeping and find something to entertain herself. In truth, I didn't even realise she knew how to turn on the television, let alone find the children's channel. She never fails to amaze me.

'What would you like to eat?' I ask, reversing the chair out of the room.

She's up and behind me a moment later. 'Well…' she says, slowly drawing out the word like it has three times as many letters, 'what I'd really like is pancakes. Could we make pancakes?'

Her chin presses down on my shoulder, and her skin feels so smooth and warm against my cheek. Despite Charlie's best efforts to make our home more accessible for the wheelchair, he's not been able to do anything with the kitchen to allow me to reach the countertops or wall cupboards. I can operate the oven and microwave on my own, but that's about the limit. He's mentioned us looking to move somewhere more appropriate, but I know we can't afford anywhere that would better meet my needs.

'Please, Mum,' Grace says, pressing her cheek further into my own. 'I'll help. You can tell me what to do.'

Despite my renewed energy, I'm nervous about agreeing to this request. It's one thing to instruct her on how to weigh flour and measure milk, but I would be taking a huge risk allowing her anywhere near a hot frying pan.

We continue into the kitchen, and I look up at the hanging cupboards. The flour and mixing bowls are in the corner in the cupboard, but even standing on a chair, there's no way Grace is going to be able to reach up to the necessary shelf.

Lifting her on to my lap, I fix her with my sincerest look, willing her not to be upset when I break the news. 'I'm sorry, sweetheart, but I don't have everything we need for pancakes this morning.' She looks crestfallen, and I'm close to cracking, when I have a fresh thought. 'I have a better idea,' I quickly say. 'We can't make pancakes now, but how about we make pancakes for dinner? That way we can nip to the shops today and buy some flour and eggs, and then Daddy can get down all the equipment we need, and then we can have pancakes for dinner instead. How does that sound?'

She crinkles her nose as if weighing up the proposal like some politician in Brussels. 'Can I have chocolate spread on mine?'

Negotiated like a true diplomat.

'Absolutely! We could even buy some ice cream at the

shops so you could have chocolate spread *and* ice cream inside your pancakes.'

Her eyes widen in excitement, and she licks her lips. 'Yay!'

I'm relieved that we've managed to find a happy compromise. After the accident, I promised myself that I would do whatever it took so Grace would see beyond the chair and my disability. I have nightmares about her being at school and the other children laughing at her because her mum's in a wheelchair. I don't want my situation to impact her any more than it already has.

She hops down from my lap, and heads over to the lower band of cupboards where we now keep plates, dishes and cereals for easier access. She pulls out a bowl and balances it on the counter in line with the top of her head, before reaching for a box of Rice Krispies and filling the bowl. I pour on milk, carry the bowl over to the kitchen table for her, hand her a spoon, and watch as she tucks in.

I don't feel hungry yet, but remain where I am, sipping from the travel mug, and watching as she shovels spoon after spoon of cereal between her lips. As nervous as I am about her starting reception class on Wednesday, I know she is ready for it. She's always been quick at learning new things; already able to say three to four words and toddling about before her first birthday. I know how lucky I am to have such a conscientious and clever little girl. Even when we'd had to tell her that her brother passed during childbirth, she took it all in her stride.

'Apart from making pancakes for dinner, what else would you like to do today?' I ask. 'It looks like it's going to be a warm day, and it would be nice to do something fun and energetic. What do you think?'

'Can I have a friend over to play?'

It sounded like a snub but I know she doesn't mean it. 'I was hoping you and I could do something together,' I offer.

'Yeah, so do I,' she says between mouthfuls. 'If I had a friend over to play with, you could take us down to the park.'

Daisy's face fills my mind: *She's not my mum.*

'I don't know who we could invite over,' I counter. 'It's a bit late notice. I could phone Ava's mum, if you—'

'No, I saw Ava yesterday. What about Daisy?'

I don't want to disappoint Grace, but I'd prefer it if we put some distance between our family and theirs, especially after Morag's surprise arrival at our home yesterday afternoon. Whilst dropping off soup could be seen as a charitable act, I can't help thinking that there is something more sinister about the way she is trying to force her way into our lives. And I'm certain she was the one who moved my box of pills behind the kettle where I couldn't reach it.

The peace is shattered by the ringing phone, but before I can turn to go and collect it from the living room, Grace is off her seat and haring past me, lifting the receiver, and telling the caller that they've reached the Donoghue residence. Whilst I'm impressed by her proactivity, I wish she wouldn't answer the phone until I've checked who's calling.

She marches back into the kitchen and thrusts the phone towards me. 'It's for you,' she declares, a hint of disappointment in her tone, as if she actually believed it might have been for her. She hops back onto the chair and tucks back in to the cereal, as I put the phone to my ear.

'Hello? Jess Donoghue speaking.'

'Ah, Mrs Donoghue, good, glad I managed to reach you before you set off,' a shaky yet warm-sounding voice replies. It sounds familiar, but it takes me a moment to place it. 'I wondered whether we could delay your appointment by a couple of hours. There's been an emergency case for me to look at, and if I could push you back from ten to twelve, you'd be doing me a huge favour.'

'Dr Tegan?' I check.

'Yes, yes,' he says quickly.

I strain to look at the calendar behind me. There are no appointments pencilled in for this month, so I don't understand what appointment he's referring to.

'Sorry, when are we supposed to be meeting?' I say, voice cloaked with confusion.

'We have an appointment for ten o'clock this morning,' he says without a beat. 'That's what I'm hoping we can push back to midday. I hate to ask, particularly if you were about to head out. Can you make it in for twelve instead? It doesn't disrupt your plans too much, I hope?'

I glance back at the calendar again. There's definitely no appointment written down, but there are no appointments recorded for the whole month, which is odd, as we are supposed to meet once every four weeks or so to assess the damage to my spine. As much as I don't want to admit it, I now have a sinking feeling that I must not have written the next appointment on the calendar.

I look back at Grace. I can't drag her with me to the hospital, as it isn't fair for her to be sitting around bored while I wait to be seen, and I know Dr Tegan won't be able to speak as freely with her eavesdropping.

'Is there any way we can move it to a different day?' I ask

There's a pause on the line. 'My calendar is pretty full for the next three weeks,' he says. 'It would be better to still see you today if possible…'

His words trail off. He's waiting for me to agree, and I can't help but feel guilty. Ultimately, it's my fault for forgetting that we were supposed to be meeting today, and had he not phoned, I wouldn't have even remembered the appointment, and would have wasted his time by not showing up.

'No, okay,' I say, my eyes clamping shut as I instantly regret the path I've chosen. 'I will see you at midday.'

Dr Tegan's office is on the third floor of the specialist spinal wing, set away from the main body of the hospital building. Built twenty years ago, this wing resembles a student hall of residence, but is relatively new in comparison with the tall grey and white block across the road from it.

His secretary greets me at the door, and promises that he won't be too long. She offers me a cup of tea, which I gratefully accept, and by the time she hands it to me, Dr Tegan is at his door, welcoming me in. The office is light and airy, and a large double-glazed window overlooks a sea of green trees from the forest that neighbours the hospital. The walls are in a neutral magnolia, and even the carpeted floor is a pattern of grey, yellow and orange fibres. It doesn't feel like a doctor's office; more like a room you would rent in a holiday park. There is a welcoming ambience to the decor.

'How have you been, Jess?' Dr Tegan begins when I've applied the brake, and he's sitting across from me, legs parted, and hands resting on his knees.

I like Dr Tegan. He had no involvement in what happened to me six months ago but has read and studied all of my medical history, and the findings of the internal investigation, and treats me with dignity and respect. In some ways, I even forget I'm stuck in this chair when it's just the two of us. He is blessed with a natural bedside manner, and charm that encourages me to believe every word he says.

'I'm okay,' I lie, not wanting to disappoint him. It's hard to explain, but he has this way about him that makes me eager to please.

It's not a sexual thing. He's in his sixties, with a receding hairline and pot belly, and I don't think I've ever seen him in anything but autumnal colours. In so many ways he reminds me of my father, and maybe that's the real reason I didn't want to cancel today's appointment. I need to hear reassurance that things will improve.

'How's that little daughter of yours? Grace, isn't it?'

I don't want to tell him that I've left her with the receptionist with a colouring book. 'She is incredible. So full of beans.'

He smiles warmly, and for the first time I notice yellow staining on his teeth. 'She must be starting school soon, right?'

My shoulders sag, but I fight every urge in my body to cry. 'On Wednesday.'

'They grow up so fast! I remember when our Jane was that age, and now look at her, married and with children of her own.'

There is a twinkle in his eye as he proceeds to share stories about his grandson, and I can hear how much he loves being a grandfather. Part of me wishes I'd brought Grace into the room to meet him.

Pulling back the white curtain that bisects the office, he helps me up onto the paper towels spread across the bed, and asks me to lower my trousers and remove my top so he can examine me. I'm suddenly transported back to that night.

I remember how heavy the rain sounded, battering the windows of the maternity ward, with occasional flashes lighting up the dark night sky. I kept telling the midwife that I thought something was wrong, that I was in so much pain, but she kept reassuring me that everything was as it should be.

When she suggested the epidural as an alternative to the gas and air, I readily agreed, having had one when Grace was delivered. I understood there were risks, but they seemed so low that I barely listened as the anaesthetist explained that less than one in 100,000 experience any kind of side effect. I just wanted my son out and in my arms, where I could properly protect him. At that stage I didn't know it was already too late.

'The needle used to deliver the epidural struck a nerve, which triggered bleeding around the spinal cord,' Dr Tegan explains, as he probes the skin of my lower back with his warm finger.

The loss of feeling in my legs was perfectly natural, the anaesthetist explained at the time. And maybe, had the midwives not become so alarmed by the baby's rapid decline, I would have mentioned the feeling of nausea and the growing pain in the base of my spine.

The memory is such a blur from there. I see flashes of movement, panicked faces, but no recollection of sound. Whatever words were exchanged between midwives, nurses, anaesthetists, and surgeons either made no sense to me or were spoken too quietly. I remember looking at Charlie for support and just watching the anxiety grow in his eyes with every passing minute. He kept kissing my hand, telling me everything would be okay, but the sweat around his temples, the shakiness of his voice, and his tight grip of my hand told me that his promises were based on hope rather than fact.

It wasn't until later in the day, when feeling still hadn't returned to my legs, that the anaesthetist started to accept that something might have gone wrong.

Dr Tegan is now pressing the tip of a needle into each of my toes, along the sole of my foot, around my ankle, all the way up to my thigh.

'Any feeling at all?' he asks hopefully.

My eyes are misting up as I shake my head.

'Okay, okay, well, it's still early days. You can fasten your trousers now.' He helps me off the bed, returns to his desk and reads the screen. 'It says here you haven't followed up on your physiotherapy appointments.'

I can see the disappointment in his frown, and I feel like a naughty schoolgirl. The truth is I don't see the point in fanning false hope. There is a fifty per cent chance that I may get some feeling back in my legs over time, but only a ten per cent chance that I will ever get full motion and control of my legs back.

I don't tell him any of this, however, nodding and agreeing that I will book an appointment in due course.

'And how are things with your marriage?' he asks, and I'm taken aback by the directness of the question.

'Fine,' I say quickly, but there is a quiver to my voice, as if I no longer believe my words. 'Charlie is my rock.'

'Good, good, and are you still taking the Citalopram we prescribed?'

I hate that I'm barely thirty and taking antidepressants to keep my mood stable. 'Yes,' I say.

'And are they helping? You're not experiencing any kind of side effects?'

'I struggle sleeping sometimes,' I admit.

'Any additional anxiety, or agitation?' he asks, watching my response closely. 'Any paranoia?'

She's not my mum.

'Um, nothing that I've noticed.'

His eyes narrow as he studies the computer screen. 'You were referred to Dr Savage for psychological assessment. Are you still seeing her to discuss your ongoing mental needs?'

I can't tell whether he's asked the question because he knows I've not been attending the appointments and is trying to catch me in a lie, or because he genuinely doesn't know.

'I haven't seen her in a few weeks,' I try, aiming for a neutral answer halfway between the truth and deceit.

He fixes me with a firm, but sincere stare. 'It's really important that you continue to get the counselling and support you need, Jess. What you're going through at the moment is not common. The brain doesn't cope well when everything needs to be rewritten, and that's why we always encourage those who suffer forms of paralysis to seek the mental health support they require. It's okay to admit that you're not finding the transition easy to adapt to.'

I know he is trying to offer supportive words, and I want to thank him for speaking so honestly with me, but there is part of me that sees he has concluded I'm struggling with things, and that leaves me deflated.

He leans closer. 'If there's anything you'd like to discuss with me now, rather than waiting to see Dr Savage again, I'm happy to listen. There'll be no judgement from me.'

What can I say? That I suspect Morag of abducting Daisy

from her true family; that I'm worried I'm losing Charlie; that I'm terrified I will never be able to lead a normal life again; that I don't know whether the rollercoaster of emotions I experience each day is perfectly natural, or whether I might be slowly losing my mind?

'I was planning to make a new appointment with Dr Savage soon,' I say hesitantly. 'Thank you for your concern, Dr Tegan, but I really am doing okay.'

He doesn't speak for a moment, continuing to watch me, before that broad smile breaks out across his face. 'That's good, Jess. I want you to promise me that you'll make an appointment with the physiotherapy team as well, as things won't improve without your determination to improve them.'

I agree without question, and am relieved when he doesn't demand anything else from me.

'She's been as good as gold,' Dr Tegan's secretary says when I emerge from his office.

Grace smiles when she sees me, and hurries over, showing off the picture of a daffodil in a flower pot that she's carefully coloured. 'Can we stick it to the fridge?'

'Of course we can,' I say pulling out my mobile as it vibrates in my bag. I don't recognise the number, but it's local, so I answer it.

'Jess Donoghue?' the irate woman practically barks down the line.

'Yes? Can I help you with something?'

'It's Miss Danvers, from Hillside Infants. I was phoning to check if you were still attending this afternoon's parent-teacher meeting?'

'I wasn't aware there was a parent-teacher meeting this afternoon. I thought that wasn't until the eighth.'

'Today is the eighth, Mrs Donoghue,' she says, but glancing down at my watch it says it's only the seventh. Either she's mistaken or my watch isn't right.

I wheel over to Dr Tegan's secretary, pressing the phone to my chest so Miss Danvers won't hear me. 'What's today's date?

I already know what she's going to say before she says it. 'Today is Monday the eighth.'

What is going on with my memory at the moment? How could I lose track of the date? I've known about this meeting for weeks. I'm sure it's to do with all those pills they've had me on. For all I know they've been making things much worse, rather than better.

'I am so sorry, Miss Danvers,' I say hurriedly into the phone. 'What time does the meeting start?'

'Five minutes ago,' she says, that frustration creeping through again.

'I'm so sorry,' I repeat, 'I'll be there as quick as I can.'

Chapter Twenty-Five

Before – Morag

This parent-teacher meeting should have started by now, and I've no idea why it's been delayed. I arrived ten minutes early, but there was already an enormous queue at the gates. I had hoped to get a seat near the front, but in the end I've had to settle for one near the back. Hopefully, there won't be anything on the overhead projector to read, as I've left my glasses at home. There must be forty or more parents in the room, but I don't know a single one of them. I had expected to see Jess here, but she's not arrived yet.

I don't really see the point of this meeting. I suppose it's the Head's way of pre-empting the slew of questions some of the parents will fire at her on Wednesday morning. It's not rocket science: bring your child to school, see that they go in, and then let these highly trained teachers do their jobs. It was never as complicated when I used to take my wee one all those years ago.

'Right, ladies and gentlemen,' the Head says, standing and clapping her hands to quiet the murmur of voices. 'We will make a start now, and anyone else who arrives later will just have to catch up.'

There are half a dozen empty seats right in the middle of the seated pack, so presumably waiting for tardy parents is the reason for the delay to the start of the meeting. There are a handful of men seated with their wives and girlfriends, but at least ninety per cent of the audience is female. I did think about asking Angus to come along, but if he had, there wouldn't have been anyone to watch Daisy for us, and there was a strictly no-children policy for today's meeting. Presumably that is to avoid disturbances, but to be fair I think Daisy would already be bored. She tells me she doesn't care about starting school, but I watch her carefully when she says it, and I can see anxiety in her hand gestures and gaze-avoidance.

'You know who's late,' I hear one of the women say behind me, 'that woman who nearly killed herself in that car accident. You remember? It was in the newspaper just after Christmas. She'd made all that fuss about the local council misappropriating funds, and then accused them of trying to kill her. She was pregnant and the accident brought on the labour. Her daughter Grace went to pre-school with my Ava.'

My ears prick up at the mention of Grace's name, and now I can no longer hear what the Head is saying.

'I'm friends with her husband, but I don't understand what he's doing with her. I suppose it could be guilt, but he could do so much better.'

'Nadine, you're terrible!' a second woman whispers loudly, and I hear the two giggle.

'Nothing wrong with keeping your options open,' the first one chuckles. 'He's young enough, handsome, works in the city, or so he tells me. Why wouldn't I be interested?'

'I know the one you mean. Charlie, isn't it?'

'That's right. I'll let you into a little secret: I caught him watching me when I was in the pool yesterday. He blushed as soon as our eyes met, but I could tell what he was thinking.'

They quieten down as the Head raises her voice to ensure everyone is listening, but then there is a commotion at the main door, which suddenly opens, and I spot Jess wheeling in like a mad thing, hot, sweaty, and out of breath. Little Grace is on her lap, and the entire room turns to stare at them.

'Find a space,' the Head encourages, and doesn't make any mention of Grace being here.

I feel obliged to wave them over and tell them there is a space near me, but Jess either doesn't see or avoids acknowledging me, wheeling to the end of the front row. I'm certainly not the one everyone is secretly whispering about. Nadine and the other woman's idle gossip has piqued my interest though. Charlie made no mention of a car accident when he spoke about Jess's last labour, and it convinces me that there are even more secrets that woman is hiding.

Chapter Twenty-Six

Now

Mike Ferry hadn't moved from the spot outside the interview room. Dr Savage had told him that Jess hadn't consented to him observing the assessment. He might not have been able to listen in, but he'd certainly heard the yelling and screaming coming from his key witness. At one point he'd almost knocked on the door to interrupt the assessment out of a duty of care to the psychiatrist, but then the yelling and obscenity had ended.

Dr Savage emerged from the room, her skin a touch paler than when she'd entered some twenty-five minutes earlier. 'She's clearly in a more agitated state than I'd anticipated,' she said, once the door was closed. 'At best guess she's been off her medication for several days, if not a fortnight.'

Mike narrowed his eyes. 'Is she dangerous?'

Dr Savage joined him, leaning against the wall, across from the door, keeping her voice low. 'I honestly can't tell you.

Historically I'm not aware of any violent episodes, but then I've never seen her this frenzied. Jess's condition is—' She paused, as if weighing up how much of her patient's confidentiality she was prepared to share, and settled for 'complicated. Presumably you're aware of the events leading to her disablement?'

Mike had no idea, but shrugged nonchalantly, allowing her to continue sharing, and hoping she would let slip some clue to confirm whether Jess could have deliberately stabbed the victim and allowed him to bleed to death.

'She was pregnant when she was driven off the road, but because of her pregnancy, she wasn't on her antidepressants, and I can't help thinking that none of that messy business would have happened had she been in better mental health.'

Mike made a mental note to see what historic news stories he could find about Jess Donoghue and this car accident Dr Savage was alluding to.

'What's clear,' Dr Savage continued, pushing herself from the wall, and straightening, 'is that she's in no condition to stay here. She is physically and emotionally exhausted. I am going to have to take her into my care and if she isn't willing to go voluntarily, then I will have to section her on medical grounds. I know you're keen to speak with her, but she's in no state to help you this evening. Once she's stabilised, we'll see, but I can't guarantee she'll even be able to give you a full account of whatever happened this evening.'

She moved back towards the door, but stopped when Mike reached for her arm. 'How long? To stabilise her, I mean?'

Dr Savage met his desperate stare. 'I'll call you in the morning with an update. Do you have a card with your number on it?'

Mike reached into his pocket and gave her his business card. 'I'll walk the two of you back to the front desk. This place is a maze of tunnels.'

Dr Savage returned to the room, emerging a few minutes later wheeling out Jess Donoghue, head buried in her hands. The baggy tracksuit bottoms and jumper they'd had to provide made her look less normal somehow. The three of them moved along the corridor in silence, and Mike could almost hear the Chief Super's indictment of his willingness to allow Dr Savage to take away his only suspect. But it was out of his hands; there was no way he could keep Jess in custody following Dr Savage's assessment, but it didn't mean they wouldn't be able to arrest her later once the evidence against her was stacked up. At least they'd know where to find her.

The front desk was closed to the public, but the shutters had yet to be lowered for the evening. Mike thanked the young uniformed officer who had escorted them from the custody suite and was now unlocking the front door for Jess and Dr Savage to leave through.

Mike started as a woman's head poked through the door when the young officer opened it.

'I want to report a crime,' the woman said, with a strong Highland accent, but then she seemed to stop herself as her eyes fell on Jess in the wheelchair.

Jess raised her head at the sound of the woman's voice, and an ear-splitting scream emanated from her mouth. 'It's all your fault. You did this!'

The Scottish woman grew deathly pale, and backed away from the door, as Jess continued to scream.

Mike pushed past the wheelchair and hurried out into the cool night air, spotting the woman in the waxed coat hurrying down the steps and into the darkness. 'Hey, wait,' he called, chasing after her. 'Hey, stop.' The woman didn't break stride, but Mike soon caught up with her. 'Hey, listen, what were you saying at the door? You said something about wanting to report a crime.'

The woman looked back up to the front door, where Jess Donoghue's screaming continued to echo. 'No, I made a mistake,' she said quickly. Too quickly for Mike's liking.

'You know that woman?' Mike asked, blocking her path. 'She seemed to recognise you.'

'Morag!' Jess screamed from behind them, and the woman's eyes widened at the mention of the name.

'I think you'd better come with me,' Mike said, indicating for her to return to the station, remembering what Nazia had told him about the neighbour's description of the people who had been renting the property in Northwood: *it was occupied by an older Scottish couple and a little girl.*

'Mrs Kilbride?' he checked, and her panicked stare was all the confirmation he needed. He offered a thankful nod skywards; it seemed the gods were finally smiling down on him. He was willing to bet this woman's prints would be a match to the unidentified pair on the blade's handle. It was almost worth calling the Chief Super to gloat, but he wasn't a poor winner, and he couldn't shake the feeling that there was still so much more he didn't yet know.

Chapter Twenty-Seven

Before - Jess

I can't tell you how tired I suddenly feel. The adrenalin was pumping as I hurried to the school, but I'm running on fumes now, having not eaten since breakfast. That's my fault, I know, but this lethargy is not how I wanted the day to finish. I still haven't done anything specific with Grace, and despite promising to cook her pancakes tonight, I'm not sure I have the energy.

It's a surprise to find Charlie's car already parked on the driveway, as it's not even three o'clock yet. He must hear us coming, as the front door opens a moment later and he appears, looking so full of life that I hate how much I envy him. He pushes me up the ramp and into our home, before lifting Grace from my lap.

'Grandma!' she squeals, as Charlie carries her to the living room, before gently lowering her to the floor.

'Surprise!' Charlie yells, for both our benefits. 'If Mohamed won't go to the mountain...' He is grinning like a Cheshire cat, and it suddenly clicks into place.

It's such a typical Charlie move. Clearly our argument yesterday morning about me going to visit my mum in Southampton has played on his mind, and he has come up with the best compromise he can think of. I do admire his pragmatism at times, and although I don't appreciate the secrecy of him talking to my mum behind my back, I know his heart is in the right place.

He wheels me into the room, and my mum springs from her seat, comes over and hugs me, the familiar scent of her rose-petal perfume filling my nose. She kisses me on both cheeks, before stepping back and telling me how well I look, and how she's able to stay for as long as I need to help with the transition of Grace starting school.

A lump forms in my throat, and my eyes sting as tears threaten to break free. I hadn't realised how much I needed to see and hear from her. There's something different about her today though. I can't quite put my finger on it, but she looks... full of life. Her hair has been coloured in rich mahogany hues, neatly cut and curled beneath her ears; she's not wearing her usual dowdy pastel shades, instead donning a vibrant blouse with large flowers, and a pair of skinny jeans I'd expect on someone half her age. In a line-up I'd argue she looked younger than Morag, even though I know Mum is several years senior.

Grace holds out her arms and Mum bathes her in kisses and a big hug. Charlie leaves the room, offering to make tea for everyone, and I just soak up the interaction between the two most important females in my life.

An hour later, Charlie has taken Grace upstairs for a bath, leaving Mum and me alone in the lounge. Tea has been replaced by sherry for Mum, and I now have a glass of water, conscious that I'm due my painkillers, but seeing how long I can last without them. All the mishaps of today – forgetting the appointment with Dr Tegan and the school meeting – have left me pondering whether I've made a mistake in stopping my antidepressants. I will make an appointment with Dr Savage to see if there is an alternative to what she's prescribed, but in the meantime I don't want to forget anything else.

Morag had waved to me at the school after my conspicuous arrival, but I had pretended not to notice, keen to avoid any further awkward confrontation. Thankfully she didn't stick around at the end to try and corner me. I spotted Ava's mum Nadine near her as well, and the last thing I needed was to hear her telling me how well I look *considering*, especially when she's clearly spent hours and a bucket of money perfecting her 'look'.

'You should have told me you weren't coping,' Mum says, catching my gaze.

Who said I wasn't coping? I want to fire back, but I let it pass. Presumably Charlie has told her my suspicions about Morag, and that's why she's offered to come and stay for a few days. If I'd known Charlie was going into London to collect her from Waterloo, I would have suggested Grace and I tag along, as I've been meaning to take her up to the Natural History Museum all summer. Of course that would have meant missing the school meeting and the appointment with Dr

Tegan, but quite frankly I don't think either has taught me anything new.

'When Charlie phoned and said you could do with a hand for a few days,' Mum continues, 'I didn't think twice before booking my train ticket.'

That's twice now she's said that Charlie intimated I wasn't coping, and I'm a little hurt if that's what he really thinks. I know I'm dreading Grace starting school on Wednesday, but I think I've done a pretty good job of keeping my emotions off display. I'd rather he weren't telling people I'm losing my mind, least of all my own mother.

'Are you okay, sweetie?' she asks, tilting her head to the side. 'You look troubled.'

I take a deep breath. 'There was something I wanted to ask you about, but I don't want you to take it the wrong way.'

Her brow wrinkles. 'It takes a lot to offend me. Go ahead and ask.'

My palms are clammy, and my pulse quickens as I will the words from my mouth. 'It's about my adoption.'

Her eyes droop slightly at the mention of the word. 'What do you want to know?'

My pounding heart feels like it will explode out of my chest at any second. 'I suppose I want to understand what the process was like. You know, like how did you choose me, or were you chosen for me? What kind of checks were run against you, and that kind of thing?'

She fixes me with a concerned look. 'Why now?'

I can't be certain how much Charlie has told her about my interactions with Morag, so I need to tread carefully.

'I'm just curious about how long it all took, I suppose.'

Her eyes suddenly widen. 'Are you and Charlie thinking about…?'

'No,' I say quickly. Maybe too quickly.

'After everything you've been through, I suppose I shouldn't be so surprised,' she says as a wistful look passes over her face. 'It's none of my business, Jess, but is it not a tad early to be thinking about things like that? There's still a chance the feeling will return to your legs and that you may be able to conceive naturally again. Don't rule anything out until you know more.'

I'm about to correct her and assure her that Charlie and I aren't contemplating adopting a child, when Charlie bursts in through the door, delicately carrying Grace, who is wrapped in a dressing gown, a towel wound tightly around her head to dry her hair. He lowers her to the sofa next to me.

'Who's up for takeaway pizza tonight?' he practically shouts.

'Me!' Grace calls, thrusting her hand into the air.

'That okay with you?' he asks. 'Thought it would be easier, and allow you and your mum more time to talk. I can collect it, maybe get some garlic bread on the side. What do you say?'

I nod, and force a smile. When I turn back to look at Mum, she's busy nattering to Grace, and I know my chance to question her further has gone for now. I reach for the home phone as it bursts into life, the display identifying the caller as from a withheld number.

I answer, ready to disconnect at the first hint that it's a nuisance sales call, but what I'm not expecting is to hear Charlie's sister Rosie's anxious voice. 'I need to see you urgently. It's about that missing girl you mentioned on Sunday.'

I feel terrible for lying to Charlie and Mum, but Rosie made it perfectly clear that she needed to meet me tonight, and I don't want either of them to know that I mentioned the Morag–Daisy situation to the police, even if Rosie is family. I push my chair down the road to the small parade of shops, under the guise of buying salad to go with tonight's pizza. The small grocers probably won't have anything resembling fresh produce, but I'm not worried about returning empty-handed. Charlie always describes lettuce and salad vegetables as rabbit food, and the expression he pulled when I suggested this trip out tells me that he'll probably be relieved if I fail in my mission.

Rosie is sitting on a public bench outside the hair salon, two doors down from the grocers. I roll over, out of breath from the exertion of the journey. I'm surprised to see a cigarette between her lips, which she quickly stubs out, before averting her eyes in shame.

'I know, I know,' she says, fanning away the exhaled smoke, 'but sometimes I just need something to balance my mood. Don't tell Charlie. You know how he feels about smoking after Dad passed of lung cancer.'

I wave away her concern; I'm the last person who wants Charlie to know about this rendezvous. 'What was so urgent? Did you find out something about Daisy? Was I right that she was abducted?'

Rosie's blonde ponytail swishes against the suit jacket she's wearing as she looks around, as if suspecting we are being watched and listened to. The charcoal-coloured business suit flatters her complexion, and covers her muscly arms, lending her a more feminine appearance than I'm used to seeing.

'I can't say too much,' she begins, occasionally glancing around us, 'but I had a look at our caseload for any missing children called Daisy.'

The suspense is killing me. I don't know why we've had to meet in such a clandestine way. 'And?'

'*And* there are no reported missing children from the area called Daisy. You said she was five, right?'

'Nearly,' I confirm, remembering Morag had said it was Daisy's birthday this Friday.

'Well, I went back over cases from the last five years, and nothing came up. I'm sorry.'

I don't understand why I feel so disappointed. I suppose if Rosie had managed to uncover Daisy's true identity, Morag and Angus would be arrested and Daisy returned to her frantic parents. I'm also even more confused about why Rosie felt she couldn't deliver this message over the phone.

'Who is this girl?' Rosie continues, leaning closer towards me. 'You were vague on Sunday, and I sense there is more you're not telling me.'

The tar on her breath is off-putting, but I focus on breathing through my mouth so I won't have to smell it. This is a crucial moment; I feel it in my bones. If I come clean and tell Rosie everything – albeit very little – that I know, it could lead to her digging further into Morag and Angus's backstory. However, it could also lead to her reaching the same conclusion as Charlie; that I am delusional.

She's not my mum.

The memory of that first encounter is enough to encourage my choice. 'Daisy is a girl Grace and I met at the park on

Thursday afternoon. She walked right up to me, looking absolutely petrified – like she'd just seen a ghost – and told me that the woman she was with wasn't her mother. The woman – Morag – is in her mid to late fifties, and I spoke to her afterwards, but she was very evasive about her past. She said she's a nurse, and her husband Angus is in logistics or something. He's the same age as her, and something has just felt off about them ever since we met. You know when you just get a vibe, and you can't put your finger on exactly why you don't trust someone? It's like that.'

'Did you confront her about what Daisy said?'

'How could I? You don't just come out with something like that when meeting someone new. Charlie suggested they could have adopted Daisy, but it just doesn't fit in my mind.'

'You said this Morag and Angus are in their mid to late fifties?'

'Yes, exactly!' I practically yelp. 'They wouldn't allow such a mature couple to adopt, would they? I mean, they'll be in their sixties when she hits puberty.'

'I don't think there's an official upper age limit for adoption,' Rosie corrects. 'If you have a look on the government website, all it states is you must be aged over twenty-one.'

I hadn't expected this, and make a mental note to double-check the site when I get home. 'Oh, I see.'

'Go back a bit,' Rosie says, 'what else can you tell me about them?'

'Both have broad Scottish accents, and she said they'd met and lived in Aberdeen for most of their lives, but had spent some time in Wolverhampton for Angus's job.'

A frown catches Rosie's hairline.

'What is it?' I ask.

'Well, the cases I reviewed are local to the borough. If Daisy wasn't taken from this area, she wouldn't appear in my search. Do you know how long they've been in London?'

I can't recall whether Morag actually said when they'd moved south. 'Fairly recently, I think,' I tell Rosie, confirming the address so she can check records to verify the exact date. 'Oh, and Daisy doesn't sound anything like Morag or Angus. I've barely heard her speak apart from what she told me in the playground, but her accent isn't Scottish.'

Doubt grips Rosie's features, and I'm almost certain she thinks I've lost the plot.

'This isn't like the last time,' I urge. 'I know that in the past... but I'm telling the truth. I am almost certain that Morag is *not* Daisy's mother, and that they're holding her against her will.'

'I don't think you're making any of this up,' she says, looking away, 'but even you must see how far-fetched all this sounds.'

'I searched for them – Morag and Angus, I mean – online,' I continue, 'but I couldn't find their names on any kind of social media. You have to admit that's a bit weird, no?'

Rosie shrugs. 'Not necessarily, given their age. What's the surname?'

'Charlie saw an envelope addressed to Mr and Mrs A Kilbride. That's what I searched for and drew a blank.'

Rosie looks so serene, but remains quiet, and I can almost hear her mind whirring as she searches for the words to let me down gently. It's funny, but Charlie pulls the same face when he knows he's going to disappoint me, like when he has to cancel plans because of one of Doug's last-minute meetings.

'I'm sorry, Jess, but there isn't enough here for me to start investigating this family. If there was something more, something I could show my DCI that warrants further digging, but four little words in a park just isn't enough. Do you realise how many children are reported missing every day in the UK? Those not found usually wind up on the missingpeople.org website, but few of those stories end well.'

She must realise how crestfallen I am at the news, as she puts an arm around my shoulders and squeezes the top of my arm. 'I do wonder whether all this – your feelings about this little girl – is serving as a distraction from an underlying problem. Charlie said on Sunday you've stopped seeing your psychiatrist.'

Is there anyone Charlie isn't discussing me with behind my back? I grind my teeth to maintain my composure. 'I didn't see the point any more. No amount of talking is going to bring'—it takes all my strength to say his name—'Luke back.' My eyes ache with tears, but I refuse to wipe them away. 'That isn't what this is about. If you'd seen how scared Daisy looked, you'd want to find out the truth. I know I don't have any solid evidence, but I am certain there is more to that family than Morag is telling me.'

Rosie passes me a tissue from a packet that appears from her pocket. 'It's okay for you to be upset about losing Luke. I still think about him every day, and I only met him that one time and for a few minutes. You didn't deserve what happened to you – none of you did. I can't begin to imagine what you went through. To carry a baby full-term and then have his life ripped from you, and then to top it all off, the epidural procedure going wrong and stealing your mobility. God knows, I'd be livid with the world if I went through that kind of pain. Nobody blames you for what happened, Jess, and I know how worried Charlie is about you.'

I finally dab the corners of my eyes. 'Thank you for looking,' I whisper.

The relief is clear on her face as we move away from the bench, and although she offers me a lift home, I tell her that I'm fine to make my own way, as it will keep Charlie from suspecting the ulterior motive for my trip out. I watch as she gets into her car and drives away. Her intention this evening was to discourage my attempts to find out the truth about Daisy, but all she's done is made me more determined. I won't let anything hold me back now.

Chapter Twenty-Eight

Before - Morag

I'm alone with only my own thoughts, as Angus has taken Daisy to the cinema. He left a note saying he would treat her to a burger and fries on the way home, and that I should send him a message if I want something too. I can't think of anything worse, and I can't handle rattling around what still feels like someone else's home. I've never been one to pay any attention to local gossip, but something Nadine said at the school meeting has been playing on my mind. She said that Jess had been in some scandal involving the local council, and I can't deny my appetite has been whetted.

With no computer at our house – Angus says they can be traced as easily as phone lines these days – I head out into town, conscious that it won't be long before the local library closes. Northwood town centre is made up of a number of banks, estate agents, and hair salons. In amongst all these are a handful of cafés, restaurants, and bars, and the occasional nonfranchised shop. The library is tucked behind the shops, in what resembles an old church. The familiar musty smell of old pages greets me upon arrival, and I'm pleased to find a woman of similar age behind the main desk.

'I want to check your newspaper microfiche records, if possible?' I say to her.

Her glasses hang around her neck by a string of pink and purple beads, not in keeping with the bright yellow cardigan she's wearing despite the heat. 'Certainly. What time period are you after?'

That's a good question. I can't be all that certain when Jess had the car accident, nor when she made her accusations against the local council. 'Last three years?' I suggest, given Grace is four, and they would have waited a year or so before trying for a second baby.

'Ah,' the woman says, frowning. 'We only use microfiche for historic records. Any newspapers from the last fifteen years are now online.' She nods at a bank of desks off to my left by the main wall.

'I don't suppose you could help me find them?' I ask, as the heat rises in my cheeks.

The truth is, I'm not all that comfortable with computers and the internet. I know that must make me sound naïve in the modern age, but my generation missed out on Information Technology at school, and has been playing catch-up ever since. My only real interaction with computers was a bit of data entry here and there at the hospital.

She considers me for a moment, before turning to the younger man behind her. 'José, can you keep an eye on the desk while I help this customer?'

The younger man, whose tight afro and pierced nose don't

look Hispanic, readily agrees, and takes the woman's place at the desk. I follow her to the bank of computers, and once we're both seated, she opens an internet page.

'Is there a particular journal you wish to review?' she asks.

I've never felt so out of my depth. What I really want to say is that I want any and all background information on Jess Donoghue, but something tells me this woman won't have any clue who that is. Maybe I should have just asked Nadine and that other mother at the meeting.

'I'm interested in a story from the last couple of years,' I begin. 'It was something to do with a local woman making accusations against the council, accusing them of misappropriating funds.'

The woman is staring blankly back at me. Perhaps the story wasn't as well known as Nadine suggested.

'Do you know the accuser's name? Or which newspaper reported it?'

I shrug pathetically. 'Sorry.'

'I really don't know how I can help,' she says eventually, glancing over at the queue of people now gathering at the front desk, where José clearly isn't coping. 'All I can suggest is you search for key terms on some of the newspaper sites, and see what comes up.' She opens three new windows, one for each of the periodicals that focus on the town and its immediate neighbours. 'Try these to begin with, and I'll come back and check on you in a bit.'

She doesn't wait for me to respond before leaving her chair and returning to the front desk.

My first instinct is to type in Jess's name in the first search box, and although a dozen links to pages appear, none of them relate to the story I'm interested in. I thought this would be a lot easier. Angus's private investigator Lawrence didn't suggest finding information about potential targets was so difficult.

After half an hour of reading and dismissing articles, I give up, and thank the woman for her help. If I want to know what really happened to Jess, and why Nadine clearly doesn't hold her in much regard, I'm going to need to confront Jess directly, or request Lawrence take me on as a private client, so that Angus won't find out.

Leaving the library, I'm surprised to see how much the sky has clouded over. A blanket of grey has me fearing a downpour as I hurry along the road in the direction of home. As I stop at the pedestrian crossing my heart skips a beat when I see a red BMW with darkened windows pull up at the lights. It's only when I read and re-read the licence plate that I realise it isn't *his*. I remain on the kerbside just in case, and as the car pulls away, my eyes watch it until it's out of sight.

Here I am, so focused on trying to find out what Jess is hiding, when my own past isn't so neatly buried. What if my casual trip to the library had resulted in him finding us? I would never forgive myself. Picking up the pace, I now can't wait to be back indoors where I can shut out the painful world.

Chapter Twenty-Nine

Now

The woman across the table from him hadn't spoken a word since he'd invited her in, and explained that whilst she wasn't under arrest, he was going to caution her prior to recording the interview. She'd shaken her head when asked if she required legal representation, and Mike had been pleased when PC Wozniak had agreed to come in as a second pair of ears.

Morag Kilbride, aged fifty-five, or so she'd claimed. Mike would have put her closer to sixty, but since she carried no kind of formal identification on her person, he would have to take her word for it. For now, anyway.

'Mrs Kilbride,' Mike began, when the formal introductions had been completed, 'can you confirm you are the same Morag Kilbride currently residing at number sixteen, Bakers Drive in Northwood?'

She looked up at him, as if trying to work out whether

admitting to an address could somehow incriminate her. Mike had only asked the question in an effort to make her feel more at ease.

'N – n – no comment,' she eventually stammered in a hoarse voice.

Mike might have expected such reluctance from the usual hardened characters he came face to face with in formal interviews, but not from someone with nothing to hide. Reaching for the tall plastic jug of water, he filled a beaker and slid it across the table to her, before filling a second and taking a long drink himself.

She eyed the water suspiciously, before her trembling hands coiled around it, and she raised it to her lips.

'I'd like to remind you, Mrs Kilbride, that you are not under arrest, and that you came here to the station this evening of your own volition. Now, I believe you are the resident at the aforementioned house in Northwood where a vicious assault has ended in the loss of life of an as yet unidentified male subject. All I want to establish is how much you know about that incident, whether you bore witness to what happened, and whether you can confirm the identity of the victim.' He paused, watching her for any kind of telling reaction. 'When you arrived at the station earlier, there was an altercation between you and another woman. Can you tell me what that was about?'

Whilst there was little she was doing to keep the fear from her expression, he had yet to determine if that fear was due to the formality of this interview, or to Jess Donoghue's earlier outburst.

'Okay,' Mike sighed, his patience already wearing thin,

'how about one I think we all know the answer to. Can you tell me who that woman was?'

She looked straight at him, her eyes filling, wanting to be unburdened, but untrusting.

'How do you know Jess Donoghue?' he asked bluntly, and this time the widening of her eyes confirmed recognition.

'Sh – sh – she... Her daughter Grace goes to the same school as my wee one Daisy,' she said, pulling a tissue from her sleeve and dabbing her eyes.

'But you know her, right?' Mike pushed. 'She certainly seemed to know you, using your name when you came into contact earlier.'

Morag nodded. 'Aye, I know her... Well, not all that well... We only met last week.'

'Tell me about her.'

She frowned at the question. 'I really don't know her all that well.'

'Tell me about how the two of you met.'

Something passed between her eyes, a memory maybe, but gone in a blink. She made no effort to answer the question.

Mike referred back to the list of questions he'd managed to scrawl in the five minutes between her being shown into the room and him joining her with PC Wozniak. 'When you arrived at the station this evening, you said something about wanting to report a crime. What crime did you want to report?'

'I d – d – don't know what you're talking about.'

'Mrs Kilbride, I know what I heard, and I'm pretty sure Dr Savage witnessed what you said also, so please don't take me for a fool. What made you come to the station so late on a Wednesday evening?'

'I – I – I thought someone was following me. I came to the station in the hope that they would turn back, and they did.'

This wasn't what Mike had expected to hear, and the statement threw him momentarily. 'You thought somebody was following you?'

'Aye, in a red car, but when you opened the door, and I turned back, the red car was gone. Probably just my eyes playing tricks on me.'

Mike had always prided himself on his ability to spot when someone was lying to him, but he couldn't say conclusively that Morag wasn't telling the truth.

'Describe the car to me. Make, model, what the driver looked like.'

'As I said it was red, a BMW I think, but I'm not very familiar with models of cars. I couldn't see the driver's face as it was so dark.'

Mike didn't like that the interview was diverging, and sought to correct the course. 'What have you been up to this evening? Where were you prior to coming to the station?'

'Out.'

'Out where?'

'My husband and I took our daughter for dinner, on account of it being her first day at school.'

'That's nice.' Mike smiled, hoping a softer approach might lull her into thinking he was falling for the story. 'Where did you go to for dinner?'

'A wee restaurant about an hour's drive away.'

'Which restaurant? Maybe I know it.'

'I can't remember its name, to be honest.'

Mike dug the nails into his hand to keep from giving away

that he knew he had her on the ropes. 'Fair enough, whereabouts was the pub? What town or village?'

'In Chalfont St Peter.'

'I know the town well,' Mike bluffed. 'My mum's from there. Was it The Crown or The Old Speckled Hen?' He had no idea if there were any pubs in Chalfont St Peter, let alone what they were called, but he sensed she didn't either.

'I really can't remember. We'd never been there before tonight, and to be honest I'm not even sure I'd be able to find it again.' She reached for the beaker and began to raise it towards her mouth, the quivering in her arm slowing.

'That's a shame,' Mike said, making a show of shrugging towards Wozniak. 'Tell me, Mrs Kilbride, when were you last at your house?'

The beaker stopped its trajectory and nearly slipped from her grasp. 'I haven't been home most of the day. I collected Daisy from school and then we went straight out for dinner.'

Mike looked at his watch. 'How old is your daughter?'

'Five – no, wait, four – she isn't five until Friday.'

'So presumably you collected her from school around three o'clock?'

She nodded. 'Half past actually.'

'Which school does she go to?'

'Hillside Infants.'

'I know the place. Up near that road with the width restriction on it. Yes, yes, I know the school. That's quite a trek from your home. Did you walk or drive to collect her?'

'Walk. My husband Angus was using our car.'

'And did he collect you from the school then?'

'Aye, and then we went on to the restaurant.'

Mike pulled up his shirt sleeve and looked at his watch,

before comparing the time to that on the recording apparatus. 'That's some meal out. I make it bang on midnight, which means you've been away from your home – or so you claim – for the best part of nine hours. Where's your daughter now?'

'With a neighbour.'

'And where is your husband?'

For the first time she looked down at her hands, but didn't answer.

Mike didn't miss a beat. 'Do you know what happened at your house this evening, Mrs Kilbride?'

Her head remained bowed.

'Are you aware that a man was stabbed to death, and bled out all over the kitchen floor?'

Fresh tears filled her eyes, as she looked up at him, her bottom lip trembling.

Mike reached for the tablet he'd brought into the room, unlocked the screen, and flipped to the photograph Dr Karen Murphy had sent over following the post-mortem. Mike slid the tablet across the table so she could see it. 'Who is this man in the photograph?'

She stared at the image for a long time, her expression frozen in horror, before the tears burst free of their dam, and she pushed the tablet away. 'I'm not saying another word until I speak to a solicitor.'

Chapter Thirty

Before - Jess

The journey home has left me physically drained. I feel awful watching my mum flutter about setting the table with plates and cutlery, while Charlie has gone out to collect the pizza. Grace is happily stretched out on the sofa, her face buried in yet another book. I envy her ability to switch off the rest of the world and get lost inside the words and magical lands she reads about.

I keep thinking about that website Rosie mentioned. Although it will be like looking for a needle in a haystack, I desperately want to search it for any sign of Daisy's face. My phone is charging in the kitchen, and with Charlie set to return at any moment, I daren't start using the laptop just yet. Maybe later. Or more likely in the early hours of the morning when insomnia comes to check on me.

I start as Charlie's phone buzzes to life on the coffee table next to me. He must have left it on vibrate. Leaning over, I see

Doug's name on the screen and that it is the third missed call from him. Grace hasn't even seemed to notice that there is any noise shattering the silence. I'm tempted to answer and explain that Charlie will be back soon, but then think better of it. Answering the call feels like an invasion of his privacy, although I have met and spoken with Doug before.

Silence returns to the room and the missed call counter increases. It's so odd that Charlie has gone out without taking the phone with him. In the past there have been calls as late as midnight. I used to joke when I'd hear Charlie's phone go that Doug had just had another brain fart he needed to share. Charlie has never mentioned it, but I am curious to know whether Doug disturbs the rest of the team as much as he does my husband.

I'm about to wheel to the kitchen to check if Mum has managed to find everything for the table when the vibration starts again. Whatever he wants, clearly Doug is keen to get hold of Charlie. I reach for the phone and accept the call, keen to protect Charlie from getting into trouble. I'll just tell Doug that we're about to eat and that Charlie will call him back after, but as I place the phone to my ear, I'm surprised to hear a woman's voice instead of Doug's gruff bark.

'Hey, it's me. Can you talk?'

I open my mouth to speak, and explain it's not Charlie, but something holds me back, and the words don't emerge. I check the display again, but it is definitely the name 'Doug' on the screen.

'Charlie? Are you there? Can you hear me?'

I'm going to have to answer, and I clamp my eyes shut to silence the dozens of questions trying to burst through: who is this woman? Why is she calling on Doug's number? Why was her first question whether Charlie could talk?

'Hi, sorry,' I say,' keeping my eyes closed, 'this is Charlie's wife. He's just had to nip out and forgot to take his phone. If you tell me your name, I'll ask him to phone you back.'

There is a pause on the line, and what I'm certain is a sharp intake of breath. 'Um, hi... Uh, sorry that's... I wasn't expecting you to answer.' Another breath. 'Can you ask Charlie to call me back?'

There's a tingle as the hairs on the back of my neck brush against the loose material of my T-shirt. 'Of course,' I say, desperately trying to keep the anxiety from my voice, as my heart thuds in my chest. 'And who should I say called?'

Another pause. 'Um... Kerry.'

The questions keep coming, and I don't want to listen to any of them.

'What number should he call you on?'

'This one's fine. I'll be here until eight, but I need to speak to him urgently about our meeting tomorrow.'

An echo of Charlie's voice from Sunday morning: *I'm away at the client's offices in Oxford on Tuesday.*

'I'll let him know you called,' I say, before the line goes dead, and I finally exhale.

You're being paranoid, I tell myself. Just because Charlie has never mentioned this Kerry before, it doesn't mean there is any reason for me to be suspicious.

So why won't the voice in my head desist?

Why has he never mentioned anyone called Kerry before? Why didn't he mention that she would be with him in Oxford? Why did her call come through under Doug's name? How many times have calls and messages from 'Doug' actually been from Kerry? Is this why he's always late home?

I need to stop. I've taken a simple phone call and developed it into a full-blown affair between my loving husband and some random woman.

'Everything okay?' Mum asks from the doorway, the wrinkles around her eyes more noticeable than usual. 'You're as pale as a sheet. Do you feel sick?'

'I'm fine,' I lie, failing to meet her stare, and fighting against the threat of fresh tears.

'Are you in pain? Are you due your painkillers soon? It's gone six o'clock.'

I slowly nod, keeping my eyes fixed on a patch on the carpet. 'I'll come and take them in a bit. Is the table set?'

'Yes, I think I've put everything out. Do you want wine with dinner, or are you happy with water?'

I blink away the building tears, and force a smile. I don't know how many times I've told her that I'm not supposed to consume alcohol with the cocktail of pills I'm required to take. 'Water is fine, thank you.'

'One little glass won't kill you,' she says, frowning.

If only she knew.

'I'd prefer water,' I repeat, looking away so she won't see how tough it is.

I hear keys jangle as the front door opens, and the delicious smell of fresh dough and melting cheese wafts into the house.

'I'm back,' Charlie calls out, and a moment later he passes the lounge door on his way to the kitchen, steam rising from the lid of the large, square cardboard box in his hands.

It's enough to catch Grace's attention, and she's off the sofa and chasing after him into the kitchen like a greyhound pursuing a rabbit.

I don't move, looking down and seeing Charlie's phone still in my hands. I quickly put it back on the coffee table, as I don't want him to think I've been checking up on him. We've always had an open policy on phones, and although he has never given me reason not to trust him, I desperately want to look at the messages he may have exchanged with Kerry.

'Everything all right, babe?' I hear him ask, and as I look up, I see him walking into the lounge and immediately reaching for his phone.

'It's been ringing,' I say. 'I eventually answered it and spoke to someone called Kerry, and said you were out but would phone her back.'

I'm waiting for any tell-tale sign that I've caught him out, but he quickly checks the display before pocketing the phone and smiling affectionately at me.

'Great, thanks,' he says. 'I'm sure whatever it is can wait until after dinner. You want me to push you through?'

Not a single tremor in his voice. That's a good sign, right? I know my husband, and he's never been very good at keeping secrets. I'm sure I would notice if my speaking to Kerry had put him in an awkward position. Wouldn't I?

'Kerry said the call was about your meeting tomorrow. You're meeting your new client in Oxford, right?'

He moves behind the chair and grips the handles. 'That's right.'

I want to ask him outright who Kerry is and whether I'm right to be feeling so on edge, but I remind myself about what Dr Tegan warned about the side-effects of my medication: *any additional anxiety, or agitation? Any paranoia?*

'Is she new? I don't remember you mentioning her name before.'

'Haven't I? She's been working in the team for three to four months, I suppose. Doug hired her to be his PA, but she seems to have become more of the office gofer, with all of us relying on her for one thing or another.'

We've arrived in the kitchen, and before I can ask anything else, he has parked me between Mum and Grace, and moved to the opposite side of the table, where he reaches for a slice of the pizza and places it on my plate. Nobody was disappointed when I returned home without salad.

Charlie is now busily chatting to Grace, and asking how her day was. Is he deliberately avoiding talking to me to cover his tracks, or am I just being suspicious? I desperately hope it's the latter, but if I'm wrong about him, does that mean I'm also wrong about Daisy and Morag? And that's when I think about what Tracy told me about her husband at lunch on Sunday: *caught him shagging some client he was working for up in Barnstaple. Apparently they'd been at it for months behind my back.*

Looking at Charlie now, I don't want to believe he is capable of such deceit, but I can't bury my head in the sand and assume he wouldn't stray. I don't think my heart could stand another hammer blow like that.

Chapter Thirty-One

Before - Morag

Clutching the handset to my ear, I count the seconds until it is answered. Gwen is out of breath as her voice comes on the line, and now I feel guilty at the thought that she has had to race to answer. She would have been expecting my early-morning call on Sunday, as I always call her on her birthday, but she won't have expected me to call back again so soon.

'How are you feeling?' I ask, knowing it is a pathetic opening question to someone as ill as she.

'Oh, I'm hanging in there. To what do I owe this pleasure? It's been hardly two days since we last spoke.'

'I guess I'm just getting sentimental in my old age.'

She chuckles at this, but there is pain there too. I sense it as only an older sister can. I still remember the day Dad brought her home, all swaddled and crying. I was nearly five and only

215

too aware that I would now have to share our parents' affection with her, but so excited at the same time. I remember Dad putting the Moses basket down on the floor so I could look in and see her. I remember taking her tiny hand in mine, and how she stopped crying in an instant, like she somehow sensed I would always be there to look out for her. Sure, we had spats as we grew up, but nothing too bitchy, and nothing that I can even recall now.

The truth is I shouldn't have snuck out again to call her, but I hate the fact that I am so far away when she clearly needs help, love, and support. I have wondered what would happen if I just got on a train and went to visit her. There's a slim chance *he* doesn't have an eye on her place, and so I could stay with her for a few months until... until the time comes for her to move on to the next life.

I'm almost at the point where I don't care if *he* catches up with me. There's nothing he can do to me that I don't deserve. Daisy is different though. She needs to be kept safe, and although I know she would survive fine without me, I know Angus wouldn't cope on his own for too long. So, I have no choice but to steal these few moments alone with Gwen, and hope they somehow help to make up for me not being there in the flesh. I'm pretty certain they don't.

'Is there a reason for your call?' Gwen asks, with a hushed sigh.

Something doesn't feel right; she's talking quietly like she doesn't want Rufus to overhear our conversation; but why?

'I just wanted to hear your voice,' I tell her, leaning back against the glass frame of the phone box. 'Did you have a good birthday? Did you go for the fish and chip supper like you planned?'

'Ah, no,' she sighs again, 'we never made it to The Black Ox in the end. I overdid it on my walk around the loch, and felt so tired that we decided to stay in for the evening. Rufus rustled me up some beans on toast, and we shared a stout before I fell asleep in front of the fireplace.'

Rufus isn't blessed with any culinary skills, and I'd be willing to put money on him having burnt the toast too. That should be me there with her, making sure she's properly fed and watered.

'You need to keep your strength up,' I gently warn her. 'You won't survive on beans and toast.'

I don't mean that to sound as cold as it does, but I also know Gwen isn't one to make a fuss, and even if she is uncomfortable or in need of greater sustenance, she will simply keep those feelings to herself, and continue as if everything is fine.

'You sounded just like Mum, then,' she says, and I'm relieved she hasn't taken offence. 'I was thinking I should probably go up and lay some flowers on her grave.'

She doesn't need to say that I've left her in the lurch tending to our parents' plots at the local cemetery. In all the time we've been running, I haven't been back there, and it pains me to consider that had we not started on this course Gwen wouldn't be in the state she now is. We'll never know for certain.

'I'm so sorry, Gwen,' I find myself gushing before I can stop. 'I should be there for you, and I'm so sorry I'm not. I promise you, I will do whatever it takes to get back up and see you.'

There's a sudden commotion on the line, and for a moment I fear that Gwen has fallen, dropping the phone in the process, but then I hear heavy breathing, and a voice that chills me to my core.

'I'm looking forward to seeing you too, Morag. Don't forget to bring my daughter with you.'

Chapter Thirty-Two

Now

The hallway light flashing to life beyond the frosted glass told Mike she'd heard his knock. DC Polly Viceroy unlatched the door and opened it a crack, tired eyes staring back out at him.

'Can I come in?' he asked, knowing she was well within her rights to tell him to get lost.

She seemed to consider the request for a moment longer than she needed to, before widening the gap. It was only as he entered that he saw the cuffs of her pyjamas – the set he'd bought her – poking through the sleeve of the thin dressing gown.

'I didn't mean to wake you,' he offered apologetically, though not sure why he'd driven so far out of his way to be here.

'What's happened?' she asked, ignoring the apology and

moving forward to the kitchen, flicking on the light as she passed and immediately filling the kettle.

'What makes you think anything's happened?'

She raised an eyebrow in his direction; her cue that she knew he was lying.

'Okay, okay, we had to release Jess Donoghue.'

Polly's mouth began to open in shock, but he continued quickly before she could interrupt.

'She's been taken into a secure facility by her psychiatrist, Dr Savage. At least we know where she is should an arrest be required later down the line.'

'So you now think she did it?' Polly asked, covering her mouth as a long yawn escaped.

'The evidence would seem to suggest as much, don't you think? We have her arriving at the house over an hour before the emergency services were called; we have her prints on the knife, and we know she handled it both before and after the stabbing; and the forensics also suggest she was in close proximity when the bleeding started. The psychiatrist confirmed Jess has been off her antidepressants too.'

Polly yawned again. 'Case closed then. That ought to keep the Chief Super off your back, and finally put to bed some of the rum—'

Polly caught herself before finishing the sentence, but he'd already picked up on what she was insinuating.

'You know I was nothing to do with all that anti-corruption inquiry. *I* was the one who blew the whistle, for pity's sake!'

Polly closed the gap between them, placed a hand on each arm and stretched to peck his cheek. 'I know, I'm sorry. And keep your voice down. I don't want you waking Sammy.'

There it was, the real reason Mike had traipsed across

town in the middle of the night instead of going home. 'Do you think I could pop my head into his room, and just see him?'

Polly was quiet as the kettle reached its crescendo. 'I don't think that's a good idea, do you? Don't want to give him mixed messages.'

'I'll be quiet, I promise. Just a quick look, and then I'll come back through.'

Polly shook her head. 'I'm sorry, Mike. Not tonight, yeah? I promise you can see him at the weekend. Maybe the three of us could go to the park or something? If he finds out you're here now, I'll never get him settled back down.'

Mike ignored the stabbing pain in his chest and nodded his understanding. After the way things had ended between them, he didn't have any right to argue about visitation rights. They weren't married, so no divorce proceedings to determine custody. He'd made such a mess of everything in the last two years, and in that second would have given anything to undo it all.

'Morag Kilbride came to the station voluntarily,' Mike continued, keen to change the subject.

'The woman renting the property? What did she have to say for herself?'

'Claimed she hadn't been home all afternoon, but when I showed her an image of the victim, there was definitely a change in her demeanour. I have a feeling she knows exactly who he is, and I'd put money on the second set of prints belonging to her. Should know for sure by the morning.'

Polly dropped a squashed teabag into the bin. 'She gave you a sample of her prints willingly?'

Mike wrinkled his nose. 'Not exactly. I bagged up the

plastic cup she'd been drinking from and asked them to process it as a priority.'

Polly scowled at him. 'You'd better be joking! You know that won't stand up in court. That breaks a dozen regulations at least! What were you thinking?'

Mike shrugged; he'd been expecting this reaction from Polly, his ever-present conscience. 'I'm not planning to use them as evidence, but I figured it is the quickest way to potentially rule her out of the inquiry.'

'And if they do turn out to be hers, then what?'

'Then we'll know I'm on the right track, and once her arrest is processed, I'll have her prints on file formally, and we can start to find answers to what really happened there tonight.'

Polly handed him the mug of tea. 'Actually, I think it's last night now. It's gone one.'

Mike pushed a stray hair behind her ear, and held his hand against her cool skin for a moment longer. 'I could stay if you wanted?'

Polly pressed her hand against his, before peeling it away. 'I thought you said you wanted to keep things professional?'

Conscience striking the keynote again, Mike nodded, only then realising that she hadn't made herself a drink.

Tightening the cord around her robe to assert that that door was firmly closed for tonight, Polly leaned back against the counter, eyeing the doorway. 'Has the victim been identified yet?'

Mike took a sip of the tea. 'Nothing yet, but I'm certain both Jess and Morag know who he is. There was a confrontation between the two of them when Morag arrived, and Jess was shouting something incoherent at her. It's only a matter of time until we find out who he was. I'm pretty sure he's too young to be Morag's husband, but we've still not managed to make contact with Charlie Donoghue. When officers called around at her house earlier her mum was there watching their daughter, but said she hadn't seen Charlie since earlier that afternoon when they'd tried to intercept Jess and confront her about not taking her meds. He went after her apparently and hasn't been seen since.'

'Did you bring the mother in for a formal identification?'

Mike sipped the tea again, before shaking his head. 'Plenty of time for all that tomorrow. I don't want to drag her to the mortuary if it's not necessary. Dental records are likely to be checked first thing, and then we'll see.'

'So is Morag Kilbride still in custody?'

Mike shook his head. 'She clammed up when I started to question her alleged alibi, and started demanding to speak to a solicitor. I told her she'd be lucky to find one so late at night, and she is going to return tomorrow afternoon to conclude her statement. I'm hoping by that point I'll have a better idea of whether she *is* involved.'

'So where is she now?'

'She asked if she could go home, and I had to tell her the property would be out of bounds until the SOCOs have finished their work. She received a message from her husband – or so she claimed – saying he'd booked them into a Travelodge near Heathrow for the night. I arranged for PC Wozniak to drive her over and ensure she went in.'

Polly yawned again, and this time stretched her arms above her head. 'You can show yourself out when you've finished that. I'm going to the bathroom and then back to bed. What time is the morning briefing?'

'I want everyone in by eight. Thanks for listening, Pol. I really am sorry for everything.'

She pecked his cheek again, and headed up, the staircase creaking as she went. Placing his mug on the counter, Mike crept out of the kitchen, along the hallway, and through the living room, to the door to the second bedroom. He'd promised he wouldn't look, but he couldn't resist. Ever so quietly lowering the handle, he cracked the door open, and peered in.

There he was, curled up in bed, but just as Mike was about to close the door, two eyes opened and stared back at him. A moment later the wagging tail was alert and the German Shepherd padded over to investigate whether his senses were correct. Opening the door wider, Mike dropped to his hands and knees, running his hands through Sammy's long fur.

'I missed you, my boy,' he whispered, allowing Sammy's long, warm tongue to brush against his ears. 'I promise I'll make things right with your mum one day,' though he couldn't be sure Polly would ever be so forgiving.

Chapter Thirty-Three

Before – Jess

The space in bed beside me is empty as I open my eyes in the dimly lit room. I must have been awake for at least three hours last night, until the battery died on the laptop and I could no longer bring myself to scrutinise the innocent faces of children I found on the missing people website. More than a hundred pairs of smiling eyes torn from the arms of parents desperate to know what happened and where they went.

I suppose it's only natural for me to think about how I would react if Grace was ever to just disappear into thin air. I'd be beside myself with worry. I know I'd do *anything* to get her back. My daughter is too trusting, and whilst open-mindedness is a virtue to be valued, in this modern world it puts her at huge risk. She must have inherited it from Charlie, because I don't think I've ever been that naïve. I know first-hand how cruel the world can be.

Mum wanders in, carrying a steaming mug, and perches on

the end of the bed. 'Morning, darling,' she says. 'I made tea.' She must spot the vacant space beside me. 'Charlie already left for Oxford?'

I nod. 'He said his meeting is at nine and he wanted to get on the road early to avoid the traffic.'

'I was thinking,' Mum continues, slurping the tea, 'we should go to the shops today. Are you up for it? I'd like to buy something for Grace as a treat before she starts school.'

I swallow hard. I can't believe the day is almost here. I'd had such plans for the summer months; things Grace and I would do together – just the two of us – so she wouldn't forget our time after she'd started at school. I don't really know where those months have gone. In fact, I don't really know where the past week has gone. Grace deserves a mum who is active and imaginative and can offer her more emotional support than I can. All I serve as is a warning not to count your chickens before they're hatched.

'Does she need anything else for school? Shoes? PE kit?'

My eyes widen in panic. I'd meant to order the required shirt, shorts, and socks online on Thursday, but never got round to it. The school sent a list to all parents of what would be required for day one, including PE kit, distinguishable water bottle, and wellies for wet days.

I push the duvet back, and shuffle until I'm sitting upright. 'I can't believe I forgot to order the blasted PE kit.'

My mum is the epitome of calm. 'Then it's settled. We'll head into the town and scour every shop until we find what we're looking for.'

I shake my head. 'I don't think anywhere in Northwood will have what we're looking for. We might have to catch the bus to Harrow.'

She stands, handing me the mug. 'Perfect! You drink that and I'll go and let my granddaughter know.'

Two hours later, and I can't remember having this much fun with Mum in ages. I can't get over this renewed energy she seems to have found, despite her advancing years. After Dad passed last year, I worried that she would soon follow. Those first few days she didn't even get dressed or leave the house. I had to organise the funeral – not that I wasn't happy to pitch in. Back then I had full use of my body and was able to juggle work and childcare with making sure Mum was eating, and that all the necessary arrangements were in place. I suppose it just shows what a difference eighteen months can make. There was me thinking she was giving up, and now she's turned over a fresh page into a new chapter of her life. I can only hope that the next twelve months bring me fresh hope.

Mum has been telling Grace stories about when I started school, and whilst I don't remember all of them, they do stir fond memories, and I can't help but chuckle when I hear Grace's high-pitched, infectious giggle. It is a relief that we have managed to cobble together a PE kit from three different shops. I'm not sure I would have had the will to do this alone, and I don't mind handing the wheel to Mum to steer us to victory.

'I'm parched,' she suddenly says, as we reach the café in Debenhams. 'What's required now is tea and cake. My treat.'

Grace punches the air in delight, and is already heading in through the entrance in search of the cake cabinet to choose her treat. I reach for Mum's hand. 'Thank you for doing this, and for coming down to see us. It means a lot.' I can't keep the emotion from my voice.

She pats my hand. 'What are mums for? Go and find us a table and I'll get the refreshments. You want tea or coffee?'

'Tea, please,' I say, heading to the table area. A woman and her son are just leaving a small, round table as I approach, and I make a beeline for it. A staff member comes over a moment later to clear their tray of leftovers and to wipe the table. I shouldn't be surprised that the café is so busy, as it's nearly lunchtime.

Grace comes charging over a couple of minutes later, followed by Mum with a tray, which wobbles as she shuffles between chairs, before lowering it to our table. There is a huge slab of chocolate sponge cake on one of the plates, a huge slab of Victoria sponge on another, and then a sliver of apple strudel on a third. Grace licks her lips expectantly.

'We couldn't decide what we wanted,' Mum says, handing me and Grace a fork each. 'So we got all three, and thought we'd share them between us. You start on the strudel, and then we'll swap plates.'

Grace digs her fork into the chocolate sponge, and manages to smear brown icing around her lips as she munches contentedly.

'You know,' Mum says, tucking into the Victoria sponge, 'if I didn't know better I could have sworn I'd just seen your Charlie. The guy was the spitting image of him. I must be losing my marbles.'

I shudder as a cold shiver ripples down my spine. I remember Kerry's call last night. 'It can't have been Charlie; he's in Oxford.'

She rests her fork on the plate and wipes her lips with a

paper napkin. 'I know, right? I would have put money on it being him, but I only saw him from behind, and he was gone before I could get a better look.'

'Ava!' Grace suddenly shouts out, waving fervently at her best friend several tables away. 'Can I go over and see her? Please, Mummy?'

Nadine looks up and nods at me. In front of her is a bowl of fresh salad and a bottle of mineral water. Her hair is set in a French plait, and her makeup looks like it was applied by a professional artist.

'Only if her mum says it's okay,' I say to Grace, wondering how much effort Nadine puts in to maintain her slim figure and perfect veneer.

Grace is straight out of her chair, a chocolate ring forming a perimeter around her lips, and darts between the tables until she reaches Nadine and Ava.

'She's a credit to you,' Mum says, bringing my attention back to our table. 'When I think about the trouble we had trying to adopt you, it really is a blessing to see how bright and clever my granddaughter is.'

Something stirs in the back of my mind. 'What kind of trouble did you have?'

She fixes me with a knowing stare. 'I know I said it is none of my business, but all your questions about the adoption process… You and Charlie are considering it, aren't you?'

I don't want to tell her the real reason I'm so interested, and simply shrug my shoulders, allowing her to draw her own conclusion.

She takes a sip of her tea, followed by a deep breath. 'We contacted the local council initially and met with a social worker assigned to our case. She wanted to know the reasons we were looking to adopt, and gave us a real breakdown of what would be involved, both physically and emotionally. At times it felt like she was trying to put us off the process. I suppose that's just the way they weed out the time-wasters. But your dad and I were adamant. The thing you have to remember is there are no guarantees you will find the child you think you're looking for.'

'Did you always know you wanted a daughter?'

She narrows her eyes. 'Honestly, no. We didn't mind what gender our child would be, but we did insist on having a new-born. I really wanted to experience those late-night feeding sessions, sterilising bottles in the early hours. Sounds silly, doesn't it? But I didn't think I would feel like a real mum without going through the extra stress a new-born brings.

'The agency at the council made us attend various preparatory classes, and then there were a number of assessments carried out both at their offices and at our house. Then at one point a check of our criminal history was carried out with the police, and then we had to provide a list of referees who would provide character references for us. Finally, we went before this panel who I think made the final decision, and then it was a matter of waiting for you. All in all, it took nearly ten months from that first meeting until we were taking you home.' She squeezes my hand. 'Worth every second and penny we spent.'

I'd never realised quite how much effort they'd gone to and have probably never appreciated either of them as much as I do right now. I squeeze her hand back in thanks for all the sacrifices they must have made for me to be here today with my own perfect daughter.

'Do you think I look like her? My birth mother, I mean.'

Mum's eyes don't leave mine, but I can see the pain as the muscles around her eyelids contract. 'It was so long ago that I really can't remember. She was younger than you are now, barely a scrap of a girl. Had she been older and had her boyfriend been more willing to take on responsibility, then maybe they would have clung onto you. I guess we'll never know.'

'Did they ever make contact and ask to see me?'

She breaks off a piece of the Victoria sponge between her fingers and considers my question as she chews. I don't understand why it takes her so long to answer. 'We received a birthday card for you once that wasn't signed. I always assumed it was either from her or your birth dad, but no other attempts were made as far as I'm aware. What's bringing all of this up now? You haven't asked about either of them since we told you on your birthday that year. Do you wish you'd made contact before she died?'

I frown. How does Mum know my birth mother is dead? And if she knows, why don't I? I'm about to ask when Grace comes haring over with Ava at her side.

'Ava's mum is taking her to the toyshop. Can we go too? Please? I want to choose what you can get me for my birthday.'

Mum stands before I can answer. 'I'll take you while your mummy finishes her cake.'

They're gone without another word, and I watch as Mum introduces herself to Nadine and then I am all alone at the table with three plates of half-eaten cake.

The lift doors ping and the young couple with the pram step aside to allow me to roll out before they enter. Their child can't be much older than six months, and is fast asleep, dummy in mouth, the picture of innocence. His dark hair is in stark contrast to that of his parents, who look exhausted.

It makes me think of how exhausted we would have been had our boy not been taken from us. Coping with a new-born and enforced paralysis would have made the last six months even more tiring, but they would have been filled with so much more joy. Deep down, I hope there is an alternative universe where there weren't complications with his delivery and where the needle in my back didn't slip. I bet that version of me is counting her blessings.

When I leave Debenhams, the humidity hits me instantly, warming my cheeks, and I'm half-tempted to roll back into the air-conditioned department store and wait for Mum and Grace to return, but I decide to plough onwards. I assume they were headed to the large toyshop we passed when we came out of the train station. Mum and I had promised Grace we would call in on the way home. I'll just have to hope that Mum hasn't gone spending-mad and bought half the shop for her persuasive granddaughter.

The road inclines, and the wheels meet greater resistance as I head up towards the main high street. This heat is making me feel parched already. Spotting a small boutique gift shop advertising cool drinks on a sandwich board by its entrance, I head in. A blast of cool air overhead hits me instantly, and I temporarily pause and welcome the refreshment. Until, that is, I feel the eyes of the uniformed security guard staring at me, and hastily move forwards.

He must be roasting in the beige woollen jumper over the collared shirt and significant paunch. His dark brown trousers and fitted cap can't be providing much ventilation either. A sign on the wall over his shoulder promises thieves will be prosecuted. He is still watching me with suspicious eyes, until I disappear behind the first shelving unit. It's funny, I don't think I've ever noticed this shop before, but it's filled with an eclectic collection of trinkets. In the air I can smell incense burning, and it reminds me of my days at university. A large cabinet to my left is filled with glass ornaments, some so intricately built that I am not surprised to see the high prices on the attached tickets.

There are Disney ornaments too. One of Cinderella's carriage, one of her glass slipper, a pair of Mickeys and Minnies, and one of Olaf the snowman. Grace would love this shop and would want all of these ornaments. Continuing along the aisle, I next come across a cascade of handcrafted greetings cards. There are some beautiful designs of flowers, cats, dogs, birds, and recognisable landscapes. I know these are printed representations of the originals, but I wish I was more creative and capable of producing such works of art.

I glance back at the cabinet of glass ornaments. Grace would so love that Cinderella carriage. It would be a brilliant present for her birthday, something special that she could put in her room, and maybe inspire more of her stories. I roll back and pick up the carriage, turning it over between my fingers. At fifty pounds it would have to be her main present, but it is so delicately painted that I can't resist. It's the size of a ping-pong ball, but it instantly brings back memories of the film, watching the animation with Mum. Growing up, I used to dream of being swept off my feet by a handsome prince. When

I think about Charlie, I suppose my dream did kind of come true.

I start as I hear an angry woman's voice behind the stands to my right, and my pulse quickens when I realise I recognise the Highland tone of the woman growling. Resting the carriage in my lap, I roll hastily to the end of the aisle, almost knocking into the stanchion at the end as I wheel around it, turning in to the next aisle, and seeing Morag hunched over, practically shouting into the phone at her ear.

Chapter Thirty-Four

Before – Morag

I ran from the telephone box as fast as my legs would carry me, arms pumping, my face a mop of sweat, as if *he* might be out there ready to grab me. I can't believe he would take our fight to my vulnerable sister. Suddenly, I understand why she was so out of breath when she came to the phone; he is capable of such evil.

I was careful to use the '141' code before I dialled her number, but he always has ways and means of getting around the rules. Does that mean he already knows the location of the phone box I used? I never should have called her again; how I wish I could be stronger.

I haven't been home just in case he's put one of his goons on lookout at the phone box. As paranoid as that sounds, I'd put nothing past him. I ran in the opposite direction to home, before boarding a bus, a Tube, and then another bus. Good luck trying to follow me now!

I can't go home. Not yet. Not until I know for certain I'm not being followed. Angus will be fretting about what's happened to me, but I daren't call him up until I'm away and out of earshot of everyone.

Somehow I've ended up in Harrow of all places, though my circuitous route took me via Eastcote, Ruislip, Uxbridge, Rayners Lane, and Wealdstone. A real tour of north-west London; roads unfamiliar to me, but my eyes have been glued to the passing traffic, searching for recurring vehicles. There was a navy blue Volvo Estate that I saw when I first boarded the bus in Northwood, and then I saw a similar vehicle when I boarded the Tube at Uxbridge, but I can't be certain the registration number was the same. I haven't seen it since, much to my relief.

Okay, it's been three hours since I heard *his* voice, and I'm sure I've managed to shake any potential tails. Pulling out my phone, I send Angus a quick text message, just to advise that I am okay, and he shouldn't worry. I keep the message short, and blasé: *Gone to the shops. Will be home for lunch xxx*

The phone feels heavy in my hand as I type in Gwen's number, knowing that Angus will probably insist on disposing of the device once I've placed the call, but I have to check that my sister is all right; that *he* hasn't done something to hurt her.

My hand trembles as I move the phone to my ear, and the breath won't pass my throat.

'I told you I would find you.' His voice is mocking, like he's just won a bet with himself that I would phone back.

'I w – w – want to speak to Gwen,' I stammer, failing to sound as assertive as I'd pictured in my mind.

'Your sister's busy.'

'I want to know that you haven't hurt her,' I say, firmer this time.

'She's fine – for now – but you're the one who'll determine how long that lasts.'

'W – w – what do you want?'

He snickers. 'I want what you took from me, and if you don't want me to make life difficult for Gwen and the rest of your clan you'll bring her back to me.'

'If you hurt my sister, or come anywhere near us, I will call the police.'

He laughs menacingly. 'And tell them what? I didn't break the law. *You* did.'

I know he's right. The police can't help us here. We're on our own.

Chapter Thirty-Five

Now

A clean shirt, shower, and shave later, Mike Ferry was back in the Incident Room, barely five hours after crawling into his own bed and allowing fatigue to take him. And when the light had started creeping beneath the frame of the curtains, he'd risen, ready to learn the truth about the stabbing in Northwood.

Writing the name 'Charlie' beneath the victim's photograph, he then drew a box with the word 'motive' at the top. If Jess's mum's statement to the officers was correct and things weren't smooth in the Donoghues' marriage, then there was every chance that she'd lashed out, but why at *that* house in Northwood? He'd seen the consequences of domestic abuse cases too many times, but the common theme in most of those had been that they occurred behind closed doors, and in the home of the couple in question. If Morag Kilbride hadn't been home since collecting her daughter from school, what the hell was Jess – and possibly husband Charlie – doing there? Why there, why then? What had happened to drive her to plunge a large kitchen knife into her husband's neck, severing the carotid artery?

Opening his laptop, he connected to the local network and logged into MOSES to check for any further updates from the Scientific Services team. No email notification that Morag's prints were a match for the unidentified set on the blade. Jess's mum said Jess had fled from their home late afternoon, and had maybe headed to Morag's to seek solace, but Charlie had come after her, and a fight ensued.

Mike stepped back from the board. It was a perfectly plausible theory, but it didn't feel right in his gut. No criminal history existed for either Jess or Charlie Donoghue, and as he now searched for the name Morag Kilbride, he again drew a blank. Three people with no previous trouble with the police had suddenly been thrust into the spotlight in the cruellest way.

He had had little choice but to release Morag Kilbride last night, but he was confident he would have her back in an interview room before the end of the day. He wrote her name on the board and scribbled notes beneath it. She'd said she was out all afternoon, but that alibi should be easy enough to prove or disprove. He would arrange for one of the team to contact the pubs in Chalfont St Peter and see if any staff could recall seeing two older parents and a four-year-old daughter. He would also ask Nazia to check her mountain of security footage to see whether there was any sign of Morag leaving and returning to the property.

He was about to log off when a fresh thought struck, and he typed in the name Angus Kilbride, excitement growing as one result was found. Opening the case history, he realised it wasn't actually directly to do with anyone called Angus Kilbride. Instead, he found himself reading about a restraining order taken out by a woman from Edinburgh against a male referred to as Tommy Chamberlain. Within the case history, the woman had provided Angus Kilbride's name as her place of residence while the restraining order was being sought. The casefile had been closed several weeks after it was opened, with the woman dropping her complaint.

Mike closed the laptop, and left the Incident Room, making sure the door was locked before heading to his regular desk to prepare for the morning briefing.

Chapter Thirty-Six

Before – Jess

Morag has her back to me, and I don't want to interrupt, but I can see she is visibly shaken by the call. There is no sign of Daisy or Angus.

Whoever she is talking to, whoever is upsetting her, is none of my business. I roll backwards and out of sight, telling myself just to find a cool drink, pay, and leave the shop. Morag doesn't know I am here, and if she does spot me, she may make some awful suggestion like travelling back on the train with us. She has already wormed herself far enough into my family; I can't inflict her on my mum too. If I just sit tight for a few minutes and wait for her to leave, I can continue on my journey towards the toyshop.

'I swear to God, I will never let you anywhere near her,' I hear Morag shout, and it is this that catches my attention.

She's not my mum.

Could the 'her' be Daisy? If so, who is on the other end of the phone? My mind whirrs with theories, none of which quite feel right. I remain still, straining to hear anything more, but Morag's voice is now little more than a murmur.

'Over my dead body,' Morag yells. 'I swear on her life, if I see you anywhere near us, I will... I will put a knife in you myself!'

I swallow hard. My body is awash with equal parts fear and sympathy for this woman who may or may not be the most dangerous person I've ever met.

I hear Morag sigh loudly, and against my better judgement take this as my cue to wheel back around the stanchion and offer her my support. Her shoulders are gently rocking, and although I can't hear her sob, it is clear she is crying.

'Morag?' I say gently, trying to include a tone of surprise, like I wasn't expecting to run into her here.

She spins around, and I can see her eyeliner has left tear-stained streaks down her cheeks. She quickly blows her nose, and forces a smile, trying to cover her crying.

'Goodness, Jess, what a small world.' She sniffs. 'How are you?'

I wish I could read her mind, to understand what secrets she is keeping and why. I desperately want to know who was on the phone and whether it had anything to do with Daisy's four little words, but I don't want her to know that I heard her side of the conversation.

'Last minute PE kit buying,' I say, pointing to the shopping bags hanging from the handles of my chair. 'Are you okay? You look like you've been crying.'

She is studying my face; I suppose trying to determine

whether I overheard any of her call. She raises the phone into the air so I can see it. 'Had some bad news about an old friend, that's all. I don't know what's wrong with me today. Must be all this humidity and the anxiety about Daisy starting school tomorrow.'

She's lying to me, but I just nod in acknowledgement. I could tell her I heard the threats she made to the other person, but I don't see what it will achieve at this stage. They say keep your friends close and your enemies closer, and for now it suits me better to keep Morag closer, until I know the real reason Daisy approached me in the park.

If I'm honest, it is taking all my willpower not to demand she tell me the truth about the phone call, and I'm hoping my patience holds out.

The phone starts ringing in her hand again, and as she looks at the display, and then back at me, I see fresh tears forming in her eyes. She declines the call, and suddenly glances around like she's half-expecting someone to jump out on us.

'I have to go,' she says, turning and racing towards the front of the shop.

'Wait,' I call out, hurrying after her, as quickly as my arms can pump. The sunshine is so bright as I bounce out onto the pavement. Morag has turned right, and is heading back down the road towards Debenhams, and I decide to go after her, until I hear a gruff voice calling out over my shoulder.

'Hey, stop!'

I nearly tumble out of the chair as it suddenly stops, and as I turn to confront whoever has grabbed the handles, I see the overweight security guard panting. A sheen of sweat shimmers beneath the peak of his cap.

'What the...?' I begin, as he starts pulling me backwards along the pavement towards the shop.

He points at my lap, and it is only now I spot the ornamental glass carriage twinkling under the intense sunlight.

Chapter Thirty-Seven

Before - Morag

I run until my lungs burn and my legs feel like they won't support my weight. I finally relent and, almost crashing to the hard concrete ground, I try to get my bearings. I am not as fit as I once was, and my feet now feel as though they are on actual fire. I'm just grateful I was wearing trainers when I snuck out of the house this morning.

I appear to have stopped near some kind of park. A playground, basketball court, and skate ramp are visible in the distance, surrounded by a sea of yellowing grass, succumbing to the continued heatwave. There are so many boys and girls rushing about that they're just a blur of colours and sounds. It's the sort of place you could slip into and just disappear.

The whole day I've been searching for tails and people who look out of place, and who should I run into in some random local shop, but Jess? She just happened to be there buying PE kit, she claimed. Really? The day before the school term starts?

I'm sorry, but I find that a little hard to swallow. Her being there has to be a message from *him*. He's showing me he knows where I am, and that if we don't do as he says, he'll be able to do whatever he likes with us. It's too coincidental that Jess approached the moment I broke off the call with him.

I can't believe I was stupid enough to fall for her sob story; did I learn nothing from Wolverhampton? At least I wasn't the only one who bought Jess and Charlie's lies.

I freeze as a fresh wave of panic hits; Jess knows where we live, and if she knows then so does *he*. Unlocking the mobile, I hold it near my face as I try and formulate a plan. He knows this number – somehow – but that means he can track it. So he can probably track any other number I dial, but what choice do I have? I need to warn Angus that he and Daisy are in danger.

Searching for Angus's name, I press dial, and listen intently, and wail in frustration when his answerphone kicks in.

Why isn't he answering his phone?

What if *he* has already gone to the house? What if his phone call to me was just to keep me out of the way?

I need to keep control of my emotions. I need to think clearly.

The taxi home is an expense I can't really afford, but I just need to know where Angus and Daisy are, and to check that they are safe. I pay the driver the last note in my purse, and don't wait for change, bundling myself out of the taxi, up the driveway, and in through the front door.

'Angus?' I call out, straining to hear any sound which might indicate where they are. 'Daisy? Where are you two?'

Only silence greets me.

Checking every room downstairs, upstairs, and the garden, I'm about to play my final card – calling the police – when I hear a set of keys, and their voices as they come through the front door.

Rushing over, I throw my arms around them both, the tears warm as they splash on my cheeks. 'Where were you two?'

'I went to buy lunch,' Angus says, waving the long baguette he's clutching near my face. 'What's gotten into you? Whatever is the matter?'

I can't answer, not at first. I just want to hold the two most precious gifts in my life and will away the bad that is to come.

With Daisy settled up in her room with a sandwich, where she won't hear us speak, I finally come clean to Angus, and tell him about my two calls to Gwen, and subsequent conversations with Tommy.

Angus doesn't say anything at first, ruminating on what I have told him. He isn't angry, maybe disappointed though. 'He phoned you on this number?' he questions.

I nod.

Without a breath, Angus switches off the phone, and removes the SIM card. 'What exactly did he say?'

'He wants Daisy back. He said he knows we won't go to the police because of what we did. He is on his way here, Angus, I know it. We need to pack up and go.'

'No.' He is so calm, but there is a hardness to his stare. 'We can't start over again, Morag. I'm tired of running, and it's not fair on Daisy. She's due to start school tomorrow, and if she doesn't show up, people will start asking awkward questions. We don't know that he knows we're here.'

I can't believe he's being so calm about all this. 'Do you not remember what he did to our cottage in Aberdeen? It's cinders and dust now. And God knows what he would have done in Wolverhampton had we not got away when we did.'

'We don't know for certain that he found us last time, Morag. We moved because you said you thought he was getting closer, but we never saw him. We both know how manipulative he is. His visiting Gwen and phoning you could just be mind games designed to drive us into an early grave. If we pack up and move again, he wins.'

'This isn't about winning and losing, Angus. This is about preservation of life: yours, mine, and Daisy's.'

He takes my hands in his. 'I will not allow anything bad to happen to you, my love. Don't worry, I have a plan.'

Chapter Thirty-Eight

Now

'You eaten breakfast yet?' Polly asked from the doorway, holding up a brown paper bag. 'Peace offering?'

He smiled at her. 'It should be me apologising. I was wrong to assume that because of what happened between us before, you would—'

She cut him off with a raised hand. 'I'm happy to forget it if you are. Did you get much sleep in the end?'

'Not as much as I probably needed. You?'

'Sammy wouldn't settle after you'd been there, so I ended up allowing him into my room, as I didn't want his scratching and howling to wake the kids next door.'

Mike winced. 'I'm sorry. I just wanted to watch him sleeping, but he must have picked up on my scent. Maybe I could have him at my place for a couple of nights so you can get some shut-eye.'

She raised her eyebrow sceptically. 'He needs to be somewhere he'll get regular walks and feeding, which my brother helps out with. Besides, your place isn't big enough to swing a cat, let alone entertain a four-year-old German Shepherd.'

He knew she was right, and decided not to push the point.

'Care to update me on the plan for today?' Polly asked, pragmatic as ever.

Mike followed her out of the room, gratefully accepting the paper bag, and chuckling as he opened it to see the maple and pecan Danish pastry. 'We'll do a full brief when the rest of the team arrives, but in the meantime, I want you to get hold of Jess Donoghue's mum and find out whether there's any word from husband Charlie. See if you can get a trace on his phone too. There was no phone or wallet found on the victim, which is unusual in itself, but if Charlie Donoghue's phone is on, I want to know where it is.'

'So you still think we could be looking at a domestic disturbance gone wrong? You think Jess offed her husband?'

Mike narrowed his eyes. 'Call it a working theory for now. I also want someone to check out Morag Kilbride's alibi as soon as possible, and when it turns out to be a crock of shit, I want her brought back in to answer why.'

Polly raised both eyebrows as she made a note of his instructions. 'My, my, someone's rediscovered their chutzpah!'

Mike was about to retort when a woman in uniform approached his desk. 'DI Ferry? I'm PC Carla Anderson. I was sent up to help view some security camera footage?'

Mike dropped the pastry back into the bag and showed her to a free desk next to where Nazia had been sitting last night. 'Good, good, make yourself comfortable. Polly can show you where you can get tea and coffee. Team brief is at eight, and then I'll introduce you to DS Nazia Hussain, who will coordinate what she needs from you.' He led Carla to the Incident Room door and punched in the code. 'We've narrowed time of death to between five and six yesterday evening, and these are the two faces you need to look for: the woman on the left is one of our suspects, and this unidentified man the victim.'

'Wait, wait, I know her,' Carla responded urgently. 'Her name's Jess, right?'

Mike's eyes widened. 'If she's a friend of yours then—'

'No, I don't know her like that,' Carla interrupted. 'What I mean is, I interviewed her here the other day. Tuesday, I think.'

This was new information. 'We checked for her on the system and there was no record of an arrest.'

'She was brought in on suspicion of shoplifting, but de-arrested when her sister-in-law came forward and offered extenuating circumstances.'

'Her sister-in-law?'

'Rosie something or other,' Carla replied. 'She's on secondment with the Misper team out of Uxbridge, I think she said. Jess claimed she had been unaware she had the item in her lap when she left the shop in pursuit of a friend. I got the impression the store security guard was a bit of a jobsworth, or on commission for catching thieves, as a look at the shop's CCTV backed up her story, but he insisted she be brought in. I think the shop owner relented and chose not to press charges, so she was released.'

'Was she interviewed under caution?'

Carla nodded. 'Of course.'

'Do me a favour and dig out the recording so I can watch it,' Mike instructed.

Carla left the room in a hurry, leaving Mike and Polly staring at the image of Jess Donoghue on the wall, wondering what other secrets she was hiding.

Chapter Thirty-Nine

Before - Jess

It's a nightmare I cannot wake from. Staring at the grimly painted, cold walls of the holding cell, it feels like I am watching somebody else's life playing out before me. I tried to explain to the overweight guard that I never had any intention of stealing the glass Cinderella carriage; that it was a huge mistake, and I'm not that sort of person.

'That's what they all say,' he told me, with a disbelieving and scornful look.

How many paraplegic shoplifters are there out there? Not as many as he seemed to be suggesting, I bet.

Every time I tried to speak, he would keep pointing at that 'Thieves will be prosecuted' sign on the wall. And it didn't seem to matter how many times I tried to explain that I'm not a thief, he simply ignored my attempts. I couldn't actually believe it when two uniformed officers turned up, and escorted me to the waiting van, before securing me inside.

So humiliating!

There was a crowd of onlookers at this point, and I can only hope that nobody I know witnessed the debacle. I couldn't bring myself to look at anyone, keeping my tear-filled eyes buried behind my hands.

I've never had as much as a speeding fine or parking ticket in my life. I've always considered myself beyond reproach as far as criminal activity is concerned, and now here I am, trapped inside a humid cell, the stale air suffocating.

What makes it worse is the fact that Mum and Grace are still out there – probably in Harrow – wondering what's happened to me. When I arrived at the police station, they agreed to allow me to call Mum, but her phone was switched off. I left a voicemail and I guess the older woman behind the custody desk took pity on me, as she agreed to keep trying the number. I can't even remember if Mum had her phone with her when we headed for the shops. It could just as easily be at home, which of course she can't get into because I have the keys. Correction: the police now have the keys.

What a mess!

As far as I can tell, I've been here for two hours, and nearly an hour of that has been spent in this same holding cell. There is a bed against one wall, but there are no windows. The only light in the room comes from a buzzing lamp overhead. There's also some kind of video camera high up in the corner above the large reinforced door. A little red light flashes continuously as it watches my every move.

The rest of my time here was spent in another small, windowless room. I declined the offer of a duty solicitor, only to reinforce the fact that I am innocent of what they are accusing me of. Yes, I left the shop with the ornament in my lap, but it was never my intention to steal. It is just a misunderstanding.

I sobbed as they informed me about what the security guard had told them. Apparently, I looked 'shifty' when I entered the store, and his 'instinct' told him to watch me. He saw on his monitor that I'd taken an interest in the glass ornaments, and how I'd moved away from the cabinet before returning and selecting the item to steal. He then told them how I hovered at the end of the first aisle, and he was studying the security camera footage trying to work out what I was doing. Again, his 'instinct' told him I was trying to secrete the Cinderella carriage somewhere on my person. Finally, he claimed that another unidentified woman ran from the store as a distraction to enable me to race away too, only he was already on to our ploy and managed to apprehend me.

As I continue to stare straight ahead at the cold walls, I can't stop thinking about Grace and my poor Mum. She doesn't know Harrow very well, and Grace won't be able to give her directions home. If she doesn't have her phone, she won't know what's happened and they'll both be so worried about where I am.

The window shutter in the door cranks as it's lowered and two beady eyes peer in and stare at me. The door clanks as it's then unlocked and swung open. I've never been so relieved to see my sister-in-law Rosie. I don't know how she found out I was here, but I'm glad she's come to talk some sense into them. If anyone can give me a worthy character reference Rosie can.

Her hair hangs loose over her shoulders, rather than in its trademark ponytail, and she's wearing the same trouser suit that I saw her in last night. She thanks the officer who has opened the door, and he leaves us.

Rosie perches on the edge of the bed next to me. 'How are you holding up?'

It's such a simple question, and although no malice was intended, the lump in my throat grows and I can't stop the tidal wave of tears.

Rosie rubs a gentle hand across my shoulders, and tells me everything will be okay, and I desperately hope she's right. She asks what happened, and I recount the story again, only this time I tell her about Morag's involvement as she already knows the trouble Morag's arrival in our lives has caused. Rosie listens without interruption, and when I'm done, her face is a mixture of empathy and concern.

'I've spoken to Charlie, and he's at home taking care of Grace,' she says. 'I told him I'd make sure you were okay and being treated properly. The good news is the shop owner has decided against pressing charges.'

I dive towards her, throwing my arms around her shoulders. 'Thank you, thank you, thank you,' I whisper, feeling fresh warm tears fill the gap between our cheeks.

'You don't need to thank me. When I spoke to the shop owner, and explained the stress you've been under, he was surprisingly understanding. Apparently, he has a niece who suffers with MS and is becoming more dependent on her wheelchair.'

'Are you going to open a formal investigation into Morag now?' I ask.

Rosie's brow furrows. 'Why would I?'

'Didn't you hear me when I said how shifty she was being? She threatened whoever was on the other end of that phone. You need to find out who she was speaking to. It could be to do with her taking Daisy.'

Rosie leans away from me, the lines in her forehead deepening. 'You need to stop with this, Jess. As your sister and friend, I'm telling you to stop. All these accusations about a woman you barely know – it isn't healthy.' She's looking at me like I've lost my mind. 'I spoke to Charlie about our chat last night, and he's just as worried about you as I am.'

All I can hear is the blood boiling in my ears. 'You went behind my back?'

She is waving her hands in a calming gesture. 'For your own good, Jess. We all love you and understand that things have been really tough on you. All this business with Morag and Daisy is—'

'Don't you dare say it's all in my head,' I snap.

'No, not that,' she replies, her voice soft and even, 'but I can understand why your mind would put two and two together and come up with ten. You're still grieving and coming to terms with the paralysis – I get all that – but you need to speak to a professional about it.'

'I'm not imagining it.'

'Maybe not, but look around you, Jess. You are in a police station cell and were arrested today. What you're doing has serious consequences. I've managed to fix things this time, but I won't be able to bail you out of trouble again.'

My cheeks are burning at the reprimand and betrayal.

Rosie stands and I feel her grab the handles of my chair. 'They need to process your release and then I will drive you home. Okay?'

I don't respond as she pulls me backwards out of the cell, and pushes me back along the corridor towards the custody suite. I know one thing for sure; I never want to wind up in a police station again.

Neither Rosie nor I say much on the ride home. I'm grateful that she's driving me in her own car, so at least my neighbours won't be aware of the shameful afternoon I've spent locked up. She hugs me as I'm about to exit the car, reminding me that the reason everyone is so worried about me is because they care. If that's the case, why do I feel like a child whose parents assume I can't understand what they're saying?

I understand everything. I understand that it's easier for them to leap to the conclusion that my suspicions about Morag are my brain's mechanism for coping with the loss of feeling in my legs and losing my baby boy. If they really care about me, why are none of them prepared to accept that I'm not mistaken about Morag and Angus? There is something not right there, but I'm the only one prepared to acknowledge it.

I don't remember everything I overheard, but there is one phrase that has stuck: *I swear on her life, if I see you anywhere near us, I will… I will put a knife in you myself!*

Maybe I should have mentioned that to the officers who interviewed me. That's a threat to someone's life and should be investigated. What troubles me most is Morag's propensity to threaten such violence so easily. I don't think I've ever threatened to kill someone, let alone describe how I would do it. If she can be so relaxed about violence, does that make her dangerous? Is that why Daisy was so terrified I would tell Morag about those four little words? Has she witnessed Morag using threatening behaviour before?

I just want to get in, go to bed, and put this sorry day behind me. It's gone six, but my appetite has yet to return. I'm dreading what Charlie is going to say, and I don't think he'll be willing to let me go to bed without dissecting exactly what happened.

Rosie's car pulls away and I don't wait to wave her off. The bags of shopping from earlier are back on the handles of the chair, and they crackle and scrunch as I roll up the ramp to the front door and insert my key. An aroma of garlic fills my nostrils as I push the door open, and I can hear the extractor fan humming in the kitchen, and shadows dancing about on the walls as Mum, or possibly Charlie, tinkers away inside.

The air is warm despite the back door being partially open. Large plumes of grey smoke fill the tiny back garden, and I'm surprised Charlie has decided to cook a barbecue tonight. Grace's giggle echoes from the lounge, and I now just desperately want to give her a big squeeze and apologise for any worry my disappearance has caused.

'Oh, Jess, thank God,' Mum says from the couch next to Grace, and she leaps to her feet, wraps her arms around me, and places a wet kiss on my cheek. 'Are you okay? I heard your message, and…' She pauses and I sense she is looking back at Grace. 'Perhaps we should chat in the kitchen.' She pulls me out of the room and we head into the kitchen, where she closes the door. 'Are you sure you're okay, sweetheart? They didn't hurt you, did they?'

The fear of the last few hours is suddenly so overpowering, and I feel a splash on my cheek. 'Oh, Mum, it was awful. They thought I tried to steal from that shop, but I swear I didn't. It was just a misunderstanding.'

She is immediately at my side, offering me one of her great Mum-hugs, just the right amount of pressure and support to silently tell me how much she loves me. I can only hope Grace feels as loved when I hug her.

'You poor thing,' Mum says quietly in my ear. 'It was fortunate I had my phone with me. We returned to Debenhams after the toy shop, and when you weren't there, I assumed you'd come to meet us, and our paths had crossed. I saw the police van pulling away, but had no idea you were inside. I tried to call you back as soon as I heard your message, and that's when the police officer answered and explained what was happening. I managed to get hold of Charlie and he let us in when he got back.'

'Does Grace know...?' I can't complete the sentence.

'I haven't told her you were arrested. She thinks you had to go for an emergency doctor's appointment. She has no clue about what happened.'

I squeeze Mum's arm against my collarbone, as relief permeates me. Charlie's face appears through the glass of the patio door. There is so much smoke that his head looks disembodied.

Mum releases her grip, removes a bottle of wine from the fridge, and heads back out of the kitchen. 'I'll leave you two to speak alone.'

Smoke fills the kitchen as Charlie pushes open the door and enters the room. The disappointment is scorched across his face, and neither of us speaks for a minute or so.

He finally sighs, and looks up at the ceiling to keep his own tears at bay. 'Tell me I don't need to be worried about this; about *you*.'

'It wasn't my fault. I was chasing after Morag, and didn't realise the thing was still in my lap. It was an accident. I'm not a thief.'

The incredulity in his face at the mention of Morag's name

reminds me he doesn't know the full backstory. 'What does Morag have to do with any of this?'

'She was in the shop on the phone to someone, threatening them. She was upset, so I asked if she was okay and that's when she hurried away. I thought she might be in some kind of trouble, so I hurried after her, and that's when the security guard intercepted me. I tried to explain to him that I'd made a mistake, but he was adamant he had to call the police. So humiliating!'

There is silence as he processes what I have just said, and then he shakes his head wistfully. 'What is it with you and *that woman*? No, in fact, what is it with you at the moment, Jess? Your behaviour has been so erratic… I'm worried about you. Last night, I found you sitting in your chair in the bathroom. Your eyes were open, but I swear you were asleep. I carried you back to bed, and you didn't stir, but as soon as your head was on the pillow your eyes closed again. It wasn't the first time that's happened either.' He pauses, avoiding eye contact. 'Maybe we need to make you an appointment for your dosage to be checked.'

I don't recall any reason I would have been in the bathroom, and I'm surprised he hasn't mentioned this before. I know I'm not cracking up. 'You didn't hear what Morag said. Whoever she was speaking to, she was angry. She told him or her to keep away and then she threatened to kill whoever it was.'

The worry lines around his eyes are deeper than I've ever seen them. 'Have you heard yourself? You're becoming obsessed with that family and I'm seriously worried about your mental health. Can't you see that this isn't normal, Jess? Please, you've got to let me in, help me understand what is going on with you. Let's make an appointment with Dr Savage, and she can help you.'

'There's nothing wrong with my mental health,' I fire back. 'Why won't you believe me? There is something off with that whole family. She's keeping secrets, and I don't believe she *adopted* Daisy. It's plausible, but there's more to it than that; I just feel it.'

'Goddamn it, Jess! No, there isn't! You're seeing conspiracy where there is none. I've met Morag, and she's given me no reason to doubt anything she's said. Only you can see trouble, because you want there to be trouble.' He pauses again. 'Is this about Luke?'

I gasp at the mention of our son's name. 'Why does everything have to come back to that question? I am not imagining this, Charlie. Why can't you just support me? I'm not crazy.'

'Really, Jess? Are you so sure about that?'

And there it is; the conclusive proof that he thinks I'm cracking up.

He disappears back into the smoke to turn the meat, and I move closer to the back door, so we can continue speaking. It kills me that he doesn't believe what I know to be true.

'We'll talk about this tomorrow,' he says, though I can no longer see him. 'I don't want Grace finding out about what happened. Is that clear? Your arrest is off-topic for this evening.'

As if I want to talk about it anymore anyway. I'd rather put the whole sorry episode behind me, and never mention it again.

Chapter Forty

Before - Morag

Mitch arrived an hour ago, and after Angus explained what had happened today, he hasn't been off his phone, talking to his so-called contacts. At least he's wearing more suitable attire, though if I didn't know better I'd have said we were speaking to a totally different person. This Mitch is in faded blue jeans, boots, and a checked shirt. He'd fit in perfectly at a line-dancing function. It really is amazing how he has transformed himself from the exercise enthusiast we met the other morning. Part of me wonders whether the change in appearance is for our benefit, so that we can feel more confident about his ability to blend into any situation without being recognised. Of course, he very well may have been on his way somewhere else when Angus called and demanded he come round.

Angus is so pale. He's trying to put a brave face on it, but there is an ever-present sheen on his forehead, and his breathing is erratic. I have to keep looking over to make sure he isn't having a heart attack. Daisy is now tucked up in bed. She can sense something bad has happened, and kept asking what was going on. I think I managed to cover, telling her that we'd had some sad news about her Auntie Gwen being taken ill. I don't want to tell her the truth; that her father has come looking for her *again*. You can pick your friends, but not your family, and it isn't fair on her to be left to face him.

I should probably cook some food for Angus and me, as I haven't eaten all day, and if he's been fending for himself he's probably only had toast, but neither of us feels hungry. Today's events have robbed me of my appetite.

Angus explained his plan to me, and whilst I think it is a noble idea, I know deep down it won't work. His hope to arrange a meeting between him and Tommy on neutral territory, and to then offer money to buy us out of this situation, seems naïve, though Angus insists it is our only option. I wish one of us had the strength and bravery just to kill the bastard, but the truth is neither of us has a violent bone in our body. Even if confronted with a life-or-death situation, I don't think I'd have it in me to end another person's life.

Can we really make a deal with the devil?

Mitch hangs up the phone and returns to the dining table where we're seated. 'I wish you'd told me all this background when you hired me. If I'd realised why you wanted me to look up Tommy Chamberlain – and you'd even hinted at exactly who he is – I probably would have thought twice about agreeing to help you.'

I feel like a naughty schoolchild being chastised by an angry teacher, and I can't bring myself to meet his gaze.

'That said, I can see how concerned you both are, and I'm

not about to leave you high and dry. We have a contract, and I will honour it.'

I can feel the tension ease in Angus' shoulders beside me.

'I have reached out to some contacts I have up north, and mooted the idea of the meet-up. They couldn't say whether Tommy would agree to it, but they did agree that nothing appeals more to him than money, so you never know.'

'Does he know where we are?' I ask, desperate to know the truth one way or another. The thought of him suddenly appearing at our door fills me with dread.

'I can't say for certain,' Mitch replies. 'As I told you the other day, the guys I spoke to suggested that he was no longer looking for you, but what you've told me today contradicts that. If you're worried, I'd suggest checking in to a hotel for the night, or even speaking to the police.'

If only it was that easy. In some way, I'd like to come clean and admit what we did, but to do so would be to give up Daisy, and I won't do that.

'What about my sister?' I ask, conscious that Gwen is at his mercy.

'I can't tell you anything about her situation. My contact said Tommy is out of town on family business, but he couldn't confirm where or why. Do you have any other family up that way you could speak to, to go and check on your sister?'

'She's all I have left,' I say, dabbing my eyes.

It's my fault she's in danger. I'd naively assumed Tommy would never go and trouble her, because she didn't know where we were, but I should have considered that he'd be willing to do anything to get his daughter back.

'When will we know if he'll accept our offer?' Angus asks, his voice strained.

'Could be tonight, but more likely tomorrow. The best thing you can do is carry on as if everything is normal, for your daughter's sake. I will let you know as soon as I do.'

'What about Jess and Charlie?' I ask, having told him about Jess's chance appearance at the shop in Harrow. 'Are they working for him?'

Mitch shrugs. 'He has a network of contacts around the country, but their names haven't come up in any of the searches I've done. If you're not sure about them, just keep away.'

That's easier said than done, I don't say.

Angus shows Mitch to the door, as I clear away the empty mugs. For some reason I can't escape the fear that tomorrow is going to be a huge day for all of us, and I can't shake the feeling that not all of us will live to see it through.

Chapter Forty-One

Now

Mike stretched his arms over his head as the video recording ended. 'Well?'

'I never took her for a shoplifter,' Polly admitted, 'but then that's probably just my prejudices. Definitely our girl though. Did you see how uncomfortable she looked when questioned?'

'Did you believe her story?' Mike asked PC Carla Anderson, who'd watched the interview with the two of them. 'You really think she was racing after a friend and forgot the item was in her lap?'

'I've seen the security footage, and there is a woman who rushes out of the shop moments before Jess does, but the angle of the camera means we only got to see the back of her head. And given how grainy the footage was, I couldn't say for certain that the figure in the coat was definitely a woman. Probably, but not *definitely*.'

'Possible decoy?' Mike asked, considering whether shoplifter Jess had a partner.

'To be honest, sir – and call me naïve if you want – but I believed her story on Tuesday, and having just watched the performance for a second time, I'm even more inclined to believe it. I don't think she meant to take the ornament.'

Mike closed the lid of the laptop. 'Did you run a background check on her finances? The poverty line is rising in the UK, and you know as well as I that petty theft is rising at the same rate.'

'We were about to pull her credit history when the sister-in-law rocked up and told us we'd made a big mistake.'

'What did you say her name was again?'

'Rosie Donoghue. I can check what shift she's on if you want to speak to her?'

Mike nodded. 'Thanks, yes. I'd like to hear from someone that knows the couple better, and might have insight into how things were on the home front.'

Carla stood and left the room. Mike nodded to two members of the team who'd arrived while they'd been watching the interview. Almost all the team were in, and he wanted to start the team brief as soon as possible. It felt like the more questions he asked, the more questions he was uncovering in response. What he needed was answers, and sooner rather than later.

'What was your take on the interview?' Mike asked Polly, leaning closer, and resting his hands between his legs.

Polly thought for a moment. 'Forgetfulness sounds like a legitimate enough excuse. I've nearly done it myself, wandering out of a shop, not realising I still have something in my hand I haven't paid for. Plus, if she's been off her medication for as long as Dr Savage claimed, then who knows what kind of state her mind was in the day before last? Have you had any kind of update from Dr Savage yet?'

Mike shook his head while double-checking his emails. 'I'll chase her up after the team brief. Still waiting to hear back from the techies upstairs on whether the prints lifted from Morag Kilbride's plastic cup are a match for those on the blade.'

Polly lowered her voice. 'Then I think you should cancel that request before it's too late. You realise that what you did'—she lowered her voice further—'is a *huge* violation of PACE? Given the inquiry you just survived, do you really want to bring Professional Standards to your door?'

Mike understood her concern came from the heart. 'I marked it for my eyes only. I don't intend to use it for anything but my own peace of mind.'

'Mike?' Nazia called over from her desk. 'Supe wants to see you in her office.'

Mike did his best not to roll his eyes. It didn't feel all that long since she'd dragged him upstairs late last night. Did she really expect that the picture would have changed so soon? The day had hardly started.

'Can you start the team brief?' Mike asked Polly, 'and I'll catch up when I come back down. You know where this thing needs to go today.'

'No worries,' she said, standing and moving towards the front of the room to gather the others. 'Good luck.'

Mike listened for the first minute as Polly updated everyone on last night's incident. A few of the team had already been at home when the 999 call had been received, and so this was news to them. Mike felt confident that with more eager minds on the case, they'd definitely make progress today.

Catching the lift up, he was planning what he was going to say when the Chief Super's door opened at the end of the corridor, and she glared out at him, her flushed cheeks and angry scowl making him want to turn back and run away. He fought the urge, and as she closed the door behind him, he sensed this impromptu meeting wasn't going to run as smoothly as last night's.

'You let your chief suspect leave the station?' she began evenly, standing against the window with the backdrop of the town's skyline in full frame.

Mike was about to respond, and explain that he'd had no choice but to release Jess Donoghue into Dr Savage's care, but the Chief Super raised her hand to cut him off. She wasn't finished.

'Then you interview a second possible suspect or witness, before allowing her to also leave, but only after you stole her fingerprints and sent them upstairs to be processed. Am I missing anything else, DI Ferry?'

Mike gulped audibly, wishing he'd heeded Polly's warning last night.

'You can imagine my shock to receive a call from Dr Emily Towser early this morning advising that you'd requested an eyes-only print processing, and asking for me to corroborate that it was in fact part of the investigation, and not some personal errand you were wasting our resources on. I told her I had to check, and when I saw no record of Morag Kilbride granting permission for her fingerprints to be taken, I realised what a terrible mistake I'd made in appointing you as SIO.'

'Ma'am, please, with all due respect,' Mike began, but she

cut him off with a sharp hand again. She hadn't invited him up to hear his side of the story.

'Did you learn nothing from that fiasco last year? I'm not condoning the behaviour of the organised crime unit you were seconded to, but braver and smarter detectives lost their jobs, pensions, and freedom for taking the law into their own hands. I warned you last night that I would do anything to prevent Professional Standards from crawling all over this nick.'

Mike wanted to shout back that it was the pressure she was putting him under to deliver a result that had led to his lapse of judgement, but in truth he knew he couldn't blame anyone but himself for bagging up Morag Kilbride's cup. It had been done with the best of intentions, but both the Chief Super and Polly were right; he'd crossed the line.

'Replacing me as SIO now will set the investigation back by days,' he argued, desperate to cling on to the chance to finish the job the right way. 'I'm sorry for what I did – I really am – and I know I've let you and the team down. You can take whatever action you want with me when the case is closed, but in the meantime, there are two women out there who know exactly what happened in that house last night. Let me bring them in and deliver justice for our victim.'

He was convinced she would kick him out of her office, demanding his warrant card, but instead she balled her fist and slammed it hard against her desk, causing the precariously balanced framed picture of her daughter to topple against the open laptop. 'You have twenty-four hours. If you don't have a suspect in custody by this time tomorrow, you're off the case and out of my nick. Do you understand?'

Mike held in the sigh of relief that desperately wanted to

escape. He nodded, and left the room before she had chance to change her mind.

He had only just returned to the office when Nazia hurried over. 'There's a woman downstairs you're going to want to meet,' she said excitedly. 'She's a former work colleague of Jess Donoghue, and she claims to know exactly why Jess was at the Kilbride residence yesterday. Wait for it; apparently, Jess was convinced that Morag had abducted the child she's claiming to be her daughter, and what's more, she has proof.'

Chapter Forty-Two

Before - Jess

She's clearly excited. Grace has always been a chatterbox – an accusation she fiercely denies – but this morning it's like the chatter has found a new level of intensity.

'And I need my hair to look just right, because you never get a second chance to make a good impression. That's what Daddy was telling me, anyway. So how should I have my hair, Mummy? In a bun? Plaited? Pigtails, or just one long ponytail?'

She pauses to shovel a spoonful of cereal into her mouth, the milk splashing onto her chin, which she quickly wipes away with the back of her hand.

I'm exhausted just trying to keep up with the explosion of thoughts flowing through her mind. I've never been great at sculpting my daughter's hair. I can only plait badly, but we certainly don't have time for that now.

'I think you should just go for the single ponytail.' If only to save me time and effort, I don't add.

'Like Auntie Rosie, you mean?'

She drops the spoon into the bowl with a clang, and fixes me with a sincere look. 'You should do something different with your hair, Mummy. Maybe you could change the colour, or have it cut differently.'

My hand shoots up to the mound of split ends near my cheek. How bad must my hair look for my four year-old to call me out on it? I make a mental note to use some dry shampoo and give it a good brush before we leave. The last thing I want is for all the judgemental mothers to encourage their children to steer clear of the girl whose mum clearly doesn't know how to look after herself properly.

'You'd better go and brush your teeth, and then we'll fix your hair,' I promise, reaching for her bowl and carrying it to the countertop next to the sink. A mound of plates and glasses are neatly stacked there from last night's barbecue.

'Do you want me to drop Grace at school?' Mum says, as she enters the room, wearing a pretty summer dress I don't recognise.

I'm dreading the blubbing mess I'll be by the time we reach the school gates, but this is the day I've been fearing for months, and I know I must face it.

'Thank you for the offer, but I want to be the one who takes her for her first day. Like a rite of passage or something.'

Mum leans in and kisses me on the cheek. 'I understand. Do you want some company?'

She's only trying to be supportive, but selfishly I don't want to share this experience with anyone. I've spent months picturing what it will be like to lead Grace into this next chapter of her life, and as painful as it's going to be, I want to be the only one she remembers in the experience.

'That's okay, I've got this. Maybe you can come with me and collect her from school later instead.'

She smiles through the disappointment. 'Of course.'

Grace bounds back into the room, and my thoughts return to sorting out her hair. She hands me a brush and hair tie and I can smell toothpaste on her breath as she busily tells me how she can't wait to see her teacher again. Before the summer holidays, all the children were invited in to the school to meet their teachers and classmates, and then the school sent photographs of the teachers and teaching assistants home so the children could memorise their names and faces. Grace's teacher is Miss Danvers, a Canadian woman in her late twenties, who seemed very enthusiastic when I met her.

'Miss Danvers said she loves reading stories too, just like me, Mummy. I like Miss Danvers. Do you think I should take one of my stories in for her to read?'

I tell Grace I will pack her exercise book of stories in her school bag, so that she can share it with her teacher. With shoes fastened, hair tied, and teeth clean, we head out of the door, down the ramp, and along the road. School is just over a mile walk from our house, and I know we have left too early really, but I want us to take our time so I can cling to those final few moments with my little girl.

It's a cliché to say that they grow up too quickly, but the last four and a bit years have flown by. I still remember the first moment I laid eyes on her, when I didn't know how she would grow, how her face would totally change shape, hair would lengthen, and what kinds of activities would interest her. That first day was so scary, not knowing what the future held, but I can't say I regret a single moment of Grace's life. She gives my life meaning. From the moment she was born, I stopped being Jess Donoghue, and became Grace's mum. For some that isn't enough, but for me it's everything.

After a few moments of nonstop chatter, Grace falls silent.

'What's wrong, darling?' I ask, slowing, and reaching for her hand so she will stop walking.

She looks down at her feet, and her lips droop sullenly, but she doesn't answer. A woman with two children in uniform, and one in a pushchair, darts around us, and I'm suddenly conscious of the wheelchair. As far as I'm aware, all the other parents with children starting at the school today are able-bodied. Although Grace has never mentioned worries about my chair, I can't stop thinking that she's worried about how the other children will react to her because I'm different to the other mums and dads. Maybe I should have allowed Mum to come with us, so that she could lead Grace through the gates while I waited and watched.

I look back along the road. We probably still have time to return and ask Mum to come with us if that will make Grace feel more comfortable.

'Talk to me, sweetie,' I say, fighting the growing ache in my heart. 'What is it that's troubling you? You can tell me anything, you know. I won't be upset.'

She slowly looks up at me, her lips now quivering, and a watery glow in her eyes. 'It's just...'

I wait patiently, not wanting to interrupt, but conscious that the seconds are passing so quickly.

'It's just...' she tries again, this time a tear escaping and rolling delicately down her warm cheek.

Suddenly she throws her arms around me and presses her

face into my shoulder. It's all I can do to keep my own emotions in check.

'What is it, darling? Please tell Mummy what is upsetting you, so I can fix it.'

A dad in long shorts and a T-shirt passes, berating his son for an unfastened shoe lace.

I rub my hand over Grace's back, and I'm about to tell her I understand her concern about my chair and that we can go home to collect Mum, when she whispers in my ear.

'I wish you could come to school with me.'

The breath catches in my throat. I've been so focused on how much I'm going to miss being Grace's world that I haven't even considered that she might miss me just as much. Happy tears fill my eyes, and I don't care when I feel my cheeks moisten. She's been so giddy with excitement this morning that I missed the probability that the chatter was masking her own insecurities. I give her an extra squeeze, inhaling the strawberry scent of shampoo on her hair, before separating us, so I can look into her beautiful blue eyes.

'I wish I could come in with you too, my beautiful girl, but this adventure is one for you to take on alone. It's an important stage in your life, and I have no doubt in my mind that you will be a huge success in school. I've never met someone so sweet-natured, tender, funny, and bright. There is no challenge you cannot overcome, and I am so proud of everything you've already achieved. You are the best person I know, Grace Donoghue, and I will be waiting in the playground when you come out, so you can tell me about everything you've done and learned today. Okay?'

She is smiling through her tears, and it's almost too much for my heart to take. She hugs me again, her shoulders relax as she lets out a sigh, and tells me we should hurry up, because she doesn't want to be late on her first day.

The playground is already filling up as we arrive. I've allowed her to travel the rest of the journey on my lap, and she only stops hugging me as we pass through the school gates.

'Are you going to be okay?' I ask, as she clambers off me, and reaches for her school bags on the handles of my chair.

She nods, with an assured smile.

'I love you, Grace, and I meant what I said. I want to hear about absolutely everything you do today, okay?'

She nods again, kisses my cheek, and hurries off to a group of three girls I recognise from her pre-school classes. I've never felt so proud and nervous, but she captures their attention immediately, and I can see the other girls hanging on her every word until the bell sounds and they hurry off towards the old brown building. She pauses only once to turn and wave in my direction, and then she is gone.

Chapter Forty-Three

Before – Morag

The sound of the school bell somewhere close by tells me I've managed to hold onto Daisy for as long as I can. I deliberately picked a scenic route to the school, different to the one I'd rehearsed taking, just in case Tommy and his people were there waiting for us.

I hardly slept a wink last night, and the lack of Angus' snoring echoing off the walls of our bedroom tells me he didn't fare much better. I just wish all of this could be over. The constant looking over our shoulders; the fear that he's always watching, waiting to strike; the inability to properly trust any other human being for fear they will let out our sordid secret. I will never willingly give Daisy back to Tommy. He isn't her father, not really. It may have been his sperm that fertilised her mother, but that is where his paternal responsibility began and ended.

There is a cool wind blowing this morning, and the sky

overhead is grey with cloud, and it's giving me such a sense of foreboding. I had considered keeping Daisy off school – phoning in to say she'd picked up a stomach bug – but I don't want her being prejudged by her teachers or children in her class.

She is squeezing my hand tightly as we head in through the entrance, and although she's hardly spoken a word all morning, I can tell she is anxious. I'm hoping it's just first-day nerves, and that yesterday's incident isn't playing on her mind. She officially should have experienced her first day at school a year ago, but we made the conscious decision to hold her back. A doctored birth certificate means everyone – including Daisy – believes she is about to turn five, when in fact it was her birthday ten months ago. All it means is she'll be one of the oldest children in her year group, and will probably develop quicker both academically and physically, but it is the only way we could think to keep Tommy and his network from her trail. He knows when she was born, but that information won't help him trace her through the education system.

Turning the final corner into the large grey playground, I immediately see Jess in her wheelchair at the far side of the perimeter, looking around, as if searching for someone; me. I knew she'd be here waiting, and that's another reason why I've waited until the last minute to bring Daisy inside the gates. I don't know how much of my conversation with Tommy she overheard, but even if she isn't working for him, I don't like that she saw me in such a vulnerable state.

The children are now lining up in front of their teachers, ready to be escorted inside. I stoop and hug Daisy tightly, but she offers little affection in return. I hope one day she'll understand why I took her away from that situation; that I only had her best interests at heart.

'Have a great day, wee one,' I whisper into her ear, holding back the urge to allow the emotion to escape the lump in my throat. 'I love you, Daisy.'

She doesn't respond, but I feel her hand gently pat my back, before pulling away, school bag on her shoulder and lunch bag in her hand, hurrying to join the line directly in front of her teacher Miss Danvers. She's Canadian, from what I recall, and such a pretty young thing. Her long caramel-coloured hair is tied in a thin ponytail; her high cheekbones and small pointy nose make her stand out from the other teachers beside her. Her beauty and thin frame wouldn't be out of place on a Parisian catwalk, but what stands out most is how young she looks. Does she really have the necessary experience to take care of a class full of four- and five-year-old children? Surely she was one of them fewer than twenty years ago. How can I be certain that she'll be able to cope with Daisy's little quirks, and give her all the attention she deserves?

Jess is still scanning the playground, searching, so I side-step, ducking down behind a couple of the other mums where she won't be able to see me, but where I can watch her, and see if she makes any kind of move on Daisy.

'Did you hear the latest?' one of the two women in front of me says to the other. 'She only went and got herself arrested yesterday. It's true, babe. I was there. Saw them wheeling her up the ramp and into the back of the paddy wagon myself!'

I catch a glimpse of Nadine, who I had the misfortune to be sat near at the parent-teacher meeting on Monday. Even at this early hour, her hair is straightened to within an inch of its life, and her lip gloss sparkles with glitter. The white denim jacket is too short in the sleeves, and doesn't cover the round bottom squashed into ridiculously tight white leggings. Anyone would think she was going out for the night with much younger friends, rather than dropping her daughter on the school run.

'I told you she was bad news. I just wish my Ava wasn't such good friends with her Grace. Don't get me wrong, babe, Grace is as sweet as they come, but if she's anything like Jess, then she's going to be trouble.'

I remain where I am, pretending to watch Daisy as she waits in line with the other children, but my attention is now diverted to the conversation between these two women.

'What was she arrested for?' the second woman asks.

'Don't know for sure, but the police van was parked in the middle of the street, and there was nothing subtle about the way they cuffed her hands and pushed her in. Here, I've got some photos of it on my phone.'

I lean a little closer as Nadine pulls out her mobile and thumbs the screen until she finds what she's looking for. It's not easy to see the image properly from where I'm standing, but I instantly recognise the boutique shop, where she happened to bump into me yesterday, in the background. Even from this distance, it's definitely Jess in the frame, but I still don't know what could have happened to lead the police to intercept her. And if they did arrest her, why is she freely moving about today?

I pull back as my conscience kicks in. There could be any number of reasons for the police to have spoken to Jess, and it isn't necessarily true that she was arrested at all. I can almost hear my own mother's words warning me of the dangers of idle gossip, particularly between mothers in the school playground.

The phone Angus has given to me beeps, and as I look at the message, I see it is from Lawrence, telling me he has arrived for our morning meeting. It was his idea to meet us at a café in town, as it's closer than me going all the way home. I also think he's keen to keep us away from that place in case Tommy has people watching it.

The lines of children are now being led into their respective classrooms. Standing at the back of the furthest line, Daisy towers above the blond boy in front of her, but there are others in the line of a similar height and build, so I'm certain nobody will question her age. As far as Daisy knows it is her birthday on Friday, so if anyone asks, she'll tell them it is so. She doesn't look back as she disappears behind a wall, and I let out the sigh that has been building inside me since I woke this morning. She is safe now. I've got her here, and for the next few hours I can rest easy, knowing he can't get to her.

Gripping the phone tightly, I back away from gossiping Nadine, and retrace my steps back out through the school gates. My gut is full of nervous energy at the prospect of the deal Angus thinks we can make with Tommy, but what choice do we have?

Chapter Forty-Four

Now

Mike headed back through the secured door, stopping when he reached the interview room, knocking twice and entering. The woman sitting across the desk wasn't what he had been expecting. In her early forties, her hair was a hive of sorts, but with loose ends straying out in all directions, making it look like she'd literally been dragged through a hedge. The half-rimmed glasses perched on the end of her nose were held by a beaded braid around her shoulders, and amazingly the woman had a scarf draped around her neck despite the late summer climate.

'I'm Detective Inspector Mike Ferry,' he said, sitting across from her and dismissing the uniformed officer who'd been standing patiently by the door. 'And you are?'

The woman confidently slid a business card across the table. 'Gail Rowson, I'm a reporter for the *Harrow Observer* online newspaper. Jess Donoghue is a former colleague and friend.'

Conscious that he only had her say-so for that, Mike chose his words carefully, not wanting to confirm or deny his interest in Jess Donoghue, nor the reason she was at the station, in case this reporter was just rustling for an exclusive. 'What can I do for you, Miss Rowson?'

'It's *Ms*, actually, but you can call me Gail. You said your name is Mike?'

'Why are you here, Gail?'

'I heard through a friend of mine that you'd brought in Jess on suspicion of murder, and I wanted to come down here and tell you it's impossible. I've known Jess for more than five years, and she wouldn't harm a fly.'

'I don't know who your source is, Gail, but nobody is currently being held at this police station on suspicion of murder.'

Pulling a sceptical frown, she reached down to her side and heaved a multi-coloured satchel, in keeping with her bohemian attire, onto the table. The bag jangled with key rings as she reached into it and withdrew a ring-bound notebook and flipped through the pages.

'My source confirmed that you, Detective Inspector Michael Ferry, have been appointed Senior Investigating Officer for the suspicious death of an as yet unidentified male at a residential premises in Northwood late last night. Jess Donoghue, a witness discovered at the scene, was taken into police custody.' She paused and fixed him with a hard stare. 'Stop me when I get it wrong.' Lowering the notepad and removing her glasses she clasped her hands together. 'I am not looking to create waves here, Mike. I have come here to help, not to look for salacious gossip. Jess is my friend, and I can tell you exactly why she was at that house last night.'

Narrowing his eyes, Mike nodded to give her the benefit of the doubt. 'Tell me what you know.'

Gail took a deep breath. 'I spoke with Jess yesterday afternoon. She called me at work and told me that she believes she has found a child abducted from Belfast, currently being raised by an older couple going by the name Morag and Angus Kilbride.'

Mike's ears pricked at mention of their names. 'Their daughter Daisy?'

Gail's lips curled upwards. 'So you know what I'm talking about? It was their house Jess was found at, wasn't it?'

Mike wasn't about to confirm any detail to a journalist he didn't know. 'Tell me about this missing child.'

Gail rifled through the satchel again, removing a handheld fan, small make-up bag, purse, cigarette case, lighter, two further notebooks, a diary, and a set of car keys. She finally removed an A4 envelope, which had been folded in half. Flattening the envelope, she pulled out two sheets of paper and handed them to him.

'Mia?' he questioned, scanning the top of the first page.

'Reported missing by her uncle after her mother was murdered in a paramilitary attack in east Belfast. Father's whereabouts are unknown.'

So much for her claiming she wasn't working on a story, Mike thought. 'And you think the Kilbrides' daughter Daisy is this missing girl Mia?'

'Jess did, and I believe she went to their house last night to confront them about it.'

It was hardly a smoking gun, but Mike wasn't yet ready to

rule any angle out of his investigation, especially with so many questions unanswered. 'Do you have anything more concrete I can work with?'

'Only my word that Jess isn't a killer. Why don't you tell me who the victim is, and then maybe I can—?'

'No, no, no,' Mike interrupted, now seeing through what he suspected was a fog of lies. 'I appreciate you coming here and telling me about Jess's suspicions about this little girl, but I'm not about to go on the record with you.' He slid his business card across the table. 'If you happen to learn anything else that might be useful to my investigation, then please do call, otherwise, I'd like to thank you for your time this morning.'

She didn't budge. 'There is one other thing you might be interested in.'

She was baiting him, and his gut feeling was to ignore it and leave the room, but time was not on his side. 'I'm waiting.'

Gail remained silent a moment longer, but clearly couldn't wait to share what was on her chest. 'After hearing how panicked Jess sounded yesterday, I did some digging into this Morag and Angus Kilbride, and do you know what I discovered?'

Mike remained silent.

'They don't exist,' Gail said triumphantly.

Mike frowned pessimistically. 'They don't exist, as in…?'

'They have no digital footprint whatsoever. No social media accounts; they're not registered to vote; and when I spoke to Bennett's – the agency they're letting through – it turns out they've paid their annual rent in advance. *In cash.*' Gail raised both eyebrows expectantly. 'Don't you find that all a little odd?'

All Mike could hear was an insatiable journalist taking

random facts and knitting them into some elaborate version of the truth. 'Not at all. There could be a hundred different reasons why this couple chose to pay their rent in advance.'

'Okay,' Gail challenged playfully. 'Name one.'

Mike thought quickly. 'Maybe they're conscientious tenants; maybe they came into some money, and decided they would invest it in their future; perhaps they don't like the stress of paying monthly. It doesn't mean they're guilty of abducting a child.'

'You must admit it does draw suspicion though. Why does anyone cover their tracks these days if not running from something or someone?'

'And who would that be?' Mike fired back.

Gail frowned, clearly not having got that far in her hypothesis.

Mike stood, keeping hold of the print-out from the missing people website. 'Thank you for your time, *Ms* Rowson. I'll have someone show you back to the front desk.'

Mike headed back upstairs and pinned the image of Mia to the soundboard near his desk. Was it possible that the Kilbrides – who he agreed looked too old to have a daughter so young – had in fact abducted a child? It seemed so far-fetched, but not impossible, and would certainly help explain why Jess was so agitated when confronted with Morag outside the station last night. What it didn't explain was how Charlie Donoghue had wound up with a kitchen knife in his neck.

Chapter Forty-Five

Before - Jess

She thinks I haven't spotted her skulking behind Nadine and Rita, but I have. I keep my eyes darting around the playground so that she doesn't realise I have her in my sights, but as she unceremoniously sidesteps away from the playground, I am on to her. Holding my breath and counting to ten, I slowly wheel away in the same direction. I need to know once and for all why Daisy uttered those four little words, and why Morag made those threats on the phone in Harrow yesterday.

Breaking through the gates, she dashes suddenly to the left, as if she knows she's being followed and is trying to escape. I have lost sight of her, and pump my arms faster in an effort to catch up. Slowing as I make it to the gates, I allow my gaze to casually scan the traffic in the road, before spotting a gap between the cars and hurrying across. I just make it before an approaching car blares its horn. The driver sneers through the window as he passes by, and I'm tempted to shout something back at him, but don't want to draw attention to myself. Stupid driver was coming far too quickly off that roundabout, and has no right to question my crossing at the island.

Morag has stopped and is looking towards where the horn blared, but she can't see me as I'm behind a stationary bus. It gives me a moment to get my breath back, and as the bus pulls away, I see that she is on the move again. We're headed towards Northwood town centre, but it's also the direction of her home, and it could simply be that that is where she's returning. I'm happy to confront her in public or on her doorstep; makes no odds to me. The more public the encounter the better.

The traffic flows slowly, the majority probably parents returning from dropping children off, and the remainder running late for work. I miss the routine of waking up with a real purpose. If I'd had the choice, I never would have quit my job at the newspaper, but it wasn't satisfactory for either party, and I'm not sure I have the energy for regular office hours at the moment. Charlie doesn't realise how lucky he is to have the freedom to escape home life for a few hours each day. I don't doubt his job is stressful – God knows Doug really makes him work for his wage – but I do envy him that.

Morag has upped her pace, and although she occasionally glances behind her, I'm pretty certain she doesn't realise I'm on her tail across the road. Heading past the art and furniture store, she scurries along the pavement like a woman on a mission, but what is she really up to?

She pauses by the flower stall at the opening to Northwood Tube station without really looking interested in the flowers. It is as if she is waiting for someone, or *something*, to happen.

After what must be a minute, she turns and stares back along the road she has just walked, but she doesn't see me as I have ducked behind a vehicle parked outside the dry cleaners, just down the hill from the station. Her behaviour is very odd. It's like watching some black and white spy movie, where the protagonist knows they are being tailed, and she is doing her best to shake it. Does she sense my presence?

She is on the move again, turning the corner past the station and proceeding towards the heart of the town. I give her a count of ten before emerging from my hidden position, and as I make it back up to the peak of the hill, I see her talking to an unfamiliar man. He is the same height as her, maybe twenty years younger and with the brightest ginger hair and beard I've ever seen. He is wearing a charcoal suit and matching blue shirt-tie combo. They are standing so close that they must know each other, but they aren't moving so I need to duck out of sight again.

And that's when the breath catches in my throat. Directly across the street from me, my eyes fall on Charlie. Bold as brass, arm looped around a Latino woman with a trim figure and tight red skirt. Her obviously dyed hair glistens despite the hidden sun, and as the two of them laugh at something Charlie has said, I watch in stunned awe as she places her hand on Charlie's cheek and rubs it intimately.

Blinking rapidly, I don't want to believe what I'm seeing. Surely I'm imagining it, or stuck in some weird dream. Not Charlie. Not *my* Charlie.

She lowers her hand, and reaches into her handbag for something, as he leans forwards and kisses her cheek, before she withdraws a set of car keys and unlocks the fancy soft-top sports car they're standing beside. The colour matches her bum-clenching skirt, and they laugh more as she heads around to the driver's side, while Charlie – *my husband* – climbs into the passenger seat.

The soft roof lowers and I can see the backs of their heads as they continue to laugh – laughing at my naivety, no doubt. The engine roars to life and they disappear up the road with a screech of tyres.

This can't be real.

My Charlie wouldn't have an affair.

We fell in love together. We had a plan to start a family and slowly fall more and more in love with one another into old age. An affair was never on the cards.

Tracy's words echo in my mind again: *caught him shagging some client he was working for up in Barnstaple. Apparently they'd been at it for months behind my back.*

How could I have been so ignorant?

It was all there before me, but I'd blindly refused to see the bigger picture: the late nights at the office; the sudden last-minute trips away; the messages on his phone that have kept him so amused; and then the call from Kerry saved under Doug's profile. Is this Latino woman Kerry? Or was that just a cover name she gave me in panic when I answered Charlie's phone on Monday night?

How could I have not seen it sooner? Why wouldn't he stray, with everything that has happened in the last year? First the accident, then losing Luke, then the paralysis and my uncontrollable weight. Charlie's still a good-looking man – why didn't I suspect that he would stray? I've done little to keep him interested. How naïve I've been to think he would stay loyal to our marriage vows, a pact made before God.

Pulling out my phone, I dial his number, keen to confront

him in his lies, but despite the phone ringing, it goes straight to answerphone.

Don't ignore me, Charlie, I want to scream into the street, and hit redial. The answerphone cuts in for a second time.

Why didn't I think to take a picture of them, so he wouldn't be able to deny what I saw? That was stupid! I won't let him get way with making a fool of me. I dial his number again, but this time the answerphone cuts in without a ring.

He's turned his phone off so he doesn't have to lie to me about what he's up to. Why didn't I see any of this sooner? The writing's been on the wall for so long, and I've been hiding from it.

The pills. Of course, it was those antidepressants and painkillers that were clouding my mind. That's why he's been so keen for me to stay on them. He wanted me not to focus on the truth of what's been going on.

Does he know?

Does he know that I'd been drinking on the day of the accident? Was that the turning point? Does he blame me for Luke dying? Of course he does, but why hasn't he let on sooner? Why has he allowed me to go on believing that we could work through these obstacles?

My heart is breaking, and I can feel every sinew as it shatters beyond my control.

Maybe he doesn't want to work through our issues. Maybe that's it. Maybe he's been looking for a way out; waiting for his chance to escape me.

But he'd never leave Grace; he loves her too much to be one of those dads who willingly walk out on their kids.

Of course! He doesn't want to walk out on Grace, he wants *me* out of the way so he can move on with his daughter. That must be why he wasn't willing to support my suspicions about Morag and Daisy's odd relationship. In fact, he probably *wants* me declared mentally unstable so it's easier for him to secure custody of Grace. That must be why he's been pushing counselling and all those pills. How long has he been planning this? Was it after Luke died, or before even?

I have been such a fool!

But no more. I know now what he is up to. Thank God I'd stopped taking the antidepressants before his plan was realised.

Turning back to where Morag and the ginger businessman had been standing, I see they have gone, but I'm not even upset. I have learned an important truth today, and now I need to do whatever it takes to stop Charlie succeeding.

Nobody will take my daughter from me. Nobody.

Chapter Forty-Six

Before - Morag

Finding a table away from the window, I can't help glancing out through the sheet of glass to make sure Jess isn't there gawping. She was distracted when we slipped away, so I'm hoping she doesn't know we're in here, but it will soon become evident that she *is* following me if she miraculously appears at one of the other tables. The café is surprisingly busy considering the time of day, and it's difficult to assess whether the proprietor relies on foot traffic or if the handful of customers are regulars.

Lawrence is at the counter, carefully rifling through the basket of teabag options the bored-looking barista is holding. Too many tea choices these days. What's wrong with a standard cup of good old-fashioned breakfast tea?

He must feel me watching, and eventually makes his choice, withdrawing a pouch and handing it to the barista before joining me at the small square table.

'When is Angus joining us?' I ask, before he's had chance to draw breath.

I already know what he's going to say, as his nose scrunches into an awkward position. 'He wanted me to tell you he has gone to speak to the bank about a loan. He wants to know how much he can afford to offer to get Tommy off your backs once and for all.'

His going without me stings, but I don't let it show, keeping my face placid as if this statement isn't news. 'Do you really think Tommy will accept a pay-off after all this time?'

He considers this question, as if trying to choose the most diplomatic response without stitching himself up should things go pear-shaped. 'There's no reason to think he wouldn't consider a fair price. He's a businessman, after all, and from what I've heard from the contacts I engaged with, things aren't going all that well for him at the moment. A reasonable offer might be just the trick.'

I don't believe him, despite his best efforts to placate me. He doesn't know Tommy like I do. No amount of money will ever be enough. Too much water has passed under the bridge for that.

The barista appears at our table with a tray of drinks, slopping my tea as she almost drops it to the table, offering no apology in return.

'What happens if he refuses Angus's offer?' I say, watching his eyes.

He can't meet my stare. 'You have two choices: you go to the authorities or you keep running, but I would strongly advise you to take the first option. From what I've heard about Tommy Chamberlain, he isn't someone you want on your tail.'

'He went to my sister's house,' I say remorsefully, thinking back to Tuesday morning's call with Gwen. 'I need to know if she's safe.'

He unlocks his phone. 'If you give me her name, address, and phone number I can look into it for you. Check that she's okay.'

It isn't enough, I want to say, but don't. That's why I haven't tried contacting her again. Even if Tommy had hurt her to get to me, Gwen would never admit it. The only thing I can do is make the journey north and physically check on her myself. But at what cost? If Tommy is still up there I'll be heading into the lion's den.

I've seen first-hand what a monster Tommy Chamberlain can be, and I'll never forgive myself for how he treated Daisy's mum while I stood by and allowed it to happen. I didn't know for certain just how bad he was, although I had my suspicions, but Sharon spoke so highly of him that I allowed myself to believe that things between them were as passionate and loving as she claimed. The occasional bruise on her arm or torso was always casually explained away as a clumsy fall or pushing herself too hard at the gym. With all my nursing experience, I should have seen that she was hiding the truth from her colleagues, and only sharing one side of their life together. I think deep down I suspected that things couldn't be as rosy as she made out, but she made it difficult to doubt her story, always so pretty and full of life, and when she fell pregnant a year later, she kept telling everyone how blessed she was. So convincing that I found myself wanting to believe in the fairy-tale.

Sharon didn't cope so well after Daisy was born. Post-natal depression can be such a heartbreaking condition, and it is so difficult to get the right treatment if you refuse to acknowledge the problem. What is it they say about medical professionals being the last to admit when something is wrong? Never truer than in Sharon's case. Maybe if I hadn't been so keen to help out with minding Daisy, Sharon might have sought help sooner, and been less reliant on Tommy to get her over her troubles.

I remember the first time I spotted the red needle-point mark on her arm. She brushed it off as a routine blood test, but when I saw her a week later, and saw the additional spots, I knew that she had a problem. Whether the addiction to heroin took hold before the pregnancy or in the aftermath I'll never know. I didn't want to confront her about it, because I'd grown quite fond of wee Daisy, but I couldn't stand by and idly allow her to put that child's life in danger.

In hindsight, I maybe could have approached it in a different way. I opted for honesty when more tact was required. I didn't expect her to physically throw me out of her flat, nor did I anticipate that she would up and leave the area without so much as a goodbye.

She turned up at our home in Aberdeen one Christmas night, wearing barely more than a jumper and T-shirt, and with Daisy swaddled close to her. She had hiked through a foot of snow to make it to our place, and was near death when she came in. She slept for two days straight, leaving Angus and me to care for wee Daisy. When Sharon did surface, she was so agitated and the track marks on her arms told me everything I needed to know about why she had sought us out. She said she wanted to get clean, and that she had left Tommy for good this time. I hadn't even known she'd tried to leave him several times before.

I told her she could stay with us for as long as she needed, and that we'd keep both of them safe. I even took unpaid leave so I could watch over Daisy while Sharon got herself cleaned up and off the heroin. She started a programme at the hospital, and several weeks later was looking more like her old, happier self. She never did tell me the whole truth about their relationship, but the wounded look she wore whenever she spoke of him said all I needed to know.

Tommy found out where she was and came calling on Valentine's Day. Despite all her earlier protestations, Sharon and Daisy were gone the next day. I never did find out how he managed to squirm his way back into her life, but that was the last time I saw her until the hospital in Manchester called and told us she was in intensive care. Turned out she'd listed me as her next of kin.

She'd been beaten within an inch of her life. For the first few days she wasn't able to speak as her jaw was wired to help the fractures heal. Two-year-old Daisy was under the supervision of social services, but they eventually released her into our care. Tommy was on the run from the police, having been identified as Sharon's attacker by a witness to the vicious assault she suffered.

Sharon was in and out of consciousness for many days, and when she did speak she vowed she would never return to him. Her priority was to keep Daisy safe, and out of his clutches. He was named on her birth certificate, and Sharon was terrified he would kill her to get to Daisy, so she made us promise to take Daisy back to our home and away from Tommy for good. We probably would have agreed to anything she'd asked that day.

The two of them moved back in with us while Sharon recuperated, and it was probably one of the happiest times in my life. We were like a proper family. I took leave from work again to help Sharon with Daisy, and then one morning, Sharon told me she was going for an interview in the city centre, because she wanted to be able to pay her way. She asked me to watch over Daisy for a few hours, and... I never saw her again.

When she hadn't returned by dinnertime, I knew something was wrong. We couldn't get hold of her, and deep down feared that Tommy had to be involved somehow. I didn't want to think that she could have ever dreamed of going back to him after everything, but when the two police officers turned up at our front door, a part of me died that day.

There had been a fire at Tommy's house in Manchester, and when it was extinguished, they discovered her body. It was impossible to say whether she'd been beaten before her body had been left in the building, or whether she had been given an overdose before the fire started, but I have no doubt in my mind who caused the fire.

It is for this reason that I know Angus's plan is destined to fail.

Lawrence is telling me not to worry when I hear my phone ringing in my bag. Hoping for good news, I answer it without checking the display, but I'm not expecting to hear the school administrator telling me I have to come to the school urgently because of an incident with Daisy.

Chapter Forty-Seven

Now

He hadn't taken his eyes from the black and white print out that Gail Rowson had provided. The girl in the image with the dark hair looked like any other sweet and innocent three-year-old, and to read the tragic story of her disappearance, he was surprised he hadn't heard of her sooner. With so many children going missing each year across the UK, the support of the public to help reunite parents and runaways was hugely important. Yet not every missing child story made it into the national press. Thankfully, most missing children were usually discovered safe and well within thirty-six hours of their disappearance, and these happy endings were rarely deemed newsworthy.

In the cases where the thirty-six-hour deadline expired, it was less common that the story ended happily. Mike had experienced enough of those situations first-hand, and understood why the Chief Super had recently put together a crew of wannabe detectives to work their way through historic cases to finally bring peace of mind to the families who still clung to the possibility that their missing relative or friend would be discovered alive and well.

'What you looking at?' DS Nazia Hussain asked, placing a fresh mug of coffee on Mike's desk.

Mike's eyes remained fixed on the print-out. 'What was your take on Jess Donoghue? Do you think she is a cold-blooded killer, a woman desperately defending her own life, or just in the wrong place at the wrong time?'

Nazia frowned at the question. 'You want my honest opinion?'

Mike nodded. 'Please.'

'Okay.' Nazia hesitated. 'I think she absolutely stuck that knife in our victim, and all the fuss she made last night was merely an effort to instigate an insanity plea, so she can walk away from what she's done.'

Mike hadn't expected such an emphatic response from someone he generally considered cool, calm, and collected. 'That reporter reckons the girl in the image is the daughter of Morag and Angus Kilbride. Claims that's the real reason Jess Donoghue went to their house yesterday.' Mike leaned over and pulled the print-out from the soundboard. 'Would you do me a favour and see what else you can find out about this girl? See who reported her missing; whether there's an open investigation with police in Belfast. It's probably nothing, but I'd hate to leave a loose end untied.'

Nazia took the print-out.

'Oh, and thanks for the coffee,' Mike added.

Chapter Forty-Eight

Before – Jess

The lactic acid burns in my arms as I reach the top of my road, and my entire body feels as though someone has been squirting me with a hosepipe. I can hear Mum pottering about upstairs when I enter the house, but she must not hear me, as she doesn't call out. I head straight through to my bedroom, the ache in the base of my spine unbearable. Pulling the chair to a stop near the bed, I launch myself forward, landing face-first on the mattress, stretched out. This is how I remain for what must be several minutes, until the pain finally begins to subside, and I'm able to push myself over and onto my back. A sweaty outline remains on the bed sheet, as if marking out where a dead body was discovered. It only serves to show how much weight I've put on since becoming confined to the chair. No wonder Charlie has strayed.

I push the thought to the back of my mind, and focus on why I was so eager to get home. The laptop is resting against the edge of the bedside table, and having sat up against my pillows and headboard, I reach for it and lift the lid. The battery indicator warns that I only have thirty per cent charge left. The charging cable is nowhere in sight, and I have a vague recollection that Charlie was using it last in the kitchen. My strength has yet to return, and so I will just have to work quickly.

Opening a fresh internet page, I type in the missing people URL. I know I'm not crazy. Proving my suspicions about Morag abducting Daisy may be the only way to prevent anyone declaring me an unfit mother.

Each of the faces on the screen before me belongs to a child who either ran away or was taken from their home against their will. Each has friends or family who care enough to have reported them missing and would give anything to see them once again. Anyone who went missing before five years ago is irrelevant to my search parameters. There are some who have been missing since the early eighties, children who would be older than I am now, assuming they are still alive. Their faces are those of children, but they would look so different to that now, making them almost impossible to find.

Using the filter, I also narrow the age range of the children I am looking for. I can only assume that Morag has been honest about Daisy's age; she certainly doesn't look or act older or younger than a four-, nearly five-year-old. I finally adjust the filter to rule out boys, and see a single page of eight thumbnails staring back at me.

My fingers are trembling as I click on the first image, and a fresh page with details and the case background opens on the laptop screen. The child in the image has fair hair, and a twinkle in her eyes. It is an exceptionally cute photograph, with a brightly decorated Christmas tree filling the frame. The girl, Cindy, was aged three when she was last seen. Reported missing by her mother, who claimed her estranged father had snatched her and returned to his native Iran. Now that I look at the image more closely, I can see the girl's skin is more golden than Daisy's, but I never would have thought to guess her parents weren't both Caucasian. I enlarge the image, and study the position of the nose, the closeness of the eyebrows to the eyes, and how the lips are curled into an excited grin. Closing my eyes, I picture Daisy's long, dark locks, the sadness and betrayal in her dark eyes. Even if Morag was deliberately colouring Daisy's hair to cover her tracks, I am fairly certain that Daisy is not Cindy.

I tab to the next case. The girl here – Jacinta – has very dark hair, but the positioning of her nose and eyes looks all wrong. She was last seen a year ago, walking to a birthday party at a neighbour's house. I quickly discover that Jacinta was nearly six years old when she was last seen, and it seems the filter has failed to block her from my list, so I tab to the next case.

The image here takes longer to load, and when it does a pair of emerald eyes fills the screen, hair a chestnut brown, but hanging just below the ears. I gasp, as three-year-old Mia gazes at something just off camera. It isn't a full-front exposure, so it is difficult to tell whether the nose is quite right, and given the image must be nearly two years old, it's possible that the tone of her skin might have changed slightly, particularly if she'd been living further north when the snap was captured. I close my eyes and picture the terror in Daisy's green-brown stare as she whispered those four little words in the playground on Thursday. My eyes snap open and I focus on the face before me.

Could it be?

The doubt in my mind is far softer than it had been with Cindy and Jacinta.

Am I crazy, or have I actually discovered who Daisy really is? I push the laptop away and take a deep breath, trying to steady my racing heart, and to consider the discovery in a more cautious manner. I try to think of all the reasons that Daisy cannot be Mia. Morag would have to have presented the local authority with a copy of Daisy's birth certificate to register her for school. How would they cover the fact that she had been born with the name Mia, but was now called Daisy? Not impossible, but it poses issues.

What would Charlie say? He'd tell me I was seeing things that aren't there. He'd say my anxiety about Daisy's confession is brought on by the medication, like Dr Tegan suggested, and the fact that I have unresolved questions about my own adoption. He doesn't know I'm no longer taking those pills, and that my focus has never been clearer.

I pull the laptop back and look at the face again. On second glance I am slightly less convinced that Mia is Daisy, but not enough not to dig further. Scrolling down I read the case history. Mia was living in Belfast when her mother was murdered. When the police discovered the body, an uncle reported that Mia was missing, and is now keen to be reunited with his niece. There have been reported sightings of Mia in the northeast and northwest of England, and even as far north as Edinburgh.

It can't be a coincidence that the public have reported seeing Mia in Scotland. My pulse quickens again. I'm not imagining this picture, the facial similarities between the girls, and the locations in their backstories. It isn't going to be enough to convince cynical Charlie and Rosie. I need something more concrete before I present them with my belief. I need someone who knows how to dig deeper and find meaning in unrelated facts.

Reaching for my handbag, which is still squashed into the cushion of my wheelchair, I remove my mobile and search for Gail's number. The phone connects after four rings.

'Hey, Jess,' she says, her voice sounding far away. 'Now's not a great time, as I'm in the middle of something. Can I call you back?'

I look at Mia's emerald eyes. 'No, I need your help right now, Gail. Please, it's important.'

The harshness of my tone has surprised even me, and I'm relieved when Gail doesn't instantly disconnect the call.

I hear keys tapped, and then her voice is louder, the phone now properly in place and her attention no longer distracted. 'What's going on? Are you okay?'

'I'm fine, Gail, but I think I've stumbled into something and I think you may be the only person who can help me find the truth.'

She listens patiently as I explain that first encounter with Daisy, how terrified she looked as she spoke those four little words, how that fear had grown as Morag had approached, and then how secretive Morag is about her past. I don't miss out a single step, and move straight into what I've found online, and the background of Mia.

'You think this missing girl could be Daisy?' Gail concludes, reading her notes back.

I'm delighted she has yet to question my sanity, but like any true reporter, Gail can sniff out great stories.

I look at Mia's face again. 'I'm not saying it is definitely her, but the resemblance is tough to ignore. It all fits: the date she disappeared, the fact that she's been spotted in areas I know Morag and Angus were based. I know I sound like some paranoid loon, but what if it is her, and we manage to get Mia back to her uncle and family?'

There is a long pause on the line. I've never known Gail be so quiet for so long. My heart sinks as the silence continues. She must be trying to find the right words to let me down.

'I'm on the site now,' she eventually says. 'I think I've found the girl you're talking about. Dark hair, from Belfast, right?'

'That's her,' I agree quickly.

'She'd be five, according to this. Does that fit?'

'She started in reception today and it's her fifth birthday on Friday from what Morag told me.'

'Leave this with me and I'll make some calls and see what else I can find out about this Morag and Angus Kilbride. Are we still meeting on Friday for payday lunch? I can share what I've found then, if that's okay?' Gail asks.

'Absolutely,' I reply, my eyes watering with happy tears.

'Great. Unless there's anything else, I really must go, Jess, I'm sorry.'

I return the phone to my handbag with a sense of satisfaction, but the laptop beeps to say the battery is nearly drained. There is a contact form for anyone with information about Mia, and without thinking I open it and type in my belief that she is alive and well and living in Northwood.

Chapter Forty-Nine

Before – Morag

Arriving at the school, I'm half-expecting to see all three divisions of the emergency services waiting for me. I could just imagine Tommy rocking up here, demanding to see Daisy and telling anyone who'll listen just what Angus and I did. The playground is empty, however, and as I make my way to the school office, sectioned away from the main school grounds, my mind returns to exactly what could have warranted the school calling me in the middle of the day.

'An incident with Daisy' could be any number of things: a bout of sickness; an argument with another child; an accident resulting in an injury requiring medical attention. My heart is racing as I approach the window into the administrator's office.

'I had a telephone call about my daughter Daisy,' I say, failing to keep the anxiety from my voice.

The administrator looks at me dumbstruck, like she

cannot believe someone as old as me could be responsible for any student attending the school. Or it could just be that we've never met before and so she doesn't know who Daisy is.

'What is your child's name?' she says.

'Daisy Kilbride,' I say, adding, 'Today's her first day.'

Something fires in the woman's mind, and she snaps her fingers at me. 'Oh yes, I remember. I was the one who called. Can you step inside here for a moment, please?'

Doing as instructed, I head through the large fire door to the right of the window, and find little more than a box room, with filing cabinets lining every wall. There are no windows in the room, save for the hatch we've just spoken through, and so the room is heavily reliant on the overhead filament, which gives off an irritating whirr, like there is a wasp's nest just beyond the stained ceiling tiles.

The administrator is the wrong side of overweight, and the long denim skirt and knee-length black boots do little to compliment her figure. The thin woollen jumper accentuates her curves, and if she'd just smile a little, her frosty exterior would quickly diminish. Instead, she has the look of a woman bored by her chosen profession and only undertaking her duties in a half-arsed manner.

'There's a problem with the emergency contact paperwork Daisy brought in today,' she says, reaching for a ring binder on the desk, and flipping through the thin plastic wallets inside, until she finds what she's looking for and removes a sheet of paper. She places it on her desk, beckoning me to sit in the other remaining chair. I recognise Angus's handwriting immediately, though the green form itself isn't familiar.

'One of the phone numbers listed – the one for you in fact –

is saying it's disconnected. The mobile number for your husband is what I managed to reach you on this morning.'

I knew Angus had removed the battery and SIM card from the previous burn phone, but I hadn't realised he'd formally cancelled the number.

'I lost my phone,' I say quickly. 'My husband has lent me his until we get a replacement.'

She studies my face, before drawing a line through the number listed against the word 'Mother'. 'So, is this now your new number, or will you be getting a new phone, and this one returned to your husband?'

I honestly don't have an answer, and still don't understand what has happened to Daisy. 'I'll probably get a new one at some point, but can you not just list this one for both of us?'

She frowns. 'We prefer to have alternative methods for contacting parents in case one of you is unavailable to talk. Well, like this morning for example. If you could let us have the new number as soon as you know it, we'll get our records updated.'

That can't be the only reason they've called me in. They wouldn't have known my old number was no longer working had they not tried to contact me in the first place. Plus, it seems a little over-the-top to call me in urgently for something so trivial.

'Was there anything else?' I ask anxiously.

She studies the piece of paper. 'Yes, there was a discrepancy with the date of birth on the form.' She points her pen at the top section of the form. 'You've listed Daisy's date of birth as 3rd November 2013, but we have it recorded as 13th September 2014.'

Angus must have tried to complete the form to save me the

effort, but he's put Daisy's original date of birth, rather than the one we'd doctored on her birth certificate. I could kill him, but need to stay composed.

Withdrawing my reading glasses, I study the date, straining to think of a legitimate excuse that won't cause this woman to question our entire story. Like a house of cards, only a little breeze will be enough to bring all the lies tumbling down.

'My husband completed the form,' I say carefully, choosing to partially rely on the truth. 'His memory isn't what it once was. Wait till I tell him he put the wrong date of birth on the form.' I chuckle light-heartedly. 'He is terrible with dates; never remembers my birthday, nor our anniversary.' I pause to check if she believes my excuse, or whether she's about to signal for some troop of police to cart me away.

Her face remains straight, giving nothing away. 'So which date is correct?'

'Her date of birth is 13th September. She turns five on Friday. Surely you've still got the copy of her birth certificate we supplied when applying for her place?'

The administrator puts a line through the date on the sheet, and writes the new date in its place. 'I'm going to need you to initial the two changes, so that our records show you wanted the changes made.'

I take the pen and scribble my initials on the page. 'Is there anything else?'

She double-checks the form again, before slipping it back into the plastic wallet in the folder. She turns back, and there is just a hint of a smile. 'That is all.'

I let out the breath I've been holding for too long, and stand to leave.

'Oh, no, wait,' she calls out just as I've reached the door.

'There was something else.' She hands me a post-it note. 'Daisy's teacher Miss Danvers said Daisy didn't bring a pair of wellington boots in with her today. It was part of the list of items each child is required to keep at the school for rainy days and the like. Can you make sure she brings some in tomorrow? Oh, and make sure her name is clearly written on the inside of the boot, in case any other child has the same pair.'

I can picture the pair of wellington boots in a carrier bag on the staircase, but with everything going on this morning, I must have forgotten to pick them up.

'I'll make sure I remember them tomorrow,' I promise, relieved to slip back out of the building. The temperature is stifling, and I can't escape the feeling that I'm being watched, though I appear to be alone by the door.

Chapter Fifty

Now

'Mike, we've got an ID on the victim,' Polly said, slamming down the phone on her desk. 'Confirmation should be coming through any minute,' she added, approaching and pulling over a vacant chair. 'That was Dr Murphy at the mortuary, and she's had a hit on the victim's dental records.'

Mike refreshed the team inbox until the new email arrived. He opened the attachment and his eyes danced across the screen, searching for Charlie Donoghue's name. He frowned when he couldn't see it.

'Who on earth is Tommy Chamberlain?' Polly asked, eyes also glued to the screen.

Mike sat back and found where she was reading. The name was familiar, but he couldn't at first place why, and then he remembered the restraining order that Angus Kilbride's name had been linked to. It couldn't be the same person, yet he didn't believe in coincidences. Loading MOSES, he typed in Kilbride's name, and pointed for Polly to read.

'There isn't a lot here,' she said. 'You think this Tommy Chamberlain knows the Kilbrides then?'

It was the only conclusion Mike could draw in the moment. 'Find out what you can about him. Phone the copper who filed the original report.' Mike pointed at the name. 'Here you go: PS Rupert MacTavish. Ask him what he knows and see if they have a photograph on file they can send down to verify Dr Murphy's findings.'

Polly wheeled her chair away, leaving Mike to stand and head into the Incident Room, and wipe Charlie Donoghue's name from beneath the dry-wipe board, replacing it with the name Tommy Chamberlain. A knock at the door caused him to turn.

'Mike? Carla and I have managed to disprove Morag Kilbride's alibi for yesterday afternoon,' DS Nazia Hussain said. 'She claimed she hadn't returned home after collecting daughter Daisy from school, right? We have her on a neighbour's security camera returning home shortly before four, and then there is no sign of her going back out. We have footage from the opposite end of the street confirming she didn't leave the property, certainly not via the front of the property.'

Mike frowned. 'What do you mean?'

Nazia stepped into the room and showed Mike the piece of paper in her hand, an aerial shot of the property. 'There is a gate at the rear of the property, which leads to a footpath, which leads into a neighbouring estate. Morag Kilbride was home by 4pm, but wasn't at the property when the first responders arrived, meaning she must have left via this rear exit somewhere between four and seven. It doesn't put her in the house when the victim entered, but it does pose the question as to why she lied in her statement.'

'We need to get her back in,' Mike said affirmatively. 'This time I want it done properly. I want her booked in, prints taken, and urgent confirmation from Scientific Services as to whether her prints match those on the knife. The blade was from a block in her kitchen, so I would expect there to be prints, but what I want to know is whether any were made post-trauma.'

Nazia nodded and peeled away.

Mike moved to the side of the Incident Room and called out to the team. 'Our victim is one Tommy Chamberlain. I want to know everything about him: where he lived; how he knows Jess Donoghue and Morag Kilbride; what he was doing in that house last night; and why he wasn't carrying a mobile phone or any identification. Can someone also tell me where the hell Charlie Donoghue is?'

'I might be able to answer that,' announced a voice from the far side of the office.

Turning, Mike didn't recognise the athletic woman in a charcoal-coloured business suit, her blonde hair scraped back into a high ponytail.

'I'm PC Rosie Donoghue,' the woman said. 'My brother is downstairs in my car and he's frantic with worry.'

Chapter Fifty-One

Before - Jess

Before I know it, the clock is showing it's half past two and I need to collect Grace from school. I haven't even eaten. In fact, the last few hours have passed with me not so much as moving from my chair in my bedroom. Have I really been sitting here thinking about Morag and Daisy for that long? I'm sure I wasn't asleep, but I can't account for the lost time.

My arms carry a residual ache from this morning's exertion, but I push through the pain, and am a sweaty mess as I wheel in through the recently painted school gates. The playground is lined by close to a hundred casually dressed parents, eagerly awaiting first-day news from their little ones. I find a gap in the crowd, and stare out across the concrete, not certain which door Grace will emerge from.

I wish I'd given myself more time to get here, so I wouldn't look such a mess. I can see Nadine – perfect makeup, hair like she's just stepped from the salon, and model-thin frame – a few metres away. She nods in my direction, before continuing a conversation with the woman next to her, whom I don't recognise. To my right there is indistinguishable excited chatter, and I feel so lonely with nobody that I know well enough to chat to.

I do hope Grace had a good day. She's such a clever and outgoing girl that she's probably managed to befriend everyone in her class already, but I remind myself that projecting my own expectations is dangerous, and I need to just wait and hear what she has to report. It is so warm today, and the sun's rays burn down on all of us. I think I'll take Grace for an ice-cream on the way home as a celebration of her surviving her first day, though that will mean having to take a detour on the way back, and I'm not sure my arms and spine can take it, but I want to spoil Grace, especially after the day I've had. At least she's not lying to me yet.

Minutes pass with no sign of Grace. The bell has sounded and the playground is filling with children, but where on earth is my daughter?

I scan the playground for any sign of her. Maybe she pointed me out to Miss Danvers while I was distracted by Nadine. It is so difficult to distinguish any children from where I am seated, as the crowd of parents have now spilled from their boundary, and the playground is filled with different colours and shapes heading in a multitude of directions. It's like watching bubbles fighting to be first to the top in a glass of lemonade.

Where is Grace?

As the crowd begins to slowly disperse, I still can't see any child wandering aimlessly, searching for their increasingly terrified parent. I need to make urgent contact with Miss Danvers. What if something has happened to Grace, and she is ill or hurt inside the school? Shouldn't they have notified me if that is the case? All the guidance we'd had to read before the first day has blanked from my mind. What if Grace signalled to me, but before she made it over someone snatched her?

Releasing the brake on the wheels, I move forward through the ever-thinning crowd, my eyes scanning left and right as I go, searching for Grace. There are so many similarly dressed boys and girls tearing around, burning off their last reserves of pent-up energy, but there is still no sign of my daughter.

'Hey there,' I hear Miss Danvers call towards me in her upbeat and jolly Canadian voice, 'Mrs Donoghue, right? Grace's mom.'

I nod feverishly at mention of my daughter's name. 'I can't find her. Where is she?'

'It's nothing to worry about,' she says, with less enthusiasm, 'but I wondered if I could have a word with you inside? There was an incident earlier, and I think it would be good if we tackled it head-on.'

'What kind of incident?' I want to shout. Does she mean an incident involving Grace? Before I can question further, she turns on her heel and ushers me towards the old brick building. My heart is racing, as my paranoia takes control of all my rational thoughts.

The classroom is so much smaller than the one I remember from my own childhood, but then I suppose that's because I'm now so much bigger. The smell of fresh paint hangs in the air, along with the scent of Miss Danvers's expensive perfume. The walls are covered with posters promoting the merits of phonetics, brightly coloured animals holding up letters and enunciating them in a visual way. There are basic sums on the dry-wipe board, suggesting that mathematics was the last subject touched upon today, and against the back wall there are a variety of painted pictures drying and awaiting hanging on a large notice board above them.

'Take a seat,' she says, before quickly admonishing herself for the slip. 'Sorry, I meant—'

I wheel to the side of the desk, next to the vacant chair that is impossibly small for an adult to occupy.

Miss Danvers slides onto her own chair beside the desk, and presses her palms onto the table top. 'Thanks for popping in, and I'm sorry we're having to meet like this so early into the term.'

The heat in the room is stifling, and as much as I want to wipe away the sheen building at my hairline, I'm reluctant to draw more attention to how inferior I feel opposite someone who is naturally pretty, and clearly not short of male attention. All I can hear is the thumping of my heart and pulse, beating out a rhythm akin to a funeral march. There's still no sign of Grace, and as I watch Miss Danvers, hunting for any hint of what might have happened, I am terrified that something awful has happened to Grace.

'How would you describe Grace's behaviour at home?' Miss Danvers asks, snapping my focus back to her.

'What? I... um, she's a very polite little girl. I don't understand.'

The question has thrown me. What does Grace's home life have to do with whatever accident has befallen her?

'Would you say she understands the difference between right and wrong? As in, would you feel confident that if she did something bad, she'd know it was wrong before she did it?'

My brow must furrow, as Miss Danvers leans a little closer, and tries again.

'I'm just trying to establish how well she is adjusted and what boundaries have been set in place regarding retaliatory behaviour.'

'Has something happened to Grace?' I try, still unable to fathom why she's so interested in things at home. 'Where is she?'

'Oh, Grace is fine, she's in the room next door, drawing a picture,' she replies, nodding to a door over my shoulder.

I crane my neck so I can see into the adjoined classroom where my beautiful girl is deliberating over which colour crayon to use next. Her head is down, and she doesn't appear to be hurt or upset as she selects a crayon and presses it to the page.

The relief washes over me, and for the first time in hours, the tension in my shoulders eases. I take a couple of extra breaths to settle my heart.

'Oh, I'm sorry,' Miss Danvers suddenly says, leaning across her table and dragging a desktop fan across the veneer. She switches it on, bringing a wave of cool air over the two of us. 'It's stifling in here today, but at least it isn't raining. The weather in this country is one of the reasons I decided to stay, rather than return to Toronto. I love its unpredictability.'

I don't want to get into a conversation about the changing UK climate, and dab my face with a tissue when she is looking down at her notes, as if trying to recall the reason she invited me in in the first place.

'Let me put it a different way,' she says, making eye contact. 'There was an incident in class just before the lunch bell rang. Grace and three or four others were at the paint workstation, and each had been tasked with painting a happy memory from their summer holidays. Generally, we see lots of beach pictures, parks, ice-cream, that kind of thing. Anyway, I was reading a story to a group when I heard raised voices, and when I came over, Grace looked upset. When I asked what was going on, she told me that one of the boys – Dylan – had called her a name. The bell sounded, and I kept Grace and Dylan behind to explain what had been said and why. Neither wanted to admit what had happened, so I told them both that name-calling isn't appropriate at any time, but especially not in school. They both apologised to one another and went to get their food. Then I spoke to a girl called Daisy who'd been at the paint workstation with them, and she told me that Dylan and a boy called Harry had said that Grace would be going to see her mum at the prison, because that's where all the bad people go.'

My cheeks flush instantly, but I remain quiet.

'From speaking to a couple of the other parents,' she continues, 'I understand that there was some kind of episode yesterday? It's none of my business, but I have a duty of care to Grace and the other children in my class to make sure that everything at home is as safe and stable as possible.'

Bloody Morag spreading rumours about me has now filtered down to the children in Grace's class.

I take a deep breath. 'I *was* arrested yesterday, but it was just a misunderstanding, and no charges were brought against me. I'm not a criminal, Miss Danvers, it was just a mix-up, that's all. Grace had no idea about it, and as far as I'm concerned, the sooner it's all behind me, the better. Was Grace okay? Did she seem upset when she came back from lunch?'

Miss Danvers' expression hardens, as the skin around her lips tightens. 'That's what I wanted to speak to you about. When I returned to the classroom to set things up for the afternoon lessons, I found that somebody had painted a large black line from corner to corner over Dylan's beach painting. I didn't see who did it, but when the children returned, I took that group to one side and asked whether any of them wanted to admit who had done it. Grace stepped forward and said she had painted the line over the image because of what Dylan had said about you.'

I must be hearing things because I'm pretty sure I just heard her say that Grace – my little angel – destroyed another child's artwork out of spite.

'There must be some mistake,' I protest. 'Are you sure that's what Grace said? She's not that type of girl. She's good and would never do something so wicked.'

Miss Danvers offers a sympathetic frown. 'The first day at a new school can be overwhelming for even the securest child. From what I understand, Dylan and Grace had never met before today, and maybe there was some unresolved tension there. I thought the conversation at lunchtime had sorted things, but I guess I was wrong. I had to tell Grace that what she had done was disrespectful and that such behaviour is not tolerated at this school. She apologised to Dylan, and I then made a point of separating them to avoid further conflict. You need to be aware that we won't be taking any further action on this occasion, but I'm keen to break any pattern of poor behaviour before it starts.'

It's as if she is talking about a different child. Grace doesn't have a malicious bone in her body, and even when things don't go her way, I've never known her lash out at anybody, or take vengeful action. I'm about to argue in my daughter's defence, when Miss Danvers rests a cold hand on mine.

'Is there anything going on at home that I should know about? Any reason for Grace to act out in this way?'

I think about the last week, and my near-obsession with finding out the truth about Daisy and Morag's relationship. Have I missed obvious signs that Grace has been unhappy or stressed with anything?

'Just the usual challenges life has to offer,' I say, hoping the throwaway line is sufficient to ease her concern.

'I remember meeting Mr Donoghue before the summer holidays. Is everything okay between the two of you?' She quickly raises her hands in a defensive gesture. 'I appreciate what goes on between a husband and wife is none of my business, and you have every right to tell me to butt out, but I'm also aware of the unseen risks that marital issues can cast on impressionable children.'

Is it possible that Grace knows Charlie has been cheating on me with that woman in the bum-clenching red skirt?

'Everything between Charlie and me is as you would expect. Sure, we have the occasional disagreement, but never in front of Grace. I don't think there's anything like that which could have caused Grace to act out like this.'

'So you're as surprised by today's incident as I am?'

'Absolutely,' I practically spit, and Miss Danvers breathes a sigh of relief.

'Thank goodness! I've always prided myself on being a good judge of character, and prior to this afternoon I'd considered Grace a bright little bee. Hopefully, today was a one-off and we can chalk it up to experience.'

With that she stands, and moves across to the door, calling Grace through to our room. Grace walks slowly, her head bowed, and she looks close to tears when our eyes do finally meet.

'Your mom and I have had a chat about what happened, and I've explained what you told me, and that you've expressed regret and remorse at your actions today. We're both hoping that we can all turn to a clean page tomorrow and start afresh. Isn't that right, mom?'

I nod eagerly at Grace, but it still feels like an out-of-body experience, as if I'm watching somebody else's child being reprimanded, rather than my own.

Grace remains silent and sullen once we are back outside in the sweltering heat. The playground is now empty, and there's a creepiness to the setting, like some plague has wiped out all the souls who were previously here. I no longer think it's appropriate to make a detour via the shop for an ice-cream, and so we head out through the gates, and make our way steadily along the pavement.

I'm the first one to crack under the strain of silence. 'Are you going to tell me what happened at school?'

She sighs heavily. 'Dylan was saying all this stuff about you going to jail and laughing. He said his mum and dad had told him to stay away from me in case I'm a thief like you.'

I want to shout and scream to the world that I'm not a thief, and to dare anyone to say otherwise to my face. It's bad enough that the parents in the playground, who don't even know me, have been gossiping behind my back, but they shouldn't be spreading such lies to their children as well. How many other children in the school will now be avoiding Grace because of the rumour Morag has started?

'That's no reason for you to destroy his painting though, is it? Especially after Miss Danvers had already told him off and asked him to apologise to you. I thought I'd raised you better than that, Grace.'

'I...' she begins, before faltering, and closing her mouth again.

'How would you like it if someone had done that to your painting?'

Her lips part again, and I cannot believe she's even going to attempt to justify what she did, but then what she does say sends my head spinning.

'I didn't do it. It was Daisy who painted the line on his picture.'

I grip the tyres tight to bring the chair to an abrupt halt. 'What did you say?'

Grace's lips wobble as she meets my gaze. 'It was Daisy who painted the black line. At lunchtime she said it wasn't fair that Miss Danvers hadn't punished Dylan. At break time he was laughing about it, and Daisy told him he was a stupid. She was really kind to me, and said I should just ignore him. When we returned to class, she put the brush across his painting, but when Miss Danvers caught us I didn't want Daisy to get into trouble, so I told her I'd done it.' She pauses to wipe tears from her eyes.

'That doesn't make any sense, Grace,' I protest. 'Why would you take the blame for something Daisy did?'

She sniffs loudly. 'You've always told me I should stick up for my friends, and that's what Daisy did for me. I'm sorry I got you in trouble with Miss Danvers, but Dylan deserved to be punished for saying those lies about you.'

I pull Grace into my arms and hug her dearly. Part of me is proud that she was willing to risk the teacher's wrath for her friend, but I am also disappointed that she found it so easy to lie to her new teacher. I'm also furious that she did it to help the daughter of the woman who caused the rumour to start in the first place.

Grace's tears are warm against my chest, and they soon penetrate my T-shirt. We remain there for several moments as I try to explain that although her decision was noble, ultimately she should have told the truth, and mustn't lie for others in future.

When we return home, there is a large Mercedes parked behind our battered Hyundai, and Charlie's betrayal flashes past my eyes as I head in and Grace tears off to her bedroom to get changed. It isn't Charlie I see first when I roll into the living room, but Mum with a tear-stained face. She looks behind me, as Charlie enters and drops a tissue filled with pills into my lap.

'Your mum was cleaning up our room and discovered these in the waste bin in the wet room,' Charlie says. 'How long have you been off your meds, Jess?'

The heat in my cheeks is intense as I look at him, and my vision mists with tears. I can't believe they've been checking up on me. And why is he challenging me in front of Mum? This should be a private conversation.

I search for a clever explanation, but my mind is suddenly foggy, and I feel lightheaded. Charlie is watching me, his expression hurt, when I should be the indignant one after his behaviour.

He points at the tissue in my lap. 'Is this the reason for your erratic behaviour, Jess? Why I keep finding you in strange places in the middle of the night? Why you were arrested yesterday, and why you've been obsessing about that woman and her daughter?'

Is this him making his play now? In front of witnesses he's going to claim I'm losing my mind, so he can take my daughter and go off with his new squeeze.

'You call my behaviour erratic?' I shout back, as the frustration reaches boiling point. 'Who is the woman I saw you with this morning looking all lovey-dovey? Tell me that, Charlie! Was that the Kerry I spoke to on the phone the other night or some other bimbo you've been shagging?'

The momentary look of shock is replaced by sad eyes. 'What are you talking about, Jess? I'm not having an affair.'

'No? Then why did I see you with some beautiful woman getting into her red sports car, so intimate?'

He turns his back, knowing I've caught him in his lies, but as much as I want to feel satisfied, it pains me to think that our marriage has come to this. I just want things to go back to where they were before that day when we lost Luke.

I start as someone knocks at the door behind me. Turning, I am surprised to see my psychiatrist Dr Savage walk in.

'Hello, Jess,' she says. 'Charlie called me and told me what's been going on. I think we need to talk things through. All of us together. Your Mum and Charlie love you dearly, Jess, and they want to make sure you get the help that you need to get things back on course. They've asked me to help them facilitate an intervention. They are concerned by some of your recent behaviour, and it is clear you haven't been taking the medication that was prescribed to treat your depression. I – *we* – think it would be best if you voluntarily came with me now, Jess, so that we can start your treatment.'

I can taste bile in the back of my throat. This bombshell has the room spinning around me. How have so many people whom I love been able to keep so many secrets from me? I need to get out of the room. I need space and air. Charlie has convinced them both I'm losing my mind.

I wheel back out of the room, not prepared to give up so easily.

Mum's hand reaches out for me. 'Where are you going, Jess? You need to stay and listen to what the doctor has to say. You'll see there's no reason to be scared.'

I'm no longer listening, as I force my aching hands onto the wheel grips and spin the chair in the direction of the front door.

'Please, Jess, don't rush off like this,' Mum calls out. 'If you'll just—'

I open the front door and I'm down the ramp before they can stop me. The fresh air feels welcome against my burning cheeks, and I suck it in as my hands pump faster and faster. I hear Mum calling after me, but I know she won't give chase. For now, I am free and on my own, but as my arms quickly tire, it feels like the world is closing in on me.

Chapter Fifty-Two

Before – Morag

The urgent knocking at the door tells me something isn't right, and as I warn Daisy to stay hidden in her room with the door locked, I push back the net curtain in the living room and look out. Jess isn't the person I'm expecting to see, but as our eyes meet, I can see how upset she is, and my heart goes out to her.

She is panting as I unlock the door. Angus's phone is gripped tightly in my hand, with 999 primed should she make any kind of move on me.

'Whatever is the matter?' I ask, but I'm not prepared for her to burst into pained tears. My previous reservations about this woman instantly diminish as the nurse in me takes control. 'You're as pale as a sheet, Jess. What's happened?'

She tries to answer, but I can't understand what she's saying through the heaving sobs. It could be an act to lull me into a false sense of security, but my instinct tells me this outburst is genuine. Wheeling her through to the kitchen, I rest Angus's phone on the counter and switch on the kettle.

She doesn't look well, and as I press my cold hand against her forehead, I recoil at how hot she is despite the pallor of her skin. 'Do you feel all right?'

Her breaths are staggered as she tries to answer again, and the last thing I want is for her to keel over in my kitchen. Reaching for the tin of biscuits we keep in the cupboard, I pass them to her and encourage her to eat. At first she is reluctant, but having devoured one, she takes two more, and her breathing settles.

'Did you come all the way from home?' I ask, assuming her blood sugar is low.

She nods as she finishes the last biscuit. 'Did Daisy tell you what happened with her and Grace at school today?' she says, with a mouthful of crumbs.

When I asked Daisy how school was, all she said was that it was okay; she likes her teacher, but some of the boys in the class are disruptive.

'One of the boys in their class – Dylan – was being rude,' Jess continues when I don't respond, 'and in retaliation your Daisy defaced his artwork, but Grace took the blame for it. Miss Danvers kept us back after the school bell to tell me.'

This is certainly news to me, and I can only accept that she's telling me the truth, as I can't understand what other angle she might be playing. Miss Danvers certainly didn't say anything to me about some clash between the children.

'What did this Dylan boy say?'

'His comments were aimed at Grace actually,' Jess says bitterly. 'It appears one of the parents has been spreading stories about me around the playground.'

I act dumb, but I can already guess what she's referring to. 'Stories? What kind of stories?'

She shakes her head incredulously. '*Someone* is telling everyone that I was arrested for stealing yesterday and urging their children to avoid Grace.'

The way she's glaring at me, I genuinely believe she thinks I'm behind the rumours. 'It wasn't me,' I almost shout. 'I overheard that Nadine woman say something about some trouble with the police, but I didn't know it was related to stealing.'

'I'm not a thief,' she says bluntly. 'After you ran from the shop yesterday, I chased after you, not realising I still had an item in my lap. The security guard thought I was trying to steal an ornament and phoned the police. I was released without charge when I explained what had happened, so there will be no further action to come either.'

I can't believe she's accusing me of something so malicious. It hurts that she could think I could be so cruel. 'I swear to you, Jess, I had no idea you'd been arrested until I heard Nadine mention it to one of the other mums this morning. I didn't even know you'd followed me out of the shop. I'm so sorry.'

My apology seems to throw her off track, and I can see the doubt creeping into her eyes. 'What about Daisy?'

My shoulders tense. 'What about her?'

'Why do you keep telling everyone that she's your daughter when we both know that's a lie?'

Oh my God, she knows!

'When I first met her in the park, she told me you weren't her mother. I need to know the truth, Morag.'

I don't respond. The house of cards we've built is too precious to knock down.

'Who were you speaking to on the phone in the shop yesterday? I heard you threaten whoever it was. You said you'd never let them anywhere near *her*. I know you meant Daisy, so who were you warning off? Your partner? The person who killed her real mum in Ireland and brought her to you? I found Mia online; her uncle has listed her on a missing people site and wants to be reunited.'

What is she talking about?

I put on a dumbfounded look, but she's not buying it. 'I don't know what you're talking about, Jess,' I say innocently. 'I don't understand what this is all about.'

She reaches into the side of her chair and thrusts out a printed page. I am stunned as I instantly recognise the child's face in the image.

'Where did you get this from?' I demand, seeing Daisy staring back at me.

There is a real look of satisfaction in Jess's eyes. 'Online. She was reported missing by her uncle two years ago, and now I know why she was so scared when she approached me in the park on Thursday. She knows you're not her mother and that you're holding her here against her will when she should be with her family back in Belfast.'

No, no, no, this can't be. Would Tommy really have fabricated a story and reported Daisy missing online?

I stare at the image again to double-check I'm not misinterpreting what I'm looking at. The page is emblazoned with branding for some missing people website. It looks genuine enough.

'I'm not holding Daisy against her will,' I insist, as a thousand thoughts vow for attention. 'We're protecting her.'

But Jess isn't listening, the bit now firmly between her

teeth. 'This poor man hasn't seen his daughter since his wife was murdered, and Mia was taken from him. The jig is up, Morag. I know Daisy isn't your daughter.'

I look up at the clock. Has Angus had his meeting with Tommy's representatives yet? If Tommy's gone to the lengths of using this website to try and locate Daisy, there's no way he'll give up on her without a fight.

'I ought to call the police,' Jess continues. 'Let them know that I've caught Mia's abductor red-handed.'

I have no way of contacting Angus, so I try Lawrence's number, but the answerphone cuts straight in.

'Where is Mia now?' Jess demands. 'I can't allow her to stay with you any longer. Don't make this any harder on her than it needs to be.'

'None of *this* is real,' I shout, catching myself off-guard, and screwing up the sheet of paper. 'Her mother *was* murdered, but not by me, and not by Angus, but by Daisy's – Mia's – father. We have been on the run for nearly two years trying to protect her. You don't realise what you're meddling in. You think Angus and I are keeping Daisy here against her will? I love that child as if she were my own.'

'But she *isn't* your daughter, Mor—'

'She's my granddaughter,' I scream, reaching for the counter to steady myself.

Jess's expression softens slightly for the first time, and she looks less sure of herself.

'Tommy Chamberlain – Mia's father – is my son,' I finally admit, defeated.

The truth feels weird as it escapes my lips. For so many years I've refused to acknowledge that that monster is my own flesh and blood, but I don't have the strength to keep running from the past.

Jess's eyes dart as she tries to process my admission, looking for holes. 'It was *him* on the phone yesterday, wasn't it? When you were upset in the shop. He's on to you, isn't he?'

I nod, and it's all I can do to keep myself upright. 'If he finds out where we are, none of us are safe.'

Chapter Fifty-Three

Now

Having been so certain that the victim in the post-mortem photograph was indeed Charlie Donoghue, the man who sat across from Mike couldn't have looked much more different. This man had a thinner, younger-looking face. The full hairline screamed of someone half his age, as did the trim waistline. But he was clearly showing the signs of stress and fatigue, his forehead glowing in the morning sunlight flooding through the window of the soft interview suite.

Rosie Donoghue sat next to her brother but was far more relaxed, acclimatised to this setting, and happy to engage in small talk with Polly, though Mike was certain the two women hadn't known each other prior to today. Mike was standing by the window, looking out as traffic passed by oblivious to the serious nature of the crime being investigated.

'Where've you been, Mr Donoghue?' Mike asked, without turning.

There was a pause, and Mike could sense Charlie glancing at his younger sister as if checking to confirm he could speak. 'My boss called yesterday afternoon and needed me to return to the office to fix an issue. I've been there all night.'

'And your boss will be able to vouch for that?'

'Yes,' he replied sharply. 'Our office is covered in security cameras, so you can watch exactly what I was doing if necessary.'

Mike turned and smiled to show he'd taken no offence to the testy tone. 'Tell me, Mr Donoghue, when was the last time you saw your wife Jess?'

In the brief time that had passed since Rosie had come in to the office to say she'd located her brother, Polly had explained that Jess was a witness to a serious crime, but she was safe and in the care of Dr Savage at the hospital. The relief on both Charlie and Rosie Donoghue's faces had been palpable.

'We... I confronted her yesterday afternoon about not taking her antidepressants,' he said, his hands trembling, as he clutched the cup of hot chocolate, blowing steam from the top, 'and she fled from the house. I've known for the last few days that she's not been taking them. She doesn't realise, but she's different when she's not on them: more like the old Jess, less docile. But the problem with that is it doesn't last, and without the pills to create a chemical balance in her head, paranoia soon kicks in, and she quickly descends into a version of herself that is as terrifying as it is dangerous.'

'Dangerous?' Mike echoed.

'To herself, yes. Her negative thoughts blow up into such a storm that she is no longer in control. She once told me it's like a nightmare from which she can't wake. Deep down she senses something isn't right, but can't quite put her finger on what or how to fix it. A bit like being in a dark room, and not knowing how close the walls are or whether there's any kind of door to escape from. That's how Dr Savage – her psychiatrist – puts it.'

'This isn't the first time she's stopped taking her pills, is it?'

Charlie shook his head, and as he looked up from his drink, his eyes were tearful. 'It's been an ongoing battle for her for years. When I first met Jess, she suffered with anxiety, and we were never really clear what would bring on her panic attacks; there wasn't an obvious underlying cause. She was resistant to taking mood stabilisers, but agreed to do so for me. But I suppose, like most problems where the cause is never truly fixed, it would resurface and grow into something more serious. The doctors never confirmed whether her depression after Grace was born was directly linked, but her pills were changed, and she managed to overcome the suffering, and become the most wonderful mum to Grace.'

He paused to wipe his cheeks with the back of his hand. 'For a time, everything was so perfect. The three of us were happy, and although we'd discussed extending the family, we knew… *I* knew it meant Jess reducing her pills, so as not to endanger the baby. I think we were all surprised when she fell pregnant again when we weren't really trying. I was terrified that she would lose control and watched her like a hawk in the early months, but she had weekly appointments with Dr Savage, and everything seemed to be going so well. But I couldn't watch her for ever, and as the pressure of work grew, I found myself less and less at home, and hadn't realised the paranoid Jess had returned. She started complaining about someone following her and was convinced it was something to do with some fraud scandal she'd uncovered through work.

'And then our son arrived, and…' Charlie buried his face in his hands, unable to continue.

'Jess was involved in a car accident on her way to hospital after labour had begun,' Rosie picked up, 'and Luke didn't survive the labour. It was devastating for all of us, and if I'm honest, I don't think Jess has even begun to really process what happened that day. She's tried to put on a brave face, but I think mentally she's still trapped in that maternity ward. As my brother said, a nightmare she can't wake from.'

Mike could see the torment reliving these memories was causing, but he needed answers. 'Has Jess ever mentioned the name Tommy Chamberlain to either of you?'

Mike studied their faces, but neither offered any signs of recognition.

Charlie shook his head, the tears temporarily stopping at the strangeness of the question.

'Who is he?' Rosie asked.

'I'm not really at liberty to say, but in the interest of giving you some context, we believe Jess witnessed the death of Tommy Chamberlain last night.'

'Jesus!' Rosie exclaimed. 'And with her so vulnerable, it's no wonder she didn't come home last night. I wish someone had called to say what had happened. Her mum has been worried sick, and we've been driving around all the local emergency wards to see if she'd been brought in injured.'

'She waived the opportunity to call anyone last night,' Polly clarified.

'She was probably worried I'd try to have her committed to hospital again,' Charlie said, his bottom lip wobbling. 'Oh God, this is all my fault. I shouldn't have tried to spring an intervention; I should have just talked to her about my concerns sooner.'

Mike handed him a fresh tissue from the box on the windowsill. 'Can you describe your wife's relationship with Morag and Angus Kilbride?'

Charlie wiped his eyes with the tissue and blew his nose. 'She's been a bit obsessed with them since they met last week. Off her pills, she's become convinced that Daisy isn't in fact their daughter.' He paused. 'Why are you asking me about them? I'm confused. What do they have to do with what is happening to Jess?'

'Tommy Chamberlain was killed in their house,' Polly said abruptly, before Mike had worked out a way to soften the message. 'You've said Jess isn't a violent person, but can you think of any reason why she would be at the Kilbride residence at the same moment Tommy Chamberlain was killed?'

Charlie's eyes widened. 'What are you implying? Are you suggesting Jess killed him?'

Mike couldn't answer, as urgent banging on the door drew all their attention.

Chapter Fifty-Four

Before - Jess

Morag is now seated at the kitchen table, and although she's gripping the handle of the steaming mug of tea, she has yet to take a sip. I'm still reeling from the revelation that the missing girl I found on the website – Mia – is in fact Daisy, and that Morag is in fact her grandmother. With Charlie's attempted intervention I'd almost started believing that I *was* losing my mind, but now my mind-set has been vindicated.

'It was maybe too much to expect that people would accept the story of adoption,' Morag says suddenly, 'but she is our flesh and blood, and we will do whatever it takes to protect her.'

'Tell me about Tommy,' I say after a moment.

She looks out of the window as if expecting her now adult son to come bursting through the door at any moment.

'Tommy wasn't... an easy child. He was something of a miracle, as I'd previously been told by the doctor that I would never conceive children, and then he suddenly arrived. We used to call him our blessing from heaven, and maybe in our eagerness to embrace the gift we were too soft with him, letting him get away with more than we should have. He ran away when he was seventeen, which was as much a blessing for us as the escape was for him. He'd been expelled from school for fighting with other students, and after countless arguments, he upped and left. I never doubted he would manage to survive on his own. He had street smarts, even at that age.

'He'd make contact from time to time, letting us know he was still alive, and then shortly before he turned twenty-three, he returned to Aberdeen and rented a place nearby. By that point, he no longer looked like the boy we'd raised and cherished. Life on the streets had taken a toll, and although he was leaner and stronger than before, his aura had darkened, and I could no longer see my son when I looked into his eyes.

'He brought his drug world into our town, setting up shop and supply lines with a network of dealers from the bigger cities. There would always be flash cars parked outside his place, and fancy jewellery around the necks of the women who swarmed around him. He thought himself Mr Big, and I suppose in many ways that's what he'd become.

'Not long after, he met a fellow nurse from the hospital – Sharon – a wee sprite of a girl who fell head over heels in love with the man she thought he was, and Daisy – Mia – was the result of their passionate affair. The relationship was... tumultuous. We didn't know until it was too late, but he was physically abusing Sharon, and then got her hooked on heroin.

She tried to clean herself up, but he had his claws inside her, and there was only ever going to be one way she would escape.'

Morag releases the handle of the mug, and dabs the corners of her eyes with a scrunched-up tissue. 'I still remember the two police officers arriving on our doorstep, and telling us about *the accident*. There'd been a fire at one of Tommy's houses in Manchester, and once the blaze was out, her body was found. The arson investigators later concluded that a chip pan had caught fire and pronounced accidental death, but I think I know deep down who really started that fire. He always liked playing with matches, you see. Even as a young boy. Shortly after we'd taken Mia in, he came for her, but we were out, and returned to a smouldering shell of our home. That was when we knew we had to properly get away from him. We changed our names, and gave Mia a new identity.

'I don't know how he manages to do it, but it doesn't seem there's anywhere we can go where he won't find us. He is charming and manipulative, and rich. I suppose he must bribe and threaten to get the information he wants. Last time, we barely made it out of the house before he turned up. We thought London was big enough that we could slip between the cracks, but it will only be a matter of time until he finds our address, and then we'll have to move again.'

Hearing Morag talk so candidly, I feel awful for ever questioning her true motive towards Daisy, and I can understand why she would fight so hard to keep her secrets buried.

Reaching out, I rest my hand on hers. 'I'm sorry for doubting you, Morag. Is there anything I can do to help?'

She looks up at me and tilts her head. 'I think you have enough problems of your own without taking on mine.'

I don't know how to respond to such a blunt statement and take a sip of tea.

'I'm sorry,' she quickly adds. 'I heard you lost your son a few months ago. It can't be easy to grieve with Grace starting school.'

She has no idea.

'There isn't a single day that's passed when I haven't thought about Luke,' I admit, 'and how my actions were probably the reason he died.'

'I'm sure that isn't true,' Morag counters, but she really doesn't have a clue about my own dark secrets.

'I suffered post-natal depression after Grace,' I say, my eyes stinging at the memory. 'It was diagnosed quickly, and I received counselling and medication, but my mental health never truly recovered. I threw myself into work to battle my demons, but without the medication, I could only last a few weeks before my condition would spiral.

'When I fell pregnant with Luke, I made the conscious decision to stop the medication. I was terrified that the antidepressants would affect his development, but I didn't tell anyone how tough I was finding it. Work, family, pregnancy – it was all getting too much. I started to use alcohol to get me through the bad days, even though it was a risk, and...'

I take a deep breath. 'I was drinking the day the labour started. I was two weeks from the due date, and it was another dark day. I just wanted to get to the hospital and let the midwife take control of my situation. I thought I could get to the hospital without an issue, and didn't want to call an ambulance, but my God, do I regret that decision! I remember getting behind the wheel, but then there is a black hole, and my next memory is being dragged from the car and transferred to a trolley, and put in the back of an ambulance. The man who'd found me said it looked as though I'd been run off the road, due to the damage to the car, and I... didn't challenge the story.'

The tears roll down my cheeks. I don't know why I'm so freely admitting my darkest thoughts to Morag. Maybe it's because she understands what it is to lose a son.

'I should have been breathalysed, but for some reason I wasn't, maybe because the contractions had started, I don't know. A policeman eventually came to my room in the days after Luke's death, but only to ask what I remembered about being run off the road. I panicked, and told him the first thing I could think, which was that a car I couldn't really remember had caused the accident. After some investigation they couldn't prove one way or another what had actually happened, and no further action was taken.'

The needle slipping and stealing my legs is the least I deserve for Luke dying. Had I not been under the influence, maybe I would have kept control of the car, and if I hadn't had the accident, maybe he would have survived the labour.

Morag dabs her own eyes. 'Thank you for being honest with me, Jess. I know it can't have been easy, and I don't think you should blame yourself for what happened. We're all guilty of actions that in hindsight weren't the wisest. I blame myself for Sharon's demise at the hands of my son, but some things are beyond our control.'

The sound of footsteps on the staircase causes us both to

turn and watch as Daisy enters the kitchen behind us. 'Can I have something to eat?'

The clock on the wall beside the stove tells me it is close to six, and I have no idea where the time has gone. I should be getting home to feed Grace, and tackle my problems with Charlie head on. There is still daylight through the kitchen window, but it won't be long until the darkness comes.

Morag stands, and hugs Daisy close, and I can see nothing but affection in the embrace. It can't be easy for Daisy to process the loss of her mother and father, and a new life, a new name, and a fresh start in a different city. Maybe that was why she approached me in the park on Thursday. Not because she was scared of Morag, but because she doesn't understand her place in this family.

'I should head home,' I say, wheeling back from the table. 'If there's anything you need, a place to stay for the night, or even just someone to talk to, please don't hesitate to ask.'

Morag smiles at me with fresh tears in her eyes. 'Thank you, Jess. I'm sure we'll be okay once Angus has spoken with *you know who*.'

My heart skips a beat, as I realise the error of my ways.

'What is it, Jess?' Morag says. 'You look like you've seen a ghost.'

How could I have been so stupid? How could I have forgotten what I'd done before I went to collect Grace from school?

I can barely get the words out of my throat. 'He knows where you are.'

Morag frowns deeply. 'What makes you say that?'

Grabbing at the scrunched-up image of Mia, I flatten the paper on the table, and point at the 'Contact' box at the top of the sheet. 'I messaged the uncle and told him where he could find Mia. He knows, Morag. I gave him your address.'

The blood drains from her face too, but before either of us can truly comprehend the implications of my actions, the front door flies open with a heavy kick.

Chapter Fifty-Five

Before – Morag

The front door swings on its hinges, the door frame splintered under the impact, and what is left of the evening's light comes pouring through. And in the middle of all that, the man I've been dreading seeing for nearly two years.

'Hello, *Mum*,' he sneers, pressing both palms against what remains of the doorframe. 'Been a long time.'

Daisy is trying to peer around me to see who is speaking, but I do my best to keep her out of his sight.

My son – it sickens me to even think of him as the baby I once swaddled – stands tall, his shoulders and upper arms like those of a body-builder, his hair long and dishevelled, and his brown beard thick and nest-like. He looks nothing like the skinny runt who ran away from home all those years ago. The blazer and trousers which struggle to hold in his monstrous frame are tailor-made, and the half-open collared shirt has a glossy sheen to it beneath the porch light. I guess he can now afford the luxury items Angus and I never could.

'Aren't you going to invite me in, *Mum*?' Tommy roars from the doorstep.

I wish he would stop calling me that, because every time he does, Daisy's face pokes out more.

'And who do we have here?' he says, stepping into the house, and giving the front door one final shove to ensure it collapses to the floor with a boom.

He's looking just past me, and I would give anything to reset the clock by five minutes and keep Daisy in her room where he wouldn't see her. I take a step back, forcing Daisy behind me, hoping I can get close enough to the back door before he realises what I'm doing.

'Get out of my house,' I shout towards him, but my voice is thickened by nervous energy and doesn't sound as forceful as I'd hoped.

I have imagined this moment so many times; it has haunted my nightmares. In none of those encounters am I on my own, without Angus. Jess is the only thing that stands between Tommy and us, but what good can she be? She is pale as a sheet, and I have a strong sense that she is off the medication I saw in her kitchen on Sunday.

'I'll phone the police,' I shout again, slightly firmer this time, but as I scan the kitchen worktops, I can't recall where I left my phone. I had it when I answered the door to Jess, but my clouded mind is suppressing my short-term memories.

'Go ahead and call them,' he sneers back, still moving forwards, his giant strides accounting for two of my backward shuffles. 'It's about time I formally had you charged with *abducting* my daughter. Mia? You don't have to be afraid of me. I'm your dad.'

Daisy's head is out again, but this time my attempts to push it back in fail, and she pulls away from me, so she can take in the man moving towards us.

He stops, drops to his knees, and watches her, a wolf in sheep's clothing. 'Do you recognise me, Mia? You do, don't you? That's because I am your father, and you lived with me for several years, before your mammy and grandma here plotted to take you from me.'

'It wasn't like that!' I yell back, but stop myself from saying he left me little choice when he murdered Sharon. One day I plan to tell Daisy the truth about her parents, but she's too young to process any of that just now.

'You always were a jealous old bat,' he says, glancing from her timid face to mine. 'Look at me now, Mammy. Your son has made a name for himself. I'm rich and powerful, and people respect me.'

I snort. 'People are scared of you, Tommy; it isn't the same thing.'

He brushes off the challenge. 'They should be scared.' His eyes return to Daisy. 'You don't need to be afraid of me, Mia. I've been looking for you for a long time. I'm going to take you back to my house, and you will have a far grander life than you can imagine. You'll be treated like a real princess. And who knows, maybe I'll even buy you a pony one day too.'

It was a mistake to lie to Daisy about her parents. After much debate we settled on telling her that her parents had both died in that fire, and that was why she would live with Angus and me. We've kept pictures of Tommy and Sharon from her, in the hope that she'd eventually begin to forget their faces and settle down. Despite how close he's come to finding us before, I always clung to the hope we'd manage to stay one step ahead of him.

God, I wish Angus was here with me now, and the breath catches in my throat. He was supposed to be meeting with Tommy today.

'What have you done to Angus?' I demand, an invisible blade passing through my heart.

A small flicker of a smile passes over his face, but his eyes remain locked on Daisy's. 'Would you like to come and live with me in my house, Mia?'

I feel her hands coil around my leg, and I rest a hand on her shoulders, relieved that she is smart enough not to fall for his routine.

'It's a much bigger house than this. You'd have your own room, a television set the size of this kitchen, and a swimming pool too. You'd be able to throw big parties and invite your friends to come and play. Leave all of this shit behind and come and be with your *real* family.'

'She's not going anywhere,' I say, grasping for the last of my inner strength. '*Daisy* is not your daughter anymore.'

He puffs out his cheeks and rises effortlessly. It's the moment I've been waiting for. Spinning, I yank open the back door, and usher Daisy outside. 'Go to our special place, my darling. Do you remember? The place I told you to hide in an emergency? Go there now, and I will come and find you soon.'

Daisy doesn't move, staring back at me, as I hear Tommy moving closer.

'Go, Daisy, go. I will find you soon. Please, just run.'

She takes off up the garden, as I slam the door closed and lock it, just as Tommy crashes me into the glass.

His breath is warm against my face. 'You made a mistake, old woman.'

I can barely breathe with his weight crushing my chest against the cold glass. 'The only mistake I made was not turning you in to the police when you first stole from me.'

'You left me no choice but to fend for myself. You were always so keen to help other people at the hospital, but you couldn't see what *I* needed. I was your flesh and blood, but you preferred to abandon me with childminders so you could go and help perfect bloody strangers.'

Is that really how he feels, or is he just saying things to try and make me feel bad, and to justify all the hurt and pain he has caused others?

Jess clears her throat, and I start, having forgotten she was still in the room. 'I've already called the police,' she says defiantly. 'They're on their way now. That's why I sent you that message through the website. We wanted to lure you out so they could come and arrest you and take you away. You've minutes at best. A smart man would get away while he still can.'

Tommy sniggers at the suggestion and, pinning me to the back door with his forearm, he turns to look at Jess. 'I suppose I should thank you for helping me track down Mia at long last. I had planned to have Daddy-o followed home after our meeting, but then I received your message through the site, and my plans changed. You gave me the perfect answer: take Dad's money *and* get Mia back. It's Jess, right? How about I offer you a finder's fee, Jess? Say twenty thousand, and all you have to do is leave this place, and never look back.'

Jess remains where she is. 'I'm not going anywhere until you're led away in cuffs.'

Tommy leans harder into my chest, and it's as if I can feel my ribs being slowly crushed, the pain so intense that I can't even scream, let alone breathe.

'I really don't want to hurt a cripple, but if you don't want to accept my generous offer, you leave me little choice.'

He releases his arm, and I can't stop myself sliding down the glass pane, slumping on the floor, as I try and get my breath back, but then something cold and hard is pressed against my eye. The long barrel stretches all the way back to his hand and long arm, and I'm waiting for the world to go black, but he suddenly withdraws the weapon, and hops away, yelping as he does.

Jess's hand is the next thing I see, as she offers to help me back to my feet while Tommy leaps about swearing, and from the way he is holding his shin, I can only assume she has driven one of the foot pedals into the side of his leg in an effort to save me.

'We need to get out of here,' she whispers, and I don't need telling twice, pulling on her arm until I am upright again, but I'm barely standing when Jess's hand yanked away from mine, and I watch as the chair flies back through the air, crashing against the wall on the far side, Jess falling helplessly to the ground in a heap. Before I can react, Tommy charges at me, and I feel the cold glass as my cheek and forehead crack into it, and this time the world does turn black.

Chapter Fifty-Six

Now

Thrusting open the door of the interview suite, Mike was surprised to find Nazia Hussain wide-eyed and stalking the corridor.

'I need to talk to you urgently,' she said, taking him by the arm and leading him out of earshot.

Polly joined them a moment later, closing the door behind her. 'What's going on?'

Nazia handed them the tablet she'd been clutching and pointed at the screen. 'Look familiar?'

Mike instantly recognised Tommy Chamberlain's face. 'Our victim. Where's this picture from?'

'It's the photographic identification provided to the missing people site when the report was submitted for missing Mia. Only the man in the picture isn't identified as Tommy Chamberlain, but in fact Adam Croft.'

Mike looked up at her. 'If you're about to tell me we're dealing with a weird twins plot twist, I may lose control.'

Nazia shook her head. 'Not twins, no, but the man we know as Tommy Chamberlain does have a string of other identities we weren't aware of. This one is Adam Croft, but I've now also located Adam Thomas, Tom Croft, Adam Chamberlain, and, wait for it... his birth name, Thomas Kingston.'

Mike stared blankly back at her. 'Is that name supposed to mean something to us?'

Nazia stabbed her finger at the screen, loading up a new page. 'Meet Morag and Angus Kingston, parents of Thomas Kingston, the man lying in the mortuary.'

Mike had to steady himself against the wall. 'Tommy Chamberlain is Morag Kilbride's son?'

Nazia nodded grimly. 'There's more.'

Mike thought back to the strange face Morag had pulled when he'd showed her the victim's photograph during their late-night interview. 'She knew he was her son and she said nothing. Why wouldn't she tell us she recognised him? Why would she allow him to remain unidentified on a mortuary slab?'

'I just finished speaking with a PS Rupert MacTavish in Aberdeen, who was the officer who was dealing with the restraining order against Tommy Chamberlain. He was very interested to learn the whereabouts of Chamberlain, as apparently, he's wanted in connection with an assault on a woman in her fifties called Gwen Barfoot, who'—Nazia took a deep breath—'is the sister of Morag Kingston. Turns out this Tommy is a real nasty piece of work, and although he has several arrests to his name, he's never been charged, on account of victims withdrawing testimony, and cast-iron alibis.'

'That explains why his prints and DNA weren't matched on the database,' Polly observed.

'But it doesn't explain why Morag or Jess would kill him,' Mike challenged.

'Maybe not, but what if the missing people report was right? What if Tommy really is Mia's dad, and Morag and Angus took her from him?'

Mike's world was spinning. Had they been looking at this all the wrong way round? One thing was for sure, two people knew the truth, and neither of them were nearby.

'Get units out to the Heathrow Travelodge, and have Morag Kilbride brought in immediately. Polly, you come with me.'

'Where are we going?' Polly asked, as he stalked away.

'The secure wing of Dr Savage's hospital. We're going to find out once and for all what Jess Donoghue knows about last night.'

Chapter Fifty-Seven

Before - Jess

Morag lies crumpled on the linoleum floor, a bloody imprint of her face on the glass where her face just slammed. She isn't moving, but she is the least of my concerns right now. I can't see Daisy in the garden, but then I can no longer see past the patio, as darkness slowly engulfs the lawn and the trampoline beyond it. I don't know where Morag told her to hide, but I hope it is far away from here, and with someone who can watch over and keep her safe.

Tommy squeezes my neck between his giant thumb and fingers, driving me back against the wall; my chair is nowhere in sight. I'm too scared to cry, and the pain in my jaw is so intense that I genuinely think he means to break it. He releases his grip but follows it up with a balled fist into my nose, and as the tears do finally escape, I can't see, because my hands shoot up to keep the rest of my face safe from his blows. I taste blood in the back of my throat as I struggle to breathe though the agony.

'You should have taken the money and gone,' I hear him snarl only inches from my ear, and it's enough to make me recoil in terror.

He stomps away, but I remain curled away from where he was standing, my hands still shielding my eyes and nose. The warm liquid slicking through the gaps in my fingers must be a mix of blood and tears, but I don't have the courage to look.

I'd hoped that telling him I'd phoned the police would be enough to make him scarper, but he's called my bluff and now we're at his mercy. Even if I screamed, there's no guarantee anyone would hear it or come to our rescue.

'Right, Mammy, now it's your turn,' I hear him groaning over near the door.

Prising my fingers apart slightly, I stare out through the bubble of tears, just about catching his shadow as he sits astride Morag. Keeping my blurred gaze on them, ever so slowly I lower my right hand, careful to keep my head and torso leaning at this awkward angle so as not to alert his peripheral vision. My handbag is to my left where it flew from the chair, and I slide my hand in, carefully feeling around until my fingers brush against my phone.

'You never should have snatched my daughter from me,' Tommy roars into Morag's motionless face.

I slowly pull my hand out and jab my thumb against the fingerprint sensor. The screen brightens, but an error message says the print wasn't recognised. A bloody mess clings to the pressure point, and I have to wipe it clean on the thigh of my jogging pants, and try again. This time it accepts the print and the home screen and apps appear.

'Throw that over here if you don't want me to come and get it myself.'

Tommy is staring at me, the long-barrelled handgun pointing in my direction. All I have to do is open the phone app and tap the 9 three times, but he is already clambering off Morag. I stab at the app with my thumb, realising this may be my final act in this cruel world, but I've only managed to press the 9 once before his hand connects with mine, and the phone flies from my grip. He follows this up with a backhand across my cheek, before driving his steel-capped boot into my side. A sharp pain erupts through my spine, as my shoulder crashes against the hard floor.

I can hear Tommy laughing above me, as he reaches for one of the kitchen chairs, presses it down over my chest, and plonks down on it. With my back pressed into the floor, and my arms pinned between the chair legs, I'm helpless to move.

'Did nobody ever tell you it's rude to stick your nose into other folk's business? You should have stayed away from here, Jess. Can't you see that this woman is poison?'

'The apple didn't fall far from the tree then,' I reply with a grimace as the pain in my nose intensifies.

He turns the handgun between his fingers. 'You know, I usually have people who take care of things like this for me, but do you know what? I'm going to enjoy getting my hands dirty for once.'

He stands and the pressure on my chest eases slightly, but my horror intensifies as I see him remove a large chef's knife from the block on the work surface. His shadow falls across my face again, and he lifts and flings the kitchen chair off into the hallway, where it makes a loud crash as it smacks against what remains of the door.

I try to shuffle away from him, but my back is aching, and I only manage a few centimetres before he drops onto my abdomen, legs either side of my arms, squeezing them against my body, the blade's point so close to my eyes that a sneeze would blind me. I can no longer see Morag, only his looming hulk over me.

'You know, they say bleeding to death is one of the most horrific ways you can die,' he taunts. 'Knowing that the grains of sand are slipping through the hourglass, and that there is nothing you can do to stop the inevitability of death.'

An image of Grace flashes in front of my eyes. My precious angel, the one thing I did in this life that wasn't a mistake. It's the impetus I need to wrestle my left arm free of his pinning knee, and I manage to wrap my fingers around his wrist, just to buy myself a few extra seconds. He is so much stronger than me, and I'm not sure even both of my hands would be enough to keep his one from driving the blade into my face.

'Please,' I wheeze. 'I have a daughter too. Don't leave her without a mother.'

'You should have thought about her before you tried to help that old bag over there. What is it with the mothers in here, putting strangers before their own flesh and blood? I offered you twenty grand to turn a blind eye. You could have been on your way home to your daughter right now. *You* chose this end. *You* chose to leave your daughter without a mother. Maybe it's because deep down you know she'll be better off without you. I know I was without mine. Made me the man I am today.'

There is a groan from somewhere behind him, and as he turns to check whether Morag is coming to, I manage to leverage my right arm out and grab his wrist with my other hand. He turns back to face me, his mouth curling into a grin. He knows I don't have the strength to prevent him, and I see the mania in his eyes as he prepares to drive the blade towards my face.

Then suddenly my hands twist as some other force takes control, and as I blink away my tears, I see a bony, wrinkled hand coiled around mine, and then the blade is moving away from my face and into the neck of the now startled Tommy.

Chapter Fifty-Eight

Before – Morag

Oh dear God, what have we done?

Tommy's prone body slumps to the side, blood gushing from the hole in his neck, splashing over Jess.

This can't be happening.

One minute we were trying to wrestle the kitchen knife from his grip, and then... I don't know what happened. Did we slip? There was a jerk, and then the blade plunged into the soft skin of his neck.

Oh God, no, not like this.

He was going to stab Jess. She was struggling; she needed my help. My hands were on hers just to keep the blade from her face, but then... I don't know what happened.

Please don't let him die.

Tommy is on his side, his hands brushing against the handle, as his slowing mind tries to process what has happened. He's trying to remove the knife, but that's the worst thing he can do.

Scanning the nearest kitchen work surfaces, I grab the tea towel from the nearby radiator, ball it up, and press it against the wound, keeping the blade where it is. Tommy rolls onto his back, but it isn't preventing the thick red liquid from escaping the wound where the knife is still embedded. Pushing the towel harder against the broken skin, I apply as much pressure as I can in an effort to stem the bleeding. If he doesn't get help quickly, he won't make it.

There's been too much pain and torment.

Jess remains frozen to the spot, her eyes so white and wide as she silently watches me scramble to help the man who only seconds earlier was threatening both of our lives. She doesn't understand that he's no longer a threat. Tommy Chamberlain is a monster; a man who deserves to die a horrible, painful death. But that isn't who I see before me now. It is my son whose skin is already taking on a deathly hue.

'Jess,' I scream to snap her out of the self-imposed trance. 'You need to press here on the wound like I'm doing. We need to stop the blood flow, to give the paramedics the chance to get here.' She doesn't move. 'Jess, please?' I try again. 'Push down on the towel as I'm doing.'

I reach for her hand to drag her over so she's close enough to reach, when Tommy's hand shoots up and grabs my wrist, forcing my hand to remain where it is. He coughs, and blood spits up onto his lips. His eyes are wet as he meets my gaze, and in that briefest of moments, I see the eyes of the boy who used to pick bunches of daisies and dandelions for me from our garden; the little boy who would snuggle beside me as I read fairy tales and poems before bed; the boy who would

363

cover his cheeks with soapy bubbles, pretending to shave them off like his dad.

Where did I go so wrong?

He's trying to speak, and I lean closer, my ear millimetres from his lips as he tries again. I'm sure he says he's sorry, but maybe that's just what I want to hear.

The tea towel is already soaked through, and I can't see anything else in easy reach I can replace it with. I temporarily release my grip on the tea towel, pull off my cardigan, and substitute it for the towel, but I already know it's too late. Even if the paramedics were at our door, they'd need a miracle and a vat of transfused blood to save him. All I'm doing is prolonging his final seconds.

How did it come to this?

For so long I've wanted this monster out of our lives to protect Daisy, yet now that I'm presented with the moment, I can't step up and take it. Maybe it's the nurse in me fighting for the preservation of life; or maybe it's because I know deep down that I'm as guilty as Tommy for where we've ended up.

I would give anything to take it all back and start again.

His face is so grey against the chestnut-coloured linoleum tiles. He can't have long left; seconds at most. My heart is pounding so heavy in my chest.

Bending my head towards him once again, I whisper, 'I'm sorry, my sweet boy,' and kiss the top of his head.

When I straighten again, his eyes are fixed on mine. Then I realise they aren't looking at me but beyond me; my son has slipped away.

Dearest God, please watch over my boy. Forgive him his sins.

Jess suddenly shuffles backwards across the floor, as if Tommy's magnetic force is repelling her. Shock can affect people in different ways. It always brings out my practical side, and do we need that right now.

Releasing my grip on the sodden material and leaving Tommy where he is, I crawl around his feet, and press a hand against Jess's cheek. She starts at the coldness of my touch.

'You need to get out of here, Jess. None of this was your fault, but if you're here when the police arrive, they're going to want to question you.'

Her stare is still so wild, and although it is fixed on my face, I'm certain she hasn't heard a single word of what I've just told her. Against my better judgement, I pull my hand from her face, and slap her cheek, leaving a bloody print. It's enough to snap her attention back to the room.

'I need to go and fetch Daisy from her secret hiding place,' I say, glancing back out into the darkness beyond the patio door. 'It is late, and she's alone. I would bring you with me but the terrain is not wheelchair-friendly.'

A distant siren heightens my panic.

'Jess, I need you to listen to me carefully. Get up, go home, and clean yourself up. I'll make sure Daisy is safe with a neighbour before I call the police and report what's happened here.'

My bloody handprint glistens on her cheek.

'Did you hear me, Jess? I'll keep your name out of this, but you can't be here when the police arrive.'

The siren is growing closer. Is it possible one of the neighbours heard or saw Tommy kicking in the door and has reported the incident?

Jess's wheelchair is on its side just inside the hallway where the carpet is now blotting the blood that has escaped from the kitchen floor

I know we don't have long. I've no idea how I'm going to explain what happened, but right now that is the least of my worries. What if Daisy forgot where the secret hiding place was, and is out there wandering the streets?

I force myself upright, my son's blood on my trousers a reminder of what has unfolded. Jess remains where she is, but I can't hang around and comfort her. Daisy is my priority.

'Jess,' I shout again, and she shudders at the mention of her name. 'For God's sake, you need to get out of here. *Now!*'

She finally stirs to life, and nods, looking for her wheelchair. It's just beyond Tommy's head, and unfortunately she's going to have to crawl alongside him to get to it, but there's no other way.

'Are you going to be okay?' I ask, concerned about her growing paleness.

She nods. 'I'm sorry, Morag. For your loss.'

I don't acknowledge her apology, as I turn and burst out of the back door, the tears exploding from my own eyes.

Chapter Fifty-Nine

Now

Mike didn't like being made to wait; patience was not a virtue he cared for. The bulky man behind reception, who looked more like a bouncer on a nightclub door than a healthcare professional, had informed them there was no access to the secure ward without prior consent. Waving his warrant card and arguing didn't make a difference. Eventually he'd settled for a conversation with the hospital administrator, who was apparently in a budget meeting and unavailable for the foreseeable future.

When Dr Savage eventually appeared, a white coat and stethoscope making her look more like a doctor than the jeans and hoodie last night, what patience Mike did possess was close to snapping. 'I need to speak to Jess Donoghue immediately.'

Dr Savage nodded a welcome towards Polly, before taking

Mike's arm and moving him away from a group of suited individuals who appeared to be on a tour of the hospital.

'I wish you'd phoned ahead,' Dr Savage said evenly.

'Why?' Mike fired back. 'Tell me you haven't let her go already.'

'Of course not,' Dr Savage replied sharply. 'I wouldn't have done that without warning you first. No, Jess is here, but I don't think she's in any condition to be interviewed by the police. As I explained last night, the pills she has been taking are designed to stabilise chemical activity in her brain, and she hasn't been taking them for several days, if not longer, and—'

'Please, doc,' Mike interrupted, pulling his most pitiful expression, hoping to appeal to her better nature, 'I need to know what she witnessed last night. The whole investigation could hinge on her testimony.'

Dr Savage considered him for a moment. 'I appreciate what you're saying, detective, and in a few days, when we've managed to get her straight, she'll be able to answer whatever questions you have, but until then, I'm sorry, there's no knowing what could happen if you started pressing the wrong buttons.'

'Five minutes,' Mike interjected. 'That's all I want. It won't be a formal interview, just me and her in a room. You can even be there too, so you can keep an eye on her well-being.'

'I'm sorry, but that can't happen.'

Mike could see he was getting nowhere, but he knew leaving the interview for a few days could mean Jess forgetting some detail, giving her more time to construct an alternative version of events; even feigning amnesia of everything that happened in that kitchen.

'They both did it, you know,' he said. 'Jess and that other woman she confronted outside the police station last night. Both of their fingerprints were discovered on the handle. They were both there when the knife broke through the victim's skin, severing the carotid artery and sending his brain into meltdown. Jess's clothes were literally dripping with his blood. Do you realise you're protecting a killer right now?'

Mike hated himself for stooping so low, but the thought of returning to the station empty-handed and dealing with the wrath of the Chief Super kept him clinging on to any hope.

Dr Savage glanced back to the security door and the rooms beyond it, before returning her gaze to Mike and Polly. 'I will allow you to ask her five questions. You won't be in the same room, for your own safety, but you can speak to her through an intercom system. I will be in the room with her, so I can monitor her reaction to those questions, *and* if I believe you are endangering her health in any way, I will terminate the interview immediately.'

Mike could have kissed her but kept it professional with an assertive nod, as if there'd been no other possible outcome to the conversation. Dr Savage led them back to the security desk, before signing them both in as her guests, and asking the Rottweiler behind the desk to grant them both visitor passes.

The security door buzzed as it opened, and Dr Savage made sure it was pulled firmly shut before leading them down the long lime-green-painted corridor, past closed doors, each bearing the name of the patient trapped inside. Mike couldn't get over how quiet the ward was, having expected to hear shouting and grumbles coming from the pained and suffering.

They finally arrived at a room with Jess Donoghue's name

on the door. 'Let me go and explain to her what is going to happen,' Dr Savage said, 'and then the two of you can head through the next door along, which houses a viewing window into the room. You will be able to observe Jess and me in the room, but she won't be able to see you.'

Mike looked along the wall and spotted a smaller brown door that looked like the entrance to a broom cupboard. Polly and Mike stepped through the door and flicked on the light. Through the large tinted window they could see Jess, her back to them, sitting by an easel and painting what looked like an accurate water-colour of a stream and fields beyond it. The room itself contained a bed secured to one of the walls, a pillow without a case and a duvet without a cover. In a corner of the ceiling a small red LED indicated that the room was under constant surveillance. A buzz in the room was followed by Dr Savage appearing through what looked like a secret portal in the wall. When it was closed, you'd be hard pushed to recognise it as a door at all.

Dr Savage's lips moved and Jess lowered her paintbrush to listen, but Mike and Polly couldn't hear a word. Scanning the area immediately around the window, Mike looked for anything that might resemble an unmute button but, not finding one, called out, 'We can't hear you.'

Neither Jess nor Dr Savage looked up, suggesting they hadn't heard. Mike began searching the walls for any other buttons, when Dr Savage's voice suddenly cut into the room. 'Go ahead, detective, ask your first question.'

Mike took a step closer to the window, so he'd feel more like he was addressing Jess directly. 'Hello, Jess. Do you remember me? I'm Detective Inspector Mike Ferry. We met briefly last night. I want to know why you were at Morag Kilbride's house last night.'

Jess's shoulders tensed at the mention of Morag's name, and she slowly shook her head. Dr Savage leaned in and muttered something unintelligible.

'Okay,' Mike continued, 'can you tell me what happened at the house last night?'

The head shaking intensified, and the easel started to shake too.

'I'm sorry, detective,' Dr Savage announced, now trying to calm Jess, 'but this isn't going to work. We need to end this now.'

'No,' Mike barked back. 'Jess, listen to my voice. All I want to know is: who killed Tommy?'

The easel toppled as Jess let out a pained cry and fought to get away from Dr Savage, as if the psychiatrist meant her harm.

'Who killed Tommy, Jess? Was it Morag? Did she kill her son?'

Dr Savage glared venomously at the mirror. 'This interview is over.'

The sound of Jess's crying stopped instantly, and no amount of shouting or demanding the truth would be heard by anyone but the two of them in the soundproofed viewing portal.

'What now?' Polly asked.

'We get Morag Kilbride in for questioning.' Mike grimaced. 'Have they picked her up from the hotel yet?'

Polly was studying her phone and didn't answer at first. 'Shit! Mike, they just went into her room, and the place is empty. Morag, Angus, and Daisy are gone. Hotel staff said they'd paid for two nights, but nobody saw them leave.'

The room seemed to spin. 'Shit, shit, shit!' Mike roared in frustration. The Chief Super would skin him alive for having let Morag escape. But he was resilient to the end. 'Let's go back to the house. Maybe they left a clue as to where they might flee.'

Chapter Sixty

Now

The outer perimeter around the Kilbride residence had now been reduced, but still blocked half the road, with access only available to police personnel and residents of the neighbouring properties who were being inconvenienced.

Mike and Polly showed their identification and signed in, before slipping on plastic mesh over-clothes, and were then led to meet the Scene of Crime Manager, who was standing by the rear doors of a van as bagged samples were being carefully loaded in.

She looked up from her clipboard and nodded at the two of them. 'Veronica Leyburn.'

'DI Mike Ferry and DC Polly Viceroy,' Mike said, lowering the thin mask covering his lips. 'How are you progressing?'

'We've completed our work downstairs, and should be finished with the upstairs by tonight,' she explained. 'No traces of blood outside, and nothing obvious upstairs. Looks like the death was contained to just the kitchen and hallway. When we're done here, the clean-up crew are going to have real job on their hands. The carpet in the hallway and the linoleum in the kitchen will probably need replacing.'

Mike nodded towards the front door, which was still barely hanging from one of its hinges. 'Any chance we can take a look around inside?'

'Sure, but please try and stay out of the way of the team, as we're against the clock today.'

Mike thanked her and replaced his mask. Polly followed him up the steep driveway and into the detached property. The hallway carpet was dotted with numbered markers, and Tommy Chamberlain's body was clearly outlined as a dark patch where the hallway met the kitchen floor. Bypassing that area, Mike veered into the long living-cum-dining room. More numbered markers were visible on the two cabinets, bookcase, and window sills.

'Doesn't look like the site of a burglary, does it?' Mike commented rhetorically. 'Given what we've learned about the victim's background in narcotics and gang violence, I'd have expected a greater disturbance here.'

'Maybe his mum tidied up before the first responders arrived,' Polly replied flippantly. 'What exactly are you looking for?'

'Anything to tell us where she might go in blind panic. Put yourself in her shoes. You've just killed – or at the very least witnessed the death of – your only son. The police suspect you of the crime, but don't yet have the evidence to arrest and charge. We know that they've fled, and that screams to me that she's panicking. So where does she go? Where would you go?'

Polly looked down at her hands. 'When things went south

with us, I went home to my mum for a few days. I've already checked that, and both Morag and Angus's parents died years ago.'

Mike looked at her. 'You really went back to your mum's when we broke up?'

She nodded, avoiding his gaze. 'I was hurting, and I didn't want to be surrounded by things that reminded me of what you'd chosen to throw away.'

Mike took a step closer. 'I had no idea. When you wouldn't return my phone calls, I assumed you were just pissed off with me.'

'This isn't the place to be discussing this, Mike,' she replied, and he could hear the pain in her voice.

'I never meant to hurt you, Polly. With everything that was going on with the Professional Standards Inquiry, I didn't want you being dragged into my mess. I'm sorry.'

Polly turned away, and Mike moved back as Veronica Leyburn entered the room, and the moment passed.

'Nothing unusual noted in this room,' she announced. 'Mrs Kilbride did ask to come in here when she stopped by earlier, but we told her the downstairs was out of bounds for now.'

Mike frowned at her. 'Morag Kilbride was here? Today?'

'Only to collect some clothes and money. Don't worry, I had one of the team escort her up to the main bedroom upstairs and made a note of the clothes she put into a bag.'

Mike's eyes widened. 'Why didn't you tell me that when we arrived? Who agreed for her to be let into the house?'

'She said you'd told her it was okay,' Veronica replied defensively. 'We hadn't had any word that she was under suspicion or not to be allowed in.'

'Tell me she didn't take her passport with her.'

'What do you take me for? Passports are still on site upstairs. She didn't even ask for them.'

Mike turned to Polly. 'Let the team know she has cash and clothes as well. It's going to make her more difficult to trace.'

Mike stopped as his eyes fell on a framed picture on the bookcase. The once silver frame was covered in black powder, the remnants of the SOCOs' search for fingerprints, but it was the volume of powder that had caught his eye. Moving across to it, he studied the image more closely. In it, a younger Morag had her arm wrapped around another woman, facial similarities apparent. In the distance, a pub sign saying 'The Black Ox' was caught in the wind blowing off the large body of water behind them.

Mike turned and looked at Polly. 'What was the name of that officer Nazia said she spoke to, PS Rupert something or other?

Polly nodded. 'MacTavish. Why?'

Mike smiled for the first time since learning Morag had gone AWOL. 'Get hold of him for me. I think I know where she's going. Home.'

Chapter Sixty-One

After - Morag

The air in my lungs is so much cleaner that I feel giddy as I march onwards across the uneven ground, the bitter wind forcing the overgrown heath to almost bend backwards. Dorothy was right; there's no place like home.

I told Angus to park in the next village over from Gwen's, in case the police are looking out for our car. Their time will come, but right now there is one thing I must do before I don't have a chance.

Poor Daisy was upset when I told her she wouldn't be going to school today, and she sobbed as I strapped her into the car. She wants to know why her dad turned up at our house when we'd told her he was dead. How do you explain to one so young that we lied with the best of intentions, that everything we've done has been to keep her safe and away from him?

I know she recognised him. The moment he looked into her

eyes and said her real name, I spotted the recognition. Poor sweet, confused lamb. What if us taking her wasn't the best thing for us to have done? What if all we've achieved is screwing up her emotional state more than ever? Angus reassured me last night that our efforts weren't in vain, and I do so want to believe him when he tells me everything is going to be okay, but how can it be after what I did? No parent should ever have to bury their child, but what kind of monster kills their child? I am the worst kind of human being, and I don't deserve to live happily ever after. My son is gone, my sister has little time left, and now my granddaughter – the one person I would give my life for – probably despises me.

Where did it all go so wrong?

A warm tear escapes my eye as the wind catches it just right.

I do wonder how our lives would have ended up had we never run. Would Tommy have pursued us in quite the same way, or would we have managed to negotiate some kind of truce, allowing him access to Mia's life? Most parents acknowledge that having a child changes you, and maybe if we'd given Tommy the chance, he could have changed too. Or maybe I'm just trivialising all my bad decisions in order to punish myself for what I did.

The heath breaks, and Gwen's wee cottage comes into sight. I'm pleased to see a plume of smoke escaping that old brown chimney pot, meaning someone is home. It is hard to believe that two days have passed since I watched my son's life ebb away. Two days in which I've barely slept, unable to find a way forward in my life, but knowing I have to for Daisy's sake. I don't think I could ever get used to calling her Mia again. Mia was a sweet angel whom her mother would bring to see me. That is like a past life now. The little girl strapped in to the back of Angus's car has changed so much, and I think for a time I did start to think of her as my own daughter rather than granddaughter. I'm sure a psychiatrist would have a field day with how messed up our family dynamic is.

The battered old wooden door opens as I approach, and I see Gwen's husband Rufus standing there, his muddied dungarees tucked into his large brown boots, and the flannel shirt catching in the breeze. I wave to him, and he nods, stepping away from the door and moving further into the cottage. The air is so much warmer inside, and I quickly unbutton my coat and unwind the thick scarf from around my neck as I step inside, closing the door behind me. The top of my hair brushes the low ceiling as I move further into the old cottage we grew up in. I can still picture the day they brought Gwen home and told me I was going to be a big sister, and I remarked that I would have preferred a puppy. I can remember my dad sitting me on his lap close to the hearth and explaining how it would become my responsibility to look after Gwen and keep her safe at school. I'll never forget the way she held my hand that first time, her tiny fingers coiling around my thumb, tugging gently, in her own way agreeing to become my wee sister.

The breath catches in my throat as I step into the living room and the evening's sun catches on the purple bruising beneath her right eye, as she sits in the tall chair beside the window. She is so much thinner than when I last saw her, and for the briefest of moments I see my ageing mother sitting there staring back at me. It's as if someone has come in and aged my wee Gwen with makeup or special effects. This is not whom I picture when I think of my sister.

I rush over and drop to my knees, taking her frail hand in mine and pressing it against my moist cheek. 'I am so sorry. What has he done to you?'

I feel her free hand drop onto my head, and she gently strokes my hair. ''Tis nae yer fault,' she says soothingly.

There is no sign of Rufus, and I can only assume he has left to give us time to get reacquainted.

I look up at Gwen, and now that I'm closer I can see just how raw the purple and yellow colouring of her eyelids is. Her lips break into a tender smile as our eyes meet, yet somehow that only increases the guilt flooding my heart in that moment.

'Are you okay?' I ask, instantly regretting the lameness of the question. Of course she isn't okay! She is fighting the cancer riddling her body, and recovering from what I know is Tommy's handiwork.

'Aye, 'tis nae bother.'

Here I am, the woman charged with taking care of this beautiful and brilliant spark, and yet she is the one – as always – looking out for me. I've never felt so hopeless, and yet blessed.

'I am so sorry for putting you through this,' I begin, reciting the words I have practised over and over since demanding that Angus drive us home to Aberdeenshire. 'I should never have left you in a position where you were at risk. You deserved a sister who could take real care of you, and I'm sorry you got stuck with me. If I could—'

She pulls her hand free, and presses both hands against my cheeks, using her warm thumbs to brush the tears from my eyes. 'You did what you had to do. Who are we to challenge what the world throws at us? I wouldnae choose any other woman in the world to be my big sister. I'm the lucky one, and don't you be forgetting that.'

I want to stay in this position for ever, with my wee sister cradling me and telling me that everything is going to be okay, but the moment is over the moment the blue flashing lights erupt through the window and flicker on the walls.

In my mind I should be terrified, and desperately seeking any means of escape, or a place to hide, but I ignore my base human instinct to flee, and remain where I am, taking in the beauty of my battling sister's smile, and knowing that if she says everything will be okay, then it will.

Heavy pounding at the door is followed by muttering and a moment later Rufus leads the suited detectives into the warm room. I recognise the tall male with the close-cropped beard from our encounter two nights ago, and the wee woman beside him, who looks embarrassed about barging in on my and Gwen's tender moment.

'I have to go now,' I tell Gwen, as her hands move to mine and squeeze. 'You said earlier that you think you're the lucky one, but I know in my heart of hearts that I was the one blessed by your arrival. I will be back, my little one, and I promise I *will* see you again before our time on this cruel world is through. Stay strong for me, won't you?'

It breaks my heart to see her eyes shining back at mine, but I feel calm, as I push my wrists towards the tall detective, and he begins to read me my rights.

Chapter Sixty-Two

After – Jess

I'm physically exhausted as the young woman helps me back into my wheelchair.

'You've made fab progress today, Jess. It's early days, but we're on the right track.'

I love and loathe her positivity in equal measure, but I know she's only doing her job. I can't imagine how much money it would take for me to remain so positive with strangers all day.

Five weeks have passed since Detective Inspector Mike Ferry advised me that the CPS would not be looking to bring charges against Morag or me for the untimely death of the man known as Tommy Chamberlain. Personally, my memory of that night doesn't scream that it was an act of self-defence, but that seems to be the picture they're painting, and I have little reason to disagree.

Members of the press are no longer camped on our

doorstep, which is the biggest relief. I now have a far greater appreciation for what celebrities go through, seeing paparazzi at every turn. Poor Grace didn't know what to do with herself. Mum has been great at taking her to and collecting her from school. I can't wait to reclaim that responsibility, as it's not the same hearing about Grace's day at school once she's home. She's usually forgotten half of the things she's done by then, and I want to be the first person she tells every day.

Mum claims there have been no more rumours about me in the playground, but I don't know if she's just trying to spare my feelings. I'll know soon enough, as I've told her I'm going to collect Grace from school this afternoon. To hell with the gossips like Nadine. If their lives are so boring that they've nothing better to talk about than me, then that just shows how small-minded they are. I've had several friend requests on Facebook from some of the other mums in Grace's class, but I haven't accepted any yet. I can't be sure how many really do want to make friends, and whether any are just hoping to cling to the coat-tails of my recent notoriety.

The biggest surprise has been Charlie. All that skulking around, sending messages, and meeting with mysterious women had me jumping to all the wrong conclusions. Last night he drove me to a bungalow on the other side of town, a stone's throw from Grace's school and the park. The woman I saw him meeting in town was in fact an estate agent.

'The woman who owned it is moving into a nursing home, and has no family to leave the house to,' he told me, as we pulled onto the flat driveway. 'As soon as I saw it, I knew it would be perfect for us,' he added.

And for once his promise of a surprise was gratefully received. The bungalow already has a purpose-built shallow concrete ramp up to the front door, as the elderly seller had difficulty with stairs after her hip replacement. The kitchen is almost double the size of our current one, and there are three bedrooms, one for each of us and a spare for when Mum wants to stay over.

'And the internal garage could be converted into a fourth room,' Charlie added. 'Several of the houses in the road have already done it, so planning permission shouldn't be a problem.'

I know why he's so keen on converting the garage. We talked about it last night, and for the first time, the thought of trying for a new baby didn't terrify me as much as it once did. I will never forget the heartbreak and grief of losing Luke, and he will remain a part of this family long after Charlie and I are gone. But maybe Grace does deserve a second chance at becoming a big sister; I know she'd be great at it.

'After some gentle persuasion, the seller agreed to lower her asking price,' Charlie continued, as he led me through to the medium-sized back garden, with beautiful raised flowerbeds along one side, and a patio that puts Morag's to shame. 'When I told her everything we'd been through in the last eighteen months, she said she'd be pleased to know the house will be filled with love and noise once more.'

Charlie's always been a good salesman, and I can just imagine him using his charm to strong-arm this pensioner into agreeing to sell the house to him. He assures me that the bank has agreed to loan us the additional money required to buy it as a replacement for our old house. As pragmatic as ever, Charlie had it out with Doug and said he would be leaving the company if he didn't get a pay rise and the freedom to work from home a couple of times a week. To my amazement, Doug agreed, and Charlie is now Vice-President of their New Business division, as Doug is looking to expand.

Sometimes, if you stop long enough to appreciate what you actually have, you realise just how lucky you are.

'Are you still okay to meet again on Tuesday?' the physiotherapist asks me now.

My entire body aches – well, the parts I can feel do – but that's why I'm here. I noticed something that day when the detective came to the secure wing of the hospital. Maybe it was the shock of seeing Tommy bleed out, how quickly his warm blood on my skin cooled and congealed; or maybe it had something to do with the way he landed on me when we struggled with that knife. Either way, I felt a warmth in my thighs that I hadn't experienced since the hospital, and I'm now filled with renewed determination.

I'm having physiotherapy twice a week, once in the outpatients' clinic here at the hospital, and on Tuesday we do work in the swimming pool. I know I'll struggle to move tomorrow, but nothing worthwhile having ever came without pain and sacrifice.

Gail has been over several times since I was released by the police. She's been speaking with the chief editor at the newspaper about me doing some freelance work from home for them, with a view to restarting my old job when I've kicked the wheelchair into touch. I appreciate her support and encouragement, but part of me suspects she's angling for me to share my story with her for an exclusive. And who knows, maybe I will. After all, who would have imagined everything that would happen based on those four little words I heard Daisy say?

Morag and Angus have been allowed to return to their

home, although from what Morag has told me, they can't wait to move. It must be weird to live in a house knowing death was the last visitor. I hope they decide to stay in Northwood. With Tommy now gone, there is no reason for them to move on, but I wouldn't blame them for wanting to return home to Scotland so she can be closer to her sister. I guess only time will tell what decision they will make. If they do move back, I will miss Morag. After everything, and in spite of my moments of irrationality, she was there when I most needed a friend.

I wave my thanks to the physiotherapist, as she washes her hands and moves on to her next appointment. The girl in the wheelchair before her now can't be much older than ten, and I recognise the pained and tearful look, as it was the same one that stared back at me from the mirror for a long time. I'm only guessing, but I would think she is newly confined to her chair, and I can't imagine how tough that must be on her emotionally. It was hard enough to accept as an adult, but to lose that feeling at such a young age must be unimaginable.

I continue to watch as the girl's mum fusses and fidgets around her, handing a file of notes to the physiotherapist and talking about the girl as if she isn't even there. I know that feeling too, but it's not one I plan to accept any longer. Being unable to walk doesn't make me, or her, any less of a human being. If you cut us, we still bleed. If you call us names or ignore us, we still carry the emotional scars. Labels like 'disabled' and 'crippled' are too easily doled out because our limbs have failed us, but we are so much more than our disability.

If I've learned anything in this last year, it's that I am more than the sum of my working parts. Whether in this chair or fully recovered, I have so much more to offer, and I will spend the rest of my days fighting to prove that I am just as capable as the next person, regardless of physical and mental condition.

I wheel over to the little girl and introduce myself whilst her mother continues to natter to the physiotherapist. 'Do you like chocolate?' I whisper.

She eyes me suspiciously at first, before nodding with just a hint of a smile.

'My daughter *loves* chocolate,' I say, smiling warmly, 'so I bought her a chocolate bar while I was at the shop earlier today. Only it was on offer so I ended up with two bars instead. The thing is, I don't really want her to eat two chocolate bars, so it leaves me with a bit of a dilemma.' I pause and check that her mum is still not paying us any attention. 'I tell you what, I will give you the second chocolate bar if you can beat me in a race to the end of the room and back. You reckon you're quick enough?'

She looks sceptical, until I pull the purple bar from my handbag. Her eyes light up.

'I should warn you that I'm pretty fast,' I add. 'You reckon you can beat me?'

The little girl nods uncertainly.

'Okay, on your marks, get set, go.'

I pull away, but not so fast that she can't soon catch up and then pull into the lead. Over my shoulder I hear her mother gasp, but it's not like we're causing any trouble, nor in any immediate danger.

The girl makes it to the wall, and is already on her way back to the finishing line by the time I reach the far side of the court. Her mother is staring at me in utter bewilderment when

I make it back. I'm not sure she's even noticed the beaming smile breaking across her daughter's face.

'Congratulations,' I whisper, handing over the chocolate bar. 'Don't ever let anyone tell you that you can't do something. If you put your mind to it, *you* can achieve anything. Don't give up on yourself.'

Her face is a picture, and despite her mother's disapproving stare, I know our little race has broken down a barrier in that girl's mind.

'What are you smiling at?' Charlie asks, as I meet him at the car.

'Nothing,' I murmur, not wanting to share the moment with anyone who wouldn't understand.

'Do you fancy stopping somewhere for a sandwich before we go home?' he asks. 'We still haven't celebrated my promotion properly, and I'm famished.'

'Lunch sounds perfect,' I tell him, as I hoist myself into the front seat unaided. 'I need to keep my strength up.'

There's something else Charlie doesn't know; the real reason why I stopped taking my antidepressants last month. And in eight months' time he'll know exactly why I took that decision. We'd better start getting some quotes for that garage extension.

Acknowledgments

Thank you for reading *Mummy's Little Secret*, and for taking the time to read about all the people who helped make this such a gripping and terrifying story. Please get in touch via the channels below and let me know what you thought about it.

The idea for the story came when I took my children to a playground in Romsey, Hampshire close to where we live. I was watching all the young children climbing and running, and laughing and lost in the safety of a place that demands all who enter to let go and have fun. I spotted parents staring on from the sides, cringing when their child looked like they might trip, and waving frantically when they heard their name being shouted. It got me thinking about what would happen if there was an imposter amongst them: someone who wasn't there having fun. That then morphed into this vision of a child approaching me with the terrifying words, "She's not my mum."

As a parent, my greatest fear is danger befalling my child. Over the course of my parenting that has ranged from the prospect of choking, drowning, breaking a limb, and abduction. Actually having the children trapped at home during the lockdowns in this unprecedented time has somewhat alleviated some of those fears. But with it has come more self-doubt: what if my home-schooling isn't good enough; what if my children fall behind in class; what if they don't understand why times are so challenging at the moment?

The thing we need to remind ourselves is: we're only human, which is why I've dedicated this book to all of you who are keeping your shit together during unprecedented times.

I want to thank Bethan Morgan and Charlotte Ledger for their creative input into this story, for encouraging me to delve deeper into Morag's character and understand why she would act in the way she does. Thank you also to the team of line editors, copyeditors, proofreaders, marketing gurus, and media whizzes who make up the rest of the One More Chapter team.

Thank you also to my best friend, Dr Parashar Ramanuj, who never shies away from the awkward medical questions I ask him. Thank you to Alex Shaw and Paul Grzegorzek – authors and dear friends – who are happy to listen to me moan and whinge about the pitfalls of the publishing industry, offering words of encouragement along the way. Thank you to Joanne Taylor for her continued support with spotting the typos in my work before it even goes to my editor.

My children are an inspiration to me every day, and as they continue to grow so quickly, I am eternally grateful that I get to play such an important role in their development. I know neither has found it easy during lockdown and home-schooling (who of us has?), but they continue to show one another affection, patience, and kindness, and make being their dad that bit easier. I'd like to thank my own parents and my parents-in-law for continuing to offer words of encouragement when I'm struggling to engage with my muse.

It goes without saying that I wouldn't be the writer I am today without the loving support of my beautiful wife and soulmate, Hannah. She keeps everything else in my life ticking over so that I can give what's left to my writing. She never questions my method or the endless hours daydreaming while I'm working through plot holes, and for that I am eternally grateful.

And thanks must also go to YOU for buying and reading *Mummy's Little Secret*. Please do post a review to wherever you purchased the book from so that other readers can be enticed to give it a try. It takes less than two minutes to share your opinion, and I ask you do me this small kindness.

I am active on Facebook, Twitter, and Instagram, so please do stop by with any messages, observations, or questions. Hearing from readers of my books truly brightens my days and encourages me to keep writing, so don't be a stranger. I promise I *will* respond to every message and comment.

Stephen

twitter.com/Writer_MAHunter
facebook.com/AuthorMAHunter
instagram.com/steph.edger

YOUR NUMBER ONE STOP

ONE MORE CHAPTER

FOR PAGETURNING BOOKS

One More Chapter is an
award-winning global
division of HarperCollins.

Sign up to our newsletter to get our
latest eBook deals and stay up to date
with our weekly Book Club!
<u>Subscribe here.</u>

Meet the team at
<u>www.onemorechapter.com</u>

Follow us!
 <u>@OneMoreChapter_</u>
 <u>@OneMoreChapter</u>
 <u>@onemorechapterhc</u>

Do you write unputdownable fiction?
We love to hear from new voices.
Find out how to submit your novel at
<u>www.onemorechapter.com/submissions</u>